W9-CYB-388

"What memories do you have of our time in Nevada?"

"Our one-night stand, you mean?" Olivia asked.

Gerald grinned. "Precisely."

She sighed, lifting a hand. "Oh, I don't know. Not much, to be honest. Tequila has a debilitating effect on my ability to retain information."

"As it does for all us mere mortals," he said with a thoughtful nod. After a moment's hesitation, he covered her hand with his free one. "I hope you don't take this too hard, but it seems on that night in Las Vegas, somewhere along the line we happened to find ourselves embedded in a wedding chapel."

Her lips twitched in wry humor. "A wedding chapel. You're kidding me, right?" When those grave, green eyes neither smiled nor strayed from hers, she fumbled. "You're...you're not? Kidding?"

Dear Reader,

I'm thrilled to give you the second book set in Fairhope, Alabama, *Married One Night*. If you have not yet read the first book, *A Place with Briar,* that's okay! You don't need to read it to enjoy *Married One Night*. If you have read Briar's book, you'll be happy to know that this is Olivia's story.

It seems that everyone's got that one friend, the hopeless matchmaker. In the first book, Olivia's cousin Briar even goes so far as to compare her to Emma Woodhouse...that is, if Emma were a forthright tavern-keeper with a bawdy laugh. It struck me that, although Olivia's character likes to match up friends and family members with their prospective mates, she's alone. A few allusions to her past reveal that her own love life has not been ideal. My editor must have noticed, too, because in her notes to me, she seemed to want to know more about Olivia's history and what it would take for her to meet her match....

Enter Gerald Leighton! He's charming, handsome, British... he's even wealthy, a self-made man (and, believe it or not, a renegade earl). Another fun fact about Gerald? He's a man not at all afraid of commitment, and from the moment he sees Olivia, he knows what he wants. When I realized that Gerald would be Olivia's hero, he struck me as an unlikely match for her. I dove in and hoped for the best... and (as Gerald would say) *blimey,* did I have a blast! Pitting the commitment-phobic heroine against the idealistic yet irresistible hero was an entertaining experience. I was surprised, too, by how much they had to learn and gain from each other. As the saying goes, opposites attract, and oftentimes it's because one gives the other something no one else can.

I hope you enjoy *Married One Night!* Stay tuned for the third book in the series—Adrian's story—coming soon...

Amber Leigh Williams

AMBER LEIGH WILLIAMS

WILLIAMS

—

Married One Night

HARLEQUIN SUPER ROMANCE®

If you purchased this book without a cover you should be aware
that this book is stolen property. It was reported as "unsold and
destroyed" to the publisher, and neither the author nor the
publisher has received any payment for this "stripped book."

Recycling programs
for this product may
not exist in your area.

ISBN-13: 978-0-373-60878-2

Married One Night

Copyright © 2014 by Amber Leigh Williams

All rights reserved. Except for use in any review, the reproduction or
utilization of this work in whole or in part in any form by any electronic,
mechanical or other means, now known or hereinafter invented, including
xerography, photocopying and recording, or in any information storage
or retrieval system, is forbidden without the written permission of the
publisher, Harlequin Enterprises Limited, 225 Duncan Mill Road,
Don Mills, Ontario, Canada M3B 3K9.

This is a work of fiction. Names, characters, places and incidents are
either the product of the author's imagination or are used fictitiously,
and any resemblance to actual persons, living or dead, business
establishments, events or locales is entirely coincidental.

This edition published by arrangement with Harlequin Books S.A.

For questions and comments about the quality of this book,
please contact us at CustomerService@Harlequin.com.

® and TM are trademarks of Harlequin Enterprises Limited or its
corporate affiliates. Trademarks indicated with ® are registered in the
United States Patent and Trademark Office, the Canadian Intellectual
Property Office and in other countries.

Printed in U.S.A.

ABOUT THE AUTHOR

Amber Leigh Williams lives on the Gulf Coast. A Southern girl at heart, she loves beach days, the smell of real books, relaxing at her family's lakehouse and spending time with her husband, Jacob, and their sweet blue-eyed boy. When she's not running after her young son and three large dogs, she can usually be found reading a good romance or cooking up a new dish in her kitchen. Readers can find her on the web at www.amberleighwilliams.com!

Books by Amber Leigh Williams

HARLEQUIN SUPERROMANCE

1918—A PLACE WITH BRIAR

Other titles by this author availabe in ebook format.

To family—near, far and dearly departed.

I respectfully ask forgiveness for borrowing a few footnotes from our respective Scottish and English (even the illegitimately royal) bloodlines. Enormous gratitude for writing down and passing on the stories. Cheers to you for the inspiration (and *hold fast*)!

CHAPTER ONE

OLIVIA LEWIS WOKE up in a Sin City penthouse amidst petal-strewn, silk sheets. She bolted upright in bed...and groaned, wavering as the world turned. And turned again.

Okay, make that silk sheets, rose petals...and the most vicious hangover of her life.

Hissing, she pressed a hand over her eyes, the other on her head to stop the contents from sloshing around. Her mouth felt like sandpaper, and her stomach writhed. Obviously the obscene amount of liquor she'd consumed the night before was turning on her in sickly rebellion.

"Oh, holy moly," she wheezed. "What the hell happened last night?" Peering around, she squinted against the desert sunlight streaming through the undraped floor-to-ceiling window that spanned the entire left wall of the bedroom. At the sight of several curiously unmentionable items scattered across the bed and floor, she became more than a little curious about the events of the previous evening. Especially when she saw the tattered remains of her red dress hooked on the wall sconce at the other end of the room.

Frowning, she lifted the covers and looked underneath. She was naked as sin. And she'd spent enough nights with men to know how she should feel the next day. With a groan, she laid back into the pillows and pulled the covers over her head.

So sometime during the night, she had snuck away from the bachelorette party for her friend Roxie Honeycutt and gotten frisky—very frisky— with an unknown man.

It wasn't her first one-night stand. Nor did she think it would be her last. But considering she'd been the hostess of Roxie's bachelorette party and it had been her idea to bring the bash to Vegas, Olivia felt shame rushing up to meet her.

She sighed, flopping her arms over her head. "Well done, Liv," she muttered at the ceiling. It was painted with a mural complete with puffy white clouds and baby-faced cherubs.

How many inappropriate things had those cherubs seen last night?

Olivia pursed her lips, thinking back hard to what she could remember of the past twenty-four hours. She and her friends had flown into Vegas, then checked into their casino hotel room. They'd gone to a bar...no, a club. The venue had been packed elbow to elbow. Olivia's other friend and invitee, Adrian Carlton, had kept ordering drinks for the three of them. Tequila shots. That would explain the gargantuan headache pounding away at the inside of Olivia's head and the base of her neck.

Then…there'd been dancing on the parquet dance floor. And a man. Olivia braved the thumping, eyes watering as she thought hard to bring him into sharper focus. She got only an impression— tall. Tailored suit. A black necktie, which she'd had fun unknotting later here in the penthouse…with her teeth?

She grimaced and focused again on the man's features. Blond hair, a bit tousled as the night wore on. There was a limo, one exclusively for Olivia and her mystery man. Some frisky business in the backseat as Vegas lights blurred together outside the tinted windows. Yes, she'd run her fingers through that gilded crown of his, raking her nails lightly over his scalp. He'd liked that. Big, skillful hands on her hips. Roaming over her back…getting lost in her hair. He'd spoken to her, sweet endearments. She wasn't usually one for sweet endearments— just the answer of skin on skin and the satisfaction that came with it.

But he'd been different. Why, Olivia couldn't say…. The accent. His sweet words had been accentuated with a devastating—British?—accent that had, quite literally, charmed the pants off her.

Olivia raised a hand to her hair as her scalp tingled in remembrance. She smiled a bit at the memory, then closed her eyes on another wave of fierce pounding. If she could summon enough energy to rise from the rumpled bed, she might be able to find her purse amidst the chaos of the room. There was aspirin in that little red handbag. She needed aspirin. ASAP.

Carefully, she sat up again and braced her hands in the thick bedding. She waited for the world to stop revolving and settle back on its axis before taking a deep, bracing breath and pulling the covers back. Instant chills racked her skin, made worse by the fine sheen of sweat courtesy of the savage aftermath of tequila drinking.

She slung her legs over the side of the bed. Her toes sank into a thick black rug. Shivering, she wrapped the white silk top sheet around her, knotting it at her collarbone so that it stayed as she stood.

It took more effort than she would have liked to stay upright. She reached forward to catch the wall as she staggered in the general direction of what she hoped was a bathroom. The floor quaked beneath her and she could feel dregs of nausea rising up from the pit of her stomach. *Yes, yes, that'd better be a bathroom.*

Before Olivia could shoulder her way through the door, it opened quickly. She felt herself pitch over, tripping over the edge of the bedsheet. Cursing, she fell against the lean, chiseled chest of the man on the other side of the bathroom doorjamb.

She heard his surprised whoosh just before his arms snagged her under the shoulders and curled around her to keep her from falling at his feet. Her cheek pressed tight against his sternum. He was so warm. The deep timbre of a chuckle trebled beneath the ear pressed to his chest and words, rough around the edges, came floating from his mouth. "Ah, she wakes."

When she tried to pull herself back, he held her fast to him for a moment longer to make sure she had her footing. With a murmured, "Easy there, love," he released her and she stepped away, seeking his face.

He was smiling. The soft expression was tense around the edges, probably from what she could guess was a good deal of pounding happening on the inside of his head, too. She drew in a breath. His eyes were a brilliant shade of green. Dimples, or laugh lines, dug in around his mouth and the corners of his eyes. A man who smiled often and laughed well, Olivia surmised. His hair was blond and wet from a shower she assumed, judging by the steam behind him. He'd combed the hair back from his forehead, leaving his high brow bare.

A towel hung loosely around his waist. She blinked. She was staring. But the longer she stared, the more she could remember from last night, and the giddy spontaneity and blistering heat of all that had transpired made her forget for a moment how miserable she felt.

And, bless him, he didn't seem to mind the staring. He was doing a good bit of his own. The smile on his lips deepened into a full-fledged grin, eyes softening further as he took her in. "Well. Aren't you a sight for sore eyes."

She found a smile curving at the corner of her mouth. He *was* British. His words were enunciated with the high-class sounds of English breeding and good humor. His voice was like fine-aged wine. Or whiskey.

Whiskey, she decided. It had a good, old-fashioned burn to it.

Keep it together. Lifting her hands to the sheet knotted just under her collarbone, she made sure it was in place before dragging a hand back through her long, curly, bedraggled tresses. "Erm…good morning?" Olivia said, unsure of herself. Usually, she knew how to navigate the awkward, morning-after interlude. But this stranger's clean-cut, unexpected appeal threw her for a loop.

He beamed and held out a hand, skimming far and above the awkwardness of the situation with good-natured ease. "Gerald Leighton. It's lovely to meet you…again."

She stared at the hand. Ignoring the wariness inside her, she reached out and took it. Again, she felt warmth. She wanted him to fold his hand close around hers until the chills deserted her. It was much larger than her own. Built for creating, shaping. A sculptor's hand. The fingers were long and narrow. Aside from the absence of well-worn calluses and wrinkles, they actually reminded her a bit of her grandfather's, a lifelong carpenter.

When she found nothing to say in return, he firmed his lips together. Scanning her face a bit more carefully this time, a frown touched his features. "Headache?"

"Uh, yeah," she said, wrinkling her nose and squinting once more at the light. "I think tequila was the culprit."

"I felt the same when I first woke," he explained, voice lowered gently. "Not to worry. A glass of water, a couple painkillers and a hot shower set me halfway back to rights." He stepped aside and lifted a hand to the marble counter of the bathroom. "Aspirin's there with a bottle of water. There's a robe, too, if you need it."

She licked her lips as they both glanced back at the torn dress. "I think it's my only option at this point."

Gerald ran a hand through his hair and she thought she saw a wink of sheepishness flash in those kind, green eyes. For some reason, her heart stumbled over itself.

She blinked. Was the tequila still in her system?

"I apologize…for the dress," Gerald added quickly. "I'll be happy to reimburse you for it. Or I can have the concierge send out for another one."

Olivia lifted a hand to stop him. "It's all right. I brought other clothes with me. It shouldn't be too much trouble. That is if we're in the same casino my friends and I are staying at. Please tell me this is the Bellagio."

"Yes," he replied. "That's what the hand towels say, at any rate."

"Good," she said with a sigh of relief. She gazed longingly at the shower. It was crooking its finger at her. Her feet were starting to feel like ice cubes and the chills were coming back with a vengeance.

"Take your time," Gerald told her. "I'll have something sent up to eat. It should be here when you're done."

"Thanks, Gerald." Olivia ducked into the bathroom. The steam from his shower hugged her as he closed the door behind her. She locked the door, crossed her arms over her chest and faced the long, fogged mirror above the marble counter. Fearing what she might look like, Olivia went to the glass-walled shower stall instead and turned the knob all the way to hot.

OLIVIA MEANT TO hurry, but she soon discovered that the shower had two jet showerheads. And the towels. Oh, the towels were so big and fluffy and, fresh off the heated rack, blessedly warm. She indulged a bit, sitting at the vanity as she took some aspirin and dried her hair with the available hair dryer. Her reflection still looked gray around the edges, but there was nothing she could do about that. She hadn't yet found her purse and she didn't carry much more than lipstick and concealer in it anyway.

Clearly, she hadn't been prepared to meet some tall, ridiculously good-looking and charming Englishman who made her tummy flutter even after a night drinking round after round of Jose Cuervo.

While showering and then attempting to make herself somewhat presentable, more memories from the night before came flashing back to her. More drinks in the casino. More kissing Gerald in the elevator. God, she hoped the hotel didn't have cameras in there. Then there was the penthouse. The penthouse sofa. The big, plush bed. Gerald. Clashing mouths, tangled limbs and staggering streams of need and pleasure.

Suddenly she was no longer cold, but instead felt nothing but the heat from last night. Looking up at the mirror, she saw that her cheeks were flushed and she scrubbed her palms over them to chase it. The Brit packed a wallop. That was for damn sure. She took several careful breaths to beat back the memories and high color and wrapped the white hotel robe around her.

Fastening it with the rope around the waist, Olivia exited the bathroom, regrettably leaving the enveloping steam behind for the bawdy, orange gleam of midmorning Vegas spilling into the bedroom through that long line of crystal-clear glass.

She, Roxie and Adrian had a flight to catch in a few hours. Bearing that in mind, Olivia grabbed the shredded remains of her strapless dress off the wall sconce, then bent to pick up her platform heels off the floor. She had to get down on her hands and knees to locate her purse under the bed…where she also found the pathetic remains of her underwear, deciding to leave them where they had fallen. *Rest in peace, Victoria's Secret.*

Instead of wrestling her bra back on, she shoved it into her purse. A quick look at her cell phone told her it, too, had died sometime in the night. She hooked the sky-high heels over her fingers and wandered into the main room of the penthouse.

The smell of coffee, toast and sausage greeted her. Gerald hadn't lied; room service was waiting for her on a covered rolling tray. A silver teapot sat next to a pot of coffee that smelled hot, fresh and strong. She desperately wanted a mug of that to push away the lingering fog of the hangover. After a few sips, she'd definitely feel closer to human.

There were covered trivets from which the breakfast smells were coming. Next to them there was a glass of orange juice and a tall Bloody Mary to top it all off. She practically whimpered at the sight.

Who was Gerald Leighton and where had he been hiding all her life?

Olivia was reaching for the coffee when the sliding glass door leading onto what appeared to be a balcony slid open and Gerald walked in. Her hand pulled back from the tray quickly as if he'd caught her stealing. While she was in the shower, he had dressed in pressed black tailored suit pants and a crisp white oxford shirt he had left unbuttoned at the collar, so the hollow of his collarbone peeked through and the tendons of his neck caught her eye. His feet were bare.

She fought the urge to lick her lips and gathered the guilty hand that had been reaching for the coffeepot back into the flaps of the robe. "Hello," she greeted as his eyes found hers. Determined to get the upper hand on the conversation this time—and make up for her earlier bumbling—she pasted on a smile.

"Feeling better?" he asked, his smile answering hers.

"Loads better," she admitted. "Thank you—for letting me use the shower. I don't want to take up too much of your time—"

"No, please," Gerald said, walking toward her in a handful of long, smooth strides. "Have a seat. Have something to eat. I didn't know what you'd like so I ordered a bit of everything."

"I can see that," Olivia said, scanning the tray admiringly. "And thanks for that, too. But I really should be going."

He stopped just shy of her and the tray, a disappointed frown touching his lips. "Are you sure?"

"Yeah. My friends and I have a plane to catch in a couple of hours. I need to get back to our room and make sure they're okay. Pack up." Out of excuses, she made herself look away from those eyes.

In addition to kind, they were wise. It was a disconcerting mix, at least for her. She gestured to the room at large. "Your penthouse is beautiful, by the way."

Gerald looked around, reaching up to scratch his chin with his knuckles. "It is rather, isn't it? I'm afraid it's new to me, too. I was staying in one of the business suites."

"Oh," Olivia said. "So you're in town on business."

"Well, for the most part." His gaze crawled back to her, that shade of timidity flashing across his face again before he hid it with a wry grin that creased the corners of his mouth and eyes and simultaneously disarmed her. "Until I met you, of course."

She lowered her eyes, pressing her lips together to hide a sly smile. "I hope I was a good distraction at least."

One of his brows arced knowingly. "Oh, quite. A worthy distraction."

She did smile a bit to herself, then sighed, realizing she was lingering here with him. *Something about him.* A pull, a tug. A compelling stir that toggled her in all the right places, particularly the area of her heart. Her smile quickly turned into a frown and she tugged the lapels of the robe together, gathering them tight against her throat. "Well, Gerald Leighton." She made herself meet his eyes again. "It was nice meeting you."

His grin turned kind again. "I couldn't be happier that we did, love."

Love. Yes, she liked the sound of that a shade too much. Olivia gripped the handle of the door and had opened it only slightly when he said, "Wait a moment."

She looked around, and her breath snagged. He was closer now. Jesus, what was this hold he had over her? She didn't know how to handle it.

His eyes narrowed on her face. The lines of his mouth were tense now, his jaw squared as he searched her expression. He reached out and took the door but didn't shut it. She was free to go if she wanted, but his gaze and the urgency she saw there hooked her and made her knees buckle. "I'm ashamed to have to ask you," he said, "but can I have your name? It seems I've forgotten it after last night's tequila-fueled debauchery."

She pursed her lips. "Why would you want to know? I mean, let's be honest. We're clearly never going to see each other again...."

Gerald lifted his shoulders and shook his head. "Not likely." He stilled and the urgency blinked into his eyes again, heightened. "But you never know, do you? Maybe...one day I'd like to find you. Or you'd perhaps like to get in touch with me. I don't know...."

As Olivia searched his eyes and the moment between them stretched, the link between them humming, she weighed his request. Weighed him.

Reaching out, she touched the arm he was using to hold the door open. His muscle tightened at her touch. She slid her fingers up to the back of his and squeezed them warmly as she memorized his face. She would be glad of it later, when she returned to her hometown in Alabama. She would remember him and her night with him in the Bellagio penthouse fondly. "Olivia," she said finally. "My name is Olivia."

"Olivia," he said, smiling softly.

She nodded, then stepped back, pulled away and broke his spell. "I think we should leave it at that."

His lids came down halfway over his eyes, hiding resignation, or disappointment perhaps. "Right. It's enough. For now."

As if there could be a later. She cleared her throat and backed away from him, through the door into the hallway. "So long, Gerald."

"Goodbye, Olivia."

CHAPTER TWO

GERALD PARKED THE rental car at the bottom of a steep incline on the main drag of Fairhope, Alabama. He frowned through the light drum of rain and the protesting whir of the windshield wipers at the barricades in front of his headlights.

It was nighttime on the snug shoreline of Mobile Bay. And according to all the local radio stations he'd scanned during the drive from the airport in Pensacola, there was apparently a large and ominous hurricane headed in this general direction. The woman at the rental car company had told him he was lucky to have found an available flight from New York to the Gulf Coast at all.

When Gerald told her he'd be driving west toward Mobile and farther into the possible cone of impact, the woman had eyed him balefully and reluctantly handed over the keys.

The inclement weather didn't faze Gerald too much. The rain was coming in bands and though the wind did slap the rain against the car at a sideways angle and tug at the wheel a bit, it was all spotty at best. Nor did the fact that he'd lost his way worry him too much. He grabbed the map from the passenger seat and flipped on the cab lights to scan it. He'd gone on drives in the New York countryside with the purpose of getting lost—lost in the scenery, lost in his head. Getting lost was nothing new to him.

What did give him pause was the fact that he had just driven through the downtown area and Fairhope appeared to be a ghost town. As he drove farther and farther away from the Florida-Alabama line and toward the bay, he had come across fewer cars on the road. By the time he got to his destination, the streets were all but deserted.

He wasn't the worrisome sort, but he would be glad for a familiar face right about now, as well as the warm, homey lights of companionship.

What better place to find it than Tavern of the Graces where he had finally tracked down Olivia Lewis, the woman who had so captivated him in Las Vegas three weeks ago. Nearly a month had passed and Gerald still couldn't get her out of his head. It might have been foolish to go flying off impulsively to Alabama when he had a manuscript due to his editor in New York very soon.

But he'd needed to see her. Something had driven him here to this small Southern town he'd never heard of, and he wouldn't rest, much less write, until he got to the bottom of it.

Gerald brought the map closer. If he was reading it right, the tavern Olivia owned and operated on

South Mobile Street was only a few blocks to the south. All he had to do was turn the car around, go back up the hill, then turn right and drive a half mile. He had made the mistake of going down the hill, which led into a park and a long pier overlooking the moody bay.

Brows raised in interest, he peered over the steering wheel, squinting through rain and wind, trying to see beyond the roadblocks. The rain was down to a light patter now. He pulled on the long wool coat he'd brought from New York and grabbed the emergency flashlight from the glove compartment. Led by that foolish, towering impulse that had brought him here to begin with, he fought the wind to open the driver's door and left the car running. He curled one arm over his forehead and bent over slightly as he walked into the brunt of the wind.

Gerald squeezed between two roadblocks. He could see why everyone had been chased into the stillness of their homes. The hungry gale wolfed off the bay, the balmy breath of Mother Nature itself. The water that he imagined was usually calm, presently chopped and slapped the eastern shore of the bay in whooshing crests. The rain seemed to slacken off as he neared the entrance to the pier and the edge of the seawall that dropped straight into briny waters. Even without the rain, the air kissed the skin with salty residue. Licking his lips, Gerald tasted it on himself already.

The wind whipped at his coat, grabbing and

tugging. A gust hit him in the middle and pushed him back from the edge of the long plunge into the bay—a fair warning. El Niño was bitter and hungry and, despite the fact that it was now getting on into fall, it wasn't giving up its hold of the Gulf Coast quite yet.

A particularly large gray wave came rolling toward the seawall and him. Gerald took several quick steps in retreat but the water sprayed up and drenched him as the wave pounded into the wall below.

Gerald laughed, rubbing a wide-palmed hand over his wet face. "Bloody marvelous," he murmured, grinning like the fool he was.

Yes, he had been right to come here. He hadn't seen it in the light of day yet, but Gerald knew without a doubt that he could write in this sleepy little bay town. Turning regrettably away from the storm's impressive display, he walked back to the rental car.

Now, to find Olivia and get the answers he'd been desperately scrambling for since she left their honeymoon suite in Las Vegas.

BLENDERS BUZZED, BOTTLE tops sucked and hissed, and glasses clinked. Speakers blared, pool balls clacked and hearty conversation all joined the tavern chorus to drown out the wind rattling the windows facing the listless bay. Only a handful of days away from Halloween, the wooden walls of the tavern were strewn with faux cobwebs.

"Jimmy Buffett, eat your heart out," Olivia announced with a wink to the gentleman on the other side of her bar who'd ordered a tall margarita.

"Hold on to your hat, newcomer," one of her regulars, Charlie, muttered, giving the gentleman a supportive pat on the back.

"How much do I owe you?" the newcomer asked her.

Olivia beamed. "On me. Didn't you hear? That storm is headed for N'Awlins. We're celebratin'."

"Though God bless all those poor Cajuns," Olivia's part-time waitress Monica Slayer said. "First Katrina. Then Gustav. Now this. They can't ever seem to catch a break."

Charlie snorted. "It's what they get for living below sea level."

"Careful, Charlie boy," Olivia warned. "We're not too far above sea level ourselves. Another beer?"

"Still nursing this one, sweetheart." Charlie's eyes twinkled. "You're pretty as your wildcat mama, you know that?"

Olivia shook her head. "You're shameless as a hound dog, old man."

"You tell Rosa I'm still waiting for her," Charlie advised before tipping his bottle back and gulping deep.

Monica nudged Olivia with an elbow. "If that

Freddie character comes on to me again, I'm gonna show him what it's like to have a three-inch heel shoved up his ass."

Olivia eyed the gangly giant in question. "Oh, come on. He's harmless. What's he doing to harass you?"

Monica rolled her eyes. "His lips are moving."

Olivia belted out a laugh. "When you first started working for me little over two years ago, you said he was pretty hot stuff."

Monica snorted. "That was before he went and married Elaine."

"You're still sore about that?" Olivia chided, brow quirked. "It's been eight months."

"Well, yeah, I'm sore! The few decent guys there are in this town get hung up in seconds…usually with the worst women."

"Ain't that the truth?" Olivia said with a doubtful glance around the room. Fairhope was as peaceful as small Southern towns got. It might be the quintessential place to retire or raise kids, but like most small towns there was a deplorable lack of good, unattached men to go around. "Don't sweat it. She'll get bored with him, and you can be the first to lick his wounds."

"I don't do seconds." Monica brooded before chugging down the shot of Jack Daniel's the wizened man across the bar had bought her. Her lips curved into a practiced simper. "Thanks, Pete."

"Hey, Liv!" someone called from the other side of the bar.

Olivia laughed fondly at the baby face of Skeet Bisbee. "Hey, cutie. I haven't seen you since you left for Tuscaloosa. What are you doing here?"

Skeet grinned, radiating collegiate charm as he sat on the vacant stool next to Charlie. "I came to order a drink."

Olivia narrowed her eyes and angled her head in scrutiny. "Does your mama know you're here?"

Skeet beamed. "I mean it. I want a black jack."

"As pretty as that face is, I'm gonna have to say no," Olivia told him.

"All right, all right." Skeet reached for his billfold and held it out to her. "Check this out. I turned legal just a few hours ago. I was lucky the DMV was open. You know, with the storm and all."

Olivia scanned the temporary license. "Hell, that ain't even in plastic yet. That can't be legal. What do you think, Monica?"

Monica glanced at the ID, then up at the hopeful, handsome face before her. "Come on, Liv. Give the man a drink." The waitress poured a jigger of Jack herself and sent it sailing across the bar with a wink. "On me."

Skeet blushed to the roots of his hair.

Olivia cackled, grabbed Skeet's face in her hands and pressed her lips to his. A chorus of catcalls went up around the tavern, and Skeet bloomed from pink to cherry-red.

"Happy birthday, Skeeter baby," Olivia said before raising her voice over the music. "Hey, everybody, it's Skeet Bisbee's birthday and I want you all to buy him a drink!"

Obliging volunteers pushed their way toward the bar and the two tavern-keepers got busy quickly.

Though Fairhope wasn't as exciting as…say Vegas, the town and the tavern had been Olivia's one and only home for twenty-nine years. It was practically her lifeblood. The minute her adventurous parents handed the reins of the business to her seven years ago to fulfill their cross-country traveling dreams, she'd found a deep sense of purpose in keeping the family trade alive and strong. Her mother and father had built it from the ground up. It was her job to nourish and sustain it. And *that* she had, even through the worst downturn of the local, small business economy.

For seven years, her life had been a chorus line of late working nights. It'd take more than a hurricane to break that chain and her love of it.

"Oh, my," Olivia heard a stunned Monica say over the jukebox crank of Boston's best. The waitress's hands were frozen in midair and her eyes were locked on the tavern doors. "What have we here?"

Olivia looked around, up over the heads of her patrons to the big, heavy, distressed-wood-panel doors. She took one look at the man who had just blown in from the windy outdoors, running a hand through his wet golden hair, his long wool jacket soaking wet, and her heart struck a drumbeat.

No. It couldn't be.

His kind, intelligent eyes scanned the shiny wood carvings on the walls and the web-strewn lights overhead before settling on the long bar. They passed over the heads of her customers and snagged on her. That drumbeat inside her kicked into a cadence as he grinned wide, knowingly, his gaze warming on hers, and inclined his head.

Monica gasped. "You *know* that piece of man candy?"

Olivia opened her mouth to speak but nothing came out. So few times in her life had she been truly speechless. But seeing Gerald Leighton walk into her tavern on the most unlikely night of the year might have been the shock of her lifetime. Shaking her head, she gawped like a fish as she and Monica both watched him walk the rest of the way to the bar and take up one of the few empty stools on the far end.

"Liv?" Monica said, snapping her fingers to get Olivia's attention. When Olivia blinked and focused on the waitress's face, Monica narrowed her eyes. "Are you okay?"

"Fine," Olivia said, glancing back at Gerald, who had eyes only for her. "Just…handle the bar for a bit. I'll be right back."

Monica looked from Olivia to Gerald and back. Then she shrugged. "All righty, then. I'd ask you to get me his name and number…but it seems he's already taken."

Olivia opened her mouth to deny it, then decided not to when Monica quickly went back to work. Clearing her throat, Olivia took off the apron at her waist and left the bar, rounding it to meet Gerald on the other side.

He smiled at her approach, those laugh lines digging in and charming her all over again. Three weeks. She hadn't seen hide nor hair of him in three weeks. She'd counted on not laying eyes on him ever again. And here he was, having the same effect on her that he'd had the morning after in Vegas. As he stood up for her, she slowed her steps and licked her lips. "Gerald," she said simply.

"Olivia," he said with a nod and a widening grin. Those green eyes washed over her like a head-to-toe caress. "You can't know how relieved I am to see you."

"Yeah, about that." Olivia cleared her throat and crossed her arms over her chest, shifting from one black-heeled boot to the other. "How *did* you find me exactly?"

"I had to call in a few favors," Gerald admitted. "In the end, it was my publicist who was able to nail down your current address. You're not an easy woman to find, Olivia Lewis. Particularly in the middle of a hurricane."

She looked toward the glass doors leading onto the veranda. Nobody had dared to brave Mother

Nature and sip their drinks outside this evening as they did most other nights at the tavern. Seeing the sturdy wooden chairs being whipped about by the wind and the soaking wet, weathered planks of the floor, she frowned at him. "You drove through *this* to get to me?"

"Yes," Gerald confirmed. And there was that hint of sheepishness crawling into his eyes. He blinked and interest filled them, chasing away the momentary embarrassment as he jerked his thumb toward the bay. "Is it always like this?"

"Only occasionally, during the latter months of hurricane season. I've seen way worse," Olivia told him. "Why?" When he looked at her in question, she added, "Why were you so desperate to track me down that you couldn't wait for the storm to pass?"

Gerald cleared his throat and dropped his eyes to the floor. "Perhaps we'd both better have a drink."

She stared at him a moment, the muscles tightening around the smile on his mouth. "Yep," she agreed with an answering nod. "You might be right about that."

OLIVIA STILL COULDN'T get over the fact that he was here. The man who, despite Olivia's best efforts, she hadn't been able to stop thinking about for three weeks. Particularly when she was in bed, alone. Or making coffee in the morning. She'd hardly been able to shower without thoughts of him rising with the steam in the bathroom.

Monica had brought their drinks to a table in the corner of the tavern, farthest away from the bustling bar and the two pool tables and televisions broadcasting sports and the weather radar. Gerald had taken off the wool jacket as well as the sports jacket he wore beneath it. The sleeves of his crisp, green, button-down shirt were rolled up over the muscles of his forearms.

Olivia watched those muscles flex as he gripped the pint of Sam Adams. Gerald brought it to his lips, tipped it back and made a sound of assent. "Bloody good draft." Shooting a glance at her over the rim, he added, "Have you always been in the tavern business, Olivia?"

She pursed her lips. "You're the one who had your publicist track me down. Shouldn't you know that already? Stalkers usually do a background check, right?"

Gerald chuckled, his shoulders moving under the shirt. What kind of material could look so soft yet be able to fold on a knifepoint as his did at the collar? It looked pricey. Olivia wondered if it had cost as much as a man like Gerald could potentially cost her. "Details aside, love, I'm not stalking you," he explained. "I actually had a very practical reason for tracking you down."

"And that is…?" Olivia asked.

Gerald jerked his chin toward her untouched pint. "You should drink first."

She gestured to the bar. "I'm a busy woman, Gerald. I don't have much time."

He leaned forward in his chair and braced his elbows on her table, those nice, solid shoulders settling over his bent arms. "What memories do you have of our time in Nevada?"

"Our one-night stand, you mean?" Olivia asked.

He grinned. "Precisely."

She sighed, lifting a hand. "Oh, I don't know. Not much, to be honest. Tequila has a debilitating effect on my ability to retain information."

"As it does for all us mere mortals," Gerald acknowledged with a thoughtful nod. He turned serious, almost grave. After a moment's hesitation, he reached out and covered her hand with his free one. "I hope you don't take this too hard, but it seems on that night in Las Vegas somewhere along the line we happened to find ourselves embedded in a wedding chapel."

Her lips twitched in wry humor. "A wedding chapel. You're kidding me, right?" When those grave green eyes neither smiled nor strayed from hers, she fumbled. "You're…you're not? Kidding?"

Gerald took a breath. "No. Apparently, Elvis presided over the ceremony. It's a bit hazy to me, too. Two ladies by the names of Roxanna Honeycutt and Adrian Carlton—who, I'm assuming, were the friends you were in Vegas with—served as witnesses. By all accounts, the entire wedding party was inordinately pissed."

"No," Olivia said. She snatched her hand out from underneath his. Her heart plummeted down to her toes. She shook her head in automatic denial even as dread crawled over her. "You're wrong. We didn't. *I* didn't."

"We were drinking, love," Gerald reminded her gently, as if he were treading on eggshells. He watched her face closely. Concern rose through the gravity as her dread became apparent. "There's no shame in it."

"No shame?" Olivia muttered, disbelieving. Damn it, how had she gotten herself into this situation? Hadn't she learned enough the first time? It didn't matter that she'd gone several rounds with Señor Cuervo. She'd gotten married. In Las Vegas. To a complete and total stranger.

"Olivia," Gerald said. He uttered her name again, reaching out to touch her shoulder and bring her back to him. "Are you all right?"

"Fine," she snapped, then checked herself and cleared her throat. "I'm fine." It wasn't his fault. If he was right, everyone involved had been plastered. There was no way her cynical friend Adrian in her right mind would have let her elope with a stranger. And Olivia liked to think, without the influence of alcohol, Roxie wouldn't have allowed her to do something that stupid, either.

She took a deep breath and gripped the edge of the table in front of her. "So…what do we do about it?"

Gerald trained his gaze on some point over her shoulder. "Well, I've already spoken to my attorney. He's assured me that he will take care of it with little fuss if we decide to go the route of separation."

"Okay, good," Olivia said, relieved. But that relief dissolved little by little as she watched him take another long sip from the pint. "Wait. You said 'if.' Why is there an *if?*"

Gerald pressed his lips together, either savoring the Sam Adams or bracing himself. She had a very frightening suspicion it was the latter. He planted his elbows on the table again and leaned toward her, smile warming the lower half of his face. "I have a wee bit of a suggestion."

"If it's not related to annulment or divorce, you might not be walking out of here in one piece," Olivia pointed out, trying to smile. He couldn't be crazy enough to suggest that they actually remain married, for heaven's sake.

Could he?

Gerald made a thoughtful noise in his throat. "Well…"

Olivia's smile fled and she looked at him as if he were crazy. "Okay, now you're scaring me."

"Just hear me out," Gerald advised, lifting a hand in plea.

"No," she said and snorted out a mirthless laugh. "No," she said again just to get her point across. "I have no idea who you are. You don't know anything about me, despite what your publicist or whoever might have told you. The only thing we have in common is one drunk night in Las Vegas."

"How do you know that, love, when, as you say, we don't know each other yet?" Gerald challenged.

Olivia's mouth dropped open. "Because *this* is me," she told him, lifting her arms to encompass the tavern. "And you're…well, you're expensive shirts and tailored suits and spicy aftershave, which I have no doubt costs more than our sham wedding. We're clearly from different parts of the world as a whole. How could you possibly think there's anything there?"

Gerald's eyes locked on hers and sobered once more. "Because of what I felt, the morning after."

Olivia fell silent. "What you felt?"

"Yes," he acknowledged with a dip of his head. "I…" He sighed, shook his head and narrowed his eyes on the windows next to the table as if trying to see the squall beyond the weeping, wind-buffered panes. "Well, suffice it to say, I felt more in that one morning than I've ever felt during any one of the lengthy relationships I've had throughout my entire adult life. And I think that's worth something."

Olivia's mouth opened, then closed and opened again. "It was the drinks, like you said."

Gerald gave her a baleful stare. "We both know we were clean and sober the next morning, Olivia. Can you honestly tell me that night or what was shared between us the following morning meant nothing to you?"

She chose to ignore the fact that she'd been thinking of little else since her flight back to Alabama with the girls, and simply lifted her hands and shoulders in a helpless gesture. "It *couldn't*. There was nothing. *It* was nothing."

Gerald studied her carefully for what seemed like an eternity. Finally, a slow grin crept over the lower half of his face, warming his eyes. The smile was like a sucker punch to her resolve. And damned if he didn't know it, Olivia thought. He took another sip of beer, leaned back in his chair and hooked one loafer-clad ankle over the opposite knee. "I'd like you to prove that."

"What?"

"A wager, if you like," he told her. "Come now, Olivia. You're a small business owner. Small business is a gamble at one time or another. And you strike me as a woman who enjoys a challenge."

"So what if I am?" Olivia asked. "How would that change anything?"

He lifted his finger and pointed at her discerningly. "There's a lovely bed-and-breakfast next door to the tavern. If my publicist's sources are correct, it's your cousin who owns it. I'll stay on there for three weeks, just long enough for you to prove to me that what we shared in Vegas was indeed nothing."

Olivia frowned at him. "If I were to agree, you realize you're betting on a losing hand, right?"

"Maybe," Gerald said with a considering nod.

"But my gut is usually right. And it tells me that the place I need to be, at least for the time being, is right here in your charming little hometown."

She narrowed her eyes as she considered him. Damn it. She did love a good challenge. Especially one where all the odds were in *her* favor. "Hmm. What are the stakes?" When Gerald's brows arched, she added, "What's a wager without stakes?"

"Oh, right." He grinned, lifting a hand to scratch his chin in a pensive manner that made her stare a moment too long at his wide-palmed hand with its narrow, creative fingers. "If you win, I will humbly admit defeat and hand over the divorce papers. And I'll pay whatever legal costs filing them incurs."

"And if *you* win…?"

Gerald's eyes shined anew with the light of promise. "Then what do you say we give this a shot, aye? You and me. I have a feeling it'll be worth it. And on a hunch I'm rarely wrong."

Olivia weighed him and his challenge. When he extended a hand for her to shake in agreement, she sighed and lifted hers to take it. "What the hell? You've got yourself a deal, Mr. Leighton. I hope you're not a sore loser."

Gerald didn't shake her hand. He squeezed it warmly and leaned forward until his green eyes yawned before hers and that aftershave of his washed over her in a splendid wave she was sure never to forget. "I rarely make wagers, *Mrs.*

Leighton. But when I do, I play to win. And I'll be damned if I don't win this one."

Olivia swallowed, then released his hand and lifted her pint to take a gulp of Sam Adams. She had a feeling she was going to need it—and perhaps a few more—if Gerald was indeed sticking around.

CHAPTER THREE

IT WAS CLOSE to midnight, but Olivia got in her old burnt-orange 1980s-model Ford pickup she liked to call Chuck and drove through the rain band currently battering the shoreline. By morning the storm would not only have made landfall but be sweeping its way west toward Texas, hopefully bringing the sun back out to dry this part of the coast.

However, Olivia didn't want to wait until then to confront her friend Adrian Carlton. The florist and single mother lived a few blocks south of the tavern in the old fruit and nut section of Fairhope. It was a quiet neighborhood, particularly at this late hour. Olivia pulled the truck into Adrian's driveway and ran to the small porch underneath the gable that crowned the front of the snug but well-kept cottage.

Balling her hand into a fist, she pounded on the door, then hugged her arms around herself, huddling as close to the door as she could to keep from getting whipped to death by wind and sideways rain.

It took several moments, but she heard the small sound of several locks clicking before the door opened and dim light silhouetted the small, red-headed woman who peered out at her in disbelief. "Liv? Is that you?"

"Yeah," Olivia said. "Let me in, will you?"

"Jesus," Adrian said as she stepped back and let Olivia stride into her tidy, shabby-chic living room. She took a moment to lock all the doors again and then turned to frown at her impromptu guest. "Why the hell are you pounding on my door at midnight? Is something wrong at the tavern? Is water getting into the shops?"

Olivia waved off the suggestion impatiently. "Never mind that. Remember when we were in Vegas?"

Adrian rolled her eyes and groaned, crossed to the sofa and had a seat. "Are you kidding? I'm still trying to live it down."

Olivia not only remained standing, she chose to pace from one wall to the other, gesturing in jerky, sweeping motions as she spoke. "Do you happen to remember the hot blond British guy who I spent the night with?"

"Yeah, we talked about him on the flight back," Adrian reminded her, placid in the face of Olivia's franticness. "You two met at the club. You danced. We all drank and you two wandered off for a night well spent from what you told us."

"It was more than that," Olivia said. She stopped in the middle of the room and spread her arms. "We're married."

Adrian raised her brows. "Married. As in…"

"As in white gown, black tie, bouquets and corsages."

"Boutonnieres," Adrian, the florist, corrected her.

"Whatever," Olivia said, waving that off, too. "Only it wasn't any of that. No, for me it was a red clubbing dress. My groom *might* have been wearing a black tie. Though I'm not quite sure because I was one shot of Cuervo shy of drooling on Elvis's gold lamé cape. And for all I know you and Roxie, who served as witnesses, by the way, carried shiny silk flowers."

Adrian winced. Whether it was from the image of shiny, silk bridesmaids bouquets or from being told she'd served as a witness, Olivia couldn't be sure. "Wow. That's…something."

"And get this," Olivia said, lifting a finger. "My hot British stranger of a husband is here, in Fairhope."

Adrian shook her head slightly as if dazed. "Wait. Now you've got to be jerking me around."

"Nope. He popped by the tavern this evening and is at this very moment checking in to one of Briar's suites at the inn. When she called just a few minutes ago, she said, 'Um, Liv? Do you know there's an Englishman here renting a room who says he's your husband?' He's *telling* people, Adrian."

"Get out of town."

"And as if that weren't enough…" Olivia laughed a sour laugh "…he wants to stay married."

Adrian frowned. She raised her hands to stop the fast flow of shocking information. "Okay. Now you've lost me."

"That's what he said," Olivia informed her, pacing once again. "He says he wants to give it a go. He wants to see if what he felt that one night in Vegas is enough to sustain a bond everlasting. I didn't know whether to pat his head and coo over his eight-year-old-worthy idea of married life or call up the deputy and have him hauled out of the bar for lunacy."

"Huh." Adrian fought a smile. "Interesting."

"So…" Olivia stopped pacing to face Adrian, and lifted her shoulders helplessly. "What do I do?"

"You're asking *me?*"

"Do you see anybody else here?"

"No, but if we don't keep our voices down, there might be."

Olivia glanced toward the hallway leading to the bedrooms where Adrian's seven-year-old son, Kyle, was down for the night. "Oh. Right. Sorry."

"I don't know, Liv," Adrian said, rubbing her eyes. "I've never been in this situation. Or anything quite like it."

"I don't know too many people who have."

"You've got that right." Adrian sighed, dropping her hands into her lap. "How long does he plan on sticking around?"

"Three weeks."

"Does he strike you as...all there?" Adrian pointed to her head.

Olivia nodded slowly, crossing her arms over her chest. "Yes. Despite the frightening optimism and the fact that he braved tropical storm conditions to tell me all this, he seems pretty lucid."

"What's your impression of him?"

"He's..." Olivia stopped, thinking of the man who'd sat across the table from her tonight. She lowered into a cozy armchair. "He's...sexy."

Adrian nodded approvingly. "Uh-huh. Go on."

"He's intellectual, but in a sexy way. Very Tom Hiddleston. Proper and upper-crust but not at all haughty. He's accessible, down-to-earth and so damned charming he can make your toes tingle just by smiling at you...."

"I'm intrigued, and also slightly confused." Adrian licked her lips. "What you're saying is...this Tom Hiddleston-esque, sexy, intelligent man-hunk walks into the tavern and has decided to stay next door for three weeks so that he can, basically, try and woo you into staying married to him. Correct?"

Olivia nodded, thinking it through carefully. "In a nutshell. Yes."

"And you, Olivia Lewis, who has no problem letting men woo her is freaking out because..."

Olivia's eyes narrowed. "He and I are married."

Adrian shrugged. "In my experience, marriage

isn't all it's cracked up to be. But, hey, some people like it. Look at Briar and Cole. Look at your parents."

Olivia made a thoughtful noise as she gnawed on her thumbnail. Her parents' partnership, which had spanned three decades and the hell-raising teen-age version of herself, was a lot to live up to. From an early age she'd known that it was the ultimate ideal—the kind of love she'd once ridiculously en-visioned for herself.

As a young adult, however, she'd learned the hard way that that kind of love and bond didn't come easily. Nor did it happen for everyone. And she was sure it never would for her. "So you're say-ing…" Olivia took a deep, steadying breath "…I should just let it ride?"

Adrian lifted her shoulders. "Why not? He'll definitely be gone by the end of the three weeks?"

"He says so. And he said he'd file for separation himself, take care of the legal fees, everything—as long as I give him these three weeks."

Tired, Adrian gave Olivia a telling look. "Then what's the harm?"

Olivia narrowed her eyes at her friend. "Usually, I can count on you for cynicism. What the hell?"

Adrian lifted a shoulder. "It's midnight. I've been up since 5:00 a.m. Penny and I threw together over a hundred arrangements at the shop today. My bed's calling me. That's all. Talk to me tomorrow after coffee if you want practical advice."

Olivia sighed. "Right." She rose. "Sorry to barge in so late."

Adrian stood. "For curiosity's sake, what's the name of this British man-hunk who intends to sweep you off your feet?"

"No sweeping," Olivia said pointedly. "There will be no sweeping. And his name is Gerald Leighton, for what it's worth."

Adrian blinked in surprise. "Gerald Leighton? The writer, Gerald Leighton?"

"That's his name," Olivia said. "I don't know what he does for a living. I don't know anything about him."

"Hang on." Adrian disappeared into the hall where she kept books on built-in shelves. She strolled back in with a dog-eared paperback, turned it over and opened the back cover for Olivia to see the black-and-white picture on the inside. "Is this him?"

Olivia gawped at Gerald's face for what had to be the third time that night. "Oh, my God. What's he doing there?"

"Liv." Adrian closed the book, firming her lips together as her eyes lit up and she clutched the worn paperback to her chest. "Your husband is Gerald Leighton."

"So?"

"Gerald Leighton," Adrian said again, a bit louder this time. "The fantasy writer. He's an international bestseller. He's won all kinds of awards

in the genre, not to mention for writing in general. He writes the Rex Flynn series."

"Who?"

"Rex Flynn." Adrian made an impatient noise. "Come on, don't you read?"

"Not really," Olivia admitted. "Just the occasional romance novel, heavy on the smut. Short ones—I don't have time for anything else."

Adrian raked a hand through the red cap of her hair. "Oy. Okay, Rex Flynn is this amazing hero who has this weird but really awesome time-traveling ability that just gets him into trouble at first but eventually becomes useful for rescuing people, spying and, of course, saving the world. But the best part about it is the love story. In book one, Rex accidentally travels to the fifteenth-century Highlands where he meets the love of his life, Janet MacMillian, and so starts this epic love story that continues throughout the rest of the series."

"*You* read love stories?" Olivia asked doubtfully. "Since when?"

"I started out reading the series because Dad suggested it for the history and time-travel elements. But it's more than all that. There's intrigue and action and magic and ancient history and love and even a little bit of smut.... Oh, it's just perfection! He is the best writer. And he's, like, a multimillionaire."

"No, he's not," Olivia said automatically.

"No, really. He's an actual multimillionaire. He

gets seven-figure advances and he does these book signings where people line up for city blocks just to meet him. They're talking even about doing a Rex Flynn movie. Liv, this is a big deal. He, Gerald Leighton, is a *big deal*."

"Calm down," Olivia ordered. She put her hands on her head and shook it in denial. "I can't process this right now. I just can't. You're right. We'll talk more in the morning. Postcoffee."

"Liv," Adrian said, snagging Olivia's arm as she opened the front door. "Can I meet him? Do you think it would be okay if I met him. I mean, meet him *again*...when I'm not drunk? Maybe he could sign a couple of my hardbacks or something?"

Olivia took one good look at Adrian's animated expression and shook her head. "For Christ's sake, Adrian. Get a hold of yourself." She walked out of the cottage, back into the rain.

If the man had Adrian Carlton of all people beaming sunshine and rainbows, Gerald Leighton was going to be far more trouble than Olivia had initially thought.

THE BREAKFAST OLIVIA'S cousin, Briar Browning Savitt, served for guests and family at Hanna's Inn was not to be missed.

Olivia walked around the tavern and the adjourning shops facing South Mobile Street. She crossed the gravel parking lot to the proud white three-story bed-and-breakfast that had been owned by the Brownings for decades. She saw her cousin's small sedan, the four-by-four owned by Briar's husband, Cole, who used the brawny vehicle to haul landscaping materials and such, Adrian's ten-year-old SUV and what looked to be a luxury sportster Olivia could only guess was Gerald Leighton's rental car.

Apparently, she wasn't the only one who had shown up for Briar's cinnamon rolls. Frowning at the blue skies scant on clouds today, Olivia mused that if not for the wet and battered leaves littering the ground and the tangled state of her cousin's climbing roses and jasmine bushes, one might never have known that the coast had had a very near miss with a Category 3 hurricane. And despite the fact that it was late October, the brush with El Niño had left the Eastern Shore warm enough for it to be mid-May.

Nobody could ever be prepared for Gulf Coast weather. It changed on a dime, rain or shine. In summer, residents suffered through weeks of dry, dusty drought followed by a month-and-a-half straight of coastal flooding. Halloween was on the horizon and Olivia was wearing flip-flops.

She smiled. The unpredictability of the weather was one thing most people around these parts tolerated. Olivia, a creature of unpredictability herself, thrived in it.

She bounded up the steps to the inn's glass-front

entry doors. The bells jangled as she opened them and the smell of cinnamon and home struck her.

Olivia followed the voices coming from the back of the house. She made her way down the hall, past the fancy dining room full of antiques and the living room with its plush, half-moon sofa and flat-screen television. Here brilliant streams of sunlight beamed unfiltered from the connected sunroom, which overlooked Briar's gardens. Cole's trim, green yard tumbled down to the rocky, sandy shore and the small dock with its Adirondack chairs and chaise longues.

The bay was still choppy but had settled back for the most part. The storm had stirred it into a murky brown. Light beamed off the surface of the crests, however, and it wasn't hard to see the gleaming spires and bottlenecked cranes of the city of Mobile beyond it.

Olivia peered through the swinging door into Briar's kitchen. Standing at the counter, a steaming mug of coffee clenched in one hand and an infant tucked against his opposing shoulder, Cole Savitt was the first to catch her eye. He grinned a lazy morning grin and tipped his mug toward her in greeting.

She pressed a finger to her lips, slipping quietly into the room. Adrian and Kyle sat at the round nook table and Olivia could hear Briar's voice floating from the open pantry doors. She walked to Cole and placed her hand gently on the baby's back. "How's our Harmony this morning?"

"I think she's out," the man said, dipping his head close to his daughter's. "She kept us awake most of the night."

Olivia got on her tiptoes to get a better view of Harmony's face. Her eyes were closed and her cheek was adorably mushed against the broad shoulder of Cole's black T-shirt. Olivia grazed her fingertip over the bridge of the two-month-old's button nose and sighed. "I was hoping for a smile this morning." Lowering herself back to the heels of her feet, Olivia asked, "Colicky again?"

"Yep," Cole said, carefully readjusting the weight of the baby so that she settled against his chest and not his arm. "It's winding down, though. She hasn't had a rough night like this in a couple weeks." His smile turned sly as his dark eyes settled on Olivia's face again. "I just hope she didn't disturb our latest guest."

Olivia groaned. "Don't. Just don't."

"Oh, come on, Liv," Cole said, setting his coffee down so he could run a tan, calloused hand over Harmony's back. "I recall a time, about a year and a half ago now, when you teased Briar and me mercilessly just for glancing at each other at the breakfast table. Now you've gone and found yourself not just a boyfriend but a bona fide bridegroom and I can't make a comment?" He smirked and shook his head. "I don't think so, cuz."

She had a hard time holding the frown on her lips when he looked so mischievous. Olivia had been raised with Briar. They were more sisters than cousins, which made Cole the closest thing to a brother Olivia would ever have. It did her well to see light and laughter in his eyes now, when a year and a half ago there had been none of that. "Just do me a favor and tell me where I can find the man of the hour?"

Cole nodded toward the pantry. "Bartering a couple of jars of Briar's homemade jam off her. She's practically fawning over him." He grabbed his coffee again, raised it to his lips with lowered brows. "If I weren't so secure in our relationship, I might feel more than a small stab of jealousy."

"You have nothing to worry about," she pointed out. "Me, on the other hand? That's a whole different ball game. I'm gonna try to rope him out of here."

"Good luck with that," Cole muttered into his coffee.

Olivia mussed a hand over Kyle's rusty brown crop of hair, leaning down to press a loud kiss to the boy's freckled cheek. "How are ya, slugger?"

Kyle beamed up at her, displaying a new gap between his teeth. "Great. Gerald gave me a euro." He raised the small European coin from the table. "Look, Liv! Isn't it neat?"

"Yeah, how 'bout that?" Olivia said, narrowing her eyes on Adrian across the table.

Adrian shrugged, though the corners of her mouth twitched. "You were right. He is a charmer."

"Oh, you, too, huh?" Olivia muttered through gritted teeth as she eyed the hardback book next to Adrian's plate.

Her friend lifted her shoulders again and lowered telling eyes to the coffee in her hands. "Yeah. You're on your own."

"Brutus." Olivia sneered. Cursing, she stalked to the pantry. It was small, but the floor-to-ceiling shelves were all stocked neat as a pin with every label facing outward. The man in question was reaching up to grab a jar of rhubarb jam off the top shelf for Briar, who beamed wide at him as he handed it to her. "Aren't you sweet?" Briar asked, a pink flush staining her cheeks. "Thank you, Gerald."

"It's my pleasure, Mrs. Savitt," he said. "Your husband's a lucky man. He has a pretty wife and envious access to all your jams, jellies and homemade treats."

Briar tittered over him. Actually *tittered*. Olivia scowled. That was the last straw. "Gerald," she barked.

Briar jumped, startled at the intrusion. Gerald steadied her with a hand on her shoulder as he turned to Olivia with a beaming smile, one arm laden with mason jars full of jam. "Well, if it isn't my gorgeous wife." His eyes dipped over her from head to toe. "You're looking fine today, Mrs. Leighton."

Olivia narrowed her eyes on him in a blistering stare. "We need to talk."

He looked from her furious, gleaming eyes to Briar's flushed face. "Your cousin's just been telling me how you used to steal jam from her mother's cupboard, which is why it's still kept on the top shelf to this day. She also says you used to steal liquor from your parents' bar. That's why they put a lock on the storeroom door."

Olivia's frown deepened as she looked at Briar. Her cousin had the gall to look innocent. "I'll be talking to you later," Olivia warned Briar. "*You,* on the other hand…" She grabbed Gerald's hand and tugged on it hard to get his feet moving. "Outside. Now."

"Thank you, Briar," he managed to say as Olivia hauled him away. "I'm looking forward to sampling each of these. Perhaps you'll make me some more of those delicious scones to go with them?"

"Of course, Gerald," Briar answered. "Whatever you like."

Muttering, Olivia got behind Gerald and pushed him out the screen door before he could respond to her cousin. Grabbing the sleeve of his oxford shirt, she pulled him in the direction of the jasmine arbor where the garden surrounded them, blocking the view from the inn's many windows. Rounding on him, she crossed her arms over her chest. "What are you doing?" she asked, indignant.

Gerald blinked and lifted a mason jar for her inspection. "Just talking jams. Your cousin's a gem. The way she talks about you...it's more like a mother. It's illuminating." His grin turned wry. "Do you need a mummy, Olivia?"

Olivia groaned. "I'm not talking about...that. This whole marriage business was to stay between *us*."

He narrowed his eyes. "I'm sorry, but I thought they were your family."

"They *are* my family—"

"And as your family, who loves you dearly, they'd have a right to know who I am and why I'm staying here. That is, unless you weren't planning on being honest with them? It was my impression that your relationship with them means a great deal more to you than that."

Olivia's mouth fumbled. She raked her hands through her hair in frustration. "You're just trying to figure me out—get inside my head." She jabbed a finger into his chest. "Stop it!"

Gerald chuckled. The laughter settled into a warm smile as he turned and set the jars in a neat row on the arbor bench. "You've a lovely family."

She opened her mouth to speak, then stopped and sighed. "Yes. I know."

"I've gathered the Savitts have had a spot of trouble with the inn over the past couple of years."

"Yes." She waved that off. "Well, the trouble started before they were together, when my aunt died several years back. Briar almost lost the business, but thankfully some investors swooped in and saved it from going under, just around the time she and Cole met. It doesn't feel right, though, not completely. Briar's still innkeeper and the inn is doing well again, but the family name isn't on the books anymore. It's a weight on them both."

"And you," Gerald surmised, wise eyes combing her face.

Olivia nodded. "Yeah, I guess it is.... Wait, why are we talking about this?"

His eyes dropped to her waist and he took a step closer to her, closing the space between them. "I realize I've disrupted your life without any warning. So, I have a proposition to make it up to you when all of this is settled."

She tried to step back to keep from getting lost in that teasing aftershave of his. Her back came up against the side of the arbor and the jasmine still blooming around it. "What?"

The light dappled onto his face as a smile warmed it. "If this doesn't end the way I want it to between you and me, I'll pay what Briar and Cole owe to their investors and restore the inn in their name."

"You'll...*what?*"

"Perhaps it will make up for my intrusion into your lives," he told her. "You're good people. Your cousins certainly don't deserve to have anyone mucking about their lives. It's the least I can do."

"No," Olivia argued. "It's too much." When he opened his mouth to insist, she stopped him. "Look, I know who you are. I know you have more money than God. But buying things isn't the way to woo me."

Gerald raised his brows. "Duly noted, Mrs. Leighton. But this has nothing to do with wooing you. This is me doing what I view is the right thing, for your family, since you are all welcoming me into your lives—even if only for a short while."

Olivia scanned his face carefully, looking for flaws. There had to be a catch. Some angle he was trying to play to win his bet against her.

He pursed his lips. "You would deny your cousins peace of mind, after all they've been through?"

She closed her eyes and pinched the bridge of her nose. "No matter what I say, you're going to do whatever you want, aren't you?"

Grinning, he lifted his hands to her face. He cupped one hand over her cheek and brushed her hair back from the other. "Look there. We're beginning to understand one another already. You know not much will stop me from getting what I want—*you*. And I know you would do anything for your family. Even if it means putting up with a gentleman like me."

Her brows came down over her eyes. "Who said you were a gentleman?"

"Do you not like gentlemen, love?"

Despite the fact that she had more than a few notches on her bedpost, Olivia didn't have much experience with so-called gentlemen. This was all new, rocky terrain. And she was very much afraid that this gentleman might make all the men she'd slept with before him dim in comparison.

She glanced back to the inn. "Do whatever you want. Just… I don't want them getting attached to you. I don't want them buying into this…" She gestured between them. "Whatever this is you're trying to make happen between us."

His eyes dimmed. "Have you so little faith in men?" Both his hands gripped her face now. "I won't hurt them. And I won't hurt you, Liv. I wouldn't dream of it."

She thought of her lack of faith more as keeping the status quo of low expectations. Raising them only meant being disappointed. She wanted to believe Gerald when he said he wouldn't hurt her—and that right there was trouble. *Stick to the status quo,* she told herself firmly. *Or you will most certainly get hurt…whether he intends to hurt you or not.*

Grabbing his wrists, she lowered them from her face and released them. "This isn't going to work, you know. I hope you're still prepared for that."

"I'm prepared to do whatever it takes to change your mind," he told her.

"Why?" she demanded. "Marriages based on

one night of passion have terrible track records."
"Trust me, I know," she almost added then closed her mouth quickly.

"I don't believe that's always the case," Gerald said thoughtfully.

She raised one brow. "Are you *always* this idealistic when it comes to relationships?" she asked.

He reached up again to brush a hand back through her hair, lowering his face close to hers so the green of his eyes all but swallowed her. "I prefer to think of it as faith."

She frowned. "Were your parents blissfully happy or something?"

"No. Their marriage was a rudding disaster and a bitter one at that."

Olivia lifted her shoulders, disbelieving. "I was wrong, then. You're not idealistic. You're just plain crazy."

"We'll find out, won't we?" he said. Before she could stop him, he bent down and touched his lips briefly to hers.

Off balance, she staggered, her mouth suddenly very dry and her heart dancing on twinkle toes.

Backing away toward the shore, he grinned at her stunned expression. "Tonight at the tavern. I'd like to see you again in your element. You can fix me a drink, and I might steal a dance." Winking, he turned away and left her standing under the shade of the arbor.

As she watched him stroll away, all confident

strides and whistling a jaunty tune, Olivia caught herself lifting her hand to her lips.

Hell. She *had* to pull it together.

CHAPTER FOUR

"LIV, I THINK you've gone and married Jude Law," Roxie said in a whispered hush as she all but crawled onto the kitchen counter to better see the man strolling around Briar's garden beyond the windows.

Olivia rolled her eyes. "I can't catch a break with this guy."

"You know—" Adrian pitched in, lifting her mug to her lips and tilting her head to better admire Gerald from the back as he turned to inspect a row of azaleas "—I think he's more Colin Firth."

"You would," Olivia snapped. "And you're no help, by the way."

"Sorry," Adrian replied. "Couldn't resist ribbing you a little. It's nice for a change."

"He's out of my league," Olivia said matter-of-factly.

"I didn't think anyone was out of your league," Roxie claimed. "You could have *anyone*."

Adrian snorted. "You *have* had anyone."

"Jerk," Olivia said, but without much heat. It was the truth. She wasn't picky when it came to the men she invited into her bed…so long as they were agreeable to leaving it the following morning. "This is Gerald's type we're talking about, not mine. Audrey Hepburn is more his speed. Not Marlene Dietrich."

"Don't knock Marlene," Cole, standing close by, advised.

"There's nothing wrong with Marlene or you," Roxie helpfully intoned. "Not that that matters because Gerald is so taken with you. When he looks at you, he just lights up."

"Roxie," Adrian said with a smirk, "you're such a romantic."

"Damn right I am." Roxie beamed. "And as far as types go, I'll warn you—it's those we don't expect to sweep us off our feet who we fall for the hardest."

Nobody would be doing any falling, Olivia determined. Least of all her. When something inside her niggled doubtfully, she frowned and turned her attention quickly to Cole. "So what's up with you and Briar?"

He frowned at her, switching Harmony's weight from one arm to the other. The baby whined, wriggled, then settled after grabbing a fistful of the dark hair at the nape of Cole's neck. "Excuse me?" he asked.

"Don't give me that." Olivia elbowed him. "You looked at her over breakfast like you wanted to slather her on your toast."

"Yeah, but you couldn't because she wasn't on the menu," Adrian added.

Cole frowned at their knowing faces. "Did she say something to you?"

"No, we're just intuitive," Olivia reminded him. "All except for Roxie here, bless her heart. She's blinded by soon-to-be marital bliss."

"Shouldn't you be blinded by marital bliss, too, Liv?" he returned with a wry smile tugging at one corner of his mouth.

"Touché," Adrian intoned, then cleared her throat when Olivia glanced askance at her. "Despite all appearances, Cole, we are known to be helpful on occasion. You should know that better than anyone."

Cole sighed, glancing the way Briar had gone. "I don't know what you could do in this case. It's been a few months since Harmony came."

"Two," Olivia said handily.

"Not that I'm counting," Cole retorted.

"And you two haven't messed around since?" Olivia guessed.

He shifted uncomfortably under their expectant looks. "Things have been busy. There's the baby. There's taking care of the inn, the new advertising initiative to bring in more guests.... There hasn't been time for messing around."

"There's always time," Olivia said.

When Cole turned stoic again, Roxie clasped a hand to her heart. "Aw. You're waiting for Briar to make the first move because you don't want to rush her. Isn't that just the sweetest thing?"

"She hasn't shot me down," Cole added quickly in defense of his wife. "We just don't talk about it."

"Who needs to talk?" Adrian asked.

"Excellent point." Olivia faced Cole, setting her mug aside so she could level with him. "Look, I'm going to tell you the same thing I told Briar when you first came to Hanna's. Get over yourself and jump her damn bones."

Cole choked on the second cup of coffee he'd only just finished. Looking around, he made sure that Kyle was still eating, safely out of earshot. "Christ."

"And I was right, wasn't I?" Olivia challenged. "It's what you both needed then, and it's what you need now. Do it. We'll all be happier for it."

A frown tugged at Cole's mouth. "And here I thought it wasn't any of your damn business."

Roxie's cornflower-blue eyes gleamed as they found Gerald through the window again. "You know, all this talk about Briar and Cole getting together…it gives me an idea…." She looked at Olivia. "You're usually the matchmaker, of all of us. I think it's time we return the favor."

Olivia didn't like where this was going. "Huh?"

Roxie smiled. "I like Gerald. I think he might be good for you. Even if that doesn't mean staying married to him, I think you should give whatever he believes you two have a chance. And, I'll be honest, if over the next three weeks I discover a way to help him convince you to do this, then I'm going to take it."

"I like this plan," Cole piped up. He slung an arm around Roxie's shoulders and squeezed companionably. "I've been waiting for the chance to give our cousin here a taste of her own medicine." He winked at Olivia. "Yeah. I like this plan a lot."

"You want revenge," Olivia told him. "It's enough having to deal with Cupid," she added, nodding toward Roxie. "I don't need Machiavelli working against me, too."

"Machiavelli is no stranger to your matchmaking ways," Adrian informed her.

"Whose side are you on?" Olivia demanded.

"Hey, I'm Switzerland," Adrian said, raising her hands. "But that doesn't mean I can't have a little fun watching you deal with Gerald and the rest of them." She swept her arm out to encompass both Cole and Roxie, who already had their heads together.

Olivia gave up trying to reason with any of them. "I'm gonna get out of here before Pinky and the Brain get too far into their plotting. I have a tavern to clean."

Before Olivia escaped through the swinging door, Briar swung it open first from the other side.

"Not so fast," Briar said. "I think I'll have a word with you now."

"I'd love to stay and chat," Olivia lied, pivoting toward the screen door, "but the bar opens early on Fridays, remember, and, frankly, I don't need a lecture."

"That's too bad." Unfazed, Briar gripped Olivia's wrist and pulled her into the privacy of the sunroom. "If it were up to you, we'd never find the time and place for me to lecture you."

Olivia held up her hands in defense as Briar whirled on her, stemming the torrent of words that her cousin had no doubt been waiting all morning to say. "Wait. Before we do this, let me ask you something. Why aren't you sexing Cole up?"

Briar balked, went pale. "What?"

"We just talked to him," Olivia said, lowering her voice to a discreet level. "He said you're not putting out."

"He *said* that?" Briar asked, horrified.

"Not those exact words, but that's the gist of it, isn't it?"

Briar flustered for a moment, then scrubbed nervous hands over her thighs, looking anywhere other than at Olivia as her face reddened. "There hasn't been time—"

"Yeah, he tried to give us that line of bull, too. What's going on, Briar? Really?"

She threw her hands up. "Nothing. Nothing's

going on, Liv. It's just… I was hoping that maybe he'd say something…or *do* something."

"Like what exactly?"

"Like…say that he wants me," Briar said with a consternated expression. "I know it sounds silly, but—"

"It's not silly," Olivia muttered. "Unless you consider the fact that he's also been waiting for *you* to say or do something, too." At Briar's helpless look, Olivia sighed. "Look, I'm begging you to put an end to it. Don't even talk about it. Just *do it*. Tonight."

"Tonight," Briar said, breathing out and looking dazed.

"That's all I have to say," Olivia said quickly.

"Wait a minute!" Briar recovered, gripping Olivia's elbow to stop her from retreating. "We need to talk about Gerald."

"I'm talked out as far as he's concerned," Olivia informed her.

"He's a nice guy," Briar said, managing a stern brow for Olivia and a small smile for Gerald all at once. "In fact…" Her eyes softened and went dreamy. "Liv, he's a wonderful man."

"Cole's right. Maybe he should be jealous."

"No, he shouldn't," Briar said firmly. "Listen, I know better than anyone that you like having your own space and your own set of rules when it comes to men. But…Gerald's different. You know that, right?"

"I know that for all his charm, brains and good looks, he needs his head examined for thinking even for a second that this has the tiniest chance of working out," Olivia said.

"I'm not worried about what he's thinking," Briar explained. "What I'm trying to figure out is why my cousin, who's never had a problem flirting with a man, can't even entertain the idea of this one sticking around for three weeks for what seems like a perfectly harmless wager."

Olivia pursed her lips but said nothing, just kept her arms locked tight over her chest. When a shape passed the glass windows on her right, her gaze snagged on it and her heart rapped when she saw it was Gerald, talking on the phone and laughing as he paced absently across the inn's lawn.

She didn't owe Briar an explanation. Neither was she going to change her views on marriage and commitment. She'd made her mind up long ago on both. Or it'd been made up for her when the last man who had proposed marriage to her left her with nothing but broken dreams and an even more broken heart.

Yes, Gerald was a perfectly good man. He might be the perfect man. But that didn't change the fact that she wouldn't—couldn't—let him in. Even if it was just for fun.

Briar patted her arm, drawing Olivia's gaze away from the man walking around outside and back to the sunroom and their conversation. "Just promise me you won't do anything drastic to chase him away. Give him the three weeks, even if you think he can't change the outcome."

"He can't," Olivia said firmly. "But a bet's a bet and I plan on keeping my word and letting him stay here."

"Good," Briar said, relief shining into her honey-brown eyes. "I've got to go clean up the kitchen and nurse Harmony before today's guests arrive."

"Let Cole do the cleaning," Olivia told her. "He'll make it shine just as much as you would. And then the both of you should try to get some rest and take some time for yourselves. Don't hesitate to call me if you need a babysitter."

"Thanks for that," Briar said with a smile. Her eyes widened. "Wow. If you'd have told me we'd be trading marital advice a few weeks ago, I would've pulled a Rochester and locked you in the attic."

Olivia rolled her eyes. "Let's not get too used to it. Gerald will be gone in three weeks." And for her, that moment could not come soon enough.

GERALD STUFFED HIS hands in the pockets of his slacks as he roamed the shoreline. Though a stiff breeze blew off the choppy bay, the sun was warm and he lifted his face to it. Where before the water had risen high on crashing, angry waves, the morning after the storm it moved in on lightly whoosh-ing crests that rolled into the sandy shore in front of Olivia's tavern and the inn. The water sluiced around the thick, wooden pillars underneath the inn's dock. He was surprised to hear the cry of seagulls and the honk of geese coming from the parks that lined the neighboring bluff.

Apparently the calm came after a storm here. It was almost like a religion, this kind of serenity. Though the main road wasn't far behind Hanna's and Tavern of the Graces and its adjoining shops, the whish and roar of vehicles didn't penetrate the quiet October morning.

Gerald's shoulders relaxed, any lingering tension left over from his journey here sliding away slowly but surely.

His instincts were right about this place. He was sure of it—as sure as he was about the woman he had married.

The morning after their alcohol-fueled romp around Las Vegas, Gerald hadn't been lying when he'd told Olivia that he had been staying there for business. In fact, he had been there for two straight weeks meeting with the motion picture studio that wanted to make his Rex Flynn book series into a film franchise.

The negotiations had been far more stressful than he'd anticipated. After two weeks of trying to hash things out with screenwriters, movie producers and potential directors, there were still too many decisions to be made, compromises to mete out.... Was it any wonder he'd been having trouble writing lately? All the noise created by the business side of his successful writing career was drowning out the quiet voice of his muse.

At the end of those two weeks in Nevada, sitting at the bar that fateful night in the club downing his Scotch like water, Gerald had wondered how the idea of making his Rex Flynn books into a movie franchise had ever seemed like a good one. The character belonged on paper where Gerald—or, rather, his muse—called the shots.

Gerald watched as two pelicans winged lackadaisically overhead, the prehistoric-looking birds in no hurry to be out on the water for their morning catch. They seemed to gaze on the quiet shore and the lone man walking it with jaundiced eyes.

His irritation with the negotiations had been compounded by the fact that he had a book due soon. Very soon, and he'd barely begun writing it. Plus, he'd scrapped most of what he'd written so far. Fears he hadn't felt since he first began to write were plaguing him. What if it didn't come as naturally as it had before? What if everything he put on the page was complete shite? He hadn't been able to connect with Rex. He'd hardly been able to envision where this next saga of Rex Flynn's story would take him.

That was…until he met Olivia. She'd been dancing so joyfully out there on the parquet floor of that frenzied dance club. Gerald had watched her dance, hardly seeing her friends or the crush of other dancers packed shoulder to shoulder with her on the floor. Scotch forgotten, motivated by a driving force that felt a lot like that exhilarating, creative freefall he'd somehow lost touch with over the past six months, Gerald had made a beeline for the blonde siren.

Though he hadn't remembered much from that point on the following morning, Gerald's mind had slowly filled in the blanks after Olivia's departure. Dancing. Drinking. More dancing. More drinking. Talking. Riding in the limo. Kissing there. Watching the fountain in front of the Bellagio rise into the night. Holding each other there. More talking. More kissing.

From there they went back to the casino. A bit of gambling. A bit more drinking. Another limo ride to the little white chapel, where he had only vague impressions of gold walls, red carpet, an organ and an Elvis Presley to officiate. He'd meant his vows. It didn't matter to him that his intoxication level had been as high as it had ever been. More than anything else he remembered about that wild Vegas night was looking into the eyes of his bride and speaking promises meant only for her.

More dancing from there. Maybe at the club. Maybe there in the chapel, for all he knew. But from the chapel, they had taken a final limo ride back to the casino, apparently rented the honeymoon penthouse suite for the night and then…well, the marriage consummation, of course, which he was fairly certain had started in the casino elevator.

From the moment he'd woken next to her in the big, plush bed strewn with rose petals and what remained of the clothes they'd in essence torn off each other hours earlier, Gerald had known despite the headache and sore muscles from the eventful evening that he didn't have any regrets. Speaking to Olivia in the morning had only reaffirmed that conviction. And after the blonde siren left him to find her friends and fly back to her stretch of sandy shore on the coast, he'd hardly finished breakfast before he'd gone back to his business suite to write.

He'd written for hours, until the light from the window began to lower, harden, then dim. All the while, the face of the woman he could now credit as his unexpected muse had stayed at the forefront of his mind. That night, as he'd made arrangements to travel back to his home in New York, he'd known that the first thing on his agenda when he got there would be tracking down the mysterious Olivia.

Gerald hadn't expected the place she called home to be as spectacular as she was. But when he'd checked into the bay view suite of Hanna's Inn the night before, he had immediately set up his notebook computer on the room's antique secretary in anticipation. He had a book due in three weeks. When he wasn't wooing Olivia or grabbing small snatches of inspiration from the Eastern Shore, he'd go back to the desk and see what the muse had to offer him.

The cell phone in his pocket vibrated. Gerald

knew who was calling before he pulled the smartphone out to answer. When he saw it was indeed his editor back in New York, he lifted his thumb and pressed the answer key.

He had avoided this conversation for weeks. Now, though, he had answers. "Dwight," Gerald greeted, putting the phone to his ear. "It's good to hear from you, old boy."

"Then why have you been dodging my calls?"

Gerald reached back to rub his neck as he walked onto the inn's dock, his footsteps loud on the hollow, wooden planks. He and Dwight had been working together for years on the Rex Flynn series, along with a few spin-off titles. He'd come to know Dwight as a friend as well as a professional. "I wasn't dodging. Just waiting for the right moment."

"To tell me what—that the book isn't finished? Tell me something I don't know."

"How do you know the book isn't already done?" Gerald ventured.

"Because this is the first book in eight years you haven't turned in two months ahead of schedule," Dwight told him. "And when the writing's going well, you're not afraid to call and chat about it. Usually, I can't get you to shut up. You haven't so much as shot me an email in a month's time in this case, which tells me you're cowering in a hole somewhere hoping I've forgotten about you."

Gerald pursed his lips and scuffed the bottom of

his shoe against a dry patch of earth. "You know I was in Las Vegas dealing with film negotiations."

"Yeah, and before that you visited your family in Yorkshire. Before that, you were, what, betting on the ponies in Jersey?"

"Are you spying on me now, Dwight?" Gerald asked.

"When you're a well-known author, people notice when you go places you shouldn't. Like Belmont."

"For the record," Gerald explained, "I was not betting on the ponies. A friend of mine breeds horses. He named one of the Thoroughbreds after Rex. I was simply making an appearance. And that could technically be lumped into the working category, you know…"

"Fine, but then your sister wrote to tell me what a good time you'd had together and thanked me for letting you fly off to England when you had a book due. I didn't have the heart to tell her I knew nothing about the trip."

"It was my niece's birthday," Gerald reasoned.

"Vegas might be forgivable at least," Dwight went on. "But let me ask you this, my friend, where are you now?"

Gerald gazed across the water toward Mobile. "I can't claim to be at the writing desk…."

"Oh, for Christ's sake, Gerald—"

"Hear me out, mate," Gerald said. "I won't deny I've been blocked. I won't lie to you and say I've not struggled with this one. In truth, piecing this story together has been like trying to carve a diamond. But that's all about to change."

"Oh, yeah? Enlighten me."

"I've found inspiration," Gerald said. "The characters are talking to me again, and I'm starting to see the pictures, the easy flow of scenes. I've also found a quiet place, one where the rush and bustle of business and city life is far enough away that I'm no longer bound to it. The words will come. And when they do, they'll come fast and hard. You'll have the book on schedule, Dwight. You can count on it."

"You're giving me your word?" Dwight asked, surprised. He knew as well as anyone that when Gerald pledged something, he meant it wholeheartedly and would rather see his soul shattered than his word broken.

"Consider it a promise," Gerald said, glancing back toward the tavern and the woman he knew dwelled within. "You won't be disappointed, my friend."

"I rarely am." Dwight sighed. "All right. If you're so sure…I'll expect the completed manuscript in three weeks."

Gerald grinned. "Give it two. Goodbye, Dwight."

CHAPTER FIVE

THE EAGLES' "WITCHY WOMAN" rumbled through Tavern of the Graces as Gerald entered it later in the evening. The establishment was packed with men mostly, he noticed. Glancing around, he admired the remarkable woodwork highlighted by tray lights on the walls. The carvings seemed to follow the history of Mobile Bay. The room was warm, battling the chill that had settled over the shoreline as the afternoon wore thin.

Appreciating the vintage rock music and more than willing to sit back, relax and enjoy the atmosphere, Gerald spied an empty table and veered toward it.

It wasn't long before the waitress manning the tables with a flirtatious smile and a finesse only experience could teach spotted him and made her way over. "What can I get you, hot stuff?"

He returned her smile of greeting. "What would you suggest?"

She raised a dark, impossibly thin brow. "Well, if you haven't already heard, we've got the finest margaritas east of The Big Easy."

"How fine is that?"

She smirked, red lips bowing and chocolate-hued eyes drinking him in. "You're not from around here, are you?"

"No." Gerald laughed. "London originally, but I'm afraid that might be a bit obvious."

"Love the accent," she purred and set a basket of tortilla chips on the table in front of him. "If you're not brave enough to try the margarita, I'd suggest something on tap."

"The house margarita is fine," he told her. "But tell your bartender to go easy on the tequila, if she knows what's good for her. And if I could, I'd like a moment of her time."

The waitress smiled warmly. "Oh, Liv's always got time for a good-lookin' guy like you. Right now you'll find her over at the pool tables. Clint Harbuck challenged her to a game."

Gerald turned in interest toward the billiards. When he saw his wife leaning over a cue stick, about to sink the black eight ball into a corner pocket, he beamed. "Who's winning?"

"Oh, Liv—by a mile."

"I wouldn't expect anything less." He chuckled, then gave the waitress a warm smile, lifting a twenty-dollar bill from his pocket. "Keep the change, love. And bring us all a round of draft beer." Shrugging off his sports jacket, he hooked it over the back of the chair and walked across the room to better entertain himself with the game and its two opponents.

Clint, the giant of a man who had challenged Olivia to a game, had a ruddy face, watery blue eyes and a rough, red beard that was days past the point of trimming. He stood with the back of his extralarge flannel shirt pressed against the wood-paneled wall. Sipping from a bottle of Budweiser, he lifted it to gesture toward Olivia. "You're never gonna make that shot, sweetheart. Not at that angle."

Olivia, focused, didn't budge as she eyed the round, white cue ball with fierce intensity. "You just shut your trap and watch how it's done, Harbuck." Pulling the stick back slightly, she tapped it hard enough against the cue ball to send it skidding into the eight ball. The eight ball spun drunkenly toward the corner pocket and sank in with a resounding clack.

A cheer went up through the tavern. As Olivia stood and turned to Clint, victorious, there was a smirk painted on her lips. "That's an even thirty you owe me this time. You'll pay up now, not like the last time when you snuck out on me and claimed to have forgotten about it next time I saw you."

"Aw, hell," Clint muttered, tossing his cue stick onto the table in frustration. In jerky movements that lent themselves toward impatience, he dug his wallet out of the saggy back pocket of his faded blue jeans and peeled three wrinkled ten-dollar bills from the fold. "Woman's a regular pool hustler," he growled, handing them over.

"Thank you," Olivia said cheerily, making a point of counting the bills before standing on the toes of her high heels to give the man a deprecating pat on the cheek. "Until next time." She spun toward the bar, then came up short when she saw Gerald in her path. Her smile fled…and wasn't that a shame?

Olivia's direct gaze was like a punch to his sternum. She'd put on enough smoky eye shadow to make the effect twice as overwhelming. He towered over her by a foot at least even after the spiky black boots that wrapped her legs to the knees before dark, taut denim took over. Both hugged what he imagined were even finer attributes. While her red halter dipped over splendid cleavage.

Recovering quickly, Gerald dipped his head to her. "Mrs. Leighton."

Olivia chanced a look around to make sure no one was eavesdropping. "I thought I told you not to call me that." She groaned as she crossed the few feet between them.

Gerald raised a brow. "Did you?"

She thought about it, then frowned. "Well, I'm asking now. So…stop. Before someone hears you."

"I was thinking of making an announcement, actually," Gerald said with a good-natured grin even as her face drained of color. "Every man in this room has taken a wayward glance at you in the short space of time since I walked through the door tonight. And while I can't blame them for admiring your many attributes, its best they not get their hopes up."

Olivia's frown deepened. He missed the light in her eyes he'd seen earlier when she was with her family. Glancing over her shoulder, she caught the eye of a tall and well-built man leaning against the bar. "Deck," she called and crooked two fingers in invitation. "Would you come here for a moment?"

Deck stood instantly at the summons and strolled over in three quick gaits. Nodding a hurried greeting to Gerald, he shoved his hands deep into his pockets and bent over to Olivia's level. "Something you need, Liv baby?"

She gripped him by the collar of his striped, polo shirt and pressed her lips to his cheek, leaving a smudge of red from her lipstick. "Why don't you come upstairs later for a drink? I want to know all about that new contracting job you and the guys were celebrating yesterday afternoon."

Deck lit up like a theme park at the suggestion. His shoulders straightened and his eyes gleamed as he grinned at her. "You mean it?"

"Of course, I mean it," she said easily, rubbing a hand over his large biceps. "Stick around?"

"You bet I will," Deck replied, clutching her around the waist. "Let me just tell the guys I won't need a ride back home."

When Deck loped happily back to the bar to relay

the happy news, Olivia crossed her arms and gave Gerald a pointed look.

He pressed his lips together. Not normally the jealous type, he was surprised by his reaction to seeing Olivia's lipstick smudge on Deck's cheek, her hand on his arm, his arm low on her waist. She'd fired her weapon, straight and true. And Gerald felt the impact of envy down to the bone. It took more time and effort than he would have liked to school his expression into one of indifference. It was harder still to wrangle another good-natured smile onto his lips. "Well played," he admitted finally.

She lifted a coy shoulder, the smirk touching her lips again. "Decker and I go way back. We met in high school. It wasn't until I moved in upstairs alone, though, that we started things up. Just the occasional hayride. You know how those things go, don't you, Gerald?"

"You might be surprised to know that one-night stands are of no interest to me," Gerald said. There was a gravelly base note in his voice he'd never really heard before. He had difficulty accepting the fact that it was the jealousy talking.

Her brows came down over her eyes. "Then what the hell was I?"

Considering her, he took his time tracing his gaze across her fair, heart-shaped face, down the blond curls tumbling over her shoulders and the shapely form she kept well in tune from the look of her. *Words, man. You usually have a way with them.* Settling on her searing, emerald eyes, he said, "That's what I'm trying to figure out, Mrs. Leighton."

"Lucky for me," she muttered.

After a moment's tension, Gerald asked, "By any chance, is Clint one of your many admirers, as well?"

She wrinkled her nose back toward the corner where the large ginger was currently trying to win his money back with an arm-wrestling match. "Just because I bring tavern men back to my place doesn't mean I don't have standards." Scowling, she looked back at Gerald and added, "Believe it or not, I haven't slept with every man you see in this bar tonight."

He cleared his throat and shifted his feet. "I'll offer my apologies, then, since mine was perhaps an unfair question."

She jerked her head in a terse nod. "Perhaps you're right."

Gerald reached up to scrape his knuckles over the small growth of stubble along his jawline. "I was sent here with a message."

Lifting a pitcher of beer and a small tray of chips from the bar, she took it to a nearby table. "Let me guess," she said. "From Briar?"

"She said something about the music being too loud," Gerald relayed, though he gleaned from the canny look on her face she'd already figured that out.

"What do you think?"

"Pardon?"

"The music," Olivia prompted, planting an impatient hand on her hip as she turned back to him. "Think it's too loud?"

How had she managed to turn this around on him? Gerald shifted his feet, glancing over at the blazing red, brightly lit jukebox in the corner. "Happen to have any Queen in there?"

She brushed by him on a wave of vanilla fragrance that toggled all those teasing memories of their time in Las Vegas.

He closed his eyes. If her outfit didn't drive him to insanity, her scent definitely would.

He watched as she leaned over the jukebox, scanning titles, flipping pages behind the glass with the buttons of the console as she wiggled her foot absently behind her. He couldn't help but admire the way the denim hugged her bum.

Many attributes, indeed.

She popped a coin in the slot and peered over her shoulder, pinning him with a very effective how-'bout-now? look as the first base notes of "Under Pressure" began to play.

She might as well have hit him over the head with a hammer.

"That just happens to be a personal favorite," Gerald told her when she crossed back to him.

"Then that makes us all happy," she said, spreading her hands. When he only looked at her, that wary shadow shifted back into her eyes. She moved her hands to her hips again and looked around. "I'm sure you're more accustomed to fancier drinking establishments than this."

"This is all pretty familiar actually," he said. "Cozy taverns and pubs have always suited me. It certainly suits you," he said with a knowing smile.

Olivia blinked. "Was that a compliment?"

"Indeed." He lifted a hand to the walls. "The woodwork is fantastic."

"My grandfather did it all," she explained after a beat of breath. "He was a carpenter, the best in the area. When it slows down, I guess I'll have to give you the verbal tour."

"Yes, you will," Gerald asserted. Especially if it meant delaying her having drinks with that Decker chap upstairs.

"I have to get back behind the bar...."

Gerald grinned, looking in the direction of the polished wood counter and the waitress behind it. "Take me with you."

Olivia's eyes snagged once again with a frown on his face. "Where?"

"Behind the bar," he expounded. When she only stared, he chuckled. "I worked at a pub while I was at university."

"You don't say," she said. "What was that, like fifteen years ago?"

Now he laughed wholeheartedly, reaching out to wrap an arm around her shoulders. "Was that a dig at me, love?"

A wry expression crossed her face. "What if it was? You couldn't keep up with the after-work rush if you tried, Shakespeare."

"You think not?" He reached down to the cuffs of his shirt, unbuttoning them one by one. "That sounds like a challenge."

"You'll just get in our way," she pointed out. "When it comes to work, I don't like people getting in the way."

"If I get in your way, you'll have the immense pleasure of having one of your score of admirers haul me out of the tavern," he promised. "*But* if I out-tip you by night's end…you agree to go on a date with me tomorrow night."

She shook her head. "You're terrible about making bets you can't win, you know that?"

"Do we have a deal, love?"

Pursing her lips, she watched him roll up his sleeves. "Sure. But when I win, you have to agree not to step foot back in the tavern during your three weeks here. Got it?"

It wouldn't come to that. Gerald was determined to make that a reality. "You drive a hard bargain. But I'll accept those terms."

She grinned widely and meant it by the light in her eyes. "Good."

As soon as they both ducked behind the counter,

an eager face emerged from the crowd on the other side. "Hey, Liv!"

"Hey there, Skeet," Olivia greeted fondly. "You back for more?"

"Sure thing," Skeet said. Gerald saw his eyes dart in the direction of the waitress.

Apparently, Olivia did, too, because her smile grew into Cheshire cat terrain. "Monica's a little occupied at the moment. What'll it be?"

"Something hard and straight," Skeet replied absently, keeping Monica in his peripheral.

"Hard and straight it is," Olivia said, reaching for a brown liquor bottle.

Gerald stopped her with a hand on her arm, flashing her a smile. "Allow me."

After a hesitant moment, she stepped back, hands raised. "Knock yourself out, Shakespeare. But remember—you break it, you buy it."

Gerald grabbed the bottle by the neck, lifting it from the shelf under the counter. He set a shot glass on the bar. In the other hand, he flipped the bottle over the back of his hand, caught it nimbly and poured the liquor into the glass. With a wink at Skeet, he passed it over the bar. "Liquid courage, my friend," he said before facing Olivia.

He was pleased when it took her a moment to find her voice. "Well, I'll be."

"Liv, you got yourself a challenger?"

Olivia rolled her eyes in the direction of one of

her regulars, Freddie. "Settle down, settle down. This doesn't concern you."

"Too rich for your blood, eh, Liv?" Clint added.

Olivia scowled at him but before she could open her mouth to retort, Gerald replied for her. "The lady and I have ourselves a little arrangement, gentlemen."

"Uh-oh," Monica muttered behind them.

Olivia narrowed her eyes on him. "Making a show of it won't help you. These are my customers. They'd side with me any day of the week."

"I made a living off tips for four years," Gerald explained, a mischievous smirk playing at his lips. "I know how to work a crowd."

Olivia blew out an unbelieving laugh. "You're a cocky son of a bitch, you know that?"

He moved quickly to toss a bottle her way. The gleam in his eyes deepened as she sucked in a breath, catching it before it shattered on the floor. "You like that about me, love. Admit it."

"Careful there, pretty boy." Olivia tossed the bottle up once, caught it smoothly, then flipped it and set it down easily on the bar. "Now I'm going to have to embarrass you in front of an audience."

Gerald offered her a come-hither motion with his hands. "Let's go, Mrs. Leighton," he added in an undertone.

"Stand back, Mon," Olivia warned, then raised her voice over the noise and spread her arms wide. "Who wants to buy me a drink?"

Men rushed for the bar. Gerald turned to the women who'd already moved forward in curiosity, and offered them a charming grin. "Ladies?"

The bet went on for several hours. Their tip jars began to flourish with wrinkled singles. Bottles flipped in the air with an encore of shot glasses and bottle caps. Blenders churned and the beer taps flowed as Gerald and Olivia tirelessly worked the Friday night crowd.

He impressed her, Olivia thought. He didn't once falter, tire or hang back for a sip of water. However, Olivia didn't begin to worry about losing until she realized that the women in the crowd were starting to outnumber the men by a hair and she caught Monica sneaking a five-dollar bill into Gerald's tip jar.

Olivia watched the smug grin spread over his face, his dimples and sexy crow's-feet digging deep. He'd rolled up the sleeves of his pricey oxford shirt and untucked it from his suit slacks. His rich laugh rose over the din, beckoning her.

If she didn't know any better, she'd have thought he'd fallen from heaven right at her feet.

Yeah, let's not go there, she thought, stifling the stirrings she was beginning to feel more and more toward him.

It was close to midnight when the crowd thinned and finally dispersed, leaving behind the lone form of Skeet Bisbee. Olivia had counted out her tips as Monica cleaned up and Gerald offered to wash glasses. After he'd worked as hard as he had, Olivia was stunned to see him still on his feet, much less cleaning up after her customers. She wouldn't argue, though. It was nice to put her feet up for a few moments after the record rush.

Word of the challenge had spread from her customers to their friends and family. Olivia couldn't remember a busier October night that didn't involve a football game or holiday. Tonight's challenge would go a long way toward her sales quota for the month.

Olivia eyed Gerald, elbows-deep in suds at the sink. She'd have to thank him for that. However, she had no plans of telling him that she'd sent Decker home early *and* disappointed.

Skeet's head was down on the bar and he was tonelessly crooning along with Bad Company's "Ready for Love." Olivia got up from her stool and went over to pat him on the back. "You all right, slugger? It's past your bedtime."

Skeet lifted his head to reveal a crooked smile and bloodshot eyes. She'd cut him off an hour ago, but he'd remained, mooning after Monica. "I'm a'right," he slurred. "And I love you, Liv. Did I ever tell you that I love you?"

"I love you, too, honey," Olivia said, kissing his puckered lips briefly before exchanging looks with Monica. "Come on now. Monica will take you home."

"Monica." Skeet gazed, awestruck, at her. "Liv, isn't she the purtiest thing?"

"The purtiest," Olivia replied, trying to haul Skeet to his feet.

"Allow me." Gerald stepped in. The scent of his aftershave teased her nostrils. "Come on, son. Let's get you back on the wagon." He hooked an arm under Skeet's shoulders and all but dragged him to the door with Monica and Olivia in pursuit.

"So?" Monica whispered, bumping an elbow into Olivia's ribs. She admired Gerald's rear as he bent over to help Skeet into the passenger seat of her old, beat-up, two-door Saturn. "What's the skinny on Mr. Shakespeare?"

Olivia shook her head. "It's complicated. I don't feel like getting into it."

"He's all over you."

"You think?" Olivia asked, curious despite herself.

"Like white on rice," Monica informed her. She dug her keys out of her purse. "I'm gonna take the little boy home."

Olivia stopped her before she could get behind the wheel. "Take it easy on him."

Monica chuckled. "I'm going to get him some hot coffee, give him a cold shower, then a religious experience."

Olivia smiled and shook her head. "No shame." As Monica shut the door and cranked the car to life, Olivia waved to Skeet. The car pulled out of the parking lot, and she turned to Gerald. "Thank you," she made herself tell him. "It would have taken both me and Mon to haul him out of there. He might be a lightweight, but he's big enough to be a linebacker."

Gerald's verdant eyes gleamed with laughter in the dark. He'd undone a couple of buttons on his shirt. Not that she was looking at the skin beneath. *So not looking...* "He revealed to me his intentions to marry her."

Olivia laughed. Really laughed for the first time that night. "I can't wait to see how that goes over." When he only eyed her in the low light, she felt that stir underneath her skin. His effect on her combined with the chill in the air made her shiver. "We'd best go inside. I'll finish cleaning up."

"And perhaps you could give me that tour," Gerald suggested, opening the door for her.

"Oh, right. Well…" She'd told him she would, hadn't she? No use trying to get out of it. Lifting her hand to encompass the west wall, she began her spiel. "The profiles are explorers and original settlers. The Spanish arrived first, around fifteen-hundred. They fought the Muskogee tribes who lived here first, circa fifteen-forty."

Gerald peered closely at a line of text under one of the more prominent profiles. "'Bahía del Espíritu Santo.' Bay of the Holy Spirit?"

"That name changed when the French came through in the early seventeen-hundreds to establish Fort Louis de la Mobile," Olivia continued, on a roll now as he looked at her with interest. "They made Dauphin Island a seaport and founded the French Louisiana capital at Mobile. Then, of course, the land was bought up by the American government. Alabama eventually became a state but decided to cede from the Union in 1861 when civil war broke out. And that led to the Battle of Mobile Bay in August of 1864."

Gerald glanced over the most intricate carvings in the room—seven late-nineteenth-century ships. "And these were the vessels lost?"

"Their wrecks still lie on the floor of Mobile Bay," she explained. "My grandfather researched the ships carefully in order to re-create them."

"It's impressive work," he mused, running his fingertips over the bow of the CSS *Gaines*.

Olivia swallowed hard when she caught herself staring at his hands—again. They were nice hands, she had to admit. But she wasn't going to think about the many things they'd done to her on their wedding night. *No sirree*. Turning, she walked to the other side of the tavern and the map etched on the opposing wall. "This is my favorite. You can see all the bay's cultural landmarks, down to the cotton. It was the bay's chief export in the nineteenth century. Here's the Fairhope Pier. And here are all the Eastern Shore townships, and across the bay the cities there and the USS *Alabama*."

"Was this fort used in the Civil War, too?" he

asked, pointing to the star shape at the bottom of the map.

"Mostly in the War of 1812," she told him, meeting his stare with a catty expression, "when you British attacked during the Battle of New Orleans."

"Ah," he said, unable to fight a grin. "Yes, well, there's no use apologizing for my ancestors. So which hurricane is this?" he asked, pointing to the large rotated eye at the entrance to the bay.

"Frederic," she answered. "That was 1979 and it was pretty catastrophic. Memories of it were still fairly fresh when my grandfather first started carving the tavern walls. That's actually sort of where my parents got the name for this place—Tavern of the Graces. They were interested in buying the property but thought that Frederic would level the building as well as Hanna's Inn when the storm came through. But by the *grace* of a higher power both were still here after Frederic passed through. They took it as a sign and put all their money into renovating it."

"And 'Jubilee'?" Gerald said, pointing to the word scrawled into the wood vertically along the Fairhope shoreline. "What does that stand for?"

"It's a natural phenomenon that takes place at night in the summertime. Fish, shrimp and crabs gather close to shore in hoards and make it easy to catch them in large numbers."

"And it only happens here?" he asked, surprised.

"It's been reported elsewhere, but Mobile Bay

is the only place where it happens regularly each year," she said. "It's the fourth largest estuary in the country."

"I had no idea this area was so rich in history," Gerald mused.

She gestured to her grandfather's work. "Lewises have been around these parts for well over a century. The area's been good to us, and my grandfather wanted to pay tribute to it when my parents opened the tavern."

"You should be proud of him," Gerald acknowledged, looking around once more for the full effect. "I'd say it's something of a masterpiece."

"It was his magnum opus." Olivia's eyes fell on the face of the clock over the bar. "I should finish cleaning."

"We don't know who won the challenge yet."

She snorted out a laugh. "I think you can go ahead and forfeit your earnings, mister. I counted over a hundred and twenty dollars in my jar."

"Did you now?" Gerald held up a discerning finger. "Just so there's no question, let me count mine, and then we'll see who deserves the spoils of victory."

Olivia shook her head as he brushed by her, unable to help the grin that stretched across her face. She could really, *really* learn to like him.

To dispel the thrall he'd cast over her, she put herself back to work cleaning tables and the floors. She shelved bottles and glasses, tallied the register, and took out the trash. By the time she completed all her nightly chores, the jukebox was softly playing its last song of the night and Gerald had finished counting. "I guess that clenches it, then," he said warily.

She smiled, tasting those spoils. "Hate to say I told you so."

He pursed his lips but couldn't quite stop the corner of his mouth from twitching upward. Combined with the resulting dimple, the satisfied smile stopped her heart. "I believe mine comes to $157.63."

After the shock wore through, a laugh belted out of her, straight from her toes. "Well, hell. You beat me."

"I successfully vanquished you, Mrs. Leighton," Gerald said, standing and offering her his cash. "This belongs to you."

Olivia frowned at the neat money roll. "What's that for?"

"It's your money," he told her. "Well earned. You're an exceptional opponent." Tracing her nose from bridge to tip with a gentle fingertip, he lowered his head and added in an undertone, "As well as an exquisite one."

It took her a moment to find her voice. "You got lucky," she muttered. "It was Ladies' Night."

"I thought that was Wednesday."

"Shut up," she said with what she could muster of a smile as she took the money and set it on the bar. Reaching for a broom, she began to sweep the floor. Again. It was better than standing a hairbreadth away from him, drinking in that maddening aftershave and feeling her lips tingle in anticipation. "Aren't you tired?"

"I should be zonked, but it's the adrenaline," he admitted. "Hasn't quite worn off yet." Reaching to grip the back of his neck with one of his wide-palmed hands, he glanced at the jukebox. "This is a good song."

It was the Stones' "Wild Horses." "It's my favorite," she murmured.

Gerald's brows lifted in surprise. "Well, blow me."

Her mouth dropped open and blood rushed to her face. *"What?"*

"I said, 'Blow me.'" When she only continued to stare, aghast, he cleared his throat. "You know? Blow me down. Knock me down with a feather. It's British. Slang, I mean."

"Oh!" Olivia said, loosening a laugh that sounded nervous even to her ears. "I thought you meant—" She caught his eye, felt her cheeks darken to fuchsia, and shook her head. "Nothing. No. Never mind."

By the look on his face, he had already caught on. He rocked back on his heels and pressed his lips together, glancing down at the floor. She thought his face might be a little red, too, but it could have been the dim lighting. She went back to sweeping and said, a little loudly, "Why does it 'blow you down'—that this is my favorite song?"

His eyes found hers again. "In addition to Queen, I'm a Stones fan, too. 'Wild Horses' has always been one of my favorites." After hesitating a brief space of a moment, he lifted his hand. "Shall we dance, then?"

Her broom stopped in midswipe as her face lifted to his. "Dance?"

"Dance with me, Liv," he repeated. "We've danced before."

Since when did he call her *Liv?* She really didn't think she could handle that kind of intimacy. Not with him. "I've got to finish cleaning."

Gerald tugged the broom away. "I think you're done, love." The words were whispered against the hair over her ear. The tingles she'd felt on her lips cascaded down her neck, back and torso until she couldn't help but shiver pleasantly.

Before she could think up a practical protest, he threaded his fingers through hers and placed her opposing hand on his shoulder. With the subtle urging of a warm hand on the small of her back, he pulled her close against him.

He was solid, steady and *oh, my God* real. A man of substance, which made him dangerous. Extremely dangerous.

Still, the words she knew she should speak were trapped on the back of her tongue and remained locked there as his chin came to rest on her head and he began to sway with her. All on their own, her arms lifted and encircled him, one around the waist, the other clutching the back of his shoulder. Her nose naturally buried itself against the lapel of his shirt.

There was nothing flashy about the dance. They simply circled and swayed. Circled and swayed. Circled and swayed until her head felt like an uncorked champagne bottle. All bubbly and translucent. The fact that he was holding her so close, right up against the heat and heart of him and had no intention of letting her go for so much as a quick spinout, didn't help matters much. She struggled to contain all the stirrings and warm sensations swirling through her as the song, that had never seemed long before, went on and on.

It didn't help that behind her closed lids, she kept getting flashbacks from the club in Vegas. At first they'd danced to the time of the base beat, breaking it down together, drawing nearer and nearer. Then as they grew more and more wrapped up in each other and the barrier between them had melted in the face of the need they'd felt, they'd wrapped their arms around each other and did just this: circled and swayed until she'd lost all semblance of time and place and rationality....

He touched his lips to her brow. "Does this not feel right, love?"

Yes. She caught the word dangling on the edge of her tongue and pulled away from him. As he stood staring at her, the song finally fading, she said nothing, just looked at him, considering.

He was upsetting the balance. Fear struck her. When he lifted a hand to touch her, assure her, she took several steps back. "No." When he looked, askance, at her, she said again, "Just...no."

The phone rang and she leaped on the chance to flee the situation. Retreating from the scene and all its emotional entanglements, she didn't look back as she rushed around the bar to grab the phone off the hook in her office. Her hand shook as she lifted it to her ear.

Damn it. She clenched her fingers hard around the receiver. "Tavern of the Graces. This is Olivia."

"Liv? He's here."

Adrian's voice quavered. Olivia's heart did a sickening lurch. "Who? What's wrong?"

"It's Radley. He's drunk. He's beating on the door. He'll break it down if I keep ignoring him."

"I'm coming," Olivia assured her. "Hold tight. Whatever you do, do *not* let him in."

She hung up the phone, all the soft feelings she'd experienced seconds before crushed under a towering surge of indignation.

"What's going on?" Gerald asked as he peered around the office jamb, concerned. "What happened?"

Ignoring him, Olivia quickly crossed the room and reached behind the couch. Grabbing the butt of the rifle she kept there for security purposes, she lifted it to the light.

He jolted in alarm. "What the bloody hell is that for?"

"This is for Radley Kennard's head, that's what," she snarled, shoving by him.

"Blimey!" he yelped. "You aren't going to shoot anybody?"

"I'll be down the street," she announced, barreling toward the door.

"You can't go off alone like this."

"Stay out of the way," she advised. "This is going to get messy."

CHAPTER SIX

CHASING A FURIOUS woman with what he feared was a loaded rifle down South Mobile Street evoked all kinds of apprehensive feelings in Gerald. Olivia hadn't thought to take a car, so they weren't going too far. Yet the implications remained.... Furious woman. Loaded weapon.

Trouble certainly wasn't far ahead, as she'd warned him.

"Where are we going?" he asked cautiously.

"Two blocks south," Olivia said. "Adrian's house."

His heart leaped into his throat. "Is someone trying to break in?"

"Her ex-husband, Radley. He can't seem to read the restraining order."

"This has happened before?" Gerald hissed as Olivia crossed the street onto a wooded avenue lined with quiet houses.

"Yes, and unfortunately he got in far enough to knock Adrian upside the head and scare Kyle half to death before the cops came. If I have anything to do with it, he'll be dead before he gets through the door tonight."

"Dear God," Gerald breathed, hesitating only momentarily before he continued on her heels.

Olivia stopped abruptly near the third house on the right.

"Is this it?" Gerald asked.

Before Olivia could answer, a bellowing shout lifted into the night. *"Adriaaaan!"*

Gerald spotted the wide-set figure standing on the small front porch, pounding at the front door of the cottage. His fear was chased by clear-cut focus. Suddenly, he understood all too well the violent gleam in Olivia's eyes. "What do you need me to do?"

"You're backup," Olivia told him. "I want you to slip around back and have Adrian let you in. If he gets past me, I'll need you to prevent him from getting to them."

"You're after facing him alone?" Gerald whispered incredulously. "You're barking mad, woman."

"I'm the one with the deadly weapon," Olivia said, giving him a look that stated clearly she wasn't relinquishing her hold of said weapon. "Gerald, tell me right now—can you do this?"

Damned if he couldn't admit by the hard look in her eyes that she was capable of defending herself. He nodded shortly, but before she could advance, he gripped her arm. "Liv? Be careful. Please."

Olivia met his gaze and offered a smile as grim

and deadly as her rifle. "It's him you need to worry about." And with that, she was off and away before he could protest further.

Gerald watched her for a moment, then locked away the fear that this could all end very, very badly. Slipping into the bushes, he maneuvered his way toward the back of the house.

"HEY! ASSHOLE!"

Radley staggered around and peered at her through watery, bloodshot eyes. Olivia remembered a time, long ago, when he'd been trim and handsome. He'd let that go to waste along with the state of his life. "'Livia?" Radley asked. "That you?"

Before the grin could break out on his face, she held up the gun. "Come away from that door or I'll blow a hole in your liver and that'll drain all that cheap whiskey!"

Radley paused, considered, then teetered toward her with a snort meant for a laugh. "Aw, you wouldn't do that. Come on, 'Livia. Don't you 'member all those good times we had together?"

She scowled. "I don't recall any good times with the likes of you."

Radley wheezed out a laugh, blowing his putrid breath onto her face and fanning the dangerous flames of her temper. He leered at her, close now. "Women like you like a man like me. Loose women. You're a loose woman, 'Livia. Just like Adrian."

The shot rang out like a blast of cannon fire

in the still night. Radley fell back on the ground, squealing like a stuck pig. He fumbled his hands over his chest, found no entry wound and glared up at her. "You could've shot me!" He tottered to his feet. "You stupid bitch!"

Before his meaty fist could take a swing at her, Olivia saw an unmanned hand catch Radley by the shoulders, spin him around fast enough to make the oaf trip over his own feet, and slam a well-tuned punch in his face.

Radley fell back on the grass and Gerald stepped out of the shadows, breathing hard. He looked to her, the sheer level of intent on his face tripping her pulse up. "All right?"

"Fine," she managed to say. "I thought I told you to get inside."

Gerald panted, lifted a nonchalant shoulder. "Couldn't leave you alone with this sad bastard." A loud snore gurgled from the ground between them and they both looked down at Radley's limp body. Gerald sneered. "Git."

Well, well. Mr. Shakespeare handles himself right nicely. Yet another pleasant surprise. Olivia saw him wince as he bent his fingers and examined his split knuckles. "Blimey," Gerald said. "Haven't done that in a while."

"There's a first aid kit back at the bar," she assured him. "I'll take care of it for you." Looking down at Radley, she kicked his boot and watched it flop back into place. "Scumbag."

The sound of a door creaking open drew both her and Gerald's attention. Adrian's white face peered out, crowbar ready in her hands, and Olivia did her best to smile. "It's all right. He's taken care of. Guess we'll call the police and have him hauled off."

THE POLICE QUESTIONED them, of course. The gun was registered to Olivia, and with Adrian's and Gerald's assurance that she had fired it in self-defense, she wasn't charged with anything. Not that it wouldn't have been worth it, Olivia thought grimly.

It was an hour later before the officers departed with Radley wailing in the back of their squad car. He'd go back to jail—where he belonged.

Cole, a former police detective, had arrived to help with the authorities at Briar's request. When the cherry lights faded, he was the one to tell the neighbors in a commanding voice that there was nothing left to see. Olivia blessed him silently and stepped back inside to join the others.

She found Adrian and Kyle sitting close together at the nook table, and Gerald at the stove making hot chocolate for the both of them. Her eyes skimmed the line of his shoulders—strong even at this late hour. *My God* had he surprised her tonight. No use denying it.

After a moment watching him, Olivia forced herself to look away. Turning her attention to the mother and child, she measured them carefully. Kyle's blue eyes were still wide with apprehension. He was wearing a pair of Spider-Man thermal pajamas and leaning against Adrian. His gaze searched each and every face for reassurances that his father would not be coming back again to harm them. The freckles spread over his cheeks were visible even in the dim light of the oven in the narrow kitchen.

Adrian looked worn, uncharacteristically ragged as she stroked Kyle's thick, dark hair as if to reassure herself that he was still there, that Radley hadn't touched him. Her dark eyes looked like bruised saucers, lined as they were with shadows. It was the state of her usually level shoulders, slumped and defeated now that the cops had been dispatched, that alarmed Olivia the most.

"He's violated the order so that'll put him behind bars for a while," Cole announced as he, too, entered the room. "After he sleeps off the serious amount of alcohol we smelled on his breath, I think he'll see fit to leave you alone."

Olivia heard Adrian's small, relieved sigh before she contained it and kissed Kyle's brow. "Did you hear that?"

Kyle pressed his face into her shoulder, hiding as he began to shake with silent sobs. Tears glinted in Adrian's eyes before she closed them and buried her face in his hair.

Sucking in a steadying breath, Olivia turned

to Cole. "Thank you for being here. You've made things a good deal easier."

"Anything I can do…" he replied, his concerned gaze straying to the pair at the table before he looked over Olivia's head at Gerald. "Thanks for helping out tonight. If you hadn't intervened, Liv here might have shot him."

"And the world would be better for it," Olivia pointed out. "Don't even deny it."

"Yes," Cole acknowledged, taking a deep breath. "But you'd spend at least a night in jail and would have wound up at the center of an investigation, whether or not it was self-defense. Your man saved you that at least. Be grateful, Liv."

She glanced at Gerald. Meeting his eyes, she crossed her arms over her chest and nodded. "He's right. You did good."

When Gerald only nodded in return, his eyes locking on hers and staying there, Cole cleared his throat and shifted from one foot to the other, awkward in the silence. "I better get home before Briar wakes the rest of the inn. Will everything be okay here?"

Olivia knew he sensed as she did that Adrian and Kyle needed to settle down, that at this point they would be better off with less activity and fewer people. Finally disengaging her gaze from Gerald's, Olivia turned back to Cole to assure him. "Everything will be fine. Go home. You're right.

Briar's probably having a panic attack, not knowing what's going on."

Cole nodded and stepped to the table. "Good night, Kyle. Good night, Adrian." He laid a hand briefly on her shoulder. "Let me know if you need anything else."

"Thank you, Cole," Adrian replied, lifting her head from Kyle's and piecing together a grateful smile. "I appreciate your help."

As Cole departed, Gerald set mugs in front of both Adrian and Kyle. "I added marshmallows," he murmured to the boy. Olivia caught Gerald's wink and the answering waver of light that flickered to life in Kyle's eyes. As a result, she wanted nothing more than to throw her arms around the man.

They all sat at the table until the hot chocolate was gone. Adrian then took Kyle's hand and asked softly, brushing the hair back from his brow, "Ready to go back to bed?" At his nod, she rose. "I can't thank you both enough for being here."

"It's no trouble at all, I assure you," Gerald said, taking the empty mugs to the sink. "I'm just thankful everything turned out right."

"Yes." Adrian offered him something of a smile. With a sigh, she faced Olivia. "Liv..."

"Go tuck in the tiger," Olivia said, patting her on the arm. "We'll lock up." Brushing her fingers over Kyle's shoulders as he passed, she waited until she heard a door creak at the back of the house before she glanced back at Gerald. "You set him at ease."

Gerald set the damp mugs in the sink-side drainer to dry. Turning to her, he frowned. "Do you think they'll be all right?"

Olivia blinked at his consideration, the kindness and worry she saw behind it. He was a marvel. "It wasn't as bad as the last time. They'll get through it. Adrian's tougher than she looks."

"Like you," Gerald acknowledged.

She sighed. She felt bone tired. The plug on her adrenaline had popped and left her to drain a while ago.

Seeming to read her, he reached for the rifle she'd set against the wall by the door. Olivia left the lamp on in the living room, knowing Kyle would creep from his room into his mother's sooner than later.

Outside, she locked up with the spare key. She turned, ready for the walk back to the tavern but stopped as Gerald reached a hand out to her. She studied him in the light of the porch.

The weapon looked so out of place in his hands, she thought blearily. Like a stick of dynamite clutched in the white gloves of Mickey Mouse. That is, if Mickey had an uppercut like Popeye's and a voice like Richard Armitage's.

Similar to the beloved character he'd crafted, Gerald looked like a time traveler, or a knight from Arthur's round table lost in the twenty-first century. The line of his brow and the fine bones of his face spoke of the high-class, English breeding she strongly suspected he hailed from. His mouth was strong, though, as was his nose and chin.

If he kept surprising her like he had tonight, Olivia would have no choice but to fall head over heels in love with him. And wasn't that a disturbing thought?

She crossed to him and took the rifle, frowning at the light drizzle that had begun to fall from the leaden sky. "Where did this come from?" she muttered.

He squinted up at the skies. "Ah, the weather's just gone soft is all. Not to worry."

"I hate to make you walk through the rain, after everything," she admitted before stepping off the stoop.

His arm halted her from going any farther. She turned to face him, perplexed. She barely had time to register the softness of his eyes in the light of the porch or the crease in his brow before he framed her jaw in his hands tenderly—so tenderly.

Her reflexes were slow. She could do nothing but watch, breath seizing in her chest, as he lowered his mouth to hers slowly, inch by inch until…

His lips brushed hers in a whispering kiss she should have barely felt. Her body lit up like a fever, heart rapping against her ribs with alarming fervor. The touch of his lips lingered as the rain fell with a sigh around them.

It was only seconds, but it felt like an eternity passed before he pulled back slightly, thumbs

sweeping over her cheeks. For once she was relieved he was holding her because she would have
keeled over sideways without him there to steady
her. Her lips fumbled open. "Wh-why…?"

That soft, soft gaze—as soft as the touch of rain
through her shirt and ten times as warm—traced
her features reverently. "You are a fascinating
woman, Olivia. And unbelievably kind." His lips
lowered to hers again and she was helpless to stop
them. Feared she didn't want to stop them.

He didn't tease her lips open nor did she open
her mouth to him, but she was sure no one had
kissed her this deeply. The testing brush hardened
by a fraction before he pulled back…then dipped
his mouth back down to hers for more, pulling in
a slow, deep breath. Yes, helpless, she could only
lift her hands to the lapels of his shirt and hold on.
Hold on for dear life.

When finally he pulled back once more, his
hands remained on her face. There they brushed
the curls back from her cheeks. As he stood looking
at her, drinking her in, the drizzle intensified into a
shower and she no longer cared that it was raining.

Thankfully, he came to his senses. Offering her a
smile as soft as his kiss and taking the gun from her
hand, he laced his fingers through hers. "Come on,
Mrs. Leighton," he murmured. "I'll take you home."

WHEN OLIVIA CALLED Gerald at the inn the following afternoon, she claimed to have work that night.

He knew, however, that this was her ploy to get out of the date he had won fair and square. After their kiss the night before, she'd avoided him throughout the day. She hadn't come to breakfast at Hanna's nor had she shown herself around the inn, shops or shoreline.

Gerald thought about waiting until the evening, then going over to the tavern to remind her she owed him a date night. Then he ran into Cole downstairs in the inn. The man told him that every morning Olivia went for a run down to the pier and back. Gerald had to admit his chances of getting through to his wife would be much better if he had the element of surprise on his side.

So the next morning Gerald left the inn far earlier than he usually rose from bed in jogging sweats and a white T-shirt. The air was crisp, but there was little wind. He didn't mind the exercise. In New York, he played tennis twice a week with his publicist. And he'd been eager to find time to do what he'd seen so many others do the previous day: walk the sidewalk that spanned South Mobile Street and led down to the pier and park beyond.

He checked his watch. Seven o'clock. Right on schedule. As he bent to retie the loose laces of one shoe, he heard footsteps crunching on gravel and looked over. He grinned as Olivia jogged around the corner of Adrian's flower shop. Standing, he placed his hands on his hips.

Her eyes latched on to him as he rose. She tripped

over her own feet, her jaw dropping open as she came to a standstill. "Gerald." She looked around, bewildered. "What are you doing up?"

"Cole mentioned that you run down to the pier in the morning," he explained. "I thought I'd join you."

With a roll of her eyes, she muttered, "Damn it, Cole." Looking him over, she said, "I run at a pretty fast clip." Bending her leg backward and grabbing the toe of her sneaker in a warm-up stretch, she added, "I won't slow down for anyone, even you."

"Don't worry about me keeping pace," he advised. "You haven't yet managed to shake me off, have you?"

Muttering under her breath, she pulled up the hood of her black running jacket and took off down the sidewalk without a backward glance. He ran after her, matching her pace.

The sidewalk was barely wide enough for both of them so he stayed at her elbow, ducking back behind her when they met other people out for a walk or run. He exchanged a few words of greeting with the people they passed. Some of them called Olivia by name and she gave short replies, keeping the pace just as she'd promised.

After speaking with an elderly woman with a shih tzu, Gerald sprinted to catch up with Olivia. "People are friendly here. A few times a month, I'll feel like jogging around Central Park. Not many people stop you or make eye contact. The hospitality seems universal here. It's nice."

She paused in her careful breathing regimen to eye him cattily. "Up there they don't even stop you for your autograph?"

He chuckled. "Not usually. I'm not a celebrity, love."

"But people do know who you are," she guessed.

"Some of the time," he conceded. "It's not as if I have paparazzi following me everywhere I go. Thank Christ. I couldn't stand the intrusion."

"You should try it sometime," she told him. "Might give you a taste of your own medicine."

He opened his mouth to respond, then his eyes fell on the bedraggled creature in the road and he lost his train of thought. Coming up short, he braced his hands on his knees, panting to catch his breath.

Olivia stopped, looked around and scowled. "What are you—" Glancing in the direction his gaze was fixed, she fell silent.

Gerald's heart reached out to the creature. Irish wolfhound or some hybrid in between, by the look of it. Its eyes were sad, its fur matted and dirty. It was shivering and looking straight at Gerald, as if begging him to put it out of its misery.

"Poor baby," Olivia said, walking back to Gerald and keeping her voice low as not to startle the dog. "He looks like he hasn't had a decent bite to eat in weeks. I hope he wasn't lost during the storm."

Gerald took a step forward, then another. When

the dog cowered, he stopped and went down to one knee, reaching out a hand. "Here, boy."

It glanced back toward the road, as if waiting for a car to come. Hoping, maybe. Gerald crept a bit closer, onto the asphalt. When the dog looked at him, it shrank back, ears flat against his head.

"I won't hurt you, mate," Gerald told it in as gentle a voice as he could muster. How someone could neglect an animal so terribly, he had no idea. All he could think was to get the dog fed, cleaned and warm. It didn't have a collar, so there was no name tag or address to go with it and it looked as if it might have some trouble with mange. "You're a right stocky lad, aren't you?"

He smiled. The dog didn't move toward Gerald but neither was it moving away anymore. Progress. Still reaching out, Gerald edged closer. "That's it. No one's going to hurt you."

The dog considered him over the few feet left between them. It made to step forward, but the whir of an approaching vehicle caught its attention and it froze. Gerald looked around at the speeding sedan in alarm. Giving up a silent curse, he stood, hoping to get the driver's attention. The dog wasn't moving.

The car didn't slow. Olivia said Gerald's name in warning behind him on the sidewalk. Gerald patted his knee. "Come now, boy. Let's get you safe."

"Gerald," Olivia said again. "They're not slowing down."

"I can see that," he said, not raising his tone so he wouldn't scare the stray. "Damn." As the car neared and it became clear the driver chose not to see them, Gerald made a flying leap for the shivering dog.

CHAPTER SEVEN

OLIVIA HEARD A horn blast and tires skirt on the pavement as Gerald dived for the stray and the car came barreling toward them. She screamed, raising her hands to her mouth as the car braked to a jerky halt in the place where Gerald and the dog had been only seconds earlier. Then silence.

"Oh, my God!" she said in horror, her heart banging away at her eardrums. "Oh, my God..." As the driver's door opened and a shocked young woman no older than eighteen climbed out of the car, Olivia rounded the hood and shouted, "Call 9-1-1! Now!"

"I didn't mean to." The girl sobbed. "I was just answering a text and I looked up and there they were. Oh, crap. Are they all right?"

Please be all right. Please be all right.... Olivia came up short on the yellow strip in the center of the road. Her lips went numb and her pulse dropped into her stomach. "Gerald?" she called, rushing to the limp man crumpled against the opposing shoulder of the road.

The dog hovered and whined, licking the man's

face. He didn't back off when Olivia ran the rest of the way to them and dropped down on her knees beside Gerald. "Gerald!" she cried, gripping his shoulder.

He groaned, rolling to his side. She saw the blood on his face and tried to stay calm. "Gerald. Can you hear me?"

"Liv…" He started to lift his hand to his head, then hissed and winced. "Bollocks. That *hurts*."

"Just stay still," she advised, placing her hands on either side of his head to stop him from moving further. "Don't move a muscle."

"Liv…" He said again, opening his eyes. They were glassy with shock. "I'll be all right. Don't you worry, love."

He was comforting *her?* "You hit your head," she told him. She felt shaking in her limbs but refused to give in to the tremors. She had to be strong, for him. "I need you to stay still."

"The dog. Is he—?"

Olivia looked up at Fido, who was sitting in the grass, panting over Gerald's condition. "He's fine. Just peachy."

"I called the police," the girl said, sprinting up behind them. "They say the ambulance is on its way."

Olivia could already hear the sirens in the distance. Still, the paramedics wouldn't get here soon enough for her taste. "Why did you do it?" she whispered. "Why in God's name did you have to save the damned dog?"

A weak smile crossed his face just before his eyes rolled into the back of his head and he passed out.

"Hurry," she murmured at the approaching ambulance through teeth gnashed so hard together, her jaw ached. "God. Please, hurry."

OLIVIA RODE IN the ambulance with Gerald to the hospital, leaving the hysterical teenager with the dog and the police on the scene. The paramedics prevented her from going any farther than triage, though, and so began a long, torturous wait for news.

She didn't think about calling anyone. Neither did she stop pacing long enough to fill out anything more than Gerald's name on the paperwork she'd been given. She didn't know his home address or phone number. She didn't know anything about his medical history or his health insurance. Neither did she know how she was supposed to sit still in one of the waiting-room chairs as an hour stretched into two and still she'd heard nothing.

He'd woken up as the paramedics were putting him on the gurney. He'd joked around in the ambulance with them, trying to draw her into the lighthearted conversation as they rode along the streets of Fairhope to Thomas Hospital. She hadn't been able to say anything as they wheeled him through the emergency room doors. No more words of comfort. Just worry—worry she didn't know how to express or contain.

The nerves swelled as the wait went on. They crawled into her throat, prickly and spiderlike. The fact that she hated hospitals didn't help matters. They reminded her of the grim visits to her aunt's bedside. Two years had gone by and the memories of what cancer had done to Briar's mother, Hanna Browning, and the emotional toll it had taken on her cousin, her uncle and her own father, Hanna's brother, haunted Olivia still.

She approached the triage nurse, unable to stand the wait a moment longer. Clearing her throat, she gripped the triage desk with white knuckles and asked, "You wouldn't happen to have any information about Gerald Leighton, would you?"

One brow arced on the woman's wide forehead. "Do you have security clearance?"

Olivia stared at the receptionist, at a complete loss. "Listen, I'm his…" She took a breath and said the words. "I'm his wife. Olivia Lewis? I just need to know if he's okay."

The woman turned to the phone next to her and picked up the receiver. "Just a moment. I'll see if there's any information."

"Thank you," Olivia said with a relieved sigh.

The nurse exchanged a few words with someone on the other end of the line, then hung up and spun her chair back to Olivia. "He's just getting patched up now. They did a few scans. It seems he's sustained a bit of a head injury."

Olivia remembered the blood and swallowed hard. "Yes. But he's going to be okay, right?"

"He's in a recovery room now," the nurse said with a nod. "Give it a few minutes and they should call you back to see him."

Olivia sighed. "Thank you. It's just…it's been hours since…"

The nurse looked sympathetic. She offered a smile. "I hope it's not too crass of me to say how much I love your husband's books. The last one—*Valley of the Shaman*… Oh!" A shudder went through her. "It was perfection."

"So I've heard," Olivia muttered.

"I hope he gets well soon so he can finish the series. It's been over a year since the last Rex Flynn book was published. He's going to write another, right?"

Olivia frowned. She didn't know anything about Gerald's work other than what Adrian had told her the night he came into town. "I…I think so."

"Thank goodness," the nurse said with a relieved sigh. "You take care of him so he can get back on his feet and get it done. We're all waiting with bated breath."

After exchanging a few more words with the nurse, Olivia wandered off. Finally able to sit down, she collapsed in a chair in the corner of the waiting room and scrubbed her hands over her face.

Olivia's stomach was tied up in knots. She'd gone completely against character and gnawed her fingernails down to the quick. Damn it, why had the stupid man dove into the road to save that dopey dog?

Because that was the kind of man he was. The kind who would risk his life to save a helpless animal. The kind who would say pleasant things like "Greetings" and "Cheerio" to those they jogged passed despite the fast pace she'd set in hopes of discouraging or losing him along the way. The kind of man who would knock a big drunken man on his ass to keep her from shooting him first and getting herself into trouble.

Drawing her legs into the chair and wrapping her arms around them, Olivia placed her head on her knees and indulged in a moment's helplessness.

If she wasn't very, *very* careful here, Gerald would win their stupid wager and she'd wind up abandoning her whole frigging belief system when it came to relationships and men in general.

She cursed fervently under her breath. She wished the man had never come here. She wished she'd never met him. And she strongly wished that he'd stayed a stranger on the back-cover flap of a book she was never bound to read.

"Ms. Lewis?"

Olivia looked up and dropped her feet back to the floor, sitting up as she took in the middle-aged doctor in front of her. "Yes?"

"I'm Dr. Woodsbrow," he explained, reaching out a hand as she stood. "Your husband's going to be just fine."

"Oh, thank God," she said, heaving a relieved sigh. Taking the man's hand, she added, "I thought… Well, I was waiting so long that I thought something was wrong."

"He's suffered a concussion," Dr. Woodsbrow informed her. "I wanted him to have a CT scan, just as a precaution. When it comes to head trauma, you can never be too careful. We also had to x-ray his shoulder. There's a visible step in the muscle there and it's painful to the touch. Although I'm happy to say nothing's broken, he does have some shoulder separation."

Olivia wrinkled her nose. "Sounds painful."

"It is, but he's very lucky. From the sounds of things, it could have been worse. We've put his arm in a sling, again just to be on the safe side. He'll need to wear it for a few days, rest the shoulder."

She reached up to touch her own brow. "He had a cut…right about here. It bled a lot at the scene before the paramedics covered it up in the ambulance."

Woodsbrow nodded. "He's got some stitches in his forehead, but other than the resulting scar, he won't have any long-term damage."

"Is there anything I can do in the meantime…to help him feel better?" Olivia asked.

"Give him anti-inflammatories. And make sure

he gets plenty of rest and quiet for the next few days. Would you like to see him?"

"Yes." The word bolted out of her before she could stop it. "I mean…if it's all right."

"Of course," he said, stepping aside and gesturing her forward. "Right this way, Ms. Lewis."

Olivia walked alongside Dr. Woodsbrow in silence as they made their way down a blank, white hall with exam room doors on either side. Nurses milled about, but nobody here in the recovery ward was in too much of a hurry. She felt her anxiety lessen somewhat and took a couple of cleansing breaths.

"Have you ever dealt with a concussion victim before?" Dr. Woodsbrow asked.

She thought about it, then nodded. "Yes. I played championship softball in high school. It gets pretty competitive at that level. People get hurt."

"So you know what to expect," the doctor concluded, taking a pen from his pocket as they came to the closed door of Gerald's room. Grabbing the chart from the wall, he made a small notation on the bottom as his brow furrowed.

"For the most part I do," Olivia replied. "He'll go through the same everyday motions but might repeat what he says." When Dr. Woodsbrow nodded in confirmation, she went on. "Um…there might be some gaps in his memory. Right?"

"He probably won't remember the accident or how it happened. He'll likely wake up tomorrow morning in a state of confusion. It'd be best if someone were there to talk him through it. As his wife, I trust you'll see to that."

Olivia swallowed. "Yes. Of course, I will."

"Very good." He reached for the handle of the door and pushed it open, crossing the threshold without any further ado. "Mr. Leighton," he announced as he entered the room with Olivia close at his back. "Your wife is here to see you."

No amount of preparation could have been enough to actually face the sight of Gerald lying on a hospital bed. Olivia stopped short, breath failing her as her eyes fell on the stark white bandage across his forehead. There was a nurse with mousy gray hair leaning over him. As Gerald's attention turned toward her, the nurse took the glass of water he was sipping from and set it aside. "Is there anything else I can get for you before the doctor discharges you?" she asked, laying a warm hand on his shoulder.

Gerald glanced from Olivia to her and a smile stretched wide across his mouth. Reaching up, he took her hand in his. "No. But thank you, Nancy, for taking such good care of me." He looked back at Olivia. "Rest assured. I'm in good hands now."

"I'm happy to hear it," Nancy said as she patted the back of his hand with her free one. Letting go, she strolled from the bed to the door and beamed at Olivia. "Take good care of him now, you hear?"

It seemed to be the battling cry of the entire hospital staff. Olivia bobbed a nod and waited until the nurse departed before forcing herself to take a step farther into the room. She ran her gaze over him more carefully. His hair was brushed back from his face. Probably Nancy's doing, or one of the other female members of the nursing staff. He was a touch pale. The brilliant green shade of his eyes was a direct contrast to the bruising around the bridge of his nose. There was a scratch on his chin and a nick on his cheek. Though he still wore the running pants and long-sleeved T-shirt he had that morning, a navy blue sling hung from his left shoulder, tucking his arm against his middle.

"Gerald," she greeted softly.

He returned the greeting with a warm, tender smile. "Mrs. Leighton."

Now at his bedside, she wrapped her hand around the bedrail instead of lifting it to his. "H-how do you feel?" she asked tentatively, unable to stop her eyes from pinging back and forth between the nicks and bruises on his face.

His expression grew wry, then a grimace took over as he shifted carefully on the bed. "I'd be lying if I said I was feeling at all myself."

Olivia ignored her unease and reached for the hand on the arm not occupied by the sling. His fingers were cold. She folded them close under hers as best she could. "You'll feel better soon. Just give it a day or two."

Gerald's eyes locked on hers. The longing she

saw in them made her feel strangely bereft. "Are we going home, love?"

Love. She sighed and gripped his fingers tighter. "Soon." They both looked to Dr. Woodsbrow in question.

The doctor tore something off the chart in front of him and crossed to the bed to hand it to Olivia. "Give him this, for pain. It'll help him sleep, too. And if you notice any changes, anything other than the usual for a concussion, don't be afraid to call or bring him back for a checkup."

"Thank you, Dr. Woodsbrow," Olivia said.

"Take it easy, Mr. Leighton," the man said as he backed toward the door.

"I'll do my best," Gerald said with an assertive nod. He winced again.

Olivia heard the door close and fought against another tide of helplessness. Her hand tightened on Gerald's in reaction. She'd never taken care of anyone before, but this man needed her now. Despite the fact that she'd been determined to dissuade him from sticking around, she wouldn't let him leave until she knew that he was all right. "Listen, Gerald…"

"The dog," Gerald said before she could finish. "There was a dog. He's all right, isn't he?" His fingers squeezed hers and a line appeared between his eyes she had never seen before. "Tell me he's all right, Liv."

"Calm down," she said in a quietly stern voice.

"He's fine. The police said that they were calling animal control to take care of him."

"What does that mean exactly?" Gerald asked, that line deepening.

Biting her lip, Olivia fought the urge to rub her thumb across it to make it disappear. "He'll probably go to a shelter for the night. They might try to find out if he belongs to anyone."

The lower half of Gerald's face tightened as his eyes went cold. "Whoever they were, they didn't care for him as he deserves. I don't want him spending the night in a kennel. There must be something I can do."

"There's nothing," Olivia said, raising her hand to his shoulder to keep him in place. He looked as though he had half a mind to get up and go after the poor creature right this minute. "Not right now. Look, if it makes you feel better, I'll talk to the deputy who was on the scene. I know him. I'll ask him where the dog wound up. Whoever has him we can call and ask for updates on his condition."

"If nobody comes for him—"

"They'll give it a couple of days," Olivia explained. "But if no one claims him, you'll be feeling better by then. And you can deal with the situation however you see fit."

Gerald sighed as he laid his head back on the raised pillow. He closed his eyes. "He'll have a roof over his head for the night. That's something."

"I'm sure they'll clean him up, too," Olivia said. "He'll have some good food to eat, as well."

"You're right." He seemed to settle finally, satisfied with her logical assurances.

"It's you we need to worry about now," she said. "As soon as the nurse comes back to discharge you, we'll go back to my place."

His eyes opened and reached for hers. "Yours?"

"Yes," she said. "The doctor thinks there should be someone with you when you wake up tomorrow. And…well, as good a caretaker as Briar is, she has enough on her plate with the baby and the inn. You'll be better off above the tavern with me."

A slow smile crept across his face, bleeding the warm light of humor into his eyes. "All right. I'll go home with you, love. You can even take advantage of me if you like."

She let out a laugh because not even a concussion could dull his charm and good humor. Latching on to his hand again, she had to admit it felt good—the laughing. The relief. She would worry about *how* good later. "You're going to be fine," she said for certain, as much for herself as for him.

"Don't I know it?" Gerald threaded his fingers through hers. His throat moved around a swallow and he closed his eyes once more. "I'm glad that you're here, Olivia."

She licked her lips. With his eyes closed, she could peruse his face again. She fought the urge to soothe those nicks and scrapes as well as that line that remained stubbornly embedded between his eyes. "Me, too," she whispered.

CHAPTER EIGHT

THE SUN HAD sunk down behind the western shore-line when Cole dropped Olivia and Gerald back at the tavern. He had given them a lift from the hospital since neither of them had taken their own vehicle there.

Because the tavern was already open for business and Monica was manning the bar, Olivia led Gerald around to the back of the building behind Adrian's greenhouse to the back door. She unlocked it and grabbed Gerald's arm, steering him into the hall-way beyond. The swinging doors at the other end of the hall divided Olivia's private quarters from the tavern. The sound of rock music escalated as she shut the door behind them. She then unlocked the first door on the left to reveal a set of spiral stairs leading up to the second level.

"You first," she said, stepping aside for him to go up the stairs. If he fell, she might be able to catch him. He may tower over her by a foot, but her re-flexes were quick and she could at least cushion his fall.

As they made their way up, he peered over the

awards, certificates and framed newspaper and magazine articles that lined the walls. "Is this all to do with your tavern?"

"Yes," she said, planting a hand in the small of his back to keep him moving. One step at a time. "Most are local accolades. Some regional."

His gaze lingered on a photograph of a couple embracing in front of the tavern entrance and the small girl who stood grinning beside them. "Look at you," he said with a fond chuckle. "All unhampered smiles and flyaway curls."

The landing was small but big enough for the two of them. She used her key again on the only door on the upper floor and swung it open, gesturing him in. "After you."

"Thank you," he said, stepping across the threshold.

"I'm not sure what state I left it in so be prepared for…" Her words of warning trailed off as she hit the light switch. The lamps on either side of a long red leather sofa lit the living area. "Huh."

"Not the state you left it in, I take it?" he asked, taking a gander around.

"Not exactly," she admitted. Briar had obviously been here. A navy suitcase sat on the floor next to the door to the lone bedroom. She smelled food and spotted the casserole dish on the stove. Shouldering the door shut behind them, Olivia herded him toward the couch. "Take a load off. You're exhausted."

He eyed her large flat-screen television on the wall opposing the sofa, the dark wood floor beams and the black wooly rug that encompassed much of the room. "Where are the knickknacks?" he asked curiously.

"What?" she asked.

"The personal photos or mementos most women leave around their living space," he explained. "You don't seem to have much of those."

"No," she agreed. "I like to keep things simple." She ran a hand over her ponytail and tried not to feel self-conscious about the arrangements of her apartment. When she had decided to move into the rooms above the tavern shortly after she took over its management, she had worked hard to make it livable. Then she had worked to make it hers. She was proud of it. It reflected her lifestyle. After long nights in the tavern, it was nice coming upstairs to her simple living space with its comfortable, over-size furnishings and to just be able to relax or crawl into bed. "There's not much to it—kitchen, dining area, living room and bedroom. I'm afraid there's only one bathroom."

"I'm sure we'll manage," he said, looking into the kitchen. The cabinets were the same dark wood as the floor, only they had a rough finish. Her appliances were clean and silver. A large granite countertop separated the kitchen from the living room. The cooking range was wide as was a sideboard full of liquor that matched the strapping dining oom table. Gesturing toward the bedroom, he asked her, "Bathroom's there, I take it?"

"Yes," she said. "I'll let you have first dibs while I heat up dinner. It looks like Briar left something for us."

When she eyed him warily, he grinned in reassurance. "It's a lovely apartment, Olivia."

"Oh." She fumbled. He'd picked up on the insecurity she'd worked hard to hide. Shrugging her shoulders back in frustration, she frowned. She didn't have to impress him, no matter who he was. She'd never felt the need to impress any of the other men she'd brought here, had she?

This was different, a voice inside her head said firmly. *Gerald* was different.

"My loft in Soho isn't much bigger," he explained. When she only nodded, he jerked his thumb toward the bedroom door. "I'll be back. Just going to spend a penny."

"Spend…what?" she asked, squinting after him. Was that the concussion talking?

He looked over his shoulder, saw her look of utter confusion and chuckled. "Spend a penny. It's a common phrase in Britain. You know—use the loo. Take a piss. That sort of thing."

"Oh," she said, waving a hand as she caught up. "Well, then…take your time?"

His grin widened as he loped toward the bathroom and offered her a casual salute.

"God, what am I going to do?" she whispered

to the walls of her living room once she heard the bathroom door shut.

Clearly, she wasn't cut out for this job. Determined to busy her hands so she wouldn't have to think about how over her head she was with him here, Olivia went to the refrigerator and opened it. "Jesus, Briar," she muttered, confronting two other casserole dishes. "Did someone die? Was there a wake since I left this morning?" Taking out a bottle of water and ignoring the soda—she was far too hyped up for caffeine—she took it to the stove where the other casserole dish was waiting with a note of instructions from Briar.

Hash Brown Potato Casserole

Pop it in the oven at 350 until the cheese bubbles.
Top with crumbled Ritz Crackers and melted butter, then bake another ten.

Let us know if you need ANYTHING!

"Yes, Mom," Olivia muttered, removing the plastic wrap and turning back the dial on the oven to preheat it.

The casserole had been in the oven for fifteen minutes when Gerald finally walked back in, a little slower this time, but his pallor had returned. When she saw the white around the skin of his lips and the tired bruises under his eyes, she went to the table and pulled out a chair for him. "Sit. You look like I could blow you." When he came up short at the assertion, her jaw dropped at his interpretation. "No. I was using slang. Your slang. Blow you down, remember? With a feather…" She sighed when he only gave a small smile. "Just sit, all right? Dinner's almost ready."

"Yes, Mrs. Leighton." He lowered carefully to the chair and braced an elbow on the table as he watched her mill about the kitchen. "It was kind of Briar to leave something for us."

"She must've been putting casseroles together all day, by the looks of it," Olivia said, nodding toward the refrigerator.

"She's lovely," Gerald murmured fondly. The small smile faded abruptly as he winced and lifted a hand to his head.

"What's wrong?" she asked, alarmed.

"Nothing. Just a slight headache," he said, shaking his head.

Knowing he was trying to make light of it, Olivia busied herself again. His skin was so pasty, it was almost translucent. She could clearly see the blue vein on his unmarked temple. "Briar's hash brown casserole is the perfect remedy to a day like today. She makes it for me when I'm sick or feeling low. It goes really well with Texas toast, which I admit is about all I can make well."

"I'll take your word for it," he said and closed his eyes. "Christ, I'm knackered."

"I'll find those pills Woodsbrow prescribed for you. That'll help with the headache. He said they'll help you sleep, too, which is what you need. Lots of sleep. Rest."

"Olivia?"

"Yes?" she asked as she pulled bowls down from the cupboard.

"Your hands are shaking."

"They're what?" She glanced down at her fingers and saw the tremor. The sight was such a shock to her, she stared at her hands for several blank seconds. Never in her life had she been so unnerved. Splaying them on her thighs, she let out a tremulous breath to match the quaver in her fingers.

A hand on her elbow turned her around. Gerald was there, looking down at her as if she was a fragile pane of glass about to shatter. He stared, that line between his eyes digging in now in concern. "You're worn thin," he said, brushing the hair back from her face with tender, steady hands. Dropping his brow to hers in a gesture that rocked her with its sweetness, he said softly, "I've placed a tremendous burden on you."

"No, you—"

"There's no use denying it," he intervened, touching his lips to her brow. "Take a minute."

She loosened another ragged breath. "This is so backward. I should be caring for you, Gerald."

Stepping back, he looked her in the eye. "I'm not going to let you wear yourself thin on my behalf. We're partners, you and I. At least for now. And I'm stronger than I look."

"So am I," she insisted, brushing his hands from her shoulders. "Let me make you dinner, please." She couldn't have said why the task was so important to her, but the plea came out on a wavering voice. It was *vital* that he let her take care of him while he was hurt.

She could still see him crumpled in the street. For a moment, she'd thought the worst. And that moment had put all the stirrings and tugs she'd felt toward him these past few days into perspective. He'd come to mean something to her despite her best efforts. She'd begun to care for him.

He gauged her face. "Did Cole mention anything about the dog?"

She sighed. "For the love of God, would you forget about the damn dog? Just for tonight?" When he simply looked at her insistently, she shook her head. "He said he'd take care of it, okay? Stop worrying. The only thing you need to worry about right now is getting food in your belly and getting some rest. Can you do that? For me?"

"For you," he agreed after a moment's pause. "If you agree to let me sleep on the couch for the evening."

She closed her eyes and lifted a hand to pinch the skin in between. "Gerald—"

"I might be your husband and I might have a bump on the head," he said, lifting his knuckles to his brow. His voice stayed steady, low, never rising as hers had. "But I'm a guest in your home. And I insist on sleeping on the couch for the night. It's rather large and long. I should be quite comfortable."

She measured him and the plea in his eyes. "Do whatever you want," she said, turning back to the stove. "You always do, don't you?"

He chuckled as he bent to brush his lips over her exposed ear. "If that were the case, I never would have let you go in Vegas."

"Don't," she said, blocking his hands from wrapping around her waist and bracing herself against the soft, teasing sensations that arose from him doing so. "Please…just go turn on the television and relax. Dinner will be ready in about five minutes. Then I'll get you a pillow and you can try to sleep."

He hovered for a moment. Then he said, "As you wish, Mrs. Leighton."

She felt him back away. A moment later, the noise of the television drifted into the kitchen and she gave into a small sigh of relief. When the casserole was done, she took it out of the oven and set it on the range, letting the heat of the dish sink through the pot holders to warm her cold hands. Then she spooned a large helping into Gerald's bowl and took it and a glass of water into the living room.

She stopped short when she saw Gerald stretched out there, his feet on the coffee table in front of him, his head leaned against the couch cushions behind him. His eyes were closed, his mouth open and that bar between his eyes was still there, even in repose.

Concern merged into the guilt she felt over brushing him off when he didn't feel well. All the mixed emotions and fatigue she'd battled over the terrible day stepped aside as she scanned his face. Rounding the couch, she set his food on the table. Then she used gentle hands to maneuver him until he was laying with his head on one of her overstuffed toss pillows. She caught herself running a hand through his hair and stopped to pry his tennis shoes off his feet. Grabbing the white alpaca throw from the back of the sofa, she folded it over his long, lean form.

Exhausted, she dropped onto the coffee table behind her, picking up the remote to mute the television. She reached over to dim the lamp, then just watched him for a moment. Watched his rib cage rise and fall soundlessly. Watched a muscle in his jaw twitch. Watched and waited, hoping the concussion hadn't in fact been worse than Dr. Woodsbrow had determined.

She had half a mind to sit here the rest of the night and watch him sleep. Just to make sure he was okay, she told herself. Again resisting the urge to reach over and brush a hand over his hair or his cheek, she pushed herself up and took the bowl back to the kitchen. Sitting down at the table, she poured herself a large glass of wine and ate in the silence.

GERALD CLAWED OUT of sleep, desperate to escape the black gulf he'd been sinking into.... Water had been dragging him down. His arms were sore. In the dream, he'd been pumping them, trying to swim for the surface. It hadn't stopped him from sinking like a weight into the depths. He was drenched from head to toe. At first he thought it was from the watery abyss of his dreams. Then, wiping the back of his hand over his face, he realized it was his own perspiration. His legs were tangled up in a white throw blanket. His breath was ragged, uneven, and his throat dry.

Tremors—they overtook him as he sat up, pulling his knees to his chest. He pressed his hands to the back of his neck, fighting for calm.

Then he looked around at the strange room and fought the panic he'd just escaped once more. Where the devil was he?

The last thing he remembered…he'd been running with Olivia. There was the dog in the road, the car coming toward them…then nothing. Fighting for calm, Gerald fumbled for a lamp in the dark. He had to get out of the dark of his dreams. Maybe then he could piece together what had happened over the past twenty-four hours.

Finding nothing, he rose, tossing back the throw blanket. He paused for a moment as he got a whiff of sandalwood.

Vanilla. Olivia. Gerald breathed the scent in deep until it pushed away the panic. This was Olivia's place. And knowing that, he felt a mite better. He rose and walked in what he hoped was the direction of the kitchen. His legs were unsteady, his ankles and knees weak.

Sod it. The dream had reduced his joints to vapor. For stability, he reached out blindly and found cold granite. There was a wall close by. He groped for a light switch and finally found one.

As the welcome hum of the fluorescent fixture over his head flickered to life, he stopped in his tracks, his eyes latching on to the figure sitting on the far side of the big dining room table. "Liv," he grated. Clearing his throat, he measured her from the top of her golden head to what he could see of the overlarge black New Orleans Saints jersey partially falling off one slender shoulder.

Judging by the disheveled state of her curls and the half-eaten package of double-stuffed Oreo cookies on the table in front of her, he'd interrupted a guilty snacking session.

She chewed for a moment, swallowed and took a long sip from a glass of milk. Then she said, "Sorry. I tried to be quiet."

He lifted a hand. "No, I... What the bloody hell happened yesterday? Or was it today?" He squeezed his eyes and pressed two fingers to them. "Blast it all. I just can't figure out how I wound up on your couch!"

"It's okay," Olivia said as she rose from the table and walked to him. "It's fine. You hit your head."

"Yes," he said, brushing his fingers over the bandage and the sore spot beneath it. "I thought that. Where?"

"On the curb," she explained, steadying him with a hand on his arm. "Does your head hurt?"

"No. Yes. But it's not too terrible..." He trailed off, seeing the hospital ID band on his wrist. "Shit. I was in the hospital. Why can't I remember that?"

"You had a concussion," she reminded him. "And some stitches."

"And my arm?" he asked, reaching up to clutch his left shoulder and the arm hanging by a sling.

"Separated shoulder," she informed him. "The doctor said it could have been worse. Way worse. You won't have to wear the sling long, but you'll have to avoid using that arm too much."

He rubbed the pads of his thumb and forefingers together, looking at them questioningly. "Feels a bit odd. Cold."

"It's normal, apparently," Olivia assured him.

He studied her. "And you brought me back here."

She nodded, crossing her arms over her chest. "I thought it'd be best.

"That was kind of you," he said. In truth, he didn't know what he would have done had he woken alone in the bay view suite at Hanna's. "Very kind."

She lifted a shoulder. "I didn't want you to be alone...after." For a moment, she closed her eyes. "I saw you almost get hit by a car today, Gerald. I couldn't let you go back to the inn, no matter how well Briar would've cared for you. I...I don't know. I somehow feel responsible for the whole thing."

"I'm fairly certain that's not the case." He frowned, reaching back to rub the nape of his neck again. "How's the dog? He wasn't hurt, was he?"

A weary laugh escaped her. "He's fine, spending the night in a shelter. We'll know more in the morning."

He nodded. Then his eyes narrowed on the package of Oreo cookies on the table behind her. "Is there a reason you're eating cookies in the dark?"

Her mouth opened once, then closed, uncertain. Then she said, "I don't normally eat sweets. They go straight to my hips. It's why I run."

Gerald scanned her. Was she wearing anything under that jersey? Inside him, a warm light toggled and he latched on to it like a lifeline. "There's nothing wrong with your hips, love. I'm rather fond of them, actually."

As she searched his face, she seemed to see more this time. Much more. Worry wrenched her features with a quick frown. "Are you all right? You don't look so great."

With a grimace, he lifted his hand to his face, scrubbing it. His skin still felt cold and clammy. His nose ached at the touch. "I'm not too certain." With no desire to rehash the dream and the confusion that had followed, he opened one of the cupboards. "I thought I'd get a glass of water."

Her hand on his elbow stopped him. "Let me. You sit. Seriously. You've got as much color as a ghost."

He swallowed, watching her fill the glass from the sink tap. "Thank you," he said when she handed it to him. She observed him as he tipped it to his mouth and gulped it. He lowered the glass, caught her staring at him still and frowned. "I'm fine, Olivia."

She raised a brow. "I might be a little more convinced if your shirt wasn't drenched like you just ran a marathon."

He looked down and cursed. The sweat had bled clean through his long-sleeved T-shirt.

Olivia's forehead creased, eyes turning thoughtful. "You shouldn't have to sleep on the couch. I don't know what I was thinking letting you."

"The couch is perfectly comfortable—"

"Gerald," she said, nonplussed. "You're nearly a foot longer than the couch. Don't try to convince me sleeping there is like a stay at the Ritz." She seemed to hesitate, then stepped forward and took his hand. "Come on."

She wound her fingers through his. He was as

surprised by the intimate interlacing as he was by the fact that she led him toward the bedroom. The light from the kitchen faded as they crossed the threshold and he frowned at the dark. "Going back to sleep isn't something I'm at all keen on at the moment."

"You need to rest," she insisted. "If you won't sleep, at least lie down."

"I'd rather stay up. Watch television. Something." *Anything* but lying down in the dark again. Letting his thoughts run right back down the rabbit hole and into the big black gulf of hopelessness.

"You're going to lie down. And to make sure you do, I'm going to lie down with you."

He blinked at her shadowed silhouette. "Are you?"

Olivia paused at the foot of the bed. "Yeah," she seemed to decide. She didn't let go of his hand as she tugged him behind her.

He followed, wordless. The turned-down satin bedspread rustled with the flannel sheets underneath as they both crawled into bed, her on the left, him on the right. He laid back next to her, sitting up slightly against the pillows stacked at his back. Raising one arm over his head, he looked up at the ceiling. There was a small circle of light there, a refraction of one of the lights on the end of the dock shining through the small bedroom window. He focused on it and swallowed, trying to settle.

Her fingers began to slip from his. He gripped them, unwilling to let go just yet.

He heard her swallow, then she said softly, "Would it help to talk about it? The accident, the confusion? Since you say sleep isn't an option?"

A headache was beginning to gnaw at his temple. Lowering his fingertips to massage his right brow, he heaved a sigh. "I don't know if I can." When she said nothing, his gaze strayed from that refracted light, but only to find the dim oval of her face on the pillow next to his. Her concerned eyes searched his. "I remember running with you, Olivia. I can almost remember the faces we passed on the way. I remembered the dog and everything I felt when I saw it standing there, shivering in the road…."

He squinted against the pulse inside his head, trying to remember more. "I remember you telling me to step back, get off the road. There was a white car…and not much else after that. Nothing at all, really. And that was the most terrifying thing about it when I woke on your couch…in the dark."

Her fingers tightened on his. "I'm sorry."

He blew out a laugh with little mirth behind it. "It's strange. I haven't woken sweating like that since I had nightmares in the nursery back home."

"You've been through a terrible ordeal, Gerald," she said. "You have every right to wake up sweating. You could even cry if you wanted to. Pretty sure I would."

He let a rueful smile lift one corner of his mouth.

"Forgive me if I don't cry in front of you, love. What little there is left of the man in me would take the mickey out of me for it."

She smiled, too. It was a small smile, as she scanned his face thoroughly. "You look tired again."

His lids were getting heavy. And, bugger it, sleep was beginning to drag him under again. Despite his wishes. What was worse, he didn't have the energy to fight it.

Her face blurred and one last wave of fear washed over Gerald. He hated the weak words that grated from his throat but was unable to stop them from tumbling out. "I don't want to go back into the dark."

The sheets rustled as his eyes began to close. God, they weighed like bricks. His arm, limp and heavy, lifted and he felt her close, her breath on his face as her head settled in the crook of his shoulder. "Shh," Olivia hushed when he opened his mouth to say…something—he forgot what it was. "I'm not going anywhere. I'll be right here if you wake up again. Okay?"

In answer, Gerald lowered his hand from the top of his head to take the one she'd laid on his sternum. It was small. He could wrap his hand around it and hide it against his chest. He did so because it was a comfort, having it balled there, warm over his heart. Turning his face into her hair, he breathed her in and what little of him that was still tense, released. Relief washed over him.

Solace. Earlier, he'd been able to stop the tremors and choke back that helpless feeling brought on by his dark dreams. But he hadn't been able to construct a true feeling of sanctuary.

Here it was now. She was the key—this woman he'd only begun to get to know.

He'd been right to come here, he thought again, knowing it now with every fiber of his being.

As he drifted off, it occurred to him that this was the first time they'd slept together since their wedding night. The novelty of the situation wasn't lost on him. He'd wanted this. Beyond the great sex and the crushing desire he'd felt for her, he wanted this hard-won intimacy that was suddenly between them.

Such a domestic thing, two people united through matrimony turning to each other in the dark. Nothing sexual. Just warmth, stability, ease and solace.

CHAPTER NINE

"I'M NOT SURE what to do with him," Olivia admitted the next morning. It was early, not quite eight. She'd left Gerald snoozing in bed to go for her morning run with Adrian who had called for Bloody Marys on the tavern terrace upon their return.

Olivia had just settled down in one of the old Adirondack chairs overlooking the bay when she caught sight of her hubby sitting on the deck out on the water, barefoot, wearing khaki slacks and a white, oxford shirt untucked. As she gazed out across the yard at him she felt a not-so-subtle stir.

He was wearing the reading glasses she'd seen hooked in his shirt pocket once before, horn-rimmed and bookish. There was an open book on his lap, but he wasn't paying it much mind. Instead, he watched the play of white, morning sunlight on the surface of the water as the mist began to break apart.

The stir quickened within her and she shifted in her chair to squelch it. No use denying she'd tip-toed around him this morning. Olivia had spent a sleepless night tossing and turning because she could still feel the press of his lips, the touch of his hands and the presence of him sleeping close beside her. The morning run to distract her had done little good. "We barely even speak the same language," she commented. "He says things like 'spend a penny,' 'bit of a tosser' and 'give it a welly.' Who *talks* like that?"

"The English, presumably. I think it's pretty cute," Adrian mused, eyeing the man on both of their minds.

Olivia thought it was pretty dang cute herself, but she was trying not to dwell on that, either. "I feel weird not having read any of his books," she admitted.

"I'll loan you a few," Adrian offered. "I know you don't read much, but I think you might enjoy them."

"Hmm." Olivia frowned. Adrian had been determined not to talk about what had happened with Radley. Olivia knew that avoidance was her friend's way of coping. Rather than bringing it up once again, Olivia said, "So are you finished with the starry-eyed bit? Can you go back to being cynical Adrian long enough for me to get a forthright opinion on this whole thing?"

Adrian lifted her shoulder. "It's definitely not your everyday marriage."

"Gee, ya think?"

"Did you sleep with him?" When Olivia turned

to her with a baleful eye, Adrian waved a hand. "I mean in the same bed. Not the horizontal monkey dance."

Olivia sighed. "He needed help falling asleep."

"Mmm-hmm. Was there cuddling?"

Olivia scowled as Adrian smirked. "Who the hell *are* you? I mean, really. This alter ego of yours is starting to creep me out."

"If the situation were reversed and it was me Gerald had married in Vegas, right now you'd be asking me the same question. Only you wouldn't have asked if we cuddled. You would have asked if he climbed on top of me during the night. And," Adrian continued, lifting a discerning finger to get her point across before Olivia could comment, "*you* would have asked me how big his manhood is."

It was hard to argue with the truth. "It's official. You and I have been friends for far too long."

Adrian's face sobered and she lowered her voice. "So how long are you going to let him stay before you get all flaky and ask him to leave again?"

"I'm a decent enough person to make sure he heals properly before I kick him out of my apartment," Olivia explained, defensive. "And…we had a deal. He could stay for three weeks. Then he's gone."

"You sure about that?"

"He's not winning the bet, Adrian."

"And is that what you really want?" When Olivia only sighed, Adrian shrugged. "Come on. There must be some reason you married him, Liv…other than the tequila's influence. What if you get to the end of the three weeks and you realize this is what you want?"

Olivia massaged her temples. "I just want to go back to being in control of my life."

"Cynical Adrian would tell you to be careful. As wonderful as he is…and he *is* wonderful, Liv— even you can't deny it—just make sure he doesn't have any underlying motives for being here," Adrian said.

"Like what?" Olivia asked, eyeing the man on the dock.

"I don't know. But if it were me," Adrian continued slowly, "I couldn't believe that some stranger I married in Vegas came all the way here for three weeks just to woo me. And that's not low self-esteem talking. It's…"

"Realism," Olivia said with a nod and a new wave of suspicion. "You're right."

"I don't think he's a bad guy," Adrian added. "Whether I've been starry-eyed or not, I haven't picked up any negative vibes on my bad-boy radar."

Olivia trusted Adrian's bad-boy radar more than anyone else's since she'd experienced her fair few. "But?"

"But…" Adrian licked her lips. "I'd hate to be disappointed in the end. So be nice…but be careful."

"I'm not going to get my heart mixed up in all

this marital turmoil, if that's what you mean," Olivia said stubbornly. "I got a postcard from my folks. They're in Charleston—what if they decide to come here for a visit? They could be here in a week or two! I'll be damned if he's not gone before they get here. No use getting anyone else involved in this, particularly family."

Adrian smirked. "The last time they were here, your dad was hell-bent on convincing you to pop out a few grandkids."

Olivia rolled her eyes and groaned. "Don't remind me."

Cupping her chin in her hand, Adrian eyed the man out on the water and smiled. "You know, your kids *would* be really cute." When Olivia balked, Adrian went on. "No, really, picture it. All tow-headed, mischievous and a little bookish. They'll be loud like you and sweet like him. Y'all would make quite the brood, I must say."

Olivia reached over and clamped her hand over the top of Adrian's Bloody Mary glass. Lifting it, she sniffed the contents carefully. "If I didn't know better, I'd say I screwed up and made yours stronger than usual."

GERALD ENTERED OLIVIA'S apartment. The morning spent on the boat dock had done him well. The pain in his head was no longer drilling, as it had been when he first woke.

He'd woken alone, he mused. Olivia had been

long gone on her morning run by the time he got up. After eating a slice of toast, drinking a glass of water and taking two pain relievers, he'd desperately needed fresh air.

The serenity of the bay had lulled the jumble of noise in his mind. The pain now felt more like a backdrop. The arm in the sling was stiff, the top of his left shoulder tender to the touch, but with the over-the-counter anti-inflammatories in his system, he could almost ignore it.

The toast had done well to tide him over, so he postponed eating anything more until brunch and fixed a cup of hot tea. Olivia was a religious coffee drinker, Gerald had quickly learned. She liked it black, which made him grimace just thinking about it. Briar must have left the bags of Earl Grey tea next to the coffeepot for him.

Olivia had no kettle, so Gerald made do with boiling the water in a small saucepan. Using one of her large mugs, he stirred a bag into the hot water and thoughtfully watched the steam rise from the surface.

Briar had brought his laptop over from the inn, too. That morning he'd set up his travel notebook on Olivia's dining room table underneath the bay windows and the blue sweep of the bay beyond them. Not that it would do him much good.

Gerald leaned back against the counter and frowned at the laptop's blank screen. It looked as if the writing would have to be postponed for a few days at least. Until the sling came off, typing was of no use to him however accomplished a typist he might be.

He thought about calling Dwight and asking to push the book deadline back. A week or two...or three. But Gerald had his pride. He'd never missed a deadline in a decade of publication. He wouldn't let even this setback derail him. He would finish the book. When the sling came off, he would write like the wind.

Until then, he'd make notes, work on the story's timeline. The fact that he was left-handed gave him some pause. The injured arm needed rest. Maybe he'd invest in that speech recognition software Dwight had been telling him about....

Restless, he walked from one side of Olivia's apartment to the other. He stopped on the threshold of her bedroom and perused its contents.

Where the rest of her apartment bordered on rustic decor, here were more feminine tones. Her scent permeated the space. He drew it deep into his lungs as he stepped farther into the room.

Her shelves were used not for books but antique beer steins and wine bottles that looked as if they'd been plucked from the ocean floor. There was also a large conch shell and a whole sand dollar. He found four framed photographs on her dresser—the same couple from the photograph in the stairway, only older. A small sterling-silver-framed portrait of newborn Harmony....

A professional, garden shot of Briar and Cole in wedding attire. He recognized the expanse of water as the bay behind them. They'd been married at the inn, he imagined. Cole was holding the hand of a small boy around Kyle's age who could have passed for the groom's son. Was this the child from his previous marriage? He'd heard the others mention the child briefly a few days before. Next to Briar holding the bridal bouquet was Olivia dressed in a strapless pale yellow sundress.

She was beaming in a way Gerald hadn't seen since their wedding night. The happy expression matched that of her cousin and the bridegroom, and it knocked the breath out of Gerald. It was a shame those full-fledged smiles were so rare.

He focused on the last photograph of a woman, older. Too old to be Olivia's mother, but the resemblance was undeniably there in the smile and her sultry, green eyes. A grandmother, perhaps?

The phone rang in the living room. Gerald hesitated a moment before walking from the bedroom. Seeing Cole's name on the caller ID screen, he picked up the receiver. "Cole," he answered.

"Gerald," Cole said, surprised to hear his voice instead of Olivia's. "How are you feeling this morning?"

"A bit better," Gerald said, rubbing the bandage on his brow. "Olivia's still out on her run. Would you like me to tell her you rang when she gets back?"

"Ah, actually, it's you I need to speak with. It's about the stray dog you found yesterday."

Gerald lowered to the sofa cushions and braced his elbow on his knee. "I'm listening."

"He's at the city rescue shelter," Cole explained, voice grave. "They've bathed him and treated his wounds. They gave him some medicine to help with the mange, as well. He's been fed and well cared for. They don't have much hope of finding an owner, however. There were no tags or chip and there's no collar. He looks like he's been pretty badly neglected for some time."

Gerald scowled, recalling the condition the bedraggled hound had been in the day before. "I noticed," he said grimly.

"They're gonna give it another twenty-four hours," Cole said. "But if no one claims him by this time tomorrow, they're putting him up for adoption."

"Adoption," Gerald muttered. Thinking quickly, he bit his lip. "Right. I owe you thanks for checking up on him and relaying the news." He looked around for a pencil and paper. "By any chance, do you have the number for the shelter?"

"Give me a sec. I'll grab it."

As Cole stepped away from the phone, Gerald located a pen and the corner of a receipt of some kind. When Cole's voice came back over the line, Gerald tried wedging the phone between his ear and shoulder to pin the receipt down with his left elbow and write a bit more carefully with his clumsy right hand. His shoulder gave a sharp protest and he cursed under his breath. Finally, he found a way to make the stiff fingers on his left hand write out the number legibly enough.

Thanking Cole once more, he hung up and dialed the animal shelter. He was finishing up with them when the door to the apartment swung open and Olivia walked in in her jogging clothes. He grinned at her. "Good morning."

"Gerald." She paused after shutting the door behind her. "How are you feeling?"

"Good," he said in all honesty. "Especially now that you're here."

She frowned as he set the wireless receiver on the counter. "You're talking on my phone."

He looked down at it, then back at her. "Does this bother you?"

She scowled. "Why should it?" she asked. Marking a wide berth around him, she made for the refrigerator and pulled out a water bottle. Sniffing the air, she unscrewed the cap. "What's that smell?"

"Tea," he told her, lifting the mug in his hand. "Would you like a cuppa? The water's still hot."

Eyeing the saucepan on the stove, she shook her head, taking a long drink from the water bottle.

He ran his eyes over her, perusing her much as he had her bedroom. Only he held himself back from getting close enough to take in the vanilla fragrance that clung to her skin—she wouldn't have liked that. Her hair was coming loose from the ponytail and her face was still flushed from her run. There was a place just above her left eyebrow where he would've liked to lay his lips.

He fought the urge, setting it aside for now even as heat gathered below his waistline and his heart stirred. Watching her eyes dodge his once more, he cleared his throat. "Is something the matter?"

Brow creased, she put the bottle on the counter. "'Course not." She veered in the direction of the bedroom before he could question her further.

Offset by her less than warm reception, he hesitated before following her. The bedroom door was wide-open as was the bathroom's with the light spilling out. He didn't see the clothes on the tile floor until it was too late.

She was in the process of pulling the loose tank top over her head. When the article of clothing was out of the way and she saw him standing, frozen, in the bedroom, she shrieked and hugged the tank to her chest. "Jesus!"

She had a tattoo in the shape of a heart resting snugly inside the curve of her waist, just above her right hip bone. The hot pants she'd worn despite the cold were now on the floor, revealing the black bikini under-thing she'd hidden beneath. The matching sports bra did little to minimize the curves of her torso.

Good God, she was built in the sexiest way imaginable.

It took him a moment—okay, *more* than a moment—to stop staring at all that silky smooth, pale skin and do an about-face. "Sorry," he said, raking a hand through his hair. That image of her would be glued to his retinas for some time.

It took a moment for Olivia to reappear, this time wrapped in a flannel robe that somehow did nothing to distill the fire in his blood. His reaction to her was so physical it nearly knocked him back a step. "I'm sorry," he said again, feeling like a complete idiot.

She muttered something indeterminable in reply as she went to the closet to fetch some real clothing.

Gerald swallowed and turned respectfully away as she dressed. He had to swallow again before he could speak words he'd thought he'd had no intention of voicing. "Ah…the tattoo?" he heard himself ask.

"I was eighteen. And stupid."

Stupid. Yes, he could relate. "Ah," he said, combing his blank mind for a complete sentence. "I'll, ah…leave you to dress. But I was wondering…"

"What?"

"I want to change the bandage," he said, lifting a hand to his brow. "But I think I might need a hand. Would you mind?"

It took her a moment to answer him. "No," she said finally. "I've got some first aid stuff in the bathroom cupboard. Find it. I'll be there in a minute."

CHAPTER TEN

OLIVIA THREW ON some clothes quickly, pairing jeans with a sweater and then a pair of flats. Tugging the band from her hair, she fluffed it impatiently over her shoulders until the curls spread evenly across them. She didn't care if she still looked untidy. He was waiting.

He'd found the first aid box and was already leaning on the edge of the pedestal sink. She went to the box next to him and flipped it open, rifling through the contents until she found a large bandage that would cover the stitches on his brow.

"When did the doctor say I should have the stitches removed?" Gerald asked.

"The day after tomorrow," she told him, taking the wrapper off the bandage and turning to him. She sighed when she had to look up too far. "You're too tall."

His lips twitched. "Sorry."

"No." She waved a hand toward the fixture behind him. "Your head's blocking the light. I need to be able to see what I'm doing."

He jerked his head in a nod. "Quite." Pushing

away from the sink, he tried maneuvering around her in the small space of the bathroom. After a moment's joggling between them, he planted his large hands on her shoulders and directed them both in a careful circle until she wound up with her back to the sink and his calves brushed against the commode. Lowering to the tank, he looked up at her. "All right?"

"Better," she admitted. "Stay still," she said when he squirmed. She saw him lick his lips, a nervous motion. "If you don't trust me, I shouldn't be doing this."

Those green eyes fixed on hers. "I have an active imagination, is all. This bandage hasn't been removed since the stitches were in place." He wet his lips again before pressing them together. "I have a few reservations about taking it off."

"I won't *rip* it off," she informed him. "It's not a Band-Aid, and I'm not eight."

"I'm not worried about you, love," he returned in a quiet voice that vibrated along her nerve endings. "I trust you. I just feel a bit squiggy when it comes to open wounds."

"Just hold still," she ordered. "Stop fidgeting." Stepping between his open knees, she laid her hand on one instinctively to steady him. "Breathe," she told him firmly. At his inhale, she set the new bandage in his offered hand and lifted her fingers to the one on his brow. "Nice and slow," she said as she began to peel it back.

His eyes remained on her face. They held fast to her features as if they were the only thing keeping him from jumping up and bolting. Trying to ignore the full force of their green depths, she took a deep breath…and smelled only him. Blowing it out, she pried the last corner of the bandage off and crumpled it into the small trash pail behind her.

"How does it look?" he asked in an undertone.

Scanning the tiny railroad track of stitches and the shiny pink skin around them, she frowned. "You're going to have a hell of a scar."

Gerald jerked a shoulder. The stiff material of his white shirt whispered with the movement. Propping one foot on the lid of the toilet below him, he said, "Scars I can live with. It's blood that worries me."

"You're not bleeding," she assured him. Taking the fresh bandage from his hand, she removed the backing and threw it away, too. When she noticed his raised knee bouncing, she laid a firm hand on it again. "Be still."

He blew out a quiet, self-deprecating laugh. "I'm sorry, love," he murmured. "Perhaps you should give me a quick snog. That should put me to rights."

Olivia lowered her eyes to his and couldn't fight a quick grin when she saw the light of humor burning through the wariness and discomfort poised in his tense face muscles. With a shake of her head, she went back to applying the bandage. "I know what snogging is."

Gerald's grin widened and the unease drained from the tight line of his shoulders. "Show me."

She had to fight hard not to let her own smile spread across her face. Damn it. She liked him a lot. "Don't you write quite a bit of violence into these books of yours? This is nothing compared to what your imagination has conjured over the years, I'm sure."

"That's fiction," he pointed out. "As real as it is to me in the moment, it's nothing a fifth of Scotch won't cure later."

"After yesterday's concussion, the Scotch isn't an option for several more days."

"And that I'm regretting," he said. When she leaned back to study her handiwork, his smile wavered and his expression sobered. "How'd you do?"

"Not bad," she said. The bruise on his nose snagged her attention. It was fading, but there was still that small, almost indistinguishable notch at the bridge of it. "What happened there?" she asked.

"Bar fight." At her doubting, arched brow, he nodded. "I told you I tended a pub while I was at university. There was a football match on. The spectators got a wee bit out of hand. I stepped in to intervene and wound up with a bottle to the face."

"Ouch," she said, running her finger over the imperfection, careful of the tender purple bruising just above it. A shame. It was a nice Roman nose.

She caught her touch lingering. The breath snagged in his chest and his gaze softened on hers.

She jerked her hand away as the tingling he'd set in motion along her nerve endings increased exponentially. Her thighs burned a bit when she saw something more than kindness and wisdom in his eyes.

Remembering the moment only minutes before when he'd caught her undressing…

He hadn't just looked at her. There had been a dark light in those intelligent eyes, one that proved he was very male. Libido and all. And speaking of libidos, hers had responded like a crazy train clambering past the station.

Far beyond the station, actually.

Her cheeks heated just thinking about it. And since when did she *blush? Damn it!* His Adam's apple bobbed on a swallow. It caught her eye. Just beneath it, almost hidden underneath the stiff collar of his pricey shirt, she saw a faint white line. "What's that from?" she asked, trying to keep her voice casual.

Gerald reached one of those wide-palmed hands up and thumbed the old scar. "Sword fighting."

She stopped in the midst of opening the cupboard to put away the first aid box. *"Sword fighting?"* she said incredulously.

He lifted a shoulder. "I was doing research for my first Rex Flynn book. I like my research to be hands-on, so it conveys more authenticity to readers. Rex was about to be forced into his first sword fight and I wanted to get a feel for it. I wanted to know exactly how a real broadsword felt in hand

and how it felt to use it against a living, breathing individual. So I hired a reputable swordsman to teach me some rough basics." A reminiscent laugh trebled from his chest and he dropped his gaze to the floor. "I advanced when I should have retreated and wound up with this."

Olivia shut the door to the cupboard hard. "He might've hacked your foolish head off."

"He might've," Gerald said with an acknowledging nod. "But where I was clumsy, he was careful. I asked for it, really. And if I had wound up with my body well shot of my head…" He lifted his good shoulder and grinned at her ruefully. "Well then, just think of the story my nieces and nephews would have been able to tell their friends… their children…their grandchildren…."

She shook her head at him. "Yes, that's quite the legacy. The tale of how their addlepated uncle was beheaded by accident."

He laughed and stood up, catching her hand before she could turn from him and escape the close confines of the bathroom. "Thank you," he said. Sincerity blazed from his eyes as well as the light of humor and more than an echo of those dark, hot intentions she'd seen earlier. "I could've done it myself, but you made the task a great deal easier."

She jerked her chin in a nod. "Let me know…if you need another hand. Later."

"Oh, I will," he said, grinning.

Olivia shook her head. If they had never married

in Vegas and he had just showed up in the tavern, she would have been all too happy to give him another wild go of what they'd had in the Bellagio penthouse. "Did anyone back home in Britain ever call you a cheeky devil? Because that's what you are."

"I was the bane of my tutors' existence," he confirmed.

"You were the class clown?" she asked as she led him from the bathroom and bedroom, back into the living room where they weren't in such close quarters and she could breathe around him again. "I would have pegged you for the brainy kid."

"I was a bit of both, I suppose," Gerald ruminated. "And you, Liv? I have the image of you in my mind as the class beauty."

"You couldn't be further from the truth," she told him. "I was physically awkward way longer than it was fair to be, so I made up for it with bawdy humor to make the boys like me. Then I hit puberty and they liked me for other reasons." She glanced at the front of her sweater, then cleared her throat when she saw his gaze follow, feeling the heat gather where she'd directed his attention. "Then I became pretty popular."

He chuckled. "And did any of those public school lads become serious candidates?"

Her mirth faded quickly. "Maybe. That was a long time ago, though—none of them matter anymore."

"Hmm." He faced her, crossing his arms over his chest. "Tender subject?"

She rolled her eyes. "You're getting inside my head again."

He studied her for a moment and crossed the small bit of space between them. Brushing the curls from her shoulder, he wrapped his arm underneath hers and gripped the back of her shoulder in a hold that felt…familiar. Warm. Loving. His fingers spread there, kneading the tight spots underneath the cashmere sweater and the titillated skin beneath it. "Whether or not you care for me being there, I'm already inside you, love. There's no denying it…so why try?"

Olivia frowned at him. "What are you really doing here, Gerald? You can't just have come all this way for me. So what other motives do you have? Do you need a green card? Are you about to introduce Rex Flynn to a flirty American tavern maid and you need some 'hands-on research,' as you say? Tell me the truth."

That darkness returned to his eyes, but it wasn't born from lust. He tipped his head back, his gaze not straying from hers, though she saw the wall come down, a veil of anger coating it thoroughly. He didn't strike her as an easy man to anger, but she had done so. "Is that what you make of me?" he asked in a low voice. "Or are you pushing me away again?" When she didn't answer, he added,

"That's all you do is push. Whenever I get close to reaching inside you or stirring something there, you push. You run. What are you afraid of, Olivia?"

"I'm not afraid of anything," she argued.

"You're bloody terrified," he accused. "I've seen you flirt with men. I know you've invited your share of them back here to your four-poster bed. So what is it about me that scares you?"

She hadn't wanted him to touch that place inside her that she'd locked away and all but forgotten until he'd come along. With him, she was very close to remembering that heartache. That gut-wrenching vulnerability she'd felt before.

His eyes softened as he searched hers, the anger sliding away to make room for sympathy. "Ah, Christ, love. Someone's done a number on you."

"No, they haven't," she said dismissively and walked away from him. "I have to get to the tavern. If you need anything, I'll be busy so call Cole or Briar."

"You don't want me to figure out what or who hurt you, that's fine," he said before she could shut the door between them. When she glanced back, she saw him slip one hand into the pocket of his slacks, both resignation and determination flashing across his face. "I won't push you there."

"I'm glad to hear it," she said, but he spoke again.

"You told me you loved me. And that's why I have come all this way."

That stopped her in her tracks. She looked back at him and the truth blazing from his eyes, and she shook her head. "No. I didn't."

"You did," he said. "I don't remember everything from the night we married, but I do remember that quite vividly. You told me you loved me. I asked you to marry me, and you didn't hesitate to say yes."

She let out an unbelieving breath, then said, "That's just...not possible."

"You doubt that's what you felt—love and the faith it takes to feel it with that much intensity? Enough to say yes to a proposal of marriage, in any case."

"I don't fall in love, Gerald," she told him firmly. "I'm sorry, I just don't."

Something of a smile moved over his lips, but his eyes didn't follow. "We'll see about that, Mrs. Leighton."

"I've gotta go," she scoffed, turning from him and shutting the door with a smart thud at her back, putting an end to the conversation.

She feared it would take a great deal more to put an end to his wager. Gerald Leighton wouldn't let her go easily. And now he was even more firmly entrenched in her small corner of the world... sleeping in her bed. Answering her phone. Telling her he could make her fall in love again.

He was wrong. She would make certain that he stayed that way.

IT WAS HARD to woo a woman while sporting a bump on the head and a sling on the arm. On Wednesday morning, Gerald took the liberty of driving himself to the hospital to have the stitches removed. He convinced Dr. Woodsbrow that the sling was no longer necessary as he didn't plan to do anything strenuous over the next week. And he also got the bandage removed.

Gerald fought the urge to reach up and rub his knuckles over the new scar as he drove back to the inn through the Fairhope streets.

By day, downtown Fairhope was a lovely, quaint place with close-built shops in bright colors and clean storefront windows. Cobbled walkways and white-painted disposals with flowers sprouting from the top added a healthy dose of old Southern charm while wrought-iron balconies brought a more New Orleans–style of architecture to the fold.

The car continued down a gentle decline draped by ancient leafy oak limbs and lazy Spanish moss. As he drove on toward South Mobile Street and the bay, the houses began to look more and more like something out of another era—sentinels awash with charm, grace and gentility.

The end of Fairhope Avenue came into view, taking a steep dive into a picturesque park overlooking the murky blue water of the bay. The long pier reached into the western horizon. Gerald squinted against the bright glow of the sun and the golden glimmer it cast across the water's surface.

The glow reached through the windshield and warmed him thoroughly. He itched to write, to be back at his computer, fingers flying over the keys without pause, fighting to keep up with the words rushing through his mind, desperate for release. The inspiration of his surroundings was beginning to build inside him. Gerald craved the adrenaline free-writing brought.

Curling the fingers of his left hand into a fist and lifting it to the steering wheel, he gritted his teeth when the muscles of his shoulder gave a protesting tug. His fingertips no longer felt cold or stiff, but no writing just yet. A few more days, he promised himself.

Instead of pulling around to the tavern parking lot, Gerald parked in front of Hanna's Inn. Glad to see Cole's truck already there, he climbed out of the Mercedes and followed the sounds of voices through Briar's garden to the wide green lawn beyond.

A chorus of barks reached his ears before he rounded the clematis. Standing on the grassy spread was Cole, Adrian and Briar cradling Harmony. They were laughing and smiling at young Kyle who was rolling over the ground with the large stray dog.

Though the wolfhound still looked too thin, his coat of long shaggy gray fur was clean and no longer matted. He was playfully rubbing his back on the grass, paws in the air as he wriggled, mouth open and tongue lolling happily. For a moment, Gerald simply stood and watched, digging a hand into the pocket of his coat and smiling. That was a fine sight. The neglected animal enjoying the attentions of the boy.

Cole was the first to see him, raising a hand in greeting.

Gerald gave a nod. Kyle yipped a hello. The dog rolled to his stomach, following the boy's attention. The pebbles of his eyes landed on Gerald and, for the space of a few breaths, he stopped panting. The hound then rose slowly and took a few steps in Gerald's direction.

Gerald swallowed at the lump in his throat. He crouched down in the grass and held out a hand. "Come here, boy," he called.

The steps quickened into a trot. The dog was a little clumsy on his feet yet. Still had some growing to do, Gerald mused, smiling easily when the wolfhound drew near enough to touch. The dog made the first move, however, licking his outstretched fingers. Gerald lifted them to the dog's ear. He tilted his head into Gerald's palm, dark eyes washing the man's face with gratitude and affection. Then he stepped into Gerald's arms.

Gerald embraced him instantly, scratching him behind the neck and across the back. "There's a lad," he murmured, lowering his head to the dog's. "You remember me, aye? Good boy."

"Looks like you've got a lifelong friend there."

Gerald grinned at Adrian. "It does, doesn't it?"

She smiled softly as man and dog fawned over each other. Then she gave a sigh. "Liv's going to love this."

"Do I detect a touch of irony, Ms. Carlton?" Gerald asked curiously.

"That's sarcasm," she told him pointedly, crossing her arms over her chest. "At its very finest."

CHAPTER ELEVEN

"LIV! LIV!"

Olivia turned from the shipment of liquor she'd been adding to the tavern inventory as Kyle skidded to a halt at the entrance to the storeroom, breathing heavily. "Whoa, slow down there, slugger. What's the hurry?"

"Gerald…" He panted, bending over double but smiling nonetheless. "Gerald got…a dog. A *big* dog." Latching on to her hand, he tugged her into the hall. "Come and see, Liv. C'mon!"

Olivia dropped the clipboard and let the boy lead her to the stairs of her apartment. Gerald. A dog. It couldn't be true. Could it?

They made it to the landing and the open door beyond. "In here," Kyle said, letting her pass in front of him. "They're in here. Isn't he cool?"

The "dog" turned out to be a mountain of gray and white fur with a lolling tongue as long as a roll of Christmas ribbon. Olivia shrieked as the animal—rabid sheep?—barreled into the living room from the bedroom where it had been exploring.

Gerald followed, bare to the waist and his hair wet. "Rex!" he called.

Before she could utter a word in surprise or denial, The Thing noticed that there was someone other than Gerald in the room. It whined once more, then scrambled across the floor. For a moment, the mustache of hair above its brows lifted along with its bounding paws to reveal adoring, gleaming black eyes. Wriggling with excitement, it made to pounce. She shrieked again, throwing her hands up with a bracing breath.

"Sit, Rexie!"

Instantly, the giant skidded to a halt, plopped down on its rear, its tail thumping loudly on the hardwood floor.

"Good boy," Gerald said. "Sorry." He glanced at Olivia apologetically. "He's well mannered. Someone trained him up nice. I'm guessing he was well cared for before he was sent off."

"What *is* it?" Olivia croaked, hands still raised to shield herself if necessary.

"This is Rex," Gerald answered, rubbing the grinning giant behind the ears. A pleasured groan emitted from its overlarge head. "The stray from the street."

"It's a dog, just in case you were wondering," Cole said flatly from behind her. As she turned toward him in disbelief, he reached around her to scratch Rex, too, and earned a sloppy kiss on the hand.

"That's not the same dog," Olivia pointed out. "This one's...huge." She lifted her hands to encompass Rex's sheer size.

Gerald chuckled as he crouched to Rex's level. "He is a bit of a stonker, isn't he? Full-blooded Irish wolfhound, as it turns out."

"Briar and I figure he's part-horse," Cole added. "*If* that horse were also related to the Abominable Snowman. I think Harmony's a little in love with him."

"He could eat Harmony," Olivia muttered, wincing as Rex's adoring face swung her way. "He could eat *me*."

"Ah, he's harmless," Gerald said, touching his nose to Rex's. "Aren't you, boy? You're just a big, hairy softy." The long ribbon of a tongue lolled out to bathe his face in kisses.

Olivia looked to Cole incredulously. He only grinned at her and pulled her into a quick one-armed hug. Then, lifting the edge of a large doggie bed, he asked, "Where should I put this?"

"He can't sleep here," Olivia said, gesturing to the living area. "There's no room!"

"We'll make room," Gerald said with a placating smile. "He doesn't need much, just a place to lay his head and a bowl of water and he's good for the night."

Olivia saw the protective hand Gerald instinctively set on Rex's massive cranium. The man was dead serious. He expected both himself and the dog to live here. "No," she said firmly.

"Come on, Liv," Kyle said, tugging on her arm. "Can't you keep him? Please?"

"Maybe he could sleep at your place," Olivia suggested, trying her best to please the boy.

"Mom would never allow it," Kyle said. He tugged on Olivia's hand more urgently. "It'll be so fun to visit, roll in the grass with him, take him for walks, teach him to play fetch.... You gotta keep him, Liv. Please, please, please."

Olivia looked from the boy's face up to Cole for help. The man shrugged and she scowled at him. Machiavelli indeed. And one look at the scrapes on Gerald's face and the glaring gash over his eye and she knew she had lost this round. Frowning, she gestured to the living room at large. "I suppose we could move the coffee table. Or the...couch."

Kyle shrieked in victory, pumping his arms in the air and jumping up and down. Gerald beamed, rising and taking her face in his hands. She wasn't prepared at all for the kiss he laid briefly on her lips. "Thank you, love," he said, rubbing his thumbs over her cheeks.

She gripped his wrists and ignored the fire that leaped to life in her belly. He smelled of Gerald... but with a strange, salty tinge. "What...what the hell happened to you?"

He ran a hand over his wet hair and chuckled.

"Ah…Rex and I were just having a game of chase on the lawn and I wound up in the bay."

"It pushed you in the bay?" she asked, giving the dog another fearful once-over.

"*He,* Liv," Cole said, nudging her in the small of the back with an elbow.

Gerald cleared his throat and nodded. "He dodged and I went flying into the waves."

"Off the dock?" she asked, shocked. "You're lucky you didn't frigging drown with your shoulder the way it is."

"Yes, well," Gerald said, "I spent several of my summer childhoods on an island in Scotland with an eccentric great-uncle. The Isle of Skye, as a matter-of-fact. There's water there for miles. Sink or swim, as it were. I wisely chose to swim."

"You named him Rex," Olivia pointed out, staring again at the massive animal. "Like in your books?"

"It's a bit of a nod to Flynn," Gerald acknowledged and grinned fondly. "But Kyle pointed out, as an Irish wolfhound, he's the biggest of his breed. Much like a T. rex."

When Gerald turned away to find a place to put Rex's bed, Olivia caught Cole's raised brow. "What's in the bag?" she asked impatiently.

Cole eyed her knowingly. His amusement outweighed the censure by a hair at least. "Oh, you know, the puppy essentials. Toothbrush, late-night snacks, shampoo, comb and bowls."

"Okay, for one, that *thing* is not a puppy," Olivia said, snatching the handle of the bag from his hand. "And second, please tell me you were kidding when you said 'toothbrush.'"

"You're gonna have fun with this," Cole said, squeezing her shoulder with a work-roughened hand. "Don't you like dogs?"

"I don't object to dogs in general," Olivia reasoned. She waved a hand toward the giant wolfhound. "But when they take up *that* much space..."

"One of these days you're going to learn that space isn't everything," Cole said sagely, then sent her a wink. "Come on, Kyle. Let's let Rex settle into his new home." He turned to Olivia with a wide smile, which didn't so much as wobble at the roll of her eyes, only widened. He led Kyle out and stopped, peering around the jamb. "There's also a big bag of dog food you can haul up for your man later."

"He's not my..." Olivia trailed off with a sigh at Cole's pointed look. "Yeah, okay." When Cole shut the door behind him and Kyle, Olivia raked her hands through her hair. "I need a drink."

OLIVIA FOUND MONICA downstairs in the tavern office just before they opened the doors for the early weekday crowd. The waitress took one look at her and frowned. "Whoa, what the hell happened to you?"

"Huh?" Olivia asked, at a loss.

"You look flustered," Monica replied. "And a little POed."

"I'm fine," Olivia snapped. *Yeah, end topic.* "How was it with Skeet the other night? I forgot to ask with everything going on around here lately."

Monica's expression lightened considerably. "I think I might keep him."

"Like a puppy?" Olivia asked. "You're robbing the cradle."

Monica glared at her. "I'm only three years older."

"Mon, he looks like he could be your kindergarten sweetheart."

"What you see on the everyday exterior is one thing." Monica grinned wickedly. "But what you don't see is all man."

Olivia shook her head. "You are so bad."

"What's wrong with you?" Monica asked, propping a hand on her hip. "Under normal circumstances, you'd congratulate me and tell me to take the puppy to bed. Knock him dead. That sort of thing. And wasn't that Beau guy you slept with three months ago in his early twenties?"

Frowning, Olivia unlocked the safe behind her desk and pulled out the cash drawers, one for her and one for Monica. Every evening, she counted what was in them at closing, setting aside a pouch of the night's earnings for her early drive to the bank the next day and leaving a small tally of each numbered bill in the drawers for the following night. "Let's unlock the doors. There's a business conference in town. We should expect several newcomers tonight."

Monica let the topic slide as they went about their opening routine. The first hour of business was relatively slow. As the clock above her struck six, Olivia was surprised to see Roxie of all people weave her wary way from the thick-paneled doors to the bar. Measuring her friend, Olivia recognized her for the burdened soul she was. "Take a seat," she said at Roxie's approach. "You look like you need a drink."

"Ugh," Roxie said, pulling off her red leather gloves and setting her large designer tote on the stool next to the one she chose to sit on. "You have no idea."

It had to be a bad day indeed if it had chased the cheer from Roxie's face. It was a rare thing to see her this low. Roxie all but collapsed on the bar, folding her head over her crossed arms. After studying the defeated crown of Roxie's head for a moment and pursing her lips, Olivia asked, "Okay, Rox. What'll it be—wine or whiskey?"

"An ice pick. Or…do you have a meat cleaver?"

Raising a brow, Olivia considered the situation. "Sorry. No lobotomies here. You might try the mental hospital down the road."

Roxie lifted her head. Her hair looked a little frazzled and her eyes were lined with strain. A kindred spirit if ever there was one. "Fix me the strongest drink you have. Wild turkey. Moonshine. Anything."

"You know what?" Olivia said as she moved behind the bar, "I'm going to make you the family painkiller."

Roxie blinked hopefully. "Sounds wonderful. What's in it? Powdered aspirin?"

Olivia tutted. "Secret recipe. But it'll make you forget all your troubles, for a while at least."

"Praise the Lord," Roxie said, folding her arms again on the bar top and hunching her shoulders forward.

As she topped the glass with a sprig of fresh mint and served it to Roxie, Olivia noted, "You're one of the privileged few who has ever tasted the Lewis painkiller. We usually save it for drastic situations."

"Trust me," Roxie said, "it's warranted."

"The other bonus of having a friend for a bartender is that you have someone to tell all your troubles to," Olivia replied, wiping her work area with a wet cloth.

Roxie took a sip, shivered a bit at the minty taste, then hummed, sighed and drank a bit more. "Amazing." Seeing Olivia's expectant look, Roxie frowned. "Why do people have weddings? Why don't they just run off into the night like you and Gerald did and find a secluded chapel? Alone."

"Your mom's still driving you crazy?"

"Oh, she's just the tip of the iceberg," Roxie said pointedly. "Though this week she's started riding me to make it bigger, more over-the-top. That's not me. That's not Richard, either. Liv, she wants a snow machine. Fake snow. *For heaven's sake!*"

"Easy," Olivia said, pushing the glass closer toward Roxie. "Take another drink."

"Thanks." Roxie obeyed, drinking deeply. She took a moment to smack her lips together and savor the taste once more before beginning again, calmer. "Somewhere along the way, it's like it became *her* wedding. This is the day I've been dreaming of and fantasizing about since I could chew. I've dedicated my life to wedding planning. It's my turn, damn it!"

Olivia watched Roxie slump forward again, beaten. "How's Richard handling the in-law hysteria?"

"Avoidance, mostly. He's dropped a few hints about pushing the date back. I can't do that again." Roxie lifted her hand to show Olivia the sparkler on her ring finger. "I've been wearing this puppy for four years, Liv. Four years." Roxie gazed at it, forlorn. "It's lonely. It needs a friend. A shiny, platinum friend."

"It only has to hold its own for a little while longer," Olivia reminded her. "Hang in there, Rox."

Downing what was left of her painkiller, Roxie waved off her troubles. "How are things going with Gerald?" Her lips bowed up into a genuine smile that was more than a little sly. "Wink, wink."

Olivia frowned and raised her eyes to the ceiling. Somewhere on the other side of it, Gerald and

The Thing were no doubt making chaos out of her living space. "He and his furry beast have moved in, all right."

Roxie sighed, her smile turning dreamy. "Can we just take a moment to appreciate just how good of a man you've got there? I mean, he leaps in front of a moving car to save a helpless animal, and *then* adopts said animal and welcomes him into his home."

"My home," Olivia noted. "Not his. Mine."

"If I weren't getting married you would have some definite competition."

"Sure. If you can live with the writer clutter he leaves all over the place," Olivia said.

Roxie pursed her lips and tapped her manicured nails against her glass. "Clutter's not a problem. Clutter could be fixed. And if not, one could learn to overlook it. Especially when the person who creates the clutter has enough charm to make your toes tingle for all eternity."

"How about dog hair?" Olivia suggested. "Great big tufts of it just floating around, collecting in corners and multiplying."

"What's wrong, Liv?" Roxie asked, swirling the ice in the bottom of her glass and tutting her lips at the watery remains of the drink sloshing around with it. "You don't like animals?"

"My mom had cats," Olivia considered. "Paw-paw had a Jack Russell that barked at the wind and chased squirrels until the cows came home...."

Roxie's eyes widened in surprise. "You've never had a pet of your own?"

"Why bother?" Olivia asked with a frown. "You get attached to them, then they wind up running off or getting killed. Then your heart's in shambles and you're a mess. Hell, Pawpaw's Jack Russell died five years before he did and he mourned the silly thing until the day he passed away, too. It was the saddest thing you've ever seen."

"Hmm," Roxie said, narrowing her eyes and considering Olivia's face closely. "This conversation is very revealing." She pouted. "I always wanted a dog, but my parents never let me get one. Heaven forbid it might lift its leg on the Turkish rug or gnaw the legs of one of the Hepplewhite chairs."

"Your parents were tight-asses," Olivia pointed out. "Me? I'm more interested in self-preservation."

"Sounds lonely, Liv."

Olivia lifted a dismissive shoulder. "A week ago, did I strike you as all that lonely?"

"No," Roxie agreed. "But there will come a point in life where you might be. And by then you might be old and gray and the young, hot bar boys won't be so inclined to sleep with you, much less keep you company."

The corners of Olivia's lips twitched. "Then I invite you to be the first person to say 'I told you so.'"

Roxie cupped her chin in her hand and stared into space. "I think a man like Gerald Leighton would age very well. Those lines in his face—

they're not like wrinkles, per se. It's more like they were carved there by well-handed masons. Those sweet green eyes full of the laughter and wisdom of all his years...." She sighed dreamily and her eyes landed again on Olivia's face. "Wouldn't you rather spend your years with someone like that instead of alone?"

Before Olivia could respond, Roxie gasped, her expression animated now as she perked up and added, "Have you read the love scenes from his Rex Flynn books?" She groaned in something not unlike envy. "In the beginning, the love affair between Rex and Janet is all about the slow-burning, cindering stuff with a few of those irresistible stolen moments in between. Then flash—*boom*—*bang!* It's all hot and heady passion and deep, gut-wrenching emotions." Again settling down with a sigh, Roxie smiled. "I figure a man who can write like that has got to be one hell of a lover."

"No," Olivia said, voice flat. "I haven't read any of his books."

Roxie reached over and covered Olivia's hand with hers, lowering her chin with a leveling gaze. "Do yourself a favor and read them. You will not be sorry. You love a good romance just as much as the rest of us, right?"

"Yeah," Olivia admitted. "But his books are different—"

"Promise me you'll read one, at least."

Resigned, Olivia finally agreed. "Sure."

"Good." Roxie patted Olivia's hand, then bobbled to her feet and dug into her purse for cash. "Richard's picking me up at the inn for dinner. If he notices I'm hammered, I'll be blaming you."

"What are friends for?" Olivia asked with a small smile.

"Indeed." Roxie fluttered the fingers of one hand in a wave as she turned for the door. "Toodleloo, dearie."

"Toodles," Olivia muttered, frowning at the change on the bar in front of her. Reaching for it, she thought about that stack of books Adrian had loaned her. She'd done little more than spend several minutes staring at his picture on the back cover. Then when he'd come to live with her, she'd hidden them from him.

Maybe it was time to give them another look. And if she didn't like the epic fantasy adventure or whatever genre the Rex Flynn series belonged to, she could always flip forward to the love scenes. Nobody ever had to know, right? Least of all the author himself....

CHAPTER TWELVE

GERALD SPENT THE next day toying with his notes on the latest novel and in turn getting to know Rex. It felt good to have a furry companion lay at his feet while he worked at the makeshift desk he'd made at Olivia's dining room table. He spent the good part of the morning at his computer nailing down the story's timeline. Without it, he wouldn't be able to write as he wanted to.

Afterward he found a tennis ball among the things he'd picked up at the pet store and took Rex to the park. It turned out the dog not only knew how to behave on leash, but he could also fetch and roll over on command. Gerald lavished the animal with treats and love to make up for the neglect the dog had suffered.

Gerald had to admit that it felt good to open his heart to a dog again. It had been several years since his retriever had passed away in his sleep at the ripe old age of thirteen. Friends had suggested he get another dog, a puppy to keep him busy and fill the silence of his loft. Many times he'd open his door and stop, expecting to hear the click of the retriever's paws coming across the tiles to greet him. Gerald had decided to buy a television instead of a puppy.

He reached down to scratch Rex behind the ears as the dog laid his overlarge head on the knee of his trousers. A smile warmed his lips as the animal swung his eyes up to Gerald's face and sighed, as if to say, "I could get used to you." Yes, three years was enough time to grieve. Rex was already making it easy to move on.

Gerald walked Rex into town to the city's public library. Behind it was the Fairhope Farmer's Market, an open-air affair. Gerald had gleaned from Briar that the market was seasonal, open once a week from May to July and then again from September to November. He'd promised to meet the innkeeper there.

He found her at a butternut squash stand and raised his hand to her in greeting. "Mrs. Savitt," he said with a nod as he approached.

"Mr. Leighton," she returned. "I was starting to think you'd forgotten."

"Never." Gerald winked and Briar smiled easily. Keeping the end of Rex's leash curled tight around his palm to keep the dog close, Gerald carried Briar's shopping basket for her and followed along as she pushed Harmony's stroller from booth to booth, loading up on everything from fresh kale to ripe tomatoes, crisp red apples and orange Satsumas.

When Gerald found a vendor with fresh herbs

he gave in, chatting up the friendly grower as he chose a few cloves of garlic and basil leaves.

"You look pleased with yourself," Briar commented.

"Suppose I am well chuffed." He held up his small bag of herbs. "Never could resist fresh herbs," he added, twisting the top of the bag so that no air could get in.

"Do you cook?" she asked.

"I've been known to when the occasion strikes," he told her. "I was thinking about going to the grocer's and picking up a few things to make Olivia supper."

"What do you need?" Briar questioned as she walked along, lifting her hand in greeting to someone in the crowd. "I might have it at the inn."

"This garlic and basil would make a good marinara," Gerald mused. "Perhaps with a few of your tomatoes, I could pull together a decent meal."

"You'll need some pasta and bread," she declared. "No need to come back into town. I've got everything you need."

"Thank you," he said, putting a companionable arm around her slim shoulders. "And thank you for bringing me here."

"It's amazing what a trip to the farmer's market does for my spirit," she said with a happy sigh. "Especially when I've been up all night with the baby. Cole's a tremendous help, but it does me good to go into town, get some fresh air. Something about the farmer's market always sets me to rights again. If I can't grow my vegetables myself, I like to look into the eyes of the person who did."

"That's exactly how I see it," he agreed with a nod. "I knew I liked you from the moment we met."

"It does me well to know that my cousin's got such a genuine guy," Briar explained, "not just some stranger she married in Vegas." As soon as the words tumbled out of her mouth, she turned to him with horrified eyes. "Oh, Gerald. I'm so sorry. I don't know why I said that."

He chuckled. "Why? It's the truth of the matter, isn't it?" When she remained silent and gnawed on her lower lip, he frowned. "I hope you're not too concerned about what I'm doing in your cousin's life."

She considered that for a moment. "Maybe at first. When you arrived at the inn and told me you were her husband, I nearly fainted. In truth, I almost had Cole muscle you out the door. But...Olivia needs you, Gerald."

He stopped walking and turned to face her fully. "How so?"

"I think there's a reason she married you beyond the influence of alcohol," Briar explained carefully. "Sometimes I see something beneath Olivia's surface. A shadow. Maybe it's loneliness, maybe something else—I don't quite know. I do know that she takes satisfaction from the way she lives her life. But she's my sister, in essence if not in blood, and

I want her to be happy. Even if you lose this wager of yours, maybe you'll make her see that she *could* be."

A smile grew over his mouth as Briar raised her eyes back to his a bit tentatively. "Just out of curiosity, if I do wind up winning her heart, will you, Cole and the others ever let her live it down?"

Briar laughed, at ease with him once again. As Gerald pushed the pram the rest of the way to the car, she hooked her arm through his. "As much as she's teased me through the years? Not a chance."

IT WAS AFTER midnight when Olivia finally came up to the apartment, expecting both Gerald and the dog to be sound asleep. Instead, the ripe scent of tomatoes and fresh herbs greeted her nostrils and sent her hungry stomach into a series of marked, empty pangs. Rex greeted her first, trotting over to coat her hand in slobber. Absently patting him on the head, she glanced into the kitchen and frowned at Gerald, who was standing at the stove.

The man turned, wooden spoon in hand and reading glasses riding the bridge of his nose. "Ah. She returns."

"Evening," she said. She'd had a damn good reason for avoiding him all day, but at the sight of those horn-rimmed glasses and the dimples digging into the corners of his mouth, all those stirrings started up again with a vengeance. "What's going on?"

"I'm making you dinner."

"You're…" She trailed off. There was a long loaf of French bread on the prep counter with a carving knife at the ready. Several plump tomatoes waited on a cutting board and spaghetti pasta boiled in a pot on the stove. "Where did all this come from?"

"The farmer's market. Briar let me tag along with her there this afternoon."

"And now you're cooking." Olivia couldn't quite take it all in.

"It's a hobby of mine," Gerald explained. "When I'm stuck in the middle of a manuscript or trying to figure out a plot kink, it helps to focus on something else. Like cooking. The solutions come more easily then."

Olivia spotted the laptop, books and notes he'd compiled on the kitchen table. "So that's why you're doing this? You've been writing."

He frowned at that. "Not exactly, no. I've been compiling some notes, though, and hope to get a jump on it early tomorrow morning."

She watched the muscles in his forearm flex as he cut the bread with the precision of a well-handed cook, while she fought the urge to lick her lips.

"And," Gerald added, "you owe me a date night. If you won't set aside your work so I can take you out on a proper date, I'll bring it home."

Olivia sank onto a stool on the opposite side of the counter. The evening and the sleepless night before had sapped her dry. If he'd been in bed as planned, starved as she might be, she didn't know if she would have had the energy to make herself something to eat before crashing on the couch herself.

His eyes rose to hers, so intelligent and so kind she could hardly breathe under their study. "I also wanted to find some way of thanking you…for letting Rex and me take up your space. I know it's important to you. And I know for now that you're simply tolerating it. I'm hoping to change your mind on that score. I would have commissioned Adrian to make you a rather large and embarrassing bouquet, but you told me not to buy you things. Plus, I don't think you're the flower type."

How had he known that? She, in fact, did not care for flowers. Anyone who loved her knew to send chocolates. Or liquor. If liqueur-filled chocolates could be obtained, all the better. Olivia skimmed her eyes down to the bread in front of him. Either Briar had revealed more than she should have or he could read every thought that passed through her mind. Both were disconcerting.

Her gaze fell on the bottle of Cabernet Sauvignon chilling by the sink. "Is that wine?"

Gerald chuckled. "I'm told you're a fan of Cab."

As he set the carving knife aside and reached for the waiting wineglass next to the bottle, she sighed. "What else did Briar tell you?"

Gerald's answering grin and deep, rich laugh warmed her through and through. He poured a splash of the dark liquid into the glass, swilled it around and lifted it to his nose to sample the bouquet before he tipped it to his mouth and wet his tongue. "Try it. I wasn't sure about the label."

Olivia took the stem of the glass and tried not to think about the fact that her mouth was watering—and not at the onset of spirits. Taking a hearty sip, Olivia watched him butter several slices of the bread. "So you have no problem writing even when you're away from home?"

"It's not usually an issue." A grim light entered his eyes. "Even when the writing is going well, though, I worry. That's why when I do write, I write quickly. The flow of words is more comforting than staring at the blank page, anxious that it won't come as easily as it has before."

Olivia nodded. "My father wrote. Some." At his curious look, she fumbled. What in the world had led her to reveal that?

"What did he write?" Gerald asked.

She shrugged. "Mostly poems about nature and the shore, since his passion, outside of running the family business, was travel and conservation. He never accomplished anything on your level, but he was proud of his work. I wish he would've tried publishing at some point, but he never did. I think writing poetry was too much a personal part of him. He never shared the poems with anyone other than my mother and me."

"It makes sense." Gerald nodded. "For a long

time, writing was a hobby, just like cooking. It was
my way of winding down from a long day—a release. It wasn't something I ever thought I'd share."

"Why did you?" she asked, unable to curb the
inquiry this time.

He grinned. "My mother. She'd written a few
books, nonfiction—mostly on history and archeology. She found one of my manuscripts and showed
it to her publisher. The rest is sort of history."

A history Olivia didn't know much about. "And
where did you learn to cook?" she asked.

"I picked it up at university," Gerald explained,
chopping the tomatoes with that same sure precision. "Along with manning a bar. I actually dated
an Italian girl who was a culinary goddess."

"What was her name?" she asked, sipping her
wine. She liked the cadence of his voice, the way
it dropped then lilted up. No doubt a woman could
be compelled to listen to him talk for hours. Olivia
was no exception.

"Carmen," he answered. "I swear she was a descendant of San Lorenzo himself." When Olivia
only blinked, he added, "The Italians believe San
Lorenzo is the patron saint of cooks. Anyway, Carmen and I dated for about three months before she
moved into my flat. I told her she didn't have to
help with rent if she cooked for me."

Olivia's lips curved into a sly smile. Lifting the
wine to her lips, she ran her gaze over him, a bit

impressed. "I never would've pegged you for the love-slave type."

"As shallow as it may sound…" he lifted his shoulders with a sheepish grin "…I repaid her cooking…well, through other means of pleasure."

Olivia laughed. "What happened?" When he raised his eyes to hers, she said, "I mean, since you and Carmen are no longer together, I assume *something* happened."

Gerald's shoulders tensed. "My father didn't care for the arrangement. I come from a distinguished English line and, therefore, was expected to marry a distinguished Englishwoman. My father was paying for my lodgings so when he found out Carmen was living with me, he had her thrown out and me transferred to Oxford."

"Poor Carmen," Olivia said with some pity. "Was she your first love?"

"Oh, I fell for her like a school lad. But it wouldn't have worked."

"Because of your father?"

Gerald nodded. "You could say that."

Olivia frowned. "So, me being a humble barmaid he wouldn't approve of much, either."

His lips quirked into a wry smile. "You're far from humble, love. And my father's opinion is something neither of us has to worry about." The amusement fled from his face. "He died, years ago. Before I was published."

She lifted the wine to her mouth for a long swig. "I'm sorry."

Grief showed itself in the grim line of Gerald's mouth and the bar between his eyes. He paused in his dinner preparations to grip the stem of his own wineglass. He swirled it, watching the liquid tornado. After a moment, his eyes lifted to hers and, amidst the rueful sadness, she saw warm reassurance. "Just as well. He didn't care for my 'scribblings,' as he called them. And at that point in our lives, we weren't close."

Judging by what she had heard so far, Olivia had a good sense that Gerald's father had not been kind to him. In the latter years, at least.

He cleared his throat, setting the wine aside and gesturing to the cutting board. "Would you mind helping me with these tomatoes while I put the bread on the burner?"

Olivia stared at the board and tomatoes he put in front of her, then gave in. "Just dice them?"

"Lightly, yes."

She washed her hands in the sink before returning to the cutting board to chop. "It sounds like you were close to your mother."

"Quite. She liked that I wrote. But she spent a good deal of time out in the field. Archeology," he informed her. "It takes you to remote locales, a lot of them dry, dusty, arid and lacking in proper civilization. My father, an earl, kept me firmly encamped at home, either in London, our country house in Yorkshire or later the boarding schools I attended before life at Eton. Although they never formerly separated, I rarely saw them together. Like me, my mother never fully conformed to her title or the role that came with it."

Gerald glanced up from the stove and over his shoulder at her. "Tell me if I'm boring you."

Olivia sighed. Though she found the stories of his early life fascinating, they put her ill at ease. *Out of her league* was turning out to be an epic understatement. "Not the, uh, *earl* part." She frowned. "Doesn't that kind of thing pass? From father to son, I mean."

"Normally, yes," Gerald explained. "But when my father died, I ran off to the States. New York. My mother was doing lectures there, and I was eager for the inspiration other writers before me had found in that city's streets. My younger brother, Bartholomew, was all too happy to take up my place as earl."

"Bartholomew?" she said with a smile.

"Barty for short," Gerald said. "My siblings and I all suffer from names that have been passed down through generations. My sister, Alexandra, for instance. She hates the moniker and insisted from a young age that we all call her Lexie."

Olivia turned, sipping her wine as she leaned a hip against the countertop and, while he had his back to her, studied his long, tall, almost wiry frame thoroughly. "How 'bout that? A renegade earl, living in my teensy apartment."

Gerald grinned back at her. "So what of your mother and father? What are they like?"

She couldn't hide the snort of laughter. "Nothing like yours, for sure."

"That might be a credit to them."

She attacked the tomatoes again, no longer trying to make them look like the ones Gerald had already chopped. "They aren't distinguished or highly educated. They are, however, remarkably loud. Opinionated. Affectionate, which is good until you overhear your friends' parents gossiping about how they were making out at the PTA meeting. But when they weren't embarrassing the hell out of me, they were a hoot. Laughter was a common sound in our home."

"You couldn't have lived here," Gerald noted, lifting the knife to the ceiling. "Where was home?"

"The cottage," Olivia explained. "The one Adrian lives in now. Around the time she was looking to get away from her parents' and start a new life with Kyle, my folks were ready to start traveling cross-country in the RV. I told them they could sell the family home to her at a fair price and I could live here in the apartment they kept for long nights at the tavern and the regulars who needed to sleep it off. The furniture was mostly theirs, from the cottage, which is why a lot of it's too big for the space."

She glanced at the brawny dining room table. "I couldn't see it all go, though."

"You've done well with the apartment. And as small as you are, oddly, the oversize furniture suits you."

Olivia smiled. "Dad always did say I was as contrary as the day is long." As she talked, the knots in her shoulders loosened. A fond smile curved her lips. "Mom swears like a sailor, and Dad belches out loud at dinner. They fight like cats and dogs, but only because they love each other and sometimes that's the only way they can express just how much. I'm afraid I'm the same way."

"You're very fond of them."

She glanced over her shoulder to find him watching her. Looking away quickly, she finished off the tomatoes. "Yes. God help me." Stepping back from the cutting board she raised her hands in apology. "I'm not much of a cooking hand." Popping one of the poor, mangled pieces into her mouth, she nodded toward the fridge. "Which is why you probably didn't find much in there other than leftover casserole."

He picked up a fork to test the noodles still boiling on the stove. "I'm pretty sure it was more than cooking skills I married you for."

When he finished with the pasta, he poured her another glass of wine. A frown touched her lips again. *Don't get used to the high-class treatment, Lewis*. Clearing her throat, she lifted her hands to the tomatoes and fresh herbs. "I'm starved, and all these yummy smells aren't helping. What else do you need me to do so we can eat?"

OLIVIA WOULD NEVER have admitted it, but the wine worked through her quickly and fluidly, making her a touch overwarm…and a bit fuzzy-headed. The tension from the long day slowly subsided as the pasta simmered in its pot on the stove and the marinara sauce imbued her apartment with mouth-watering fragrance. She watched Gerald brown mushrooms on the burner next to hers as she sat on the countertop, stirring the sauce.

Winding a figure-eight pattern through the tomato-red depths with a wooden spoon, she breathed in deeply. The smell was hearty, succulent. The perfect answer to a busy night like she'd had. She couldn't imagine coming home to anything better.

Neither had spoken for a while, but the silence was a comfortable one. Except for Rex's snores, the sound of the noodles boiling, and the clomp of the knife as Gerald sliced more mushrooms before dropping them into the sauce, the apartment was quiet, peacefully so. Studying Gerald's profile, she measured the steady line of his shoulders and admired the place in his cheek where a half-moon dimple wore in when he smiled. She took note of the horn-rimmed glasses riding the bridge of his nose, which he adjusted regularly to keep them from riding over the lingering bruise there. The nicks and scratches on his chin and cheek had nearly faded away. The red scar above his eye near his hairline, however, wasn't going anywhere for some time. It was still fresh, pink.

Olivia fought the urge to soothe it and turned her attention to the intent set of his eyes. It puzzled her how they could go from studious to tender in an instant. The shift was never abrupt. The warmth always hovered close underneath the intellect.

It struck her now that she'd never been with a man like Gerald. And in his contrast to all the men she'd been with lay his danger to her.

Gazing at him, something inside her curled into a snug circle and radiated from the center out. Her limbs tingled from its welcome heat. She did love danger, she had to admit....

He turned at her shudder. "Cold?"

Anything but. "You know what I think, Gerald?"

He grinned at her wine-flushed face. "What's that, love?"

Olivia lifted a finger. "Correct me if I'm wrong, but your father was an earl...and your grandfather was an earl...and all the Leightons in your direct line going back hundreds of years were earls, yes?"

He chuckled at the winding rhetoric. "Yes, generally speaking."

"Then that would make you...like...royalty or something. Generally speaking."

"No." He smiled, eyes winking with laughter

as they found hers. "Aristocratic, maybe. But not royal. Unless you count a distant Scottish ancestor who *claimed* to be the son of the Duke of Berwick who was, of course, the rumored illegitimate son of King James II."

"Uh-huh." She licked her top lip. "Illegitimate royalty. Still out of my league."

Lifting the wooden spoon to her mouth, he cupped a hand underneath to catch any excess. "Taste this for me."

"Mmm, yes. Ply me with food to keep me from talking. Well played, Mr. Leighton."

He chuckled. "I try."

Maybe she was glutton for punishment, but she didn't take her eyes from his as she closed her mouth around the spoon and the sauce exploded on her tongue. "Wow. That's incredible. Is this one of the recipes you learned from Carmen?"

"No. I came across this myself while on holiday in Rome."

"Rome," she hummed. "I'd kill to go to Rome."

"I rent a villa there every so often when I need a break. If you lean out the second-floor window, you can see the Trevi Fountain. I think you'd love it. Not near as much as you'd love Africa, though, I'd wager. I spent some time there with Mum while she was researching her second book on archeology. Perhaps that's where we should spend our next honeymoon, you and I."

She frowned at the honeymoon mention…and

over the excited spark she felt at the idea of riding through the bush on safari with Gerald. Or watching an African sunset in a tree house—him holding her. Yes, Africa sounded much more her style. Not that she should expect that sort of thing.

She'd have a better chance of walking on the moon before she'd find herself on safari with the man standing in front of her. He'd be gone soon.

The thought made her sad.

Doing her best to shrug the honeymoon images off and another wave of ensuing warmth, she pushed off the counter. "Plates are behind that door there."

"The sauce needs to simmer a little longer," he said. "Stir it for me. I'll grab the plates."

After setting the table, Gerald walked back to her. Reaching around her, he covered her hand on the spoon. "Like this. Slow circles all the way through to the bottom." His other arm came around her to turn down the heat of the stovetop.

The warmth of his arms encircled her. His aftershave enveloped her until she had no choice but to lean back into him, laying her head on his uninjured shoulder. "You always smell so good."

He turned his nose into her hair. "You smell like vanilla. And a hint of whiskey."

"Someone spilled whiskey on my jeans at the tavern. And there's vanilla in my shampoo." She wanted to turn into him but refused the urge because she knew being blocked between the stove and his surprisingly hard body would elicit any number of inappropriate responses. "Thanks for doing this. I needed it."

"Maybe tomorrow night I'll teach you to make something else," he suggested.

"Like stones—or whatever it is you British folk eat?"

Gerald chuckled and the deep sound vibrated through both their shirts into her back. Into her bones, where it kept going, trembling pleasantly until she felt her nerves tingle in answer. Was it Roxie who had warned Olivia that Gerald was the kind of man who could make her toes tingle for all eternity?

Lowering his head next to hers, he murmured against her ear, "I think you mean scones, love."

The rusty sound of his voice kicked the spark kindling inside her into a flame. When he let go of the spoon and touched her elbow, she turned to him willingly. His mouth was there. She took it.

The impact of the kiss knocked her back against the stove. She locked her arms around his neck and held on for dear life.

The sauce on the stove behind her didn't simmer as hot as the heat that built to crescendo between them. Needs, thick and tangled, threatened to drag her down into the depths of something just as dangerous as he was.

She wanted to sink. As the kiss stretched on, she drank from his gentle lips, relishing the lazy flick of tongue, the almost hesitant nip of his teeth. Thirsty for more of this delicious, languid torture.

His hands drifted over the soft material of her sweater, skimming to the hem and then under. A strangled noise stirred in her throat as his touch moved over skin. He trailed his hands lightly up her sides, deepening the stroke of his tongue against hers. She felt linked to him by the engulfing heat between them. It was more than a physical bond. To her detriment and far beyond her control, it was purely emotional.

CHRIST, SHE FELT like a heater. Gerald's touch cruised over Olivia's buttercream skin. Their mouths moved in a natural rhythm, as if they'd been made to meld this way. His hands were shaking, but it wasn't from weakness. He hadn't meant for the kiss to go so far. He'd only wanted to taste her—steal a wee nibble.

The response of her mouth and her body as she pressed tight to his, as her hips arched underneath his hands, booted his gentlemanly intentions out and left only need.

My God, such staggering need. Where had it all bloody come from? It was as if his very life depended on her—them, this way.

On a shuddering wave, her body bowed against his, her navel thrusting unbidden against the center of his hips. The pang of arousal that ignited from her movements knocked out what little breath he had left in him. It sang clean into his groin. Feeling the low, telltale throb and the blood that had sunk from his head to his middle, however, he sucked in a shocked breath.

The movement must have jarred Olivia, too, because her eyes opened wide, latching on to his. She made a noise, one caught between arousal and alarm, and pulled back. It did no good to look at her, the stunned expression of uninhibited pleasure fading from her features, her parted wet lips tempting him further into damnation.

They watched each other for a moment, breathing raggedly. The connection he'd felt to her hung like a taut, thrumming strand between them, some invisible hand plucking it incessantly like a well-tuned guitar string.

Such heat—blistering heat. His body knew her, all right. It was the only explanation for that blaze leaping to life after simmering too long in wait.

She dropped her hands from around him and shifted away. "Have to get my breath," she managed weakly. Turning from him, she scooped her hands through the curls his hands had mussed moments earlier.

"Yeah," he returned in a voice that sounded much more uneven than usual. She was his kerosene, and he, an open flame, needed to step back. Way back.

Finesse. Control. He wouldn't take her to bed until he could be sure what she felt for him matched his feelings for her.

But if they went on kissing like that, he'd have no choice but to haul her over his shoulder with all the finesse of a caveman and cart her to bed.

Breathing carefully, he looked around at the sauce that was about to boil over. "Bugger." He quickly took it off the stove, burning himself in the process. Cursing, he set the pot safely aside. "Can I pour you more wine?"

"No!" she shrieked. At the quick turn of his head, her mouth fumbled and her eyes dodged his. Her cheeks were flushed pink and she looked thoroughly rumpled. Ravaged.

God. Don't think like that, Leighton. You prat.

"No," Olivia said again, more carefully. "Just tea for me. Please."

"A cuppa it is, then." He should warn her he'd been drinking tea all day and it had done absolutely nothing to quench his thirst for her.

After he shuffled aside his notes, books and computer, they sat down to dinner at the table. Now the silence wasn't easy. After a few savoring bites, she ate quickly as if ready to be done with the intimacy of their first sit-down meal together. In the end, she pushed her empty plate away after mopping up what remained of the marinara with the last bite of bread and swallowing it. Wiping her hands, she washed it down with her glass of iced tea. He knew she liked it cold and sweet so he'd made her a pitcher before starting the meal tonight. Clearing her throat, she stared thoughtfully at a small knot in the wood of the table. "I think we can safely say that's all there was to it in Vegas."

He chewed, watching her face as her brows drew together and the frown that was becoming far too comfortable on her lips deepened. Eating the remains of his spaghetti, he sat back in his chair and leveled with her. "I told you there was more."

"Then how come the only thing I can remember is the heat?" she asked, looking up at him with the grim light of challenge culling to life in her eyes. "The sex? If I didn't know you better, I'd say you were lying to me when you say there was more to it than that."

He ran his tongue over his teeth. It was a shame. After the fine meal and the fine moment they'd shared prior to it, he now had a bad taste in his mouth. "Well. I guess that's something."

"No need to get moody," she pointed out. "For the most part, you're still a stranger to me."

He narrowed his eyes and scowled. Then he shoved his plate aside in frustration and scrubbed his hands over his face. "By God, Olivia Lewis. You are by far the most stubborn female I have ever met."

"Oh, really?"

"Really," he said, dropping his hands with a discerning nod. "Let me tell you something, love. Strangers don't know each other like I know you. I know the taste of you, the smell. I know the workings of your mind. I was starting to think I was beginning to know your heart as well or maybe some small piece of it—"

"Don't bother."

"I'm not bloody finished."

"You talk too much," she accused.

"I speak my mind, and so do you. A little bluntly at times, but you value honesty above all else, I've found. So here it is, Liv. The truth. My body knows yours. It remembers you. It craves you."

She closed her eyes and gripped the edge of the table hard. "Stop."

"Not this time. For whatever reason, I need you like ink needs the page. Like the tides need the moon."

"You have a way with words," she reasoned carefully. "But it's fiction. Just like your books. You make stuff up for a living. That's what you're doing with us."

"You'd be very wise not to insult me again," he warned, his voice low and his jaw rigid.

"Or what, Shakespeare?" she asked, her voice rising. Somewhere in the living room, Rex whined. "You'll leave? Door's over there. Have a nice flight."

"I won't go," he told her. "I'm determined to get to the bottom of whatever it is we have because I'm starting to think it's vital to me. You're a part of me, whether you want to be or not, Olivia."

"Look," she said, rubbing her fingertips over her temples. "I'm sorry that you have these…these…

feelings for me. I really am. But, Gerald, you need to face facts. You're putting your heart on the line for this to work, and the only reason you'd do something that stupid is because you haven't fully assessed the risk. Maybe you don't even know what the risk is because you've never been hurt. You've never been heartbroken."

"I have, actually," he said quietly. At her surprised look, he nodded in confirmation. "I know all too well about the risk."

"Then you have to know as well as I do that *I will hurt you* in the end. And I don't want to be responsible for that."

He crossed his arms over his chest and took a steadying breath. "I'm responsible for my own heart and my own faith, something of which you know nothing about."

"Your faith is blind," she said. "It's irrational."

He rose quickly, scraping his chair against the wooden floor, and planted his hands on the table. "If you must know anything about me, love, know this," he said in a low voice but no less promising tone. "Number one—I'm not stupid. Neither am I rash nor impulsive. *That's* how I know what you meant to me in Las Vegas. I wouldn't have asked you to marry me if I hadn't known it was right. Number two—when I gamble, I weigh the risk carefully. I measure what it is I have to lose if I do and what I have to lose if I don't. In this case, I decided to show my cards, go all in, because above all else, the thought of letting you slip through my fingers terrified me. You are the woman I have always dreamed of. And I will not give you up without a fight."

For the first time since Gerald had arrived, Olivia was completely silent. Completely still. Completely vulnerable. The words had knocked out her defenses and her soul lay bare before him. And there he saw how great her fear of him and whatever he represented to her was.

He thought of kissing her again in hopes of making that fear disappear. Instead, he reached for her hand and wrapped it in his, studying the link as he smoothed his thumb over the back of her hand. With a whisper, he said, "I'll take the couch tonight."

Her lips parted but she said nothing, lowering her eyes to some spot on his chest. There she apparently found no comfort because she continued to look like she'd been set adrift alone on some turbulent, yawning sea without hope of rescue or respite. He leaned down to her and brushed his lips over her brow. Giving her hand one last squeeze, he released it and picked up both of their plates to wash.

CHAPTER THIRTEEN

THE RAIN FELL on the Eastern Shore, not in the spotty bands Gerald had seen there before, but in steady torrents. There'd been a time when he would have happily confined himself to the indoors and written as the light rumble of thunder and the monotony of precipitation served as a pleasant, creative backdrop. But with the woman he wanted engrossed in the tavern next door, he frowned at the downpour from the windows of the inn.

He'd forgone his usual cup of Earl Grey and taken the mug of Briar's black coffee Cole had offered him. Gerald had only drank a few sips of the brew, the substance going cold even as he continued to clench the handle of the mug and watch the rain from the sunroom that was empty except for him.

The bay view suite was vacant once more. He could pack up his things and return to Hanna's and its hospitality. It would certainly be easier than weathering Olivia's silence and his own damnable writer's block that was back in full force. He'd had to call Dwight to tell him it would indeed be

another week before he'd be turning in the manuscript…if not more.

Gerald was a patient man. He liked to think he
was an understanding one, too. But Olivia Lewis
tested him. She'd turned his life upside down and
refused to grant him the time he needed with her
to reconfigure it all, to find out what it was about
her that made him reach for her.

And as long as she kept him at arm's length, the
more tangled up he felt inside.

He could've gone flying off the handle. He
could've cursed and scowled for all the woman
made him a nutter. Instead, he stood and watched
the rain come down in buckets on the Eastern
Shore.

His free hand wandered into the pocket of the
jeans he'd picked up several days ago in town. He'd
never found much desire for wearing jeans before
coming to Fairhope. But something about the laid-
back quality of life he'd found here on the shore
called to the need for Wranglers. His fingertips
came up against something warm and metal at the
bottom. Delving a bit farther, he hooked the small
circle on the tip of his middle finger and pulled it
out into the dim light of the rainy day.

The band was too small to fit any one of his fingers. The gold shined like new, unmarked by a single blemish. He'd put it on Olivia's finger the night
they were married in Vegas. It was after her departure from the Bellagio penthouse that he found

the wedding ring under the bed while looking for his cuff links.

And so the chase began. Though now he had to admit, he was growing weary. He kept the larger, matching band he'd found in the pocket of the suit trousers in his wallet, tucked safely behind his identification.

However, when he'd come to Fairhope to find her, he'd needed Olivia's closer. Of course, he had hoped to find the right moment to present it to her again. Now…

Now the landscape looked a great deal different. It looked as if he might do what he'd told Olivia he'd known he might be doing at the end of the three weeks: dragging his heart right back to New York without ever placing the ring on her finger again.

On the floor next to him, Rex stirred. Though he didn't lift his resting head from his paws, the dog's tail thumped twice in greeting. Gerald's hand quickly dived back into the pocket of his jeans to hide the gold band from view before he turned and saw Briar standing in the sunroom's entrance.

Her eyes, wide and searching, lingered for a moment on the pocket before pinging back to his face.

He cleared his throat. She'd seen the ring. "I thought I was alone."

Briar's eyes roamed his face. Then a slow smile curved over her lips and she stepped into the room. "I was just putting Harmony down for a nap." She walked to the windows, bending to pet Rex on the head before she straightened and, standing shoulder to shoulder with Gerald, looked out at the rain as he had been doing. "It's come a-flood."

He trained his gaze on the window. "That it has."

They stood for some time in the silence with only the accompaniment of Rex's snuffling breath and the drill of the torrent outside. Then she took a deep breath and said in a quiet voice, "Don't give up on her, Gerald."

His head turned quickly in her direction. "Pardon?" he asked, unsure if he had heard her right.

Briar turned and pinned him with a stern gaze. "Olivia. Don't you dare give up on her."

He searched her determined, honey-colored eyes and frowned. Sighing, he moved his shoulders in an impatient gesture and lifted the mug still clenched in his hand to his lips. He winced at the mouthful of cold coffee. "Your cousin has refused my every advance."

Briar reached up and pried the mug from his fingers. "You know what that tells me, Gerald? That it's working. You're getting to her. If you weren't, she'd have already slept with you and sent you off with a pat on the back." At the doubting noise he made in the back of his throat, she added, "I know Liv better than anyone else…aside from maybe her parents. I'm telling you to keep pushing. Keep pressing at that wall. If you press long and hard enough, sooner or later it's going to start to chip

With you being as sweet and charming as you are…
I'd bet on sooner. And I don't bet, mind you."

"At this rate, I'm going to need a forklift…maybe
a bulldozer to get through to her in time."

Again Briar's gaze looked at the pocket where
his fingers still clenched Olivia's ring. "Talk to
Adrian."

"Adrian?"

Briar nodded. "I think she tells Adrian more than
she tells me. We all do. Adrian's experienced more
than any of the rest of us, and she has risen from
it. She's the one we all go to when we need good
advice."

Gerald narrowed his eyes as the idea sank in
and took root.

Briar saw his silent agreement and heaved a sigh
of relief. "Rexie can stay here. There's some left-
overs from dinner I think he'd enjoy."

Pulling the fingers from the jeans pockets sans
ring, Gerald reached for Briar's hand and lifted it
to his lips. "If I had met you first…"

Briar cackled at that. "You might be sweet and
charming, Mr. Leighton, but you'd be out of luck
there. I'm a happily married lady, and my husband's a rather large man." She ran her eyes over
his frame. "You might be sturdy, but I don't think
you could take Cole in a fight."

"My ego is thoroughly bruised," Gerald said, but
let go of Briar's hand. "Rest assured, Mrs. Savitt.
My skin bruises easily, too, so I'm not after getting

into a tussle with your husband. Though I'll have you know that I'm a fair swordsman. But it's easier and much less painful to vanquish an enemy with words rather than fists."

Briar lifted a knowing brow. "There you might have him beaten."

Gerald lifted his chin as he weighed the words, watched the shadow pass over her face. He would have a word with Cole. Give the man a friendly push. A woman as lovely as Briar deserved words along with all the usual feminine delights. Flowers, chocolates, et cetera. And though Gerald suspected those yellow-orange roses in the crystal cut vase on the dining room table had been a gift from her husband, he aimed to make sure that Cole found the right words to say to his wife to cleanse her of that shadow.

He let Briar make him a cup of Earl Grey to ward him against the chill the cold rain was bringing to the shore before he sought out Adrian. He managed to catch the florist at the door of her shop, just as she was returning from her lunch break. "Adrian!" he called as he jogged through puddles to reach the dry overhang in front of the bright display window.

The woman jerked around to him, her hand fumbling from the keys she'd been twisting in the lock. "Gerald," she said in obvious relief. "I'm glad it's you."

"I didn't mean to startle you," he said, touching a hand to her arm.

"No. It's fine." She shrugged in a jerky motion. "It's my fault. My mind's all over the place." Searching his face, she added. "Is there something I can do for you? You look very determined."

"Oh." He paused, frowned. "It shows, does it?"

Adrian nodded. "You're an open book. Pun intended."

Gerald chuckled. "Perhaps we should go inside first."

"Right." She finished unbolting the door, then swung it open for him with a welcoming ding. "Come on in."

"After you," he said, gripping the door over her head. When he motioned for her to duck under his arm into the shop, she did so and he followed, letting the door whoosh shut slowly at his back.

Her shop, Flora, smelled like the season—cinnamon, pumpkin and a whiff of hay. Neatly lined on open curio shelves were candles in glass jars with Flora's logo stamped on the front. Homemade, he surmised, and also the source of all that seasonal fragrance. A glass countertop on the left with an old-fashioned cash register stood among lush potted plants and novelty, hand-painted birdhouses and mailboxes. "There's much more to your shop than I imagined," Gerald admitted, peering into the back where her prep counter and storage space was set up.

"I expanded a few years after I opened shop," Adrian told him, shrugging off her safari-style jacket. "I added another cooler so I could order flowers in bigger bulk and keep up with production."

As Gerald watched her move things around to make room, he realized he and Adrian had not had a proper conversation since her ex's run-in with his fist. "How are you?"

"I'm doing fine," Adrian said with a short smile. He would have found it convincing if not for the sleeplessness rimming her eyes. "Busy. Kyle's Pop Warner season is winding down." At his lowered brows, she laughed shortly. "Football for peewees."

"I see." He grinned. "And business is good, I hope?"

"Oh, yes," she told him. "Fall has become a busy time of year. A few years ago, I started doing Halloween decorations. The word got out thanks to a feature in the local paper and ever since I get orders coming in right and left during October. And November also brings in a good haul. Cornucopias, Thanksgiving centerpieces, that kind of thing."

It was small talk, but he sensed she needed it to feel at ease alone with him. "Is there anything I can do to help?" Gerald asked.

Adrian's gaze narrowed. "Are you in the floral business, too?"

He reached up to scratch his chin, thoughtful. "Can't say I am or ever have been. But I can be useful every now and then. Even if it's just shuttling a young lad off to peewee football."

Surprise filtered over her face. "Thank you for offering, Gerald, but I've got it all worked out."

For a moment, they stood facing each other across the big room. She was Olivia's closest friend and confidante. Gerald wondered momentarily if asking Adrian to help would be crossing some line....

"What is it that you wanted?" she prompted, spreading her hands when he continued to say nothing.

Gerald frowned. "It's about Olivia." Looking around, he found a wooden stool in the corner and lowered into the hard seat. "I don't by any means want you to betray her confidence. I know what your friendship means to her. But I'm at a loss for what's wrong."

"Wrong?" Adrian asked. "With Olivia?"

"I was hoping you could tell me what it is exactly that's making her distance herself from me. I get the sense that somewhere in the past someone hurt her rather badly."

Adrian's brow creased as she thought about it. "Hurt Liv?"

Gerald gave a small nod and dropped his eyes to the white-tiled floor between them. "I'm fairly certain that's the case."

"She's never said anything to me," Adrian told him. "And she doesn't hide much. So if there's something in her past holding her back from you, I don't know about it."

Gerald ran his tongue over his teeth as he fell silent, thoughtful again.

She sighed at his consternated expression, giving in and lowering herself to the stool next to her prep counter. "What I do know is that Olivia is the most confident person I know. It seems that, with you, for some reason or other, that confidence has taken a hit and she's…fumbling. For a long time on a daily basis she's juggled all kinds of different balls and she's done it with finesse. But now for the first time I think she's afraid that someone might be capable of upsetting that balance."

"Have you ever seen her like this before?" Gerald asked.

"No."

Gerald's frown deepened. "It's because of me, Adrian. We both know it. There's no use pretending otherwise. It's pretty clear that commitment, outside of the tavern business or her friendships with you, Roxie, Cole and Briar, terrifies her. I wondered if I could get to the bottom of it, whether I could tip the scales and make her start believing in something other than what she already knows."

Again, Adrian shrugged. "I don't know. She's been living her life the same way for years. There's a pattern there, and when it comes to men it's not a very healthy one." She rolled her eyes. "Though she'd say the same about me, I'm sure."

"As her friend," Gerald said, bracing his hands on his knees as he leaned toward her in confidence, "do you think there's any chance that she might learn to make room in her life for me?"

"As far as your bet is concerned, I'm Switzerland," Adrian explained. "As much as I like you…" She paused, bit her lip a little as she eyed him. Then she gave in with a sigh and said, "I know that she cares about you. A little more than she'd like to. A *lot* more."

He frowned. "Caring about someone and loving someone is significantly different."

"Love?" Adrian fumbled. "What does all this have to do with…" She stopped, mouth falling open as his eyes rose back to hers slowly. "Oh." She let out a shocked breath. "God. Gerald—"

He raised a hand to stop her. "You've made things clearer even if you couldn't give me all the answers I need. Thank you for that."

Adrian watched him rise and turn to walk out. She shot to her feet. "Gerald. Wait."

He stopped and made himself look at her as she caught up with him. "Yes?"

After a moment's pause, she laid a hand on his arm. "You're a good man. And I don't say that lightly."

Gerald forced his mouth into a smile. There was pity there in the deep, dark saucers of her eyes. "Thank you, Adrian."

"Liv's a strong woman," she warned. "But I will say that she's questioning herself at this point."

"So I should give her the space she needs?" he

asked, feeling heavy and hollow all at once in his chest. He scrubbed the heel of his hand over his heart.

A pensive expression moved over Adrian's face. "I don't think space will give either of you answers...."

He blinked in surprise as his gaze rose back to hers. "You don't?"

Adrian weighed the situation carefully, then bit off a curse. "She's going to kill me for this but... look under her bed."

Gerald frowned. "Her bed?"

"That's what I said." Adrian's face held the flicker of mischief. "She told me something. When you moved in. She put something there, to hide it from you. You should look. See. Maybe... I don't know...it *might* help. That's all I can offer you, for now, as her friend."

"Ah...thank you?" he said, puzzled by the clue. God only knew what a man might find under a woman's bed, particularly Olivia's. Though the idea wasn't without intrigue.

"Don't mention it." She sobered. "Really. Don't. She might actually kill me."

Gerald chuckled and lowered his head to hers. "I won't let that happen." Giving her shoulder a squeeze, he said, "If you need anything, Adrian, I'm here for you. Know that."

She beamed at him. "You're too nice for her. You know that, right?"

With a fond shake of his head, he walked back toward the door and the rain beyond. "Give my best to the peewee."

THE RAIN BROUGHT more than a fair scattering of customers to the tavern. People, especially the single variety, didn't much like being confined to the interiors of their homes with their nightcaps on rainy nights. They tended to stop by the tavern for a companionable pint and entertainment.

Especially when the blues were live like they were tonight. The musicians lent a good dose of atmosphere to the damp evening. It wasn't so busy, though, that she had to call Monica in on her night off. She worked the bar in solitude, a rarity she preferred on evenings like this.

Olivia couldn't face another night upstairs with Gerald where tension hung in the air and she let it because she didn't have the first damned clue how to dispel it. How to get rid of him and all the promises she saw in his eyes....

"Hey, Liv, can I get another Corona Extra over here?" Freddie asked.

"Bottle or tap?" she asked.

"Bottle."

"Just a minute. I've got some in the back." She walked through the swinging doors and her steps hitched at the sight of Gerald leaning against the jamb of her office, Rex at his knee. "Oh. I didn't know you were down here."

"I just got back from dinner at the inn," he explained, looking all too appealing in the freshly ironed oxford shirt with two buttons undone at the collar, giving her a good gander of the tendons of his neck and a teasing glimpse of rugged collarbone. Those horn-rimmed glasses were hanging from his breast pocket. "Briar sent over one of the steaks Cole prepared. I put it on your desk."

Olivia peered around him and the jamb and saw the covered platter waiting on her desk. Judging by his casual stance—one ankle hooked over the other, his shoulders relaxed against the frame of the door—he'd been waiting for her. The affable expression on his face as he looked at her didn't at all hold up against the strain that had existed between them since the dinner he had made for her. "That was…nice," she said after several beats of silence. "Thank you."

He eyed her in a way that went straight to her toes. It was chased by a tingling sensation that lingered in an area she refused to think about.

This was exactly why she couldn't spend more than a handful of seconds with him. His potency was subtle but absolute.

"I wanted to talk to you about something," he said.

"I'm really busy, Gerald," Olivia said, gesturing toward the swinging doors. "I have customers."

"It'll only take a second." Gerald lifted a hand and Olivia's mouth gaped at the dog-eared paperback he was holding. "Does this look familiar?" he asked.

Olivia swallowed. "Should it?" she said in a choked voice.

"As I found it along with several others under your bed, yes."

Drawing up her shoulders, she demanded, "What were you doing under my bed?"

"I didn't think it was too much of an invasion of privacy as we *are* married and have shared the bed on several occasions," Gerald said pointedly. For some reason, a self-satisfied smile stretched across his mouth.

Olivia threw her hands up. "So what? I read them."

"All of them?" he asked, the gleam in his eye amused and a little surprised.

"Yeah. Am I not supposed to read your books?"

"No," he said carefully, "but you didn't have to hide the fact that you were reading them."

Now that he said it like that it *did* seem ridiculous.

"What did you think of them?" he asked, lowering the book and opening it absently to a page somewhere in the middle.

"What does it matter?" she asked.

"Don't be defensive, Olivia. I just want to know your opinion. It means a great deal to me."

She sucked in a steadying breath because she *was* being defensive and there was really no reason to be. "I liked them. Which is weird because I rarely read for pleasure, except for the occasional romance novel...."

Gerald smirked. "You don't normally read for pleasure, but you read every one of my books?"

"The Rex Flynn series, yes," she admitted.

"And you liked them?" he questioned, smile broadening.

"Half the world likes them," she reminded him. "Otherwise you wouldn't be an international best-seller, would you?"

"Yes, but you're my wife," Gerald told her. "You don't know what it means to me that in your limited downtime you read my books despite the fact that you don't like to read. It's rather touching."

"I'm hardly your wife, *and* it's not that big of a deal." Olivia checked herself when he looked a bit put off. "Okay, it *is* a big deal because they were unbelievable. I couldn't put them down. I desperately need to know when the next book will be out because I'm probably going to buy it the day it is. First in line, money in hand."

"Olivia..." Gerald beamed. "You're blushing."

She swiped the back of her hand over her hot cheek as if that would chase away the telling color. "I don't know why," she muttered, frustrated with herself.

To set her at ease, he offered her the book. When she took it, he shifted away from the jamb to place both his hands in the curve between her neck and each of her shoulders. "Not to worry," he added. "The next book is nearly done…and I'm suddenly more determined than ever to finish it."

"Because of me?" she asked, brow creasing.

"Yes," he laughed, moving his hands up to cup her pink cheeks. "Because of you."

"No need to rush it on my account." It was a lie. Olivia wanted the book like the carnivore in her wanted that steak on the desk…like the woman in her wanted him. "I don't know why I hid the books. I've never been guilty about guilty pleasures—like hot baths, Captain Morgan, Dwayne Johnson movies, Patrick Swayze in *Dirty Dancing*. You." Her eyes widened and she fumbled as he laughed again. "Your books, I mean. Rex Flynn, Janet MacMillian—that whole crazy, time travel, ill-fated love story sort of thing that you've got going there."

"Trust me, I'm flattered."

"You shouldn't be," she accused, slapping him on the arm with the abused paperback. "Only a sadist would keep those two apart. Why do you do it? It's just heartrending. I don't know how your readers have put up with you this long."

Gerald's smile softened and tenderness flared to life there, catching her off guard. He moved one hand from her face back through the hair at her brow and farther, cupping the nape of her neck, warming her through and through. "It's the promise of tomorrow, love. There's always the promise of tomorrow. The next page. The next book. Trust me,

I don't delight in keeping Rex and his Janet apart. But I do believe in the promise of all their tomorrows, which they will have. I promise you that."

Olivia sighed, trying to content the new, rabid reader in her with that much at least. "All right. I guess I believe you."

"Now…before you charm me into giving away anything else about our intrepid lovers' future, tell me, do you need help manning the bar? I didn't see Monica's car in the drive."

"I've got it," she said, pocketing her hands as he lowered his from her and she could breathe somewhat regularly again. "But if you want, you can take a seat and listen to the band. They're pretty good."

The smile that curved Gerald's lips thrummed through her because he wasn't laughing at her anymore. It was as if her invitation touched him. "I'd be happy to."

Olivia gestured toward the swinging doors. "Go ahead. I need to grab something from the cooler." When he moved past her, she indulged that flagrant need to breathe him in. "Gerald?"

He turned. "Yes, Olivia?"

She smiled tentatively. "I see a lot of you. In Rex Flynn, I mean. Even if you don't intend for it to be that way…you're there, on the page. In him."

Gerald's eyes searched hers. "And…do you like him—Rex?"

She sucked in a long breath. "Yeah. Usually nice

guys don't do it for me. But Rex I like. A lot. Maybe a little too much."

Gerald's smile couldn't have been wider, warmer or sexier. He chuckled and the sound pleasured her in more ways than she could define. Her heart skipped a little as those mirth lines dug their way into the corners of his eyes and mouth. At his answer, though, it simply melted. "You know, Olivia Lewis, I think you might be my muse."

Her eyes widened. "Me?"

He grew serious. "Yes. I'm starting to think that's how it was meant to be all along."

When he turned and disappeared, Olivia stayed glued to the wood floor of the hall beyond the tavern, unable to move toward or away from him and what she sensed might be the author's own promise of tomorrow for himself and her.

CHAPTER FOURTEEN

THINGS IMPROVED BY a marked degree between them. It wasn't just Gerald's imagination. There had been a cup of Earl Grey waiting for him when he woke the following morning. Then there was easy small talk when she returned from her run. When she went down to work at the tavern, Gerald found himself pacing the floors, all the restless energy finally leading him to the makeshift desk he'd set up on Olivia's dining room table.

He wrote like the wind, brand-new material swamping him, begging for release. The words came in profusion and he was helpless to stop them. He sat for hours getting it all down. Relief chased them. He had thought the well had dried. For the first time in weeks, maybe more, he was writing again the way he'd wished to be writing all along.

As the fresh, new stream finally trickled out, Gerald leaned back in the stiff dining room chair, closing his eyes for the first time in hours. They were tired, as were his neck and shoulder muscles. And still there was that familiar sense of accomplishment—the thrumming of his temples signaling a good, long day at the computer doing what he did best.

Removing his glasses, he rubbed the bridge of his nose and looked out the window, surprised to see dark pressing against the pane.

Olivia. He had her to thank for this. He knew it as certainly as he knew that he would be back at the computer in the morning, raring for a fresh go at his new work in progress. His surroundings, the contentment that came so easily with them now and, he had to admit, even the sexual frustration he'd begun to feel living here in close quarters with the woman he wanted, all lent themselves to this creative surge.

Gerald took Rex out for a short, refreshing walk, glad the rain had stopped. Then he called down to the tavern and asked Monica if either she or Olivia needed a bite to eat. When the answer came back no, he fixed a small plate of sandwiches and, sliding his glasses onto the bridge of his nose again, did what he could to edit the new material.

Before he knew it, the door to the apartment opened. Rex woofed low in his throat, startled out of sleep by the clack of heels on hardwood. Gerald glanced up as Olivia rounded the corner, looking spectacular in heeled boots and an emerald sweater-dress with a deep V-neck. As he took off his glasses, he observed the tired bruises under her eyes and rose quickly to cross the room to her. "I didn't realize it was so late."

"You're on your own there, pal," she said, opening the fridge and taking out what remained of the chilled Cabernet he had bought for dinner the other night. "Tonight I felt every waking minute."

Taking the bottle from her, he lowered his free hand to the small of her back and ushered her to the couch in the living room. "Long night, eh?"

"Most nights are long in the tavern," Olivia said, sinking into the deep cushions with a sigh, moving only to unzip her knee-length boots. She kicked them off and they clattered to the floor. Rex bumped his head against her hand and she obliged him by scratching him on the nose, lowering her head against the back of the couch and closing her eyes. "This one, though… It's rare, but I hate nights like these."

Gerald crossed back to the kitchen to retrieve a glass. Pouring the Cab into the crystal, he handed it over the back of the couch. "Did you eat?"

A small, sour grin touched her face as she lifted the glass to her lips. "Careful. You're starting to sound like Briar. And, yes, I had dinner, thank you very much." Laying her head back again, she turned it slowly to face him. "You look pleased with yourself."

His brows drew together. "Do I? Huh." At her questioning look, he explained, "I wrote today."

"Ring-a-ding-ding." Her eyes warmed, sleepy as they were, and her lips curved. "Congratulations."

"I know for certain now that you're my muse."

The glass stopped halfway to her mouth. "Do you?"

"Yes." Reaching up, he traced the line of her cheek, brushing back a wisp of hair that had loosened from the knot at the nape of her neck. "I wrote well today. Really well, for the first time in…I can't remember. And I have you to thank for it."

"I wasn't here," she pointed out.

"Yes, you were. You're always here. I'm surrounded by you here and down in the tavern. Every wee little bit of who you are, from the scent of your perfume to the pulse of your spirit, motivates me."

"You say the damnedest things." Her lids were at half-mast and he saw a small but no less distinguishable flame beginning to cull around her pupils. Heat leaped to life in his groin as he watched her tongue dash quickly over her lips. "The nicest things," she added, stretching her arms over her head, yawning as she did so. "They should pay you to talk, not write."

As she relaxed again, he touched his knuckles to her chin and lifted it, so her face was directly underneath his. The way she was, loose and limber, he could conjure up all sorts of ways to talk her into bed with him. But she was knackered, and he had more than enough decency to staunch the burn inside him…as he had before. Many times before, as far as Olivia was concerned. "What made your night so terrible?" he asked her.

The mirth left her face. "Clint. He picked a fight

with Freddie and there was a brawl. Had to have a couple of deputies haul him out. Could've used your left hook to help break it up."

"I'm sure your rifle did well to end the dispute," Gerald commented, turning his attention to her shoulders. There he began to knead the knots he felt under her skin.

"Nah, I only bring out Betty when there's a real threat."

His lips quirked. "Betty."

"Tonight I used Glinda."

"I'm almost afraid to ask. Who's Glinda?"

She yawned again. Long after her jaw cracked and the yawn ended, however, her eyes remained closed and her head nestled into the cushion behind her. "The aluminum baseball bat—from my softball days."

"I had no idea you played softball," he commented. Because he was losing her to sleep, he gently plied the wineglass from her hand.

"High school. Shortstop. Best batting average on the team. They wanted to give me a college scholarship for it, but you know how those things go...." She waved a hand, sweeping it under the rug. "Anyway, the fire marshal showed up sometime after the brawl. Decided I was overcapacity. We had words."

"Please tell me he didn't get wind of either Glinda or Betty."

"No, but he did fine me. Bastard. Then just when

I think I'm going to get through the rest of the god-forsaken night without any more unwelcome company, Skeet Bisbee shows up near to closing."

"I thought you liked Skeet."

"I love the squirt." Her head came down on his shoulder with a sigh. "But then, so does Monica and she's not afraid to show it. Goes around peacocking for him. Gets his dander up. I turn my back for five minutes…catch them in the back room going at it on my desk."

"You don't say."

"Hmm. Not a sight I'll forget soon enough. Then she goes on and on about how much she's in love with him."

He frowned. "So what if she is?"

Olivia's scoff was halfhearted but telling. "Because she's Monica. And he's Skeet. Before he came home from Tuscaloosa, she spent half her time harping on about how love doesn't exist. And he's still half-green around the gills."

Gerald lowered his head against hers, his lips brushing her temple. "That doesn't mean they aren't compatible. People find love in all sorts of places. Look at us."

Her brow puckered. "Us?"

"We met in Vegas, far from either of the places we call home. We fell in love and decided to get married jolly on the spot. I've heard stranger love stories yet."

She sighed again. This time the soft sound came with a sleep-infused snuffle. "It won't last."

His hand stopped in the midst of combing her loosened ponytail. "Me and you or Skeet and Monica?"

She didn't seem to hear him. "...doomed from the start..."

He lowered his lips to her hair. "We'll see."

"Hmm." Whatever she had meant to say next came out on a muffled snore. She was out like a light.

Gerald closed his eyes a moment, enjoying the feel of her against him. It struck him that this was another first for them. Rehashing the day, relaxing on the couch...resembling something of a normal, matrimonial couple.

"Rest well, love," he whispered, indulging himself by turning his face into the soft curls that fell across her temple. He waited until he was sure she was good and asleep before shifting away from her.

Rex had already found his bed and wagged his tail in one acknowledging thump when Gerald turned to check on him. Touching a finger to his lips, Gerald rose to his feet. When he was sure the dog would remain, he turned off the lamp next to the couch, then bent down to tuck his arms under Olivia's shoulders and knees. Lifting her, he carried her into the dim bedroom.

After he laid her down and covered her with a blanket, she quickly fell back to sleep. Unable to return to the couch, he removed his shirt and slipped on a pair of sweatpants before joining her.

For the first time in what felt like an eternity, he slept well, waking only once to tuck his chin against the top of Olivia's head when she turned to him late in the night.

"YOU HAVE NO idea how great the view is back here."

Olivia snorted, looking over her shoulder as she jogged down the sidewalk overlooking the bluff of the Eastern Shore. "Something tells me you don't mean the bay."

"Don't I?"

She shook her head and let a grin bow wide across her mouth. "I think it's time to pick up the pace, Mr. Leighton."

"I would, Mrs. Leighton. But I'm a bit out of shape, you see."

"Rex is jogging faster than you are. The both of us could run circles around you."

"Now, that was uncalled for."

Still smiling, she pivoted so she was jogging backward. Gerald's face was flushed, sweat had started to dot the front of his T-shirt, and he was definitely short of breath. But she was assured by the amused glint in his eyes and the fact that he was only a few paces behind her. He, too, was smiling. "Close your mouth. You're more aerodynamic that way."

"No wonder the others refuse to exercise with the likes of you. You're a regular beast."

"Honey, I'm just doing my part to whip America back into shape."

"Whipping indeed." His grin widened and the glint in his eyes sparked into something suggestive. "And 'honey,' is it? I like the sound of that."

Olivia sighed, turning back around so she could kick it up a notch. "Don't get used to it, mister." Letting out a piercing whistle, she held out a hand for Rex's leash. "Come on, boy. Let's show this loser how it's done."

"Show-offs!" he called from behind them, laughing breathlessly.

She might egg him on, but Olivia was content with him running at his own pace—it was his first run since the accident. And she had to admit that his pace was picking up. He seemed refreshed, energized.

Olivia reached the park first. The path led down the steep hill to the pier that disappeared into the mist hovering like a ghost over the stone-gray flat-top of the bay. There were a few walkers and runners out, but the circular parking lot was empty.

She slowed to a walk until he caught up with her at the bottom of the hill. "I love days like this," she said, spreading her arms wide in the still hush of the fresh November morning.

Breathing hard, he bent over double and replied,

"Yes. I like it better when there's no one around to witness my suffering."

She handed him the water bottle pinned to her belt loop. "Have some water."

He straightened, took the flask. "I'm all right, by the way."

"I know you are." Despite the heavy breathing and sweat, his coloring was good. "You're just out of practice."

"Truth be told, I feel like I could run the length of the pier and back."

She raised a brow. "I might just have to see that. Race you!" Challenge leveled, she took off across the parking lot.

Footsteps pounded after her. "Now, wait. If anyone deserves a head start, it's me."

Olivia heard his footsteps closing in behind her as they hit the first leg of the pier. Looking back, she saw him catching up. She picked up her pace.

"Close your mouth, Mrs. Leighton," Gerald chided when he was level with her and caught her gaping at him. "For aerodynamics' sake."

"Oh, it's on, Shakespeare." She broke out into a full-out run. As they chased headlong into the thick of the cool mist, they remained neck and neck, their footsteps pounding in unison, echoing back to them along with the cry of gulls and the groan of boats moored at the marina. Olivia shrieked with laughter as Rex broke the hold she had on his leash and bounded ahead with a happy chorus of barks.

246 MARRIED ONE NIGHT

The pier widened into a T at the end and they slowed together, relinquishing the lead to the hound. She reached for the railing, bracing a hand on her hip as she caught her breath. "Wow. That felt great."

"Yeah," he agreed, smiling through pants. "Well?"

She ran her eyes over him, considering. "You're a better opponent than I pegged you for."

"If I were still playing tennis on a weekly basis, we wouldn't be having this conversation," he advised.

"Tennis." That explained the great calf muscles and underlying stamina. "Right."

Gerald took up Rex's leash, petting the dog on the head. "There's a good lad."

"You wouldn't think something as big as he is could run that fast," Olivia said, reaching out to scratch Rex behind the ear. The dog leaned into her hand with a satisfied groan. "He made us both look bad."

"I think the trash talk amped him up," Gerald said, dropping to a bench. He looked at the mist swirling in slow circles around the pier. The heel of his running shoe tapped against the concrete. "It's too bad I don't have my notebook. This is the perfect creative environment."

Instead of crossing to the bench to sit next to him, Olivia pulled herself up onto the ledge of the railing. "How so?"

"Careful there, Mrs. Leighton," he advised, getting quickly to his feet and crossing to her. He laid his hands on her thighs. "We wouldn't want you to take a swim."

"I'm fine," she said, tightening her grip on the ledge at his touch.

"I'm talking about the kind of creativity that comes with the *new,*" he explained, looking out to sea. "The exhilarating unknown that comes with free-writing—the adrenaline."

"This isn't enough adrenaline for you?" she asked with a smile.

"It certainly helps," Gerald told her with a grin that might have been a tad suggestive. "It's a different kind of rush. I wish I could show you."

His gaze lingered on hers and she licked her lips, ignoring the fire in her belly. Under his hands, her thighs warmed far more than they should have. Maybe she'd had a little too much adrenaline for one day. Clearing her throat, she straightened, looking over his shoulder toward the park. "Let's keep it to a walk on the way back."

Gerald hesitated a moment before he slid his hands from her thighs and stepped away. She hopped down from the rail and began to stroll with him, retracing their steps back to the shoreline.

It was early enough to explore more of the park that led into the picnic and beach areas. Rex took gleefully to the sand when Gerald produced a tennis ball. As man and dog tussled on the beach, Olivia lowered to one of the swings on the playground and watched. The ball wound up in the small, lapping bay waves by mistake. Before Gerald could stop him, Rex charged into the spray to rescue it.

Olivia cackled as Gerald took off again at a dead run toward her. Rex, wet and filthy, gave chase. The laugh died in her throat when the man called "Run for it!" and she realized she wasn't safe, either. Shrieking, she made a break for the duck pond and the thick trees surrounding it.

"Oh, God," she said when she heard Rex galloping through the grass. She was going to end up covered in giant, wet dog for sure....

Gerald dived out from behind a tree, snagging her by the waist and swinging her around so he was between her and Rex. As the dog closed in on them, Gerald outstretched his arms. "You can get me, but you won't get her, you git."

Rex leaped gleefully at Gerald. They both tumbled to the grassy grove. The dog wound up on top, coating Gerald in sandy filth and drenching the front of his clothes. Gerald covered his face, but it didn't keep Rex from spreading sloppy kisses over his cheeks. "Rex!" Gerald yelled, laughing. "All right, you got me!" He looked to Olivia. "A little help, Liv?"

She could hardly stand upright she was laughing so hard and held up her hands helplessly to show it.

"I saved your life!" He groaned when Rex landed a kiss on his mouth. "Off with you. Happy mon grel." Gerald managed to sit up. Rex plopped down, grinning, beside him. "Thanks a lot," Gerald called over his shoulder to her.

"I'm sorry," Olivia said, unable to stop the laughter. Plucking at the sleeve of his T-shirt, she snorted. "Now you both smell like dog."

He eyed Rex. "What do you say we get her?"

"No," she said, backing up when both man and beast gained their feet and started after her. "No!" She took off for the parking lot.

They chased her all the way back to the tavern. Out of breath, Olivia bobbed and weaved through Briar's garden before making a dash for the door.

"Oh, no you don't!" Gerald's arms wrapped her around the waist and hauled her back with a growl as feral as Rex's.

Her heart leaped into her throat as she found herself on the ground beneath man and dog. She tried to close her smiling mouth and stem the flow of laughter before Rex overwhelmed her with kisses, but she couldn't. By the time both rolled away from her, she was soaking wet with sand and dirt clinging to skin and clothes. And still she couldn't stop laughing. "I'm…going to kill…you both…." she managed finally.

Gerald mirrored her on the grass with arms flung overhead, staring up into the blue-tinged sky. The fog and mist were lifting to unveil a clear, fall day. "I'd believe you, if you weren't grinning like a fiend."

"Can't stop," she admitted. Frankly, she didn't want to stop. She'd thought she had been living carefree for years, but she hadn't felt quite this airy and…hell, downright childlike in way too long. Shifting, she found Gerald's face turned toward her. His eyes were still bright with laughter.

The urge to spread kisses across his face as Rex had and rub herself all over him until her scent overwhelmed all else formed out of something other than childlike giddiness. The woman in her wanted at him again. It took a level of self-discipline she didn't know she had to tear her gaze away from his. "We gotta get up. Briar has guests."

"We've probably woken the house."

Olivia pointed at Rex. "That mutt can't come inside smelling like that."

"It's called 'wet dog,' love. And I'm sorry to say, you smell like that, too."

To fight a grin, she got up and attempted to wipe herself off. "There's a hose over by the greenhouse. Adrian won't mind if we use it."

The water was ice-cold, but there wasn't much they could do about that. Olivia did her best not to pay attention as Gerald stripped off his sodden jogging clothes, leaving nothing but the boxer-briefs behind. While he ran the hose over Rex, she made sure they were out of sight of the inn windows and stripped to her sports bra and undies.

Gerald turned to her with the hose as if he were about to open fire. She raised her hands to shield herself from what she thought would be an icy torrent. Instead, he stopped and stared, heat culling in his eyes.

"Hell," she muttered. Folding her arms over her chest, she sighed. "You really shouldn't look at me like that."

"I can't help it," he replied. "You first?"

She sucked in a bracing breath and stepped to him. "Do me a favor and make it quick."

He lifted the hose over her head and squeezed the nozzle only enough for a fine spray to trickle over her. Her teeth clattering, she worked fast to scrub the dirt and sand from her scalp. After a moment, she felt Gerald's hand on her back, rubbing the filth away.

He really shouldn't do that. The warning voice in her head didn't penetrate the purring need to be touched. The purr made it all the way up into her throat when his stroking hand reached around to her abdomen, rubbing the soot away.

Don't turn around. She clenched her teeth to keep from turning into him. Her limbs obeyed the command, but that didn't stop them from stepping back into him. His hand came to rest on her navel, warm, as her hips fit into his and her head dropped back to his chest. A sigh spilled out of her as his hand moved to her waist and his arm wrapped around her.

He had a good foot on her in height, but still they fit together nicely.

His head lowered and she felt the press of his lips on her temple. The chill of her skin and the rising heat underneath it made her feel feverish....

"What's going on back here?"

Rex let out a short woof and Olivia jumped like a red-handed criminal. The cold chose then to kick in, freezing her in place as Cole stalked around the corner. Thankfully, Gerald had enough sense to back away from her, disengaging the water hose.

Cole stopped. By the alarmed look on his face, he'd gotten a good gander at the scene before Gerald lifted his hands from her. Olivia flushed to the roots of her hair, utterly embarrassed. To add to it, she stuttered in her quick attempt to explain herself. Nothing came out but a fount of unintelligible words.

Cole firmed his mouth into a careful line. From the look of things, a grin wasn't far behind it. "Sorry. Briar said she heard something out here, and I came to check out the er...situation."

Situation indeed. Olivia frowned, unable to look at either of them.

Gerald cleared his throat. "Sorry for the noise. We were just wrapping it up."

"Yeah, okay." Cole caught Olivia's eye and lifted his brows knowingly. "Good to see you, Liv. Gerald."

"Cole," she muttered through gnashed teeth. She didn't wait until he rounded the corner before scooping up her clothes and heading for the door.

OLIVIA ATTACKED THE task of cleaning the bar with gusto. She could use the mops, but she felt like getting down on her hands and knees and scrubbing until her fingers were red and raw. Or until the fire in her burned out.

She'd put money on the red and raw happening first.

Over the next couple of hours, she missed lunch and ignored the sound of the phone ringing. By the time she was done polishing the floor's wood beams, she was sore but above all she was cranky and in no mood for company.

When all three of her pals walked through the double doors of the tavern, Olivia all but snarled. "Go away."

Adrian held up a bottle. "We brought Cab."

"And strawberries," Briar said with a hesitant smile, holding up a miniature picnic basket. "Fresh from the garden."

"I'm not in the mood."

"I'm sorry, Olivia." Roxie held up her hands. "Did you just say you're not in the mood for Cab?"

"And strawberries," Briar whispered, aghast. "This is worse than I thought."

Adrian sighed. "Just back away slowly. I'll handle this." She walked partway across the room, stopped. "You know, if I'd been caught Adam-and-Eveing in the garden this morning, I'd be a lot more festive than you are."

"We were *not* Adam-and-Eveing." Olivia scrubbed her hands through her mussed hair.

"You're cleaning," Briar pointed out from a safe distance. "Which means you're frustrated. So I know you didn't have sex."

"How would you know that?" Olivia asked incredulously, rubbing her raw hands.

"Because I do the same thing," Briar reasoned. She crossed to the bar and set the basket down. "All I've done for the last two months is clean. Still, the fact remains that Cole did say you and Gerald were…naked—and touching."

"This is a nightmare." Olivia dropped a bar stool to her newly polished floor and lowered herself to it. "We weren't naked. Not technically."

"But there was touching," Adrian surmised. She had the decency at least to not look amused.

"Harmless petting." Olivia scowled.

Roxie went around the bar for glasses. "This is your husband we're talking about. It would be weird if there wasn't *some* petting involved."

"Even under the circumstances," Adrian added.

When Olivia only grumbled, Briar sighed and opened the basket. "Here, have a strawberry. You'll feel better."

"Oh, right. I forgot you grow sin-absolving fruit. Though it probably doesn't help that I thought seriously about sexing the writer in residence up underneath your strawberry bushes." Olivia took the berry anyway and stuffed it in her mouth. "I wanted to drag him down onto your husband's freshly mowed lawn and ride him like a prized stallion at the rodeo."

"Hot damn." Adrian lifted a strawberry to her own mouth. "You're not the only one who's sexually frustrated so let's keep the visuals to a minimum."

Briar's cheeks were red, but she licked her lips anyway and spoke again. "Nonetheless…I owe you both thanks for *not* doing it. Let's just say we were lucky nobody in the inn decided to take a walk but Cole."

Roxie tittered as she poured herself a glass of Cabernet. "A little birdie told me that your stallion has an impressive package."

Olivia groaned. "Adrian's right. Cool it on the imagery. In fact, I think we should cool it on this topic altogether."

"That would pretty much defeat the purpose of our powwow," Adrian said.

"Powwow?" Olivia snorted. "More like an ambush."

"Hey, we brought wine," Roxie reminded her, "which makes it less of an ambush and more of a—"

"Alcoholic inquisition," Olivia filled in. She looked to Briar. "If you'd brought the baby, I would have felt better about it."

"Dad visited this morning," she explained. "He's still rocking her. I wanted to give him some time with her. *And,* I'm sorry, but Harmony doesn't need to hear about her aunt's petting or sexing or whatever it was you and Gerald were doing in the garden this morning."

"Petting," Olivia decided.

"With a little bit of sexing," Roxie added with a wink. "I'll never look at the strawberry patch the same again." With that, she popped one into her mouth, closed her eyes and hummed.

Despite everything, Olivia felt the corners of her lips twitching. "Are you done?"

"Not quite."

"Richard's still away, huh?" Adrian presumed.

"Unfortunately, yes," Roxie admitted.

Olivia turned to Briar, who remained pointedly neutral. "And you? Did you and Cole get it on?"

"Almost," Briar murmured, lifting the glass to her lips. When the others only looked at her, waiting, she lowered it. "We weren't very far into it last night before the baby started crying…and that was the end of it." She lifted her hand in a helpless gesture.

"Oy," Olivia sighed.

Adrian poured herself another glass of wine. "It's nice, in a way." When Olivia, Roxie and Briar frowned at her, she shrugged. "I'm the lone single lady in the group now. It's nice knowing I'm not the only one not doing the sexy dance all the time."

"I know a lot of tavern regulars who could change that," Olivia told her.

"Oh, now, another drunken disaster. Just what I need."

Olivia lifted a shoulder and mumbled, "Works for me. Usually."

Briar hesitated before lifting a hand to Olivia's arm. "We came here to tell you that…it's okay. Whatever happens with Gerald, it'll be fine. More than fine."

Olivia looked around at them all. "You think I'm going to lose, don't you?"

Roxie lifted innocent eyebrows at the suggestion. "Did we say that?"

Olivia gaped when Adrian avoided her gaze. "You think I'm going to fall for him and that—what?—we're going to live happily ever after? *Are you frigging nuts?*"

Briar pursed her lips. "It wouldn't be the worst thing."

Pushing away the wine and strawberries, Olivia rose to grab a wet cloth and start wiping down the bar. "Judases. The lot of you."

Roxie frowned as the others began gathering up the offerings. "You won't even stay in touch with him if the divorce does happen?"

"What's the point?" Olivia asked impatiently. "He lives up there. I live here. He and I are from two different worlds. How could that ever work? Long-distance relationships suck."

Roxie nodded acquiescence. "I'll grant you that. But I was thinking as more of the occasional dalliance sort of thing when it's convenient for both of you. That seems much more like something you'd be open to. You two obviously have something. Whatever that is, big or small, it'd be hard to cut it off completely after everything you've been through. Don't you think?"

Olivia sighed. "Maybe. Maybe," she said, more strongly the second time. "He might not feel that way by the end."

"What do you mean?" Briar's eyes narrowed. "You're not going to do something horrible, are you?"

"Liv," Adrian said, seeming to hesitate. "Don't do anything to hurt him, okay? He's—"

"—a good guy," Olivia finished for her. "Yeah, I know. Which makes this whole thing a million times more complicated."

"So you know he has feelings for you?" Adrian questioned.

"Aw…" Roxie began, then trailed off when Olivia sent her a squelching look. Burying her face in her wine, she murmured, "Sorry."

"Do you know something you're not telling me?" Olivia asked, pointing to Adrian.

"No." Adrian failed to look nonplussed.

She failed miserably, leading Olivia to growl, "What is it?"

Adrian carefully picked a strawberry from the basket, looked it over discerningly. "If you're already determined to end it, maybe you don't deserve to know."

"And maybe you're not so Switzerland after all," Olivia said.

"Let me just say this," Adrian said, lifting a finger. "If it was me in your shoes, as many doubts as I might have about the long-term and as negative as I feel about relationships, I would be thinking about how I might be able to make it work, rather than a clean break—unless something was stopping me from doing so."

Briar lifted her hand to cup her chin, leaning against the bar for support. "What's stopping you, Liv?"

Olivia clenched the cleaning rag in her fist and sucked in a breath, tightening her hold on her fast-slipping composure. "Here's the deal. He only has a couple of more days, and then he'll be on his way home. Maybe you should all just resign yourselves to that. Clearly, you guys are gonna miss him far more than I will."

"That's a lie," Adrian mused. "A really bad one."

Olivia shrugged, trying her best to look careless. "Look on the bright side, Adrian. When he and I are divorced, you can make a play at him. You're so full of his praises." Before any of them could say another word, she whirled and walked out of the tavern into the hall through the swinging doors, letting them slap shut behind her.

CHAPTER FIFTEEN

OLIVIA SLEPT BADLY, tossing and turning through most of the night before finally succumbing to dreams.

She dreamed of a warm body next to hers and she turned into that warmth in the night. Strong arms enfolded her, pulled her in, and she cozied up to the welcome heat and the intimacy their criss-crossed limbs kindled. She dreamed of little else but the arms wrapped around her back and the endearments whispered to her in the dark in a brogue from way across the pond.

Until morning, her consciousness didn't penetrate enough for her to realize that the man she dreamed of was without a doubt Gerald. And as she roused the following morning, at first she couldn't bring herself to care.

Then light hit her in the face and, with it, noise.

"Oy, lazy cheeks, out of bed."

"What the…" Squinting against the blinding sunlight, Olivia watched the figure next to the bed come into slow focus. She pulled a pillow over her head. *"Are you kidding me?"*

"Are you kidding *me?*" Gerald countered, tugging the pillow away. "It's past ten, and you're the one still abed. Knock up!"

"Knock…*what?* Do you even know what you're saying?"

Gerald tugged the corner of the sheet, but she had a death grip on it. "It means 'wake up.'"

"No, it means… Ugh, never mind." Olivia thought about whimpering but she settled for a growl. "It's *Sunday,* Gerald."

"There's coffee."

Throwing an arm over her head to block the obscene light, she shook her head. "You make godawful coffee."

"I had it sent over from the inn."

Oh, now he was playing dirty. Cursing, she lowered her arm. "If you're lying, I'll drive a rusty blade through your heart."

"Good morning to you, too." When she sat up, scowling, he handed her a mug. It was the only thing that could have saved him. And judging by the amused smirk on his face, he knew it.

"Damn you," she muttered before cupping her hands close around the mug and letting the heat sink into her bones. "You better have a frigging good reason for getting me out of bed this early on my day off."

"I couldn't have let you sleep the day away," he told her, earning another growl. Chuckling, he lifted her hand and brushed his lips over the inside of her wrist. "Rex and I have a surprise for you."

"If he chewed a pair of my shoes, you're replacing it," she mumbled, tugging her hand out of his grasp and scrubbing her tingling wrist over her sternum. "And buying me another pair. Just because." She began to follow Gerald from the room when she realized she was wearing nothing but a tank top and undies.

Sometime in the night, she must have gotten hot and pulled off the sweater and jeans she'd crawled into bed in after an unexpectedly long night at the tavern. Yep, there was her shirt. On the floor.

Gerald turned to her, saw her dilemma, and his eyes dropped to the clothes on the floor, too, cheeks coloring modestly.

The man blushed. How the hell was she supposed to resist him when he turned that sweet shade of pink in the face of her polka-dotted cheekies? "You could solve this problem really quickly by handing me that robe on the back of the door," she informed him.

"Right. Robe." His gaze skimmed over her in a deft once-over that she felt to the tips of her toes. Shivering pleasantly, she crossed her arms over her chest as he looked away, grabbed the robe and tossed it her way. He cleared his throat and added, "Carry on, then."

No, they had to *quit* carrying on like this before

she tugged his blushing, ridiculously cute bones back into her bed.

Shrugging the robe around her shoulders and tying it tight at her waist, she ignored the sparking heat she felt somewhere around the area of her womb. "So where's this surprise?"

His expression changed from blank to brisk, and he smiled anew. "Get dressed, Mrs. Leighton. We're going for a drive."

THE DAY WAS warm for November, so much so that Rex rode in the back of Olivia's old Ford as Gerald cruised through town. They bumped into some churchgoing traffic on Section Street so she directed him through back roads until they wound up on 98 again.

Gerald kept Chuck's tires on Alabama tarmac, letting the truck ramble past fields of late season crops. The beautiful spread of cotton snagged his attention. "I see why it's called 'Southern snow.'"

"Hmm?" Olivia, distracted, looked away from the passenger mirror where she'd been studying Rex. The dog was leaned over her side of the truck bed, the wind peeling the wool back from his eyes and mouth. She saw Gerald gesture to the cotton and said, "Oh. Yeah, cotton's about as close as we get to snow this far south of I-65."

"I'll take this over the real thing," Gerald told her. "I've always been one for a more Mediterranean climate. Even New England's a bit too cool for me this time of year."

"Huh." She picked up the thermos of coffee she'd insisted on bringing with them. "Well. You'd fit right in around here. That is, if you can stand country living. You're a city boy, aren't you?"

Gerald lifted a shoulder. "Growing up, I kind of straddled the line between city and country. Honestly, I think I'm more keen on country living. The wide-open spaces, the breathable air—"

She snorted. "Breathable air. If this was July, you'd be singing a different tune…with an oxygen tank. And a respirator. And down here, the word *country* usually brings to mind rednecks, hicks, hillbillies and the like."

Gerald pursed his lips, intrigued. "Can't say I've ever met a hick. Or a hillbilly, for that matter." He peered at her closely. "Are you a redneck, Olivia?"

She met his stare, then burst out laughing. "No need to wrinkle your nose up at me. *Redneck* doesn't imply *leprosy.*"

"But you *are* one?" he surmised.

"Maybe," she said with a short shrug. "I spent a good deal of my time in the country at my grandmother's while Mom and Dad worked late nights. She lived out on 181 in between Fairhope and Daphne, just south of Silverhill. When my grandfather was alive, they grew pecan trees, harvested them, then sold the pecans locally. If I had a nickel for every pecan I harvested alongside them, I'd be retired by now. Pawpaw even let me drive the tractor on occasion."

Gerald's lips twitched. He wondered if Olivia knew that while she reminisced about her country living that her vowels lengthened and the bottom dropped out of her *o*'s, making her sound very much like a country bumpkin. "Is it still there? Their acreage?"

"Yes," Olivia said. "Though the house has survived better than the pecan grove and Birdie's garden. The land's gone wild, overrun with weeds and vermin. My parents and I only go out there on occasion to pick up a few pecans and carry them back to Briar. She uses them for holiday cooking and baking. It just isn't the same without Birdie. She lived there a good fifteen years after my grandfather passed."

"You loved her," Gerald noted. He could hear bittersweet nostalgia and a thread of grief on her voice. "Very much."

Olivia shrugged again. "She's been gone a long time. Eight years now."

"What do you say we go there?" At the lift of her head, he added, "To the house on 181. Sounds like the right place for Rex to stretch his legs and explore. I brought us some sandwiches. We can picnic in the pecan grove and you can tell me more about your childhood there."

She scrunched her nose up. "You wanna go to my grandparents' house?"

"Why not?" he challenged. "Is it too painful?"

"No, I just…" She nodded to the picnic basket between them. "It looks like you had plans."

"My plan was to get us both out of your apartment for a day," Gerald told her. "And perhaps find a nice picnic spot. I've driven us a fair distance from home and now it sounds like I've found us a good place to picnic. What say you, Liv?"

Still a bit hesitant, she lifted her hands. "It'll probably bore you to death, but if you're so determined, be my guest."

"Excellent," Gerald said with a grin. "Can you navigate?"

She rolled her eyes. "What kind of question is that? I know these back roads like the back of my hand. Turn left up ahead. That'll take us back toward 181. Just watch your speed and keep Chuck between the lines, will ya?"

They bickered a bit along the way. He chastised her fondly over her directions and she poked fun at his driving. It struck him not for the first time that he was seeing more and more glimpses of coupledom between them. Finally, she told him to turn off 181 onto a narrow two-lane road. Already he could see pecan trees on either side, impressive sentinels gathered together in their shady groves of overgrown brush. From the bed of the truck, Rex barked.

"Squirrels," Olivia explained. "They've taken

over. If we're not careful, they might gang up and carry Rex off."

Gerald chuckled. "That'd be a sight."

She directed him down the lane until the truck rumbled onto a single dirt track. Another hundred yards and the house came into view. The windows were boarded up and the shingles of the roof had faded a good bit, but it still looked like a fine house, built to last with its sturdy brick walls and a wide chimney thrusting through the roofline. Vines of all shapes and sizes slowly crept their way up the walls. As he parked and got out of the truck, he heard Olivia say, "Mind you don't fall into some kudzu. You'll disappear forever."

Gerald surveyed the house. It had a double-door entry. The mahogany panels still looked nice and smooth and welcoming. Light dappled nicely through the pecan trees around them, shining onto the vines—*kudzu,* as Olivia had called it—and what little of the garden had survived it. To the left, there was another Ford truck, this one from the '50s. It was faded and rusted and the kudzu had hidden most of it from view, but what little of the hood was still intact showed a few lasting specks of the red it had once been.

"I can see you here," Gerald mused as he watched Olivia walk from the truck, Rex's leash in hand. The dog strained at the end of it, yanking her toward a patch of kudzu. Something rustled inside it and the dog tugged the leash out of her hands and dived headlong into the vines.

She rubbed her hands together where the leash had scraped against her palms and looked around. "I had the run of this place, back when Birdie and Pawpaw were still here. I ran and climbed until dark and I was forced to go back inside. Birdie would have something yummy on the stove and Pawpaw would be kicked back in his chair by the fireplace with a newspaper. I'd curl up in his lap and we'd read the obituaries." At Gerald's frown, she gave him a small smile. "It was nice actually. It was about acknowledging those who'd passed on and the lives they led."

The smile stayed on her face, warming her expression. Gerald watched as she hugged herself. Before he could wrap her in his arms, she turned and walked toward Rex, who was leaping gleefully through the kudzu like a white-wooled porpoise.

"Was your grandfather the carpenter who crafted the walls of the tavern?"

She nodded, pointing behind the house. "His wood shop was back that way. In the latter years when the arthritis took over, he mostly worked with models—trains, planes, automobiles. He had a booth at the Arts & Crafts Festival in Fairhope every year and he'd sell the models to youngsters."

"He was a skilled man, and a kindly one, it seems," Gerald guessed.

"Yes. You don't get that a lot anymore," she murmured as they strolled through what had been her Birdie's garden. "Not in my experience."

Gerald was caught up in the overgrown world, its mysticism and enchantment. Yes, he could see Olivia here, and, strangely enough, he could see himself here, too. "No one's lived here since Birdie's passing?"

She looked around again as the wind gusted through the high limbs of the trees. "Just the squirrels. Why?"

"No reason," he said thoughtfully, turning to walk between two wooden pillars attached to bird-feeders above. The wood shop was just ahead, the roof caved in but the walls still intact. Before he could venture farther, however, Olivia shouted, "Don't move!"

Gerald stopped short, his heart banging against his chest. Looking up from the feet he'd been focused on to avoid tripping over kudzu, he saw the giant, neon spider inches away from his face and stumbled back, arms milling. "Jesus H. Christ! What the bollocks is that?"

"Banana spider," she noted, laying a hand on his shoulder to balance him. "Big one."

"Mother of God," he muttered, lips numbing as he watched the spider's spindly legs skitter up a length of its web.

"Calm down, she won't hurt you," Olivia told him. "But let's not mess up her web. It's pretty."

He stared, aghast, at his wife and the spider in

turn as the former took his hand and led him away. "You all right?" she asked.

Gerald swiped his hand over the top of his head. "Feel all spidery—like it's on me."

She pressed her lips to hide a smile. It didn't work. "Afraid of spiders much?"

"Only when it comes down to giant, mutant spiders the size of my godforsaken fist. That thing should be in a laboratory somewhere."

"They're pretty common around here. Particularly in wooded areas."

"Forget what I said about living in the country. Christ." Seeing an oak tree larger than all the rest ahead, Gerald tugged on her hand. There was a tire swing attached to one of the high thick knotted arms. "What's this?" he asked as he spied something carved into the trunk. It was a large heart with the initials *O* and *W* twined in the middle. "Who do the initials stand for?" he asked.

"Olivia and Ward," she told him. "My grandparents. They must have carved it sometime in the '50s when they first bought the place."

"I thought your grandmother's name was Birdie."

"That's what everyone called her. She was smallish—she had bird bones so she was always cold come winter. Her mama nicknamed her Birdie. It stuck."

"You were named for her."

She nodded. "Olivia Rose. Olivia for Birdie, Rose for my mother, Rosa, Birdie's daughter."

"Olivia Rose," Gerald said. Looking her over, he beamed. There could be no other name for her. He wanted to hold her here on her family's land, underneath the limbs of the tree the grandparents she had loved so much had carved their initials into. "Come here, Olivia Rose," he said as he drew her into his arms.

She leaned back in his embrace with a wary sigh. "I don't see Rex. There's a creek just up the way. There might be cottonmouths—"

"You can tell me what a cottonmouth is later," he said, banding his arms doubly around her waist, so their navels pressed together. The scent of vanilla drew him. He lowered his lips to nibble the spot below her ear and indulged himself as he hadn't been able to before, either from her resistance or his own. "If it's anything like a banana spider, though, you might have to spare me," he murmured against the warmth of her skin.

"A cottonmouth's a snake. The bad kind."

"Is there a good kind?"

Olivia snorted, but sounded a bit breathless nonetheless. "You're right about one thing. You'd be hopeless living in the country."

Gerald turned his attention to the space of her shoulder, revealed by the wide-necked cowl sweater she had chosen to wear. "Hold still, love," he said in a soft, low voice, "and put your arms around me."

"Gerald—"

"No, hold me," he insisted. "I'm still shaken from the near-miss with the mutant."

It made her laugh. She considered him, searching his face, then finally gave in and lifted her arms around his neck. Before she could protest, he planted his lips on hers.

No sooner had he kissed her than the wind picked up and swept through the grove. The limbs of the tree above creaked. The leaves that littered the ground around them stirred into a makeshift tornado. The tire swing swayed back and forth.

"Blimey," Gerald said, lifting his chin to the top of her head as he watched the spectacle. "It's like someone's trying to tell us something."

Olivia frowned at the branches tossing around above them. "Or knock us over."

On the wind came the strong smell of wood smoke. "Do you smell that?"

Olivia lifted her nose to the air and he watched her brows lift in surprise. "Smells like…cigars. And lavender." A shiver went through her.

Gerald tightened his arms around her. "Okay?"

"Yeah." She hunched further into his embrace. "Just…weird feeling, is all."

"Bad?" he asked, raising a questioning brow.

She shook her head but said nothing more.

He held her closer, spreading his arms over her back as he turned his face into her hair. The wind lifted high for a moment before everything began to settle gradually back down to earth.

She breathed a sigh. He felt it move through her more than heard it. "I'm glad that's over."

The skin around her mouth looked a touch white. Framing her face in his hands, Gerald tipped her chin up until her eyes met his. "Are you sure you're all right?"

"I'm fine. It's just…for a moment, I thought I heard…something."

"What was it?" he asked, rubbing his hands down the length of her spine in hopes of soothing the unsettled look in her eyes, the stiff rise of her shoulders.

Olivia opened her mouth to answer. Nothing escaped. Doubt flared to life in her eyes as she searched his. Finally, she pushed out a ragged breath and, with it, words. "I thought—"

Rex's bark startled them. Gerald jerked in reaction and Olivia damn near came off her feet. He settled his hands on her shoulders as he turned his head to watch the dog race toward them. "Where have you been?" He frowned. "What's that in your mouth?"

"Oh, God," Olivia groaned, hand coming up to shield her nose with her sweater's cowl as Rex laid the animal at their feet. "It's an opossum."

Gerald gaped as Rex bounced happily to show off his prize. *You killed an opossum?*

Olivia gagged and took several steps back. "Nope. That one's been dead for a while. And he's been rolling in it, from the looks of him."

The smell overwhelmed Gerald and he took a step away, too. "Rex, where did you find that?"

"Probably from the road." Olivia shook her head. "He's just found himself some Alabama roadkill and tried to pass it off as his own."

"Rex," Gerald groaned, shaking his head. "You're going to need a bath. *Two* baths."

"Yeah," Olivia said as she turned and traipsed back toward the truck. "Good luck with that."

Gerald watched her go, mouth firming into a scowl. She hadn't got around to telling him what had unsettled her.

Rex drew his attention by plopping down on his wide rump and beating the leaves proudly with his tail. Gerald ran his hand over his face when the dog only smiled at him. "Come on with you," Gerald said, motioning in the direction Olivia had gone. "Let's get you home. Nope, no," he instructed when Rex looked back at the opossum. "Leave the road-kill. Just…leave it.

CHAPTER SIXTEEN

"HE JUST HAULED me out of bed for a day schlepping in the country. It was barbaric."

Adrian rolled her eyes. "Oh, would you please stop bitching?"

Olivia stopped pacing the flower shop long enough to turn a baleful eye on her. "Excuse me?"

"You heard me." Adrian shot back, crowning a large centerpiece with a long stem of purple iris. "For the last thirty minutes, you've done nothing but complain because the man took you on a picnic. To your grandparents' house. Where he kissed you under their favorite tree where they'd carved their initials. Your bosoms should still be heaving, for Christ's sake."

Olivia, caught between amusement and frustration, shook her head. "Did you really just use the word *bosoms*?"

"Your grumbling has caused my vocabulary to sink that low, yes," Adrian replied.

"Sorry I'm late," Briar said, rushing in from next door with Cole on her heels. "What's going on?"

Olivia eyed the two of them, suspicious. "Why are you out of breath?"

"Um, we ran," Cole told her blandly. He held up his cell phone. "You texted 'EMERGENCY.'"

Adrian snorted. "If this is an emergency, I'm Pittypat Hamilton."

"Put a cork in it, Adrian," Olivia retorted. She whirled on the other two. "And if you want to be a good liar, Briar shouldn't have buttoned her shirt wrong."

"What?" Distressed, Briar looked down at her silk blouse and saw that she'd missed the top two buttons. "Oh, God. No wonder Mr. and Mrs. Higgins looked so surprised to see me." Turning away, she fumbled with the pearly snaps.

Adrian shook her head at Cole's sheepish grin as he helped his wife with her buttons. "Well…looks like Briar's out of the club."

"Who started a club?" Roxie wanted to know, clacking in on three-inch pumps. "And what did I miss?"

Adrian gestured their way with the sprig of baby's breath in her hand. "Olivia's bitching, and Briar had sex."

Roxie gasped, eyes brightening on the couple trying not to look embarrassed in the corner. "You *hussy!*" she shrieked, then delightedly clapped her hands in celebration.

As Briar fumbled for something to say, Cole

raised a hand. "Permission to curl up and die now?" he asked.

"Why are you ashamed?" Olivia wanted to know. "You had sex. Have a cigar!"

Briar, agitated, raised her voice to be heard. "Listen, the baby's got about fifteen minutes left on her nap and, yes, we haven't exactly been baking cookies since she's been out. So can somebody please tell us what the fuss is all about so we can get back to it?"

Everyone rounded on her in surprise. Cole cleared his throat, beaming as he lifted a loving hand to the small of her back, tugging her close.

Olivia walked to her cousin and threw her arms around her.

Briar returned the tight hug but muttered softly, "What's wrong, Liv? You're scaring me."

"I'm just so proud. Because I love you. And you," she added, glancing at Cole. "I'm sorry I cut into your sexy time."

Briar eyed Adrian over Olivia's shoulder. "No really. What's going on?" Briar asked.

Adrian stopped arranging flowers and caught Olivia's eyes as she turned back to the room. "You're not upset because Gerald carried you off to your grandmother's house, are you?"

"No," Olivia said with a sigh. "While we were there something weird happened. We were…"

While Olivia sought the right words, Roxie smiled, reading her thoroughly. "Canoodling?"

Olivia frowned. "Something like that." Becoming impatient when they all looked pleased at the news, she blew out a breath. "I took your advice, all right? I indulged him. We had a moment—a nice moment."

"Aw," Roxie said, placing a hand on her heart.

Olivia chose to ignore that. "Anyway, we were underneath the tree where I used to swing. The one with Birdie and Pawpaw's initials, and the wind picked up. I mean, it really started blowing."

Cole's eyes narrowed. "I don't remember it being windy yesterday."

"It wasn't," Olivia pointed out. "Maybe the occasional breeze, but not like this. This was like tropical storm wind…out of nowhere. And it just kind of swirled around us. At first it felt like it would knock us over. Then…I don't know. Then it seemed more like it was pushing us together…."

Briar's eyes were riddled with confusion. "What are you saying, Liv?"

Olivia ran her hands through her hair. "I don't know. It was weird, okay? And it got even weirder. Gerald said he smelled wood smoke. There hasn't been smoke in the chimney of Birdie's house since she died. Well, before that even because she spent over a month in the hospital with pneumonia."

Briar nodded. "I remember. Eight years ago."

"Yeah," Olivia said. "And there aren't any more houses around there. Not for half a mile or more. It was all Birdie and Pawpaw's land for acres…."

"Still," Adrian considered, "a good wind can blow the smell of a fire for miles."

"That wasn't the weirdest thing," Olivia admitted after some hesitation. "Gerald was the one who smelled the wood smoke. Right after he said that, I sniffed the air, too, and it hit me. The scent of lavender." She looked to Briar again. "Birdie lined all the drawers in that house with lavender. She wore lavender perfume. She even grew lavender. Only it's all dead now." When her cousin nodded slowly, Olivia continued. "And then, right on top of the lavender came the smell of cheroot. Pawpaw smoked one cigar every evening after dinner. He'd go out to the wood shop and I'd often be watching him tinker with whatever he was carving with those rough, working hands when Mom or Dad came to pick me up."

Adrian squinted. "Couldn't this have been a figment of your imagination, Liv?"

Olivia lifted her arms. "I don't have an imagination like that. I know the smell of lavender and cheroot. I remember them all too well. But there's a difference between remembering and smelling. And then, I swear to God, I heard her laugh. Birdie's laugh. That high, almost witchy cackle that isn't like anyone else's. It was faint, but I heard it. Like she was sitting on the front porch drinking her tea, watching us struggle with each other…."

"Spooky," Roxie whispered, shivering a bit.

"Yeah," Olivia nodded, rubbing her hands over

her upper arms. "I've been out to their house every year since they've been gone and I've never had an experience like that. But I got the strangest feeling…an impression, I guess. Gerald said it was like someone was trying to tell us something, and I think he was right. I think Birdie—maybe her and Pawpaw both—was there. She was trying to tell us something."

"Both of you?" Roxie asked. Her face softened. "Oh, so sweet…."

Olivia sighed, looking at Adrian. "Go on. Tell Roxie her bosoms are heaving."

"Bosoms?" Cole echoed.

Briar scanned Olivia's face slowly, looking for something more. "What do you think Birdie was trying to say?" she asked in a quiet voice.

"I don't know," Olivia lied.

"Yes, you do," Briar said after a beat. And she smiled. "Birdie used to come to the inn all the time," she told Cole. "She'd sit on the front porch and chat up the guests. She was a pretty good judge of character. She was blunt, too, and funny as all get-out."

"Sounds familiar," Cole muttered, offering Olivia a small, consoling smile.

Briar considered for a moment, her own grin deepening. "Birdie would have loved Gerald."

Olivia caught herself hugging herself. It was warm in Adrian's shop but, still, she was chilled to the bone and had been since she and Gerald left the pecan grove. "I can't…I can't make myself believe that she actually conjured all that mess just to prove a point."

"What point?" Adrian asked.

Frowning, Olivia paced. "Damn it. When I was little, she said a man would come along. She said he would sweep me off my feet when I least expected it. She said I would meet my match and I'd be all the happier for it."

Roxie tapped her fingers to her mouth. "Would that be considered wisdom or foresight?"

"I met Birdie once," Adrian told them. "She informed me very matter-of-factly that I would marry a man with blue eyes, a Cessna and the mark of a pirate."

Olivia lifted a hand in a sweeping gesture, relieved. "Thank you, Adrian. You've just proven that foresight had little to do with it—more like gin and Splenda." Sighing, she rubbed her hands together to warm them. "Maybe I'm overanalyzing the whole thing. Maybe what's between Gerald and me is making me as batty as Birdie was at times. That's it." She nodded her decision. "I'm going to ask him to leave."

"What?" Briar asked, alarmed. "That's the exact opposite of what this experience should have taught you."

"It's the end of the three weeks," Olivia pointed out. "We had a wager. He's a man of his word. He'll go if I ask him to."

Before Briar could argue with her, a keening wa
went up through the room. Briar reached into he
pocket and produced a baby monitor. "She's up,
she said to Cole.

"I'll take care of her," he offered and lowered hi
lips to her cheek and grazed it with a tender kiss
"You take care of this," he added. Frowning back a
Olivia, he moved around his wife toward the doo
"Good luck, Liv."

"Don't ask him to leave." When Olivia gape
at Adrian in horror, the latter lifted her hands i
defense. "He told Kyle he would bring Rex to th
Lighting of the Trees Festival. He's been telling hi
friends about nothing else all week."

Olivia resisted the urge to tug at the ends of he
hair. "He told…" She trailed off, took a deep, sta
bilizing breath. "See? This is exactly what I didn
want. He's making plans to *stay*."

"Liv…" Briar scoffed as Olivia barreled for th
door. "Where are you going?"

"I'm ending this, right damn now," Olivia tol
her, pushing through the shop's door. The bells ra
tled after her as she tore out of the shop, workin
herself up to a fine, good tirade.

GERALD WAS LOST—in one of the best possible way.
The world of Rex Flynn and the enduring minc
set of his favorite character had taken him away, hi
imagination painting a vivid place he knew onl
existed in his mind and the hearts of his reader:

In moments like these, it seemed so tangible that it was him walking in Rex's shoes through the mud on the familiar trek to the village in the Highlands where his bonny lass dwelled. Time gave them so little of the moments together that defined all the rest. But they were worth waiting for. Worth dying for.

Of course, before Gerald's wary time-traveler could reach his lover, he would be thwarted by a violent band of the laird's henchmen. That was the nature of conflict, which was fundamental to any well-told tale.

Rex was pulling out his jewel-encrusted scabbard when the apartment door opened and slammed. Gerald's facial muscles twitched but his fingers continued dancing across the keys, too ingrained in the rhythm and beats of the scene to be foiled. Eyes glued to the screen, he barely heard the fall of boots on the kitchen floor or the sound of his name when a shadow fell over him.

"Gerald."

He grunted in reply as Rex parried the thrust of one of the clansmen's swords. The deadly clang of a swordfight echoed in Gerald's ears, drowning out all else. Five against one. There was no way Rex would make it out of this scuffle unscathed—

"Gerald!"

He blinked as the shout muffled the story's beat, the song of swords. Frustrated that they were slipping away along with the rhythm he'd set, he glanced up and saw Olivia's stony face. "It's you."

"Yeah, it's me," she snapped. "Who were you expecting?" When he only went back to typing, she planted her hands on her hips. "We need to talk."

"Now?" he asked absently, mind already reaching back into the story, tuning into the action rhythm and beats again. They didn't come as easily as he'd have liked, though. He needed fuel. Desperate, he picked up his coffee cup and thrust it at her.

She jerked back to keep from getting clocked in the face by one of her own ceramic mugs.

"How long have you been sitting here?" she asked.

Finally he looked up and found Olivia's face flushed as red as a beet and her green eyes were flashing as she obviously surveyed his appearance.

He ran his tongue over his top teeth, then caught it as concentration became more difficult to manage. If he could just get to the part where Rex was forced to use his time-warping gift, the excruciating ability that shifted his soul from one body to another's, in order to escape a severed head or sword through the heart, Gerald could give Olivia all his attention. But not just yet....

"Have you eaten anything at all since I left?"

Silence but for the rushed clatter of keys and the battle sequence raging in his head.

She threw her arms out. "Say something, for Christ's sake!"

"Tea."

She let out a dangerous sound that made Rex, the wolfhound, jump in his sleep under the table. "I'm not your damned maid!"

"For the love of God, woman!" Her shouting had chased the time-traveler Rex Flynn and all the deadly clansmen far away from the Highland hills and—farther—out of his subconscious. Curling his fingers into his palm, Gerald calmed himself and turned to her. "Olivia, I've been running on nothing but adrenaline for hours. I need caffeine. Food. Peace and quiet for just another half hour. Is that too much to bloody ask for?"

Olivia's irises had heated to raging, boiling sea foam. A lesser man might have quavered, but Gerald was too far beyond his usual level of exasperation for that murderous, slightly mad gaze to faze him.

Without rewarding his spiel with so much as a word, she snatched the mug from his hand and stomped toward the counter like an ill-mannered child. Relieved and not a little bit flustered, he blew out a breath and raked a hand through his mussed hair.

He read over his last paragraph, trying to get a grasp of where he'd left off. Before he could do more than lay his fingers over the notebook keys, however, Olivia was standing over him again.

"Thank you," he said, reaching up to take the mug from her hand.

Gerald hadn't lifted his but a few inches when she tipped the mug upside down. A cold torrent of water from the new teakettle he'd warmed hours ago poured over his lap. He leaped up with a yelp, his chair crashing to the floor. Rex barked out of sleep, growling fiercely in his throat at the sudden racket.

Gerald turned shocked eyes on Olivia's smug face. "Are you off your trolley?"

"Who are you to talk to me like that?" she demanded to know.

"Like *what?*"

Eyes firing again, she closed the gap between them, going toe-to-toe with him. She might have been a mere five-two, but she was a force to be reckoned with. One that thundered in his blood, caused it to swirl and sing. "Like I'm just a pawn! Like you can move me left, right, front, back, center—wherever it is you want me! Wherever's most convenient for you!"

"You are off your trolley," he confirmed with a decisive nod. "Crazy. Mad. Bonkers. I haven't the faintest idea what you're talking about. Rex, leave off barking!"

Rex subsided and ducked back underneath the table, but Olivia refused to back down. "No, you wouldn't, would you? You're too busy pounding at your computer to notice the slightest bit of what's happening around you."

Didn't she think he wanted to know what the

bloody hell was going on inside her? He'd done everything he knew to get a handle on her thoughts, to know what it was that troubled her so. He'd had enough. His voice rose to the same wall-rumbling level as hers. "You leave me to guess what's going on inside your heart because you haven't got it in you to tell me. I've had enough, Liv! Tell me, what will it take to ever figure you out because I've hit every block I possibly could trying to find what it is you need from me."

After a moment of taut silence, her lips finally came together on the words, "What I need *from you?*" Letting out a ragged breath, she threw her hands up. In that moment he saw just how fragile, how close to breakage, she really was, and it shook him to the core. "Gerald…you're perfect. You're…." She lowered her eyes, and he thought he caught a wet gleam in them. "You're…everything that I never dreamed about before because men like you don't exist. Maybe buried in Rex Flynn books, but not out here in the real world. The fact that you do exist makes me more afraid than I've ever been because a lot of the time you look at me like I see you. And I'm not perfect. I'm so far from perfect, Gerald, there's probably no redeeming me. You need to know that."

His hands were in her hair, framing her face and lifting it to his. When she closed her eyes, he sucked in a frustrated breath. "Look at me, Liv." He said in a rigid voice that made her lids lift, her eyes focusing on his. "Whatever you think you've done, whatever's made you feel so inadequate, it's time to let it go. You've done absolutely nothing to make me believe you are anything less than what I want—what I need."

She began to shake her head in denial, but he stopped her. "No," he said firmly. Running a thumb over her full bottom lip, he shook his own head and lowered his mouth to within an inch of hers. "No," he said again before covering her lips with his in a kiss that pounded at the depths of his soul.

Her mouth opened to his, her hands coming up to fist in the hair that had begun to grow over the nape of his neck. It was the first time she had received him this way, mouth to mouth, and it was potent. She smelled of the fresh, windy shore he walked by day. Need beat in his blood. He wrapped her in the hard circle of his arms. To let go might have killed him.

And she didn't let go as she had all the times before; she didn't back away from the live wire that was between them…that had been there all along. Olivia came alive against him, and suddenly he was the one holding on for dear life. She unlocked, finally giving way to the passionate woman he'd sensed within her all this time.

As his mouth tangoed with hers, lips, tongue and teeth moving in a primitive dance, that sound that had so devastated him before lifted from her throat, uninhibited. He snarled at the full-hearted moan of well-pleased female, hands moving in a possessive sweep from her face over her shoulders and down the front of her body. She keened again, back arching as she moved with the surge of his slow, full caress.

His hands dipped into her waist, then rose and fell with the sweet curve of her hips. Lower, he spread his fingers until they found the backs of her thighs. Then, mouth still locked, rising, falling over hers, he bent her legs until they left the floor and her arms circled his neck for support. Finally answering the urge that he'd held off more and more reluctantly with each passing day, he lowered her to the kitchen floor.

Pillowing the back of her head with his hand, he moved the other to cup her cheek and easily lost himself in her kiss. Her thighs cradled his hips and he surged against her in one upward motion that snagged his breath. Hers rushed across his face along with an agreeing hum. The sounds she made alone could drive a man to insanity. Combined with the devastating kiss and curvaceous body... For the first time in his life, Gerald knew why Paris had risked war and all damnation for Helen of Troy. It was here, right here.

Her hands skimmed his shoulder blades, moving down over his back. Her touch found skin as they burrowed beneath his shirt. If he'd had half a mind, he'd have peeled it off so her hands were free to roam wherever they liked. But that would require lifting his mouth from hers. Not yet, he thought. Maybe not ever....

She arched up to him, head falling back as he answered the rising wave of her body with the mirroring surge of his own. The heat radiating from their center hastened to flashpoint. Judging by her gaze that was fused to his, stripped of anything but undiluted need, he'd driven his point home. He wanted her, needed her....

"No," she said suddenly, tensing. "No. This isn't... I don't want this."

"The bloody hell you don't," he mumbled, grasping her chin to bring her mouth back to his. "Stop fighting and kiss me."

"No," she said again, pushing him back. "I came here to tell you to go. To leave. Three weeks are over. You lost."

He let out a panting laugh. "You think this isn't working? That it won't? Look at us, Liv. Look where we are. Think where we were yesterday at Birdie's."

She shook her head hard. "Don't talk about Birdie. Don't. And as for this..." She took several careful breaths, closed her eyes. "We've been stuck in this apartment together for too long. It's sexual tension. If we slept together, it'd be gone and there'd be nothing left."

"I have half a mind to prove you wrong on that score," he said, his voice grating.

"Why don't you, Shakespeare?" she challenged. "Take me. I'm yours."

As he scanned her face and the new wager behind it, desire simmering in his blood and threatening to go on a tear inside him if he didn't appease it, he made a noise in his throat. He was sorely tempted to take her up on her challenge.

Fighting it, he rolled off her and dragged himself to his feet. He took a moment to calm himself, pacing as he straightened his clothes and combed his hair back from his brow. "I'm not one of your tavern regulars, Olivia Rose. I'm not going to be another flash in the pan gone the next morning." He glanced back at her as she rose to her feet slowly. He studied the desperation hiding underneath the tension on her face. "And you know it, don't you? That's why you came here to tell me to go. Because you're starting to feel, to need. Because I'm starting to make a believer out of you." When she opened her mouth to argue, he saw the weary way she did so and stopped her, shaking his head. "I won't go, love. Not that easily."

"It's over," she said, spreading her hands in a helpless gesture. "The three weeks. I gave them to you."

He frowned. "Then I'll go back to the inn. And if by the end of this week, you still want the divorce, I'll serve you the papers."

"That wasn't our agreement."

"It is now," he determined and walked toward the bedroom to pack his things.

She made a frustrated noise. "How long are you going to drag this out? How long are you going to drive me crazy?"

"As long as it takes," he said over his shoulder. "It won't be long now anyway," he added in a promising undertone.

CHAPTER SEVENTEEN

"ANY DOG OVER twenty pounds should ride in the bed of a truck," Olivia argued, bracing her elbow on the ledge of Chuck's driver's side window. "It's just common sense."

Gerald, riding in the tight bucket seat with his knees drawn up to his chest and his elbow digging into her ribs, grinned. "Rex is special. And it's cold. Come on, look how happy he is."

She slid her narrowed gaze from the windshield, around Gerald to the gigantic canine in the passenger seat—or rather the canine's rump. The rest of the dog was hanging out the passenger window, tongue flapping in the wind like a wet, red streamer. "People are pointing and laughing."

Gerald laughed himself. "Come now, love. He's behaving himself."

"He's barking at cars, Gerald."

The chuckle deepened and he nudged his arm out from between them to lay it across the back of her seat. His hand came to rest warm on her left shoulder, thumb smoothing across her collarbone. In a matter of seconds, her body went from chilled

by the open window and the crisp bite of November
air to flashing hot. The good humor emanating off
of Gerald was contagious. Still, she couldn't shake
the dregs of the argument and sexual haze they'd
gotten good and submerged in only days before.

He'd moved back into the inn. He and Rex both.
And she'd gone four days without him there when
she came home to her apartment, though they'd
run into each other plenty. He came to the tavern
most nights. He was there for breakfast at Briar's
in the morning, waiting for her in the kitchen with
a mug of coffee ready when she came in through
the screen door.

She wouldn't admit that she missed him. She
wouldn't admit that the space of her apartment
seemed to yawn and echo without him and Rex.
She sure as hell wouldn't admit that she missed
finding his warmth there in the night when she
needed it in her dreams....

He wanted another week. Well, fine, she was
giving him another week, especially now that he'd
moved out and she could tell herself it was easier.
He didn't have to know she hadn't stopped thinking about him.

The Lighting of the Trees Festival took place
in downtown Fairhope every November. Locals
and late-season tourists gathered in the square
to watch the trees that lined the streets come to
life with holiday lights. It did well to ring in the
Thanksgiving and Christmas season, even for the

humbugs among them. Olivia felt fairly humbug herself. Even though she'd been forced to ride into town with Gerald and Rex because the others had "conveniently" left early for the festivities, she was looking forward to tonight's distraction.

They managed to find a parking spot not too far from the central hub of activity in the middle of town. The streetlights and storefronts were dimmed to make way for the vivid display. As Rex tugged Gerald onward by way of the leash and Olivia practically jogged to keep up, they neared the platform where the mayor, his family and five local Magnolia Trail Maids would ring in the hour. The sound of Christmas carols played by the local high school jazz band grew louder as they joined the throng of people in the square.

Olivia stood on tiptoe to scan faces. "I told Briar we'd meet them by the old clock."

"Over there?" Gerald asked, pointing from his tall vantage. "I think I see Kyle and his pint-size crew of miscreants."

Just as they found the small pack of boys near the corner, Kyle's voice pealed over the crowd and music. "Rex!" he cried, running toward them.

"Don't you run farther than I can see you, Kyle Zachariah Carlton!" Adrian shouted after him. She subsided as her eyes fell on the dog and the couple tagging along behind. "Oh, hi, guys. Join the party."

"We have hot chocolate," Roxie tempted, holding up a foam cup in one gloved hand. The other was tucked in the elbow of a staid man in a tweed jacket. "Gerald, I don't think you've met my fiancé, Richard Levy."

"Mr. Leighton," Richard said, reaching out to take Gerald's hand. "I enjoy your work."

"Thank you." Gerald shook, nodding his head at the man. "You're a lucky man," he said, smiling at Roxie who lifted her hot chocolate in toast. He glanced around at Adrian. "How are *you* this evening?" he asked her, relinquishing the dog's leash to Kyle.

"Cold," she said, hugging her scarf closer around her neck. "The weatherman said nothing about a stiff breeze."

"Aye, it's blowing tonight, isn't it?" Kyle and the other boys caught Gerald's attention. "Careful, lads. Keep a steady grip. Rex will drag you ten blocks if he finds something interesting enough to chase." He chuckled, turning back to the circle of adults as the young group bent down to Rex's level to lavish him with attention. "He's in heaven."

"The kid or the dog?" Olivia ventured.

"Both," Adrian said, smiling as she took a sip of her own hot chocolate. "Thanks for bringing him."

"I wouldn't have it any other way," Gerald told her. "Neither would Rexie boy."

"Where're Briar and Cole?" Olivia asked, searching the crowd.

"They wanted to keep Harmony out of the cold for as long as possible," Adrian explained.

"What's all this?" Gerald asked, nodding toward a girl dressed in a blue ruffled frock and matching bonnet.

"Trail maids," Olivia told him. At his creased brow, she sighed. "It's just one of the oddities of the South. They're pageant girls. They win scholarships, dress up like Scarlett O'Hara and ride in parades and such."

"Fascinating," he muttered. He glanced from the dress to Olivia with amusement. "Ah, did you ever—"

"No," she answered before he could suggest such a thing. "I was too busy stealing bases to trouble myself."

"And stealing hearts," Gerald added with a smirk, making her roll her eyes in response.

"I was a trail maid," Roxie piped up.

"Of course you were," Olivia said, the corner of her mouth quirking up.

"Were you now?" Gerald asked, brows raised in interest.

"Yellow," Roxie boasted, gazing at the maids with whimsy. Looking to Olivia, she added, "And the scholarship money got me through my freshman year of college."

"And you, Adrian?" Gerald asked.

Adrian let out a sour laugh. "Yeah, right. The truant officer was a regular visitor to my parents' door. I'm pretty sure I would've been banned by pageant officials. My mother was one, though." She wrinkled her nose. "Green, just like her disposition."

Gerald chuckled. His eyes lit on someone over Olivia's shoulder. "Ah, here are the Savitts now."

Olivia turned to watch them weave their way through the crowd, Cole pushing Harmony in a stroller bedecked with holly and twinkly lights. "Aren't you festive?" Olivia noted, eyeing his reindeer antlers.

"Briar tried to get me to wear the ones that lit up," Cole admitted. "I had to put my foot down."

Briar, wearing a long pointed elf's hat that drooped over her shoulder, reached up and straightened the antlers. "It's for your daughter," she reminded him, grinning widely at Harmony who was dressed in a fleece red-and-white-striped head-to-toe one-piece complete with Santa hat. "And you know you don't mind this nearly as much as the Peter Pan costume for Halloween."

Cole grimaced. "Yeah, I've blocked that one out."

Olivia smirked. "The rest of us certainly haven't."

"Oh, yeah," Adrian remembered with a teasing grin. "You look great in tights. I have the pictures to prove it."

Cole muttered something dark under his breath when feedback from the speakers surrounding the stage drew their attention. There the trail maids were beginning to squeeze in with the adolescent trumpet and saxophone players, and the mayor and his family. "Looks like they're about to get this show on the road," Cole said.

"Let's hold her up so she can see," Briar suggested, reaching down to unlatch the stroller restraints from Harmony's waist.

As Cole lifted Harmony, Olivia noticed that the chill in the air had gone down significantly. Tucked underneath Gerald's arm and against the long line of his torso, she forgot all about the winter's chill. She felt as cozy as she would curled up to him in front of a big, roaring fire. She should've shrugged out of his grasp but couldn't bring herself to do it. Not so much because she disliked the cold, but because she liked him this close—as much as she hated to admit it.

The scent of his aftershave brought to mind brandy and libraries. She resisted the urge to turn her nose into the lapel of his long black wool jacket and sniff like a hound in heat. Looking down, she saw her fingertips had somehow found their way into the hip pocket of the jacket. She frowned. *How did that happen?*

She jerked like the guilty when the clock over their heads chimed the hour. Soothing, his other arm came around her and suddenly she found herself right up against him, her nose pressed into that lapel she'd been so determined to avoid. For days, she'd tried not to think about how solid he was. Or how his embrace seemed to fold her in like eggs

in cake batter until they were one and the same—
a bunch of messy ingredients that, once combined,
made something delicious.

Finger-lickin' good, as her Birdie had once said.
At the time, she hadn't been describing cake assem-
bly...but a man jogging shirtless down the street
in front of the tavern. She'd waited for that jogger
on the inn's porch with a pitcher of Hanna's sweet
tea and a folding fan every afternoon. Birdie was a
happily married woman for fifty-some-odd years,
but she would be the first to admit that looking at
ripped men in running shorts never hurt anybody.

Olivia had to admit the memory was one of the
reasons she loved to run so much. Every time she
saw a hot man in running shorts, she had a good
laugh on Birdie's behalf.

Briar had been right about one thing, Olivia
mused, Birdie would have loved Gerald Leighton.
From his amazing books to his *finger-lickin' good*
cooking to his collegiate charm and, maybe especially, his tight butt. Her approval rating would
have been a solid ten.

Olivia shook her head. Birdie's opinion of Gerald didn't matter. The woman was long gone.
Olivia might have thought she'd heard her grandmother's laugh tinkering away on the wind at the
pecan grove. But over the past few days, she had
chalked it up to lunacy. The strange wind sweeping through the grove had spooked her and spurred
on her imagination.

True, she hadn't known her imagination could be that vivid. But it was the only logical explanation....

Birdie and Pawpaw were gone. As Gerald would be soon.

The dual thoughts coated her in regret. A grim veil of sadness fell over her.

Frowning, she caught herself nestling farther into Gerald's chest, all but crawling inside his jacket, as the crowd joined the mayor's countdown. His arms tightened as if knowing she needed the comfort of the close embrace. Lifting her face from his chest, Olivia looked out over the square to the trimmed Bradford pear trees lining the streets.

A united, pleasured cry lifted from the crowd as the square suddenly filled with festive, golden light. Gerald expelled a surprised, "Blimey." Olivia couldn't help but watch the lights bathe his features as he scanned the illuminated square. "Incredible," he breathed with a shake of his head, smile curving his lips.

Again unable to help herself, she wound her arms around his waist. He glanced down at her, smile widening until the dimples and laugh lines dug in and his eyes warmed until she felt steeped in their depths.

His hands swept from her back to her shoulders, then down her arms and back up. "You're shivering. Are you cold?"

"Mmm…hmm? Cold?" She searched for a more articulate response and settled for a shrug.

His smile stretched into a sly grin. "Mrs. Leighton…you really shouldn't look at me that way."

Remembering their cold shower in Briar's garden, Olivia felt that same shocking heat sidling into her bones. "Can't help it," she murmured, eyeing his mouth. Call her crazy, a glutton for punishment, whatever—she wanted to kiss him. Right here in front of her friends and family. In front of the whole town. Maybe even Birdie and Pawpaw…if they were indeed watching. That old reckless streak she'd put on the back burner for far too long flared up.

This time, though, it wasn't the heat that enticed her most. It was the feeling of rightness. Despite time and place and circumstance, he felt right. Being with him here in this moment felt…meant to be. Just as it had in the pecan grove.

His expression softened, those pensive green eyes reflecting everything she wanted, needed. The feel of his hand roving up to cup the side of her face made her lashes lower over her eyes, a curtain to the outside world.

Damn circumstances. He was hers and she was his—there was no denying.

His lips brushed hers but lifted quickly at a shrill, happy shriek. Olivia broke from her reverie as Gerald started against her. They both glanced over to see Harmony smiling in her father's arms, delighting both her parents with her first laugh.

Rex barked beside Kyle, lifting himself onto his hind legs, as ecstatic about the lights as everyone else.

"Rex," Gerald called, arms reluctantly loosening from around Olivia. He shifted away, looking at her regretfully. "Sorry, love." Removing his jacket, he hooked it on her shoulders before moving away to rescue boy from dog. "Rex! You silly git, get down before you knock someone over."

"He's taller than I am!" Kyle exclaimed.

"He's taller than everybody." Roxie laughed as Rex reared onto his hind legs again. "Richard, we should get one."

The man eyed the wolfhound doubtfully. "Like that? All that fine china you put on the registry would never survive."

"Maybe a small one?" Roxie asked plaintively, with a pretty pout. "I've always wanted a teacup Chihuahua. They don't take up much room. I could tote it around in my purse and bring it to work with me."

As Richard and Roxie debated dog breeds, Olivia took a deep breath. Something wet landed on her face and she frowned at the sky. "Is it raining?"

"Snow machine," Adrian supplied. "They turned it on with the lights. Didn't you notice?"

Olivia's eyes narrowed on her friend's knowing face. "Your sarcasm needs a little work."

Adrian raised a brow, nodding sideways toward Gerald, who was untangling Kyle and his friends from Rex's leash. "Oh, I think it's just fine."

Olivia opened her mouth to respond, but then she was almost bowled over by an excited wall of gray-and-white fur. As Rex leaped on her, she managed to twist around and catch his paws in her hands. It wasn't enough, however, to avoid getting licked thoroughly in the face. "Urrrg, Rex!" she protested, doing her best to keep her eyes and mouth shut as she batted him back. "Yes, yes, I love you, too! Now down!"

"You heard the lass," Gerald said, hauling Rex back by the collar. "She confessed. Now calm yourself." One hand dived into his pants pocket. "Sit," he instructed, producing a dog biscuit. When Rex obeyed, Gerald handed it over. "Good boy." Scratching the dog, he grinned at Olivia. "So you love him, do you?"

She wiped her face with the back of her hand. "I only said it to get him off me."

"You love him," Gerald prompted. "Come on, say it again."

She began to deny it once more, but the light in Gerald's eyes stopped her. Rolling her eyes, she lifted both hands, palms up. "What can I say? He grows on you…if you can get passed the doggie breath. And the fact that he has enough gas to fill a hot air balloon, and he still smells like opossum."

Gerald chuckled. "I need my glasses but I've got

my hands full. Can you reach into my inside jacket pocket and get them for me?"

"Yeah, get a good look at the fake snow," she agreed, feeling under the flap of the jacket for the horn-rims. "Real snowflakes have as good a chance around here as snowballs in hell."

"You have this way with words that's so inspiring," he said, smirking.

"Wait a minute. There're no glasses in here." She pulled out a long, slender box. "Just this…a jewelry case?" When he didn't take it, she glanced up to see his soft smile. Dread culled within her as understanding sank in like a stone. "You didn't…"

Her paralyzed shock didn't faze the sweet glint in his eyes. "Open it," he said, gesturing to the box.

"I…" She shook her head and held the box out to him. "I told you, I don't need anything. You shouldn't *buy* me anything. Ever."

"Just this once," he insisted, pushing the box back at her. "Trust me. You'll love it."

Glancing around at the others, who were watching with a great deal of interest, Olivia fumbled the box. Clutching it tight to her chest, she hesitated. Already she knew by the expectant look on his face that she had no choice but to open it.

She pried back the lid and almost grimaced as she looked inside, expecting something outrageous. Diamonds. Rubies. Sapphires. Though the golden glow from the branches above did glimmer off the surface of the trinket inside, she was shocked to find that it wasn't a bracelet or cuff or some other extravagant ornamentation.

"A watch?" she blurted, reaching for the pretty timepiece. She pulled her hand back because despite the simplistic quality of the slender white band and the mother-of-pearl face, she knew by the name brand etched underneath the glass that Gerald had spared no expense.

He took the box from her and pulled out the watch. Slipping the empty box into his pants pocket, he lifted her wrist gently, turning her hand palm-up as he carefully hooked the watch into place. His head leaned close against hers and his brow brushed her hair as he lingered. "You're always asking for the time," he reminded her, taking her fingers in his and tilting them until the face shimmered with light once more. "I thought it would suit you. I'm pleased to see it does."

Her mouth gaped. Looking around at the others, she caught Briar's eye. Her cousin gestured for her to speak, say "thank you," anything. Olivia had never before been this speechless.

Clearing her throat, she looked at the watch again, summoning words. She settled for the truth. "I, ah…I don't know what to say."

He eyed her uncertain expression. "Why are you so embarrassed? It's a bloody watch."

Olivia shook her head. "You shouldn't have bought me anything." Blinking, she realized her eyes were wet.

What in God's name...? She never cried.

His fingertips touched her chin, lifting her face to his. After studying the wet sheen over her eyes, his brow creased. "What is it, Liv?" he asked softly, so the others wouldn't overhear. "Tell me, love."

Shaking her head again, she fought to contain her emotions. She shoveled out a breath, hating that she wanted to reach out to him, assure him everything was okay. "You shouldn't have given me this," she said simply.

"Bollocks to that," he said on a laughing breath. "You're my wife."

Perilously close to sobs, she sought escape. "I can't..." Brushing past him and the others, she walked briskly away, refusing the urge to look back.

CHAPTER EIGHTEEN

IT WAS SOMETIME LATER—Olivia couldn't be sure how long exactly—that she stared up blearily at the heavens, watching stars bleed through tiny wisps of cloud. It was after she came back to the tavern and snuck in while Monica was manning the bar. She grabbed a bottle of tequila and went to the dock where Roxie and Adrian had met her. Several shots later, here she was squinting at the sky. It didn't appear to be the clouds moving but the stars themselves.

When the sky altogether seemed to tilt and revolve slowly, she closed one eye to see if it would stop. *Nope, still spinning.* With a sigh, she raised her arms in defeat. "I'm a terrible person."

It took more than a moment for either of her companions to speak. It was Roxie's voice that tinkled cheerily into the quiet lull. "I think you're perfectly nice." The words were a bit slurred but heartfelt.

Another moment passed before Adrian seemed to catch up. "I don't know about nice, but I've known you a long, long…" Adrian wrinkled her nose as if trying to remember how far back exactly her friendship with Olivia went "…long time. You're not too terrible."

Olivia shook her head. "No, somewhere I turned a curb. Curve? No, curb."

Roxie sat up and swayed. She put her hands on the arm of the chaise longue and waited for her own world to stop revolving before saying, "Listen, honey, everybody deserves a little bit of happiness."

Olivia chuckled at Roxie's sloppy grin. "You're a cheery drunk, Rox."

"I've never known *you* to be a gloomy one," Adrian pointed out. "That's me."

Olivia raised her arms. "People change. I've changed…. I'm not rightly sure how it all happened, but I'm a bitch all the same." She grimaced because no amount of tequila could drown out the look on Gerald's face when she'd walked away from him tonight. "I mean, did you *see* the way he looked at me? Like I killed his dog or something."

"I think he loves you," Roxie interjected.

Olivia squeezed her eyes. "Go away. You're not helping."

"No, no, I mean it," Roxie said, determined to inject some cheer into Olivia's pity party. "I think the man's hopelessly in love with you."

"He doesn't know me," Olivia reasoned. "If he did, he'd run screaming. His big dog, too."

Adrian rolled her eyes. "Look, why don't you go and tell him that? Tell him what he apparently doesn't know about you, why you're undeserving

of him. Whatever. If he still wants you after…well
you'll know he's the real deal. Right?"

"I'm tired of hurting him," Olivia muttered, mo-
rose. "I don't want to screw him up, at least not any
more than I probably already have."

Roxie jumped at the sound of her bouncy ring
tone. She snorted out a laugh as she dug the vibrat-
ing phone out of her back pocket. "That tickles."
Grinning stupidly at the screen where her fiancé's
pensive face stared back at her, she lifted her finger
and had to press the answer button twice before she
succeeded. "Hello?" she asked, putting the phone
to her ear. "Oh, hi, Squigglekins."

"Squigglekins?" Olivia mimicked.

"Don't ask," Adrian warned.

"Oh, no," Roxie continued, "I'm with the girls
still. Are you lonely? Do I need to come home?"

"Oy," Adrian muttered when Roxie's grin turned
mischievous. "Rub it in our faces a little more, why
don't you?"

"Leave her alone," Olivia said without much con-
tempt. "She's happy—and plastered."

"I'll see if one of the Savitts can drive me home,"
Roxie continued, reaching for her purse. "If not
I can call a cab. I'll be home soon. I love you,
too, Squiggles. Kisses." She pressed her lips to the
phone and puckered, making kissy noises.

"Oh, make it stop," Adrian groaned.

Roxie giggled again and said, "Buh-bye." She

ended the call then stood up, stumbling. "I have to go home."

"For heaven's sake, don't fall in," Adrian advised, watching Roxie weave her way around the chaises they'd arranged in a circle for their drinking session. On her toothpick boot heels, she tottered precariously close to the edge of the dock.

"Yeah," Olivia remarked. "We're not going in after you. It's cold. And I'm pretty sure we'd all sink at this rate."

"I'm all right, dearies." Roxie leaned down and pecked a kiss on both of Olivia's cheeks. "Cheer up, Liv. I can't stand to see you so low. He loves you. You'll make up and have lots of babies. I just know it."

"I'm glad you think so," Olivia drawled, wishing she could engage in her friend's drunken optimism. "Go wake up Cole. He'll take you home. Just try not to kill yourself on the stairs."

Roxie lifted her fingers in a wave to Adrian, who was now on the far side of the circle of chairs. "We'll have lunch tomorrow, okay? I love you both."

Adrian snorted as they watched Roxie pick her way across the inclined lawn to the inn. "She's gonna fall on her face. I'm gonna laugh when she does."

"Me, too." Olivia pursed her lips. "I guess that makes us both bitches."

Adrian nodded. "You're in good company there.

Me, though? I get it naturally. Mom was a bitch and her mother was a bitch. Your mom ain't no bitch—she's a hoot. You've got no excuse."

Olivia smiled sadly, thinking of her mother. Once a hellion, still a pistol—one her father lived to keep pace with. But Rosa Lewis didn't have a mean bone in her body. "Did I ever tell you about the time me and Rhodes Phillips eloped?"

Adrian blinked. "Wait a minute. You eloped with your high school boyfriend?"

"That's what I said," Olivia said, fumbling blindly for the tequila bottle under her chair. There was no way she could tell this story without another shot of Cuervo. She frowned when she lifted it, tipping it upside down. A single drip spilled from the uncapped lip. Cursing, she tossed it onto the dock.

"How did this happen?" Adrian asked, sitting up a bit straighter. "And why am I just now hearing about it?"

"We didn't tell anyone. Or I didn't. He would've loved to tell all his friends before my daddy ran his sorry ass out of town."

"You were crazy about Rhodes," Adrian remembered.

"Yes, I was," Olivia said bitterly.

"How long did you two date? A year?"

"And a half," Olivia added. "All through junior and half of senior. I saved myself for that jackass."

"That doesn't sound like you."

Olivia narrowed her eyes on Adrian's doubtful

ace. "This was before I joined the hussy league. I
believe you were already there, so don't you judge."

Adrian lifted her hands. "There's no judging.
Just trying to wrap my head around this. How did
you two wind up eloping?"

"He waited, grudgingly. I wanted to do it on
my eighteenth birthday. Even though it was still
six months away, he said he would keep waiting nonetheless. Then one day out of the blue he
said we should elope. We were hyped up on some
äger we stole from the tavern. And, frankly, I was
drunk stupid on Rhodes himself. So we drove to
Biloxi, found a chapel, and got ourselves good and
hitched."

"Sounds familiar."

Olivia nodded grimly. "One of the many reasons
I chide myself for this whole thing with Gerald.
The difference with Rhodes is I wasn't messed up
enough *not* to know what I was doing. Call it youth
or idealism, whatever. I liked the idea of being married, especially to him. It wasn't until after Daddy
found us in a fly-by-the-night motel off I-10 mid-
way through the next morning and we got back to
Fairhope that I found out my groom wasn't nearly
as sincere."

"Why not?"

"Well," Olivia said, staring out over the bay
where fog drifted over the water, obscuring the
bright lights of the city on the other side, "Rhodes's
buddies had been riding his ass for months about

me making him wait. Apparently they bet him thre
hundred dollars that he couldn't pop my cherry be
fore graduation. He knew the only way to get m
to give it up before I turned eighteen in July wa
to marry me. It was a bold move and it paid of
He might have left town early for summer course
at Troy, but he left three hundred dollars riche
and, luckily for him, wifeless. Daddy had the who
thing annulled quickly, for my sake as much as hi
It was the one time in my life I was completely ar
utterly humiliated."

Adrian made a thoughtful sound. "So is that wh
you started sleeping around?"

Olivia lifted a careless shoulder. "I guess
thought that if the person I'd loved so much coul
treat my virtue so carelessly, why should I valu
it? I hold myself in higher esteem than that nowa
days, trust me. I'm a grown woman. I have need
and I enjoy sex. But it started out for different rea
sons entirely." Seeing the contemplative look on he
friend's face, Olivia added, "And, yes, the who
Rhodes experience is probably the chief reason I'v
not been in a meaningful relationship since." Snif
ing, she crossed her arms over her chest becaus
she was getting a chill, and the memories weren
helping to warm her. "So there you have it."

"Hmm." Adrian cleared her throat, looking at th
hands in her lap. "Well, since we're sharing pa
transgressions...."

Olivia turned to Adrian with a raised brow. "You think you can top that?"

"Oh, I think so," Adrian said, wincing a little. "I got pregnant at seventeen, right?"

"Right," Olivia said slowly, waiting as Adrian took a deep breath.

"I told everyone that Radley was the father...."

As Adrian turned to her with a bracing expression, Olivia sat up fully in her chair. "He isn't Kyle's dad? You're sure?"

It was Adrian's turn to stare blandly at her. "Okay, I might have been a hussy but that summer there was only one man I was sleeping with."

"Do I know him?" Olivia asked.

"You probably did at the time."

"Wait," Olivia said, thinking back. With alcohol blurring the edges of her memory, she had to think harder than usual to bring it into focus. *"That summer!"* she exclaimed suddenly, realizing finally what Adrian was reluctant to tell her.

Adrian turned red, looking anywhere but at Olivia's knowing face. "Damn it. I didn't think your memory was that good."

"I don't think anybody could forget a guy like *James Bracken.*"

Adrian winced at the name. She cursed under her breath. "Oh, trust me, I've tried. He was serving his community sentence time at my parents' nursery. Otherwise, it never would have happened. He never would have looked twice at me."

"But then there would be no Kyle," Olivia pointed out.

Adrian nodded slowly. "The best thing that ever happened to me came out of one of the biggest and most bitter regrets of my life."

"Did Radley know?"

"I was five months pregnant when we got married," Adrian informed her. "Pretty sure he noticed."

"Is that why you stayed with him?"

Adrian sent her a cool look. "When you think so little of yourself, it's easy to let people mistreat you, maybe because you think that's what you deserve. Isn't that why you just told me you slept around after your annulment?"

Olivia nodded. "That's fair, I guess."

"The things we do for love are just plain dumb."

Olivia shook her head, unable to take it in. "James Bracken." At Adrian's exasperated look, she barked out a laugh. "Hey, I'm not judging, either. It just makes so much sense now. Kyle looks nothing like Radley."

"Yeah, thanks for never bringing that up."

"It's a credit to the kid." Olivia gazed out at the horizon. "James Bracken."

Adrian made a distressed noise in the back of her throat. *"Would you stop saying his name?"*

Olivia pressed her lips tight together to hide a smile. "Sorry. And, hey, thanks for sharing."

"Feel better now?" Adrian sobered quickly a

she studied Olivia's face. "Admit it—you love him. Gerald."

Olivia sighed, long and forlorn. "More than I loved that prick Rhodes Phillips. I'll say that much."

"You should tell him that, too."

"Oh, like you would tell James Bracken you loved him if he showed up here tomorrow?"

Adrian shuddered at the thought. "God, no. But this is different. He ran off, a lot like Rhodes did. He doesn't deserve to know what I felt about him. Gerald's feelings for you are stronger than you'd like to admit. There's love on both sides. If there were a chance all this could work out—"

"There isn't."

"*If* there were," Adrian continued, a bit more loudly, "a chance that you two could make something real of this, wouldn't you want to give it a try?"

"Roxie's hopeless optimism is rubbing off on you, the eternal pessimist. I'm disappointed." Olivia gripped the back of her chair and stood, trying very hard not to waver. She eyed the distance to the tavern and, particularly, the water hazard surrounding it. "I think I can make it. You?"

Adrian didn't bother to rise. "I'm crashing at the inn. No way am I going home. Mom's there watching Kyle."

"No, you're right. Go to the inn. Edith and her guilt trip can wait until morning. Need help?"

Adrian pulled the big wooly blanket Briar had

brought earlier from the inn to her chin. "I think
might sit here and sulk for a while longer."

Olivia carefully began to walk back to the wa
ter's edge and the safe lawn beyond. "You do tha
'Night." She folded her coat around her as a stif
cold breeze cut through the sweater underneath
She stopped in the deserted bar long enough t
throw out the empty bottle. Sweeping one loo
around the place, she saw that everything was nea
and put away and headed back down the hall to th
stairs. There seemed to be more of them than usua
She was a bit winded when she got to the top.

Silently, she pushed through the apartment doo
The lamp was on but dimmed. The first thing sh
saw—and heard—was Rex snoring. She frowned
looking wildly around the room.

Yep, there was Rex sleeping in the corner…an
Gerald on the sofa with a book. Both were oblivi
ous to her.

Olivia closed the door as quietly as she could
Shocked as she was that he was here, she wante
to look at the man for a moment. Just look.

His hair was growing longer. With his head ber
slightly forward over the pages, she had a clea
view of the blond strands that were starting to fin
ger the nape of his neck and curl outward a bit un
tidily as they did at the tips of his ears, too. Sh
wanted to go to him, to tease those little waves, t
run her fingers through those on the back of hi
neck until they lay straight.

An odd and very strong instinct had her taking a step toward him. Then another. And another. Her hand lifted, unbidden, and fell to his shoulder.

Gerald jerked hard. As he turned to look at her, he blew out a self-deprecating laugh. "Christ, love," he said as he scrubbed the heel his hand over his heart. "You gave me a start."

Love. The word seemed to echo in the silence.

He loves you.

She closed her eyes. She feared both Roxie and Adrian were right—Gerald loved her. The thought burned, but it gave her hope, too. A tiny speck of hope she couldn't quite bring herself to grasp yet. But hope nonetheless. Maybe they could make things work....

As she searched his gaze, his light expression sobered quickly. She skimmed her eyes over his face, reaching out to rub her thumb lightly over his jaw where the dim lamplight shone through the stubble there, making it look like burnished gold. She heard his breath quicken at her touch and let her hand fall away.

He loves you.... For once that night, her sigh wasn't one of defeat. Maybe he did love her. If the slow-burning look in his eyes was any indication. Yes, yes, he did love her. And for one night, she wanted to be that woman that he saw. Just once.

She lowered her mouth to his slowly and kissed him as she had too often hesitated to do before. He made a noise in his throat that climbed right up into her heart and warmed it. That warmth turned into a flame and spread quickly, a brushfire. She'd been so cold moments before. Hadn't she?

As she tilted her head to deepen the kiss, his hand lifted to gently grasp the back of her neck. His mouth opened and his tongue greeted hers. She hissed as arousal swept through her, following that cindering trail already lit up inside her. Dear God. The man might be bookish, but *damn* could he kiss.

She pulled away after several moments, gnawing on her lower lip when it tingled in protest. His eyes flicked down to her mouth before veering back up to hers. And from there they refused to stray again, seeming to read her every explicit thought.

Something passed between them. Silent words of understanding. The next thing she knew he was on his feet. Wrapping his arms around her shoulders and hooking the other underneath her knees, he lifted her into his arms and carried her to the bedroom.

No SOONER HAD Gerald entered Olivia's bedroom than he set her down on the floor, tugging at her coat without preamble. There was a fire in his blood and he was beyond the point of want or need. His wife had kept him at arm's length long enough. Now was the time to claim her. Despite the fact that he'd come here tonight to talk about what had happened at the festival…he was giving in and taking what he wanted.

Something had passed between them as she kissed him. Like an agreement. An offering. *I'm yours,* she had seemed to be telling him.

Finally, he thought, as she jumped to the pace he set, yanking at the buttons of his shirt before sweeping her hands over his chest and down to loosen the snap of his jeans. His touch fumbled at the bottom hem of her sweater when she loosened his belt enough to reach inside and get a feel for what he was struggling with underneath.

"Bloody hell," he growled, discarding tenderness. There was too much at stake here for gentleness. He grasped her wrists, yanking her hands free and lifting them high over her head. In restless movements, he easily removed her sweater and threw it over his shoulder before he wrapped his arms around her and, mouth firmly lanced to hers, spun her toward the bed.

Somehow amidst their spinning, she managed to trip him up, so when they landed together on the bed, he was underneath her. Before he could right that situation, she had in turn grasped him by the wrists and yanked his hands above his head. They remained there, cuffed, and him helpless and burning as she spread openmouthed kisses along his jaw, then down his neck over his Adam's apple and, further devastating him, over his shoulders and collarbone.

While her tongue teased one of his nipples, his hips jerked against the snug confines of hers. Be-

fore she could turn her attention to his sternum o
anything farther south, he levered himself, flippin
her underneath him.

Quickly cloaking her mouth with his, he cuppe
her breasts. She gasped and he grinned, nippin
her lower lip. "Let me," he murmured against he
throat as he tugged the waistline of her pants fror
her hips. "Just let me, love. Let me have my wa
with you."

"Okay," she agreed, mindless and without hesi
tation. "You...just—hurry."

"Blimey," he said, molding her hips with hi
hands. He dipped them into her waist then up agai
over her torso. "I've always thought you were pe
fect, but...by God, woman. You're tidy, aren't you?

"Thank you?"

"All that bloody running," he mused, absently
Before she could use her leg to leverage hersel
over him again, Gerald placed his hand on he
knee, keeping her firmly in place. "Wait a momen
Something I've been wanting to..." His word
trailed off as he ran his mouth down the center o
her torso, down to her navel and the heart someon
had inked into the recess of her hip. "You'll hav
to tell me more about this here...." He flicked hi
thumb over the small tattoo. "Later," he decided
"Much later." He traced the shape with his lips, nib
bling a little here and then there, taking his time...

"Damn you." She wriggled underneath him
twisted. "Damn it." Finally, she grabbed a chunk o

his hair and raised his mouth back to hers. "Come here, cheeky devil."

"Sorry." He grinned, blowing a panting laugh over her face before kissing her deeply, openly. He hooked his fingers into the band of her knickers and tugged them down. "I'll hurry it along for you. Just this once—I'll hurry."

"Please."

"You're begging, Olivia."

"Don't care."

His grin faded as he lowered himself fully to her. There was absolutely nothing between them, just the heat of their skin and the slight sheen of perspiration that had gathered between them. His voice was lower, deeper and edged with need when he spoke again. "Put your arms around me, love. I need to feel your arms around me."

When they twined around him, her hands pressed tight to the blades of his shoulders, he wrapped his hand beneath her knee, fingers stroking the sweet spot there when she made a sound of assent. Lifting her knee, he buried his face in her hair and surged against her, breaching her in one fell swoop.

Breath burst from them both. He groaned, his eyes closing tight as he choked back a reverent curse. He stayed for a moment, buried to the hilt as she vibrated around him. He lifted his palms to her hair, balling handfuls in his fists. Then he moved again, unable to bite back the oath this time.

Pleasure, biting in its intensity, threatened to top-

ple him into upheaval too soon. Her quick and bla-
tant cry of completion slammed into him. Moving
faster now, he took her up again, gritting his teeth
to fight against the rising tide of release. *No. No.
yet. Not yet....*

Moments later, the sounds of her sobs broke
through the pounding drumbeat of blood pulsing
in his ears. In a last attempt at the gentleness he'd
wanted to show her before, he touched his lips to
the place where her heart raced against her throat
whispering her name against her skin. He said it
once more as he sailed over that fine line between
heat and weakness, his breath washing out of him
like a rogue wave—a ragged, involuntary rush.

She laid her hand on the back of his tousled head
as he lowered his brow to her breast and, panting,
stayed there for a while, trying to recover some
semblance of himself.

After they'd both cindered in the aftermath for a
good, long while, Gerald rolled, wordless and careful not to let her go. Pulling her with him into the
pillows at the head of the bed, he touched his lips
to hers in a soft, whispering kiss. His arms winding loosely around her, he let exhaustion rush up
and claim them both.

CHAPTER NINETEEN

IT WAS SOME time later when Olivia woke with her head on Gerald's shoulder. Light burned from the living room. She could hear the muffled snort of Rex's snores through the open door. More, she could hear the thump of Gerald's pulse. It was slow and strong. His breath fell over her brow where his lips had been pressed when she fell asleep.

A wash of contentment moved through her, as deep as the marrow of her bones. She felt no need to move away, even though they were both still naked. Even though his arms were around her. Even though this time she remembered every detail of their lovemaking in stark detail.

That's what it had been. No denying it. He'd made love to her in a way no one ever had before. She'd been through the same motions with other men. But with Gerald, there had been an intensity as well as a certain softness. Tenderness might not have been at the forefront of their minds through most of it, but beyond the smoldering need had been nothing but soft oceans of passion.

She felt as if she'd been bobbing on the surface

of stormy seas for weeks now. Here, though, finally was the calm she'd needed. She had thought that his leaving would bring it about—that return to normalcy and clarity she'd so desperately wished for from the moment he moved in.

Now she realized he was what she needed and his departure would bring nothing but more tumult.

She closed her eyes tight. There was a headache nibbling at her temples. Her mouth was dry—chalk that up to tequila. She shifted to rise, trying not to wake him as she did so.

They were too closely entangled. As soon as her arms fell away from him, he sucked in a breath and woke. "Liv?"

"Sorry," she whispered. "Go back to sleep."

"Where're you going, love?" came his quiet answer in the dark. "It's not yet day."

"I'm just going to clean up a bit."

Before she could shift her legs over the side of the bed and rise, his hand reached out and caught hers. "Wait a minute." He sat up, the flannel sheet falling to his waist, and peered more closely at her. "Something's wrong. What is it?"

"It's nothing," she lied. "I just need some water or something."

"You've a headache," he said. After a moment's study, he lowered his head and touched his lips to the temple that was thumping hardest.

How had he known? When he lingered, she closed her eyes, allowing herself to sink into those warm, calm waters again. Who needed Africa or Italy when she could have *this?*

He must have sensed the tensing of her shoulders because his hands came up to them, rubbed, thumbs kneading that tight spot at the curve of her neck. "You stay," he said finally. "I'll get what you need."

"Gerald, I can—"

"Stay," he insisted. The covers rustled as he pulled them back and beat her to the edge of the bed. "That's an order, Olivia Rose."

She wasn't used to taking orders, but she sat tight, drawing her knees to her chest and the covers to her chin as she lay back against the headboard and watched his naked figure disappear into the bathroom.

It was a shame she hadn't had time to bite one of those buttocks. Just one playful little nibble...

She caught herself smiling and cleared her throat, wincing as it protested. She shouldn't have gone the rounds with Jose again.

In addition, all the aches and sweet pangs from sex were starting to announce themselves. Not that she minded those. How much she would come to regret later was hard to say because now...now she needed this time with him. Later...later all the worry and doubt could come tossing her back into that storm, if needed. But not now.

He returned from the bathroom, bringing her a hot, wet towel and some painkillers before leaving again to get her a glass of water from the kitchen. She mused over the towel until he came back, handing her the glass. "Thank you," she murmured after washing down the painkillers. "For all of it."

"I can't have you hurting, love." He watched her down the rest of the water and took the glass when she was done. "More?"

She shook her head. "That was plenty."

He looked at her, measuring her expression. "How are you feeling?" he asked hesitantly.

Her smile grew into a full-blown grin. "Gerald, this was hardly my first time."

"Yes, I know," he said, "but I usually go about things with a little more finesse. I was afraid I might have hurt you in some way."

She met his gaze. "I'm fine. Minus the headache, I'm actually feeling kind of great."

"Thank God."

The words, expelled on a shoveled breath, made her look more closely at him. Seeing just how worried he'd been, she lifted her hand to his face. "And you? How are you, Gerald?"

The corner of his mouth twitched wryly. "Pretty bloody fantastic."

A laugh belted out of her. It halted, though, when need flashed in his eyes again, a sheer, hard glint that took her breath away. Before she could gather that same breath, his mouth was on hers. He kissed her with the intensity he had earlier, his hand spread on the space between her shoulder blades, bringing her in close. Need, thick and tangled, robbed her thoughts, and love, swift and true, reared up in their place.

By God, did she love this man?

She lowered her hands to his shoulders, pulling away. "Gerald," she said. She took a second to inhale and exhale carefully and calm her racing heart.

His eyes searched hers, seeking. Almost bracing.

She frowned. He'd told her he knew she could hurt him. But seeing him now…preparing for the blow, it nearly rent her in two. Unable to voice any of the doubtful words she'd been ready to say moments before, she reached for him.

He expelled a relieved breath as he wrapped his arms around her, holding her tight.

She kissed him once, twice. His eyes were open, on hers, drinking in the emotions washing over her face. Knowing he could read her like an open book, she still couldn't bring herself to look away.

He caught her chin in his hand. "That's right. Look at me, woman. Look right here, into me, and see what it is you've caused."

"Gerald…"

"Look," he repeated, tucking an arm low around her waist and lifting her until her legs splayed over his lap again. Not once did his eyes stray from hers. "Just look."

She obeyed. This was the first time in her life she could remember ever being so obedient. But she looked, and she saw. Testing him, she grazed her lips over his, nibbled his top lip, then the lower dragging it into her mouth and tugging.

His lids lowered to half-mast, his arms tightened around her.

Still watching him, she touched his face, moving her hands up his jaw, over the sides of his face and into his hair. Her small nails teased his scalp, and he made a noise in the back of his throat.

Planting her hands on his shoulders, she pushed. Reluctantly, he lowered to the pillows behind him. When he reached for her, she took his hands, intertwined their fingers, but didn't follow his urging to lay down with him. Instead, she lowered her mouth to the underside of his chin and began a small kissing trail from his neck to his sternum. She heard him suck in a breath as she went lower, to his trim waistline.

"Liv," he said in warning.

She raised her gaze to his face. His lips were parted, his eyes nearly closed. Still, she could see the plea in them. It didn't ask her to stop but to keep going, drive him crazy.

With a small smile, she let go of his hands as she nuzzled lower. His hips jumped under her hands as she turned her attention to his arousal, already hot and thick and raised. She wrapped her hand around it. Glancing up, she watched him as he had asked her to. Watched the muscle in his jaw pulse as he clamped it tight. Watched his chest rise and fall rapidly. She teased him with her lips, then with grazing teeth before she nipped her way around to his bottom.

"What the *bollocks?*" he yelped as she took a bite of his hind quarters. He let out a breathless laugh before it lifted and trebled. As he continued to laugh, she relinquished her hold on him and sat up, grinning like a fool.

"Minx." When she only grinned at him, he asked, "What?"

She lifted her shoulders. "I've never heard you laugh hard like that before."

"I wasn't expecting you to take a bite out of my arse now, was I?" When she only smiled, he moved in a quick motion. Before she knew what was happening, he'd snagged her by the waist and was rolling her underneath him. "My turn," he announced.

"No," she said, fighting his hold on her as he followed the same path she had taken on him—chin to sternum, sternum to waist and farther. She let him pry her legs apart and nuzzle for a moment, sighing as he did so. But when his grip on her tightened and he began to nip his way around to her butt, she resisted, snorting as she fought laughter. "No, *no!* Gerald!"

He took a bite nonetheless and she shrieked, hysterical laughter pelting out of her. "Stop it! Stop it! I didn't bite you near as hard, you bastard!"

He lifted his head with a raised brow, gaze finding hers. "Bastard, am I?" In another quick motion, he'd lowered his head again and was taking another chomp. She screamed in protest, wriggling to get away, but snorted with repressed laughter, tears gathering at the corners of her eyes. "I surrender!" she cried, giggling so hard she could hardly get the words out. When he lifted his head again, grinning, she flopped back and shook her head. "You're mean."

"You started it." Hair charmingly tousled, he craned his neck to get a gander at the bite mark on her rear. "You've a cracking arse. Has anyone ever told you that?"

She snorted once more. "Do you have any idea what you just said?"

He grabbed her beneath the knees and yanked her across the mattress to him. Planting one hand on either side of her shoulders, he raised his face back to hers. "It means it's the best arse I've ever laid eyes on. Now hold still, Mrs. Leighton. I'm going to ravish you thoroughly."

She hadn't thought it was possible, but he seduced her all over again. At his touch, she discovered the skilled finesse he'd spoken of earlier. He took her up again and again until she was putty in his hands once more. Then, sweating, he slipped inside her, cupped her face in his hands and demanded she watch. Watch him as they took each other up, glided over the edge together and clung through the long, hard spill back to earth.

THE SOUND OF low woofing broke through Gerald's dreams. He groaned, not yet wanting to relinquish his hold on sleep. Olivia was there. His dreams were filled with her. They were in some opulent penthouse with panoramic windows overlooking the bright lights of a city by night. There was champagne flowing, rose petals strewn everywhere.

When the far-off sound of barking grew louder and began to pry him from the penthouse suite and back into the present, he called out a mumbled, "Bugger off, Rex," before rolling to shove his head under the pillow.

He managed to nearly roll off the side of the bed. Cursing, he threw an arm out to catch himself. Another arm tightened around his chest, underneath his shoulders to keep him in place. "I'm sorry," Olivia said, voice muffled against the back of his shoulder blade. "I'm sorry. My fault."

"Blimey," he said, sitting up with her. He glanced over the scant bed space she'd managed to corner him into, then at her with a rueful grin. "We're going to have to talk about this bed-hogging business of yours."

"If it's any consolation, you steal covers," Olivia told him, pulling the sheet up to fight the chill. She frowned as Rex's barking became more insistent. "What's wrong with him?"

Gerald listened and heard over the dog's racket

the distant sound of knocking. "I think he's trying to tell us someone's here."

She sighed, throwing aside the covers. "At six o'clock in the morning? Really?"

Gerald watched her rise, admiring her bare form as she snatched up the first thing at hand—one of his oxford shirts. It was soft and wrinkled and fell nearly all the way to her knees. She buttoned it wrong, he noticed but didn't say a thing about it as she ran a hand through her wild hair. "Tell whoever it is they can either go away or face the wrath of Betty or Glinda," he told her. "Then come back to bed. I'm not nearly finished with you, woman."

She beamed over her shoulder as she left the room. He listened as she calmed Rex. Gerald could hear the dog's wagging tail thumping against the walls as Olivia maneuvered him out of the way of the apartment door. "Just a second," she called in answer to the next knock. The door squeaked on its rusty hinges. A beat of silence. Then Olivia's voice again, "Can I help you, sir?"

Another pause. "Yes," a clipped, male voice said. "I'm looking for my brother. I was told he would be here."

Gerald's heart missed a beat. He quickly wrested back the sheet wrapped around him. His feet hit the floor and he shrugged on the jeans he found at the foot of the bed. Not bothering to hook them, he walked quickly into the living room, eyes lighting on the man standing in the door. "Barty," he said and smiled in greeting.

Bartholomew Leighton cut a lean and impeccable figure in a dark blue tailored suit. Though he wasn't nearly as tall as Gerald, he had the same high brow, green eyes and strong nose. Puzzled, he gave Gerald a once-over, the corners of his lips twitching at the corners wryly. "I say, Gerald. It may be warmer here than it is in New York. Still, that isn't any excuse to parade around with no shirt."

Gerald laughed as he crossed the room and enveloped Barty in a strong-armed hug. Thumping him on the back, he asked fondly, "How are you, you bastard?"

"The question is," Barty said, stepping back to measure Gerald's face, his eyes lingering on his brow, "how are you?"

Gerald lifted his knuckles to his scar. "Well enough."

Barty's expression turned stern. "I had to hear about the accident from your editor, of all people. Alexandra's all but sick with worry, I'll have you know. She made me fly out on the red-eye. And to Alabama, of all places. What's going on, Gerald? Why haven't you called? And why in God's name are you here?"

Clearing his throat, Gerald motioned for his brother to come inside the apartment, stepping back over the threshold himself. He turned to Olivia, who had done well to fade into the woodwork by shrinking back against the wall opposite the door, her arms crossed tightly over her chest as she surveyed the brothers' reunion. Gerald smiled at her in earnest as he clapped a hand on Barty's shoulder. "Barty, there's someone I'd like you to meet."

"I believe I already have, somewhat," Barty said with a polite nod to Olivia, his eyes rushing briefly over her tousled hair and bare legs. "Sorry, miss. I called, but this git doesn't answer his phone half the time."

She lifted a hand. "It's okay. Really. It's...nice to meet a member of Gerald's family. He talks about y'all a lot."

"Y'all?" Barty asked, brows drawing together.

"Olivia's my wife," Gerald said without further preamble.

Barty's face dropped as it turned up to Gerald in shock. "Wife?" he asked, punching the word out in disbelief.

"Yes." Gerald nodded. "We've been married for some weeks now. I've been staying here, for the most part. In her home."

Barty blinked from Gerald to Olivia. He held a hand up as if to steady himself. "You'll have to forgive me. This is the first I'm hearing of this, too."

Gerald saw Olivia's gaze rise to his quickly in surprise. He cleared his throat and explained to Barty, "We met in Las Vegas and married there. Then I left the loft in Soho and came here to be with her."

"Did you?" Barty scanned Gerald's face, then glanced over Olivia once more. After a moment's study, he said in a flat voice that spoke volumes, "I see." Clearing his throat, Barty shrugged off his suit jacket. "It seems we have much to discuss, don't we?"

"Indeed," Gerald said, taking his brother's jacket. "I'll hang this, then get you some tea. You've had a long journey."

As he ushered Barty into the kitchen, Gerald caught Olivia's eye. Seeing the shadows in them and doubts culling there for the first time since the festival, he reached for her hand. Raising it, he lifted her palm to his lips. "Don't worry about Barty," he whispered against her skin. "He's harmless."

She moved a shoulder. "I'm not worried about him," she said. She jerked her head toward the bedroom door. "I'll get dressed. You know where everything is, right?"

"I do." Frowning at her quick departure, Gerald worried about the wall he thought he'd seen rising between them again in her emerald eyes. Rex bumped his head against Gerald's knee, distracting him. He reached down to pet the hound. "Let's make our guest at home, shall we, boy?"

AS EARLY MORNING stretched into midmorning then lunch and the brothers caught up on everything from the marriage to the accident to Gerald's latest book news and deadlines, Olivia wrestled with the itch to escape and let them have time to themselves. But every time she so much as looked at the door, Gerald reached for her and she lingered.

He hadn't told his family he was married? She bit her lip over the news as she listened to the cadence of British voices talking family back home across the pond in London, Yorkshire.... Their mother was apparently on some important dig in China. Olivia listened with only half an ear as they ate the sandwiches she threw together for them and drank every bit of tea Gerald had left at her place when he had departed days before for the inn.

Still, the thought niggled. If she was so important to him, why hadn't he told his family?

It was close to one o'clock in the afternoon when Barty expressed some desire to take a walk. Instead of getting the break she thought the news would herald, Olivia found herself cornered into going with him when Gerald received a phone call from his editor and he asked her kindly if she would mind escorting his brother around the grounds of the inn.

She grabbed a coat from the closet by the door, ignored both Barty's and Gerald's looks as she led the former out of the apartment, and remained silent, unsure of what to say to her husband's younger brother—the earl—as she led him down to the rocky shore.

The wind was high and it carried more than a touch of winter with it. She flipped the collar of the North Face coat up to shield her neck and chin as she and Barty made their way toward the dock.

"It's quite pretty," Barty said, breaking the silence. "Your town."

"Thank you," Olivia said for lack of anything better.

Barty waited until they had reached the end of the dock and the railing there to say anything more. "My brother's always been a bit of an odd duck."

She looked at him, surprised. When he only gazed out over the murky bay and the city that looked so small beyond it, she asked, "How so?"

Barty lifted a shoulder. "Only that he's always carved his own path. Even when he'd hit bedrock, he'd chip away at it endlessly until he found a way around it or underneath it. It's admirable, that kind of determination. I admire him for fighting against my father's wishes and giving up the family title. It took courage, not the cowardice or lack of responsibility so many of our peers thought he showcased by doing so."

Her brows drew together. "He's his own man." She'd known this for weeks now. Why was Barty trying to drive this point home to her? "And he's a good one."

"Yes." Barty nodded, leaning a bit over the railing to see down into the depths of the shallow bay. "But Gerald also has a few unfortunate habits... particularly when it comes to matters of the heart."

At this, Olivia's eyes rose to his face. She waited

for the man to say more. When he didn't, she couldn't fight the impatience or the curiosity and blurted, "Such as?"

Barty's gaze finally returned to her face, direct and stern. "He loves *suddenly*. Recklessly, as well. Love has a tendency to make him blind. And it's gotten him into trouble in the past. Did he tell you about the last woman he considered marrying? A fellow writer, not nearly as successful as he was. It seems after a time that she grew weary of his accolades and instead of ending the relationship as she should have, she sold a large number of pages of his next Rex Flynn book to a leak site. Made quite the profit even as she broke my brother's heart and left the loft they shared. He may have learned to put his heart on the line again with you, but since the day she betrayed him, he hasn't shared his work with anyone—family, friends, *anyone*—until he's forced to turn it over to his editor."

Olivia's mouth parted. She stopped herself from speaking, thinking back over the past three weeks. Though she had seen Gerald at work, it had been in stolen moments when he'd thought he was alone. Soon after learning she was there, he'd shut his computer and walk away from it. He'd spoken of writing, but never of what he was working on.

She cleared her throat because Barty was eyeing her expectantly. "And you think that Gerald's love for me, as it is, is going to get him hurt again." It was what she'd thought, too, a day ago. Hell, a few short hours ago. But still, she didn't like that this stranger before her, brother or no brother to Gerald, would automatically assume such a thing. "Why? Do I look like a heartbreaker?"

"No," Barty said carefully. "But looks can be deceiving. Particularly when you consider the fact that you met my brother in Las Vegas and were married the same night. Then he dropped everything to come here and be with you. By your request or not, I'm not sure—you could have lured him, baited him for all I know."

Her teeth clenched at the implication. "And why would I do that, Barty?" she asked, every word falling off her tongue like broken shards of glass. Delicate but deadly.

Barty turned thoughtful eyes to the low-flying clouds above. "Gerald's a rich man. He's obtained wealth even his family can't imagine. He's also well-known. Connected in the business world, in society. You're a small business owner in a town not too many people have ever heard of. You have ambitions, Olivia, I'm sure. You'll understand why I'd feel the need to speak to you in this manner if you had a sibling such as Gerald."

She stared at him for several beats of silence, carefully leashing the need to lash out at the man. No. Better to deal with his kind as he was dealing with her. Firmly and placidly. "I don't want anything to do with your brother's money. Three generations of my family have made the Lewises and our tavern what it is. I like to think I've earned the legacy and the success I've made of it since it passed into my hands."

Barty nodded sagely, pursing his lips. "As one who knows the value of legacy quite well, I can understand that."

"And I get that Gerald is your brother and he's made some bad calls in the past," Olivia went on. "You want to protect him. Well, you go on and do that." She closed the distance between them. "But if you're going to insult me, you better back up your so-called implications with some hard evidence. Otherwise, you're just some a-hole in a suit."

He lifted a smooth hand. "Olivia, I didn't want to start a row—"

"Who's rowing?" Olivia asked. "My cousin owns the inn next door. Your brother's staying in the bay view suite there. I suggest you get yourself a room, Mr. Leighton, or else find out when the next flight back to London is. You'll have to forgive me for not much caring which."

CHAPTER TWENTY

GERALD WAS STILL ON the phone when Olivia returned to the apartment. He heard her pacing from one side of the living room to the other as he wrapped up the call. "Yes, I'm sending the manuscript," he explained, glancing back at her briefly. She was alone. Where had Barty disappeared to? he wondered vaguely, then tuned back into the conversation with his editor. "I told you I would finish by the original deadline. You were wrong to doubt me, Dwight."

"I've never been so happy to be wrong," Dwight said on the other end of the line. "Hey, I've got a couple of other writers suffering from writer's block. Where's this place that's inspired you so much? Maybe I'll send a few of them down."

"It's a little town on the Eastern Shore of Mobile Bay called Fairhope," Gerald said, pushing the send button on the email with the completed Rex Flynn manuscript attached. "I highly recommend it. It's the perfect place to get the creative juices flowing and finish a novel."

"Sounds ideal."

"It is," Gerald said. The pacing behind him had slackened. He looked around to see Olivia standing in the doorway to the kitchen, staring at him aghast, her arms limp at her sides. He cleared his throat. "Listen, Dwight, I'll talk to you later."

"I'll call you when I've given the manuscript a read," Dwight replied. "Enjoy the rest of your stay down south."

"Sure thing." Gerald ended the call, carefully setting the cell phone down on the tabletop. As he stood, gripping the back of his chair at the dining room table, he noted the sinking feeling in the pit of his gut. Olivia's face was pale and coated in echoes of disbelief and something close to fury. "Liv," he said, taking a step toward her. "What's wrong? What have you done with Barty?"

Her brows shot up onto her forehead, one of them forming a high-backed arc. "What have I done with your little brother? I hope I've sent him packing. He's under the impression that I'm a gold digger out for your blood."

Gerald let that sink in for a moment, then cursed under his breath. "Damn it, Barty."

"Let me ask you something, Gerald," Olivia said, taking several threatening steps toward him. "Who was that on the phone?"

"Just now?" he asked, looking back at the cell phone on the table. "My editor. Dwight Howard."

"Your editor," she said in a low, cool voice. "I see."

His eyes narrowed on her. Her backbone was

amrod straight and her shoulders were set in a steely line, a posture a heavyweight boxer might find too intimidating to challenge. "I can see your wheels turning," Gerald said, trying to blow out a laugh with the words and ease whatever had gone amiss between them in her absence. Dropping his voice to the level of hers, he walked the rest of the way to her and cupped the side of her face in his hand. "You've let me inside you. Don't put those walls up again."

"You want to know what's going on inside me?" Olivia challenged, eyes like fire. "You might be sorry you did, but here it is. Here's what I'm thinking. I was right from the beginning. You're a fraud."

His mouth fumbled and his hand lifted from her skin. "What—"

"You didn't come here for me," Olivia asserted. She pointed to the phone sitting on the table next to his notebook. "You came here for that, right there. Your work. Your writing. Rex Flynn. You had a deadline, from the sounds of it, and you came to the bay and Hanna's Inn not to court me but to gain the little bit of inspiration and atmosphere you needed to finish your damned book. Me? I was just an extra. The bonus feature. You thought you could smooth your way into my home and into my bed and that would give your imagination that little bit of extra push you needed to finish the book."

He stared at her. "Christ. What else did my brother make you believe?"

"To hell with your brother," she said, her voic[e] rising an octave as her ire became more and mor[e] apparent. "I can think for myself. I'm not blind. [I] can see things just fine. I can see how you used m[e,] how you used every one of us!"

"Olivia," Gerald said, trying to stay calm. Sh[e] had taken a marked step back from him. Severa[l] marked steps. All he had to do was cross back t[o] her and make her see that what she was sayin[g] was drivel. "I've asked you before not to insu[lt] me. If you must push me away, do it when it's war[-] ranted. Not because you're afraid, once again, [of] what we've made here."

She let out a mocking laugh, latching her fin[-] gers into the hair on top of her head. Her eye[s] peeled. "I can't believe I let you in. I can't believ[e] I bought into this whole stupid scenario you'v[e] woven around me. You're so good, Gerald. You'r[e] so damn good at making people believe what yo[u] want them to."

"Olivia," he said again, this time with more tha[n] a hint of warning. "Do *not* test me."

Crossing her arms over her chest, she shook he[r] head. "No, you're right. Because seduction won'[t] work on me this time. You won't get me on th[e] floor beneath you again. For once, you and me ar[e] going to talk about what's really going on here." Lifting her wrist, she began to tug at the band [of] the watch she'd fastened there the night before.

"What are you doing?" he asked, brow creasing as he watched her fight to remove his gift.

"I don't need your things," she said, finally managing to unlatch the band. She tossed the watch at him. "I don't need your money or your connections. I don't need your gifts. I don't need you, Gerald. I never did."

Before he could intervene again, she held up a hand. "You know, all you had to do was give me the divorce. You could have had me, just like that, so long as you left afterward."

"That's not what I wanted—what I *want*," Gerald told her. "We've been through this."

She shook her head again, on a roll now as she started pacing the kitchen. "No, I've finally figured you out. You wanted three weeks. I bet the end of them lined up nicely with the deadline for your book." Leveling an accusing finger at him, she stopped and said, "I dare you to deny it."

He lifted his hands in a helpless gesture. "Liv, the deadline—the book—had nothing to do with you."

Her gaze sharpened. "I'm right, though, aren't I? You had over three weeks to write your book, then you'd be on your way. Back to New York or London or wherever it is you call home between your jaunts to Italy and Africa. Vegas. Do you find inspiration in a local woman's bed wherever you go, Gerald, or am I the only one?"

Gerald closed his eyes. He'd lost her. Somewhere along the way, he'd lost her and he had no idea how.

He had no idea how to fight her now that she was so convinced of his wrongdoing. "There's no one but you," he answered in a weary voice. He was tired, so tired of fighting her. "There's never been anyone like you."

"Not that writer chick you lived with?" Olivia asked. At his blank stare, she nodded, "Oh yeah, Barty told me all about that one. The other one, I should say. She's the reason you won't let anyone see your work. It makes sense. Every time I come into the room and you're writing or talking on the phone with your editor, you shut it down quickly or let me know I'm not welcome. Just like the other night."

"Liv…"

"I'm your wife," Olivia said. "You've claimed I'm your muse. You put so much stock into what we have but you won't let me near your work? How does that add up, Gerald? Not to mention your family. You love them. They're so important to you, but you didn't so much as call to tell them that you're married?"

Gerald raked a hand through his hair, trying to see through the murk of her accusations. "I was going to. But then the accident happened. I got distracted, and it slipped my mind."

"Oh, sure," she said with a roll of her eyes. She propped her hands on her hips and fought to catch her breath. If he didn't know any better, he'd have said a few of her inhales snagged in her throat or what could have been a sob, barely restrained. "Say you're not lying about having so-called feelings for me. Say you did come here at least half of the way to find out what we have. That's another problem altogether. You're desperate for a meaningful connection or relationship with someone because your mom was always away on some dig or your father only wanted you around because you were the oldest boy and you were destined to take over as earl. And your brother and sister? I don't know. You could never connect with them on a deep level because you went to some remote boarding school. Right?"

"Now, wait a minute," he said, unable to stand her throwing his words back in his face to drive her false point home. "My family has nothing to do with this—with us. You're grasping at straws."

"Just stop and think about it for a second. It's why you bribed Carmen into living with you in college. I bet it's why you were with *writer girl*. It's why you married me to begin with. Because you want something to be there, but it's not, Gerald. It's just not."

As the words echoed around them, he clenched his jaw. A muscle ground against the bone there as the last bit of what she'd said sank in. "Is that really what you think? After these past three weeks together? After last night?"

She gave an assertive nod. "Yes," she said in a broken voice.

He exhaled slowly, the hurt melding into disappointment. The weight in his heart doubled and he took a moment to breathe through the despairing sensation. Heartache. He'd known it before. Here it was again. "That's a shame. Because despite all appearances, despite what you've led yourself to believe, the two of us have something. If you can truly make yourself believe it wasn't from what we started in Vegas, that's one thing. But you can't for one second make me believe that these last few weeks meant nothing to either one of us.

"I love you, Olivia. And that has nothing to do with who my father was or who my mother is. It has nothing to do with where I come from or what happened there. It has nothing to do with my work or yours. If I didn't love you before I came to Fairhope, what we've shared since has made me love you in the way my parents should have loved one another, in the way you've told me your own parents do. And last night you made me believe that you could accept that—and maybe that you meant those same three words you said to me the night we were married."

When she only shook her head in automatic denial, he sighed. "You're determined not to believe it. You're doing your best to shut me out—of your mind, your heart. You've lost that faith in us I saw blazing in you last night. If you truly believe that it meant nothing—that none of what's happened over the past weeks means anything—then tell me so. Because I can't take another moment of disappointment."

Raising a hand to cover her mouth, she let her eyes fall to his chest. After some thought, she seemed to collect her resolve. "If you're disappointed…" She swallowed and seemed to have to force herself to raise her gaze back to his. He might have imagined the shadow of doubt he saw there. "If you're disappointed it's your own fault. Not mine."

He lifted his chin. And so it was, he thought, frowning back at his computer and notes. At the cell phone. At Rex watching the exchange from the floor. He took a good look around at the life they could have made together. At the life he'd begun to envision for them. The heartache and disappointment mingled and became too much to bear. "Shame," he said again. Looking at Olivia, he saw the quaver of her chin and thought once more about trying to breach that gulf she'd forced between them. What would be the point, though, if she found some other way of refusing him down the road? As she had every day since he entered her life.

Rubbing the back of his hand over his mouth, Gerald went to the table and packed up the notebook and papers. He grabbed Rex's leash from the counter. Bending down to clip it in place on the dog's collar, he focused hard on the task at hand as the silence pressed against his eardrums. His brows knit together, pulling at the scar on his temple, and he kept his breaths even, his hands steady.

Giving the dog a pat on the head, he rose and hesitated. Olivia's arms were locked over her chest as if they were the only things keeping her in place. She didn't glance at him as he approached her, as he stood over her, taking one last, lingering look. He curled his hand in a fist around Rex's leash to keep from reaching out to her. "Look at me, Olivia," he said in a near-whisper. "You owe me that at least."

He heard the audible click of her swallow before her eyes roved from some space over his shoulder and landed on his face. After a moment of searching his features, she finally found his eyes and blinked several times as his gaze held hers.

He blew out an unbelieving breath. "You have no idea how hard it is not to kiss you goodbye."

Blinking again rapidly, she shook her head but said nothing. Her eyes grew damp, shocking him. He'd never seen so much as a tear escape her.

She was strong, he mused. *Too bloody strong.* Making a quick decision, knowing it was right, he reached into his pocket with his free hand and pulled out the wedding ring he'd been keeping there. Holding it up for her to see, he watched it catch the light. Watched the wetness in Oliva's eyes double and threaten to spill. "I was waiting for the right moment to give this back to you." He sniffed, closing the gold band in his fist. "I guess there's no point in my doing so now."

Holding on to it for a moment more, he tightened his fingers around it. Then in a quick motion that startled her, he tossed it on the counter beside her. It bounced once with a resounding *tink,* then spun loudly before it settled, still.

Gerald fought the emotions filling him to capacity, despair at the crest of the usurping wave. Clearing his throat, he said, "Don't spend your life alone, love. Learn to share it with someone. Even if you don't regret this…you'll regret not having something like it eventually." When she frowned, he gave in to the scowl pulling at his lips. "Goodbye, Mrs. Leighton," he told her and made a quick exit with Rex at his side.

CHAPTER TWENTY-ONE

"YOU LOOK LIKE you need this more than I do."

Olivia stopped sweeping the floor long enough to peer over her shoulder at her lone customer. Clint lifted his pint and wagged a knowing brow. Looking away, she went back to sweeping. "Why aren't you at home? It's Thanksgiving. I'm sure the wife's expecting you."

Clint snorted, leaned back in the chair and propped one foot on the other underneath the table. "I'm hiding from the in-laws."

Olivia rolled her eyes. Right now she could be sitting down at her cousin's table, digging into Cole's smoked turkey and shooting back a glass of wine. Briar had made it a point to invite her, as she always did. They'd spent every Thanksgiving together since Hanna Browning's death.

Olivia had decided to cancel at the last minute. Where she'd got it into her head to open the tavern doors on Thanksgiving, she had no idea. Everyone was toasting and giving thanks in the comfort of their own homes today—there wouldn't be much business. But she hadn't been able to stand the thought of sitting down with family or moping around in her apartment, either. Work. She'd needed work. When all else failed, work would sustain her.

Or it had…until Gerald Leighton came along.

Rolling her shoulders, she did her best to chase away the thought of him. An impossible feat. He was always there. Always hovering on the cusp of her mind, looking just as he did the day he left.

Shattered.

She rolled her eyes as Clint began to sing tunelessly along with the jukebox's "Ain't No Rest for the Wicked." Gritting her teeth, she gave in to the towering urge to shut it up and kicked the machine hard with the heel of her platform boot. It stuttered, fell quiet for a moment. Clint let out a whining, "Hey, what's it to you?" Then Otis Redding began to croon "These Arms of Mine" through the speakers. Giving up, gritting her teeth, Olivia finished sweeping the floor and retreated behind the bar.

She poured herself a glass of cold water and drank deeply, trying not to think about the right hip pocket of her jeans where for some reason she'd been carrying around her damned wedding band for two weeks straight. She'd met the courier Gerald had sent from New York a handful of days after his promised departure. The divorce papers had been sitting on her coffee table ever since.

All she'd been able to do late in the evenings and mornings—between her morning run and afternoons working at the bar—was stare at his signature and fiddle with the ring.

Two weeks of this. Still, she couldn't sign. She couldn't see the end of this brood she'd been sunk down deep in since she saw the disappointment and deep, deep hurt the words she'd been so convinced were true had caused the man she'd desperately wanted to chase away.

Regret. Gerald had been right about that at least. Over the past fortnight, she'd grown accustomed to the bite and bitter tang of regret.

The doors to the tavern opened. *Oh, good,* she thought without much cheer. More customers to distract her from her circling thoughts.

"Hey there, sugar bean!" someone called over the music.

Olivia looked around wildly. At the sight of her father's beaming face, she nearly fell to pieces.

Harrison Lewis lifted his arms. "Well? What are you waiting for, darlin'? Come 'ere and give your old man a kiss."

Olivia all but leaped over the bar into his embrace. As she buried her face in his barrel chest, he lifted her off the floor and whirled her around before setting her down and rocking her side to side. "How's my Livie?" he murmured, touching his lips to her brow.

She swallowed the cries that wanted to well out of her. Suddenly, she was a young girl, eighteen, all over again and he was comforting her after her first heartbreak. "I'm so glad you're here."

Harrison pulled back, grabbed her face in his hands and looked his fill, his emerald eyes dancing over her face. "We couldn't let our girl spend Thanksgiving alone, now could we?" His smile sobered when he saw the tears that were on the brink of release. "Don't you start those waterworks, now. Your mama might be tough as jerky, but you know with me weeping's contagious."

Burying her face in his flannel coat again, she let out a long, ragged breath. "I missed you both. I missed you so much."

He laid his cheek on her head and soothed her by rubbing a fatherly hand over her back. "We're here now, sugar bean."

No sooner had Olivia's mother parked the RV in the parking lot of the tavern than Rosa Lewis shooed Olivia from behind the bar and got to work herself. Knowing she'd just get in her mom's way, Olivia parked herself on one of the stools and watched her mother work. "You've been driving all day. Aren't you tired?"

Rosa sent her a stern look. "I've been stuck in a metal container with your ol' crow of a father for too long. We've done nothing but sit and hike and argue for the better part of a year. Trust me, I'm right where I need to be. 'Specially from the looks of you."

Olivia dodged her gaze. While Harrison, the wanderlust, seemed satisfied taking things at face value, Rosa always delved deeper, sometimes cleaving underneath the surface to get at the heart of the problem. It was part of what had made her so good at bartending.

Something thunked down on the bar in front of Olivia. She looked up to see a tall glass filled with a white substance she recognized instantly—the Lewis family painkiller. Glancing up at her mother's face, she saw the knowing glint in Rosa's eye.

"To chase the pain," she said, patted her hand and went back to work.

"Thank you," Olivia murmured. Yes, Rosa saw, knew all. Olivia wrapped her hands around the glass, let the cold sink in and fought the urge to weep again. Damn it, she wasn't like her father. Weeping had never been a problem. She hated tears, always had. Downing half the Lewis painkiller, she chased the sting of them away.

Rosa passed a draft beer over the bar, exchanging it for rumpled singles. "There you are, Charlie. You doin' all right?"

"I'm doing just fine, Miz Rosa." For the first time in Olivia's memory, the tavern regular smiled. "You're looking mighty pretty tonight. Prettier than I remember. I'll buy you a drink. How 'bout a shot of Crown…so long as you don't tell that randy husband of yours."

Rosa winked. "He never has to know. Crown, it

is." She poured a jigger full of Crown Royal. Olivia watched with a half smile as the woman swooped it down, sighed and shivered. She laughed again and poured herself another. "God, it's good to be back. Damn good."

"Just remember, it's my bar now, Mama," Olivia warned with a fond grin. "I keep the exchange of ownership papers in a safe-deposit box, so you can't change your mind and go tearing them up, either."

Rosa began to reply, then came up short, her gaze seizing on something over Olivia's shoulder. "Oh, dear Lord. Looks like that card shark's gone and found himself a game."

Olivia groaned as she watched her father slap a fifty-dollar bill on one of the tables. "I'll flip you for it, Mama."

Rosa smirked, digging in her pocket for change. "You're on, sugar bean."

"None of your two-faced coins," Olivia advised. "I'm inspecting it this time just to make sure."

Olivia lost the toss. Resigning herself, she got up from her stool and weaved her way through the tavern to her father's table. "Hello, gentlemen!" she called over a Dave Matthews tune.

"Hey, Liv!" Decker greeted her. "Your old man's all right."

"Old man," Harrison muttered, scooping his deck off the table out of sight. "Hey, sugar bean. Why don't you get me and the boys a round of Corona?"

"Daddy," Olivia said, making a grab for the wad of cards. "You know you're not supposed to be gambling anymore. The sheriff's a regular, and he's the one who arrested you the last time. Remember?"

Harrison waved her off. "This here ain't gambling. We were just going to have a nice little tournament is all. Nothing illegal."

"Daddy," Olivia said again, inclining her head. "You should know that patronizing tone doesn't work on me now any more than it did when I came up to your knees. I'll get you a round of Corona if you hand me the cards."

"Aw, hell." Harrison handed over the deck. "Eyes like a cat."

"That's right," she said, lowering her lips to the thinning crown of his head. "Why don't you help me get those beers? Charlie's trying to talk Mama into leaving you."

Harrison's eyes zoomed to the bar. "That son of a gun! He can't let it go, can he?"

"Go remind him who won her fair and square before he tries talking her into the back of his grandson's truck," Olivia told him.

She had to admit the night went over smoother than she would have wagered. The old running jokes and routine with her folks helped her forget Gerald's face for a while at least. Until closing time, that is.

"So what's this I hear about a British boy giving you trouble?" Rosa pried as she stacked chairs on tables.

Olivia looked up, surprised. "How did you know about that?"

Rosa lifted a shoulder. "Briar might have called."

"Briar," Olivia said with a shake of her head. "Damn it. Is that the reason you two came home?"

"We were halfway here." Rosa brushed off the specifics. "She seemed pretty worried about the state you'd gotten yourself in over it."

"Yeah, well, Briar worries about everything. It's who she is."

Harrison peered up from the jukebox where he was flipping through titles and crooning Hootie and the Blowfish out loud. "Briar. That little girl she's got…" He let out an appreciative whistle. "Pretty little thing steals the heart right out the ribs. When are you going to give us some grandkids, Livie?"

As Olivia groaned, Rosa shook her head. "Harrison, turn the music down. You're already deaf enough as it is. And grandkids?" She snorted. "Lord help us all. You'd have them sipping beer from a bottle and running with scissors—down the street—naked!"

Harrison jerked his thumb at Olivia. "That one turned out just fine."

"If she turned out decent, it's my doing. Not yours."

"You two can't be in the same room for more than two seconds without starting in on each other,

can you?" Olivia asked wonderingly before her
father could retort.

"Of course, we can't," Harrison jabbed. "You
know us better than that."

"Thirty some odd years of marriage and you'll
be doing the same thing," Rosa asserted. "What
else would we do but bicker?"

Harrison quirked his bushy, silver-tinged eyebrows. "I can think of something."

"Oh, dear Jesus!" Olivia pressed her hands to
her ears. "I'm not listening. I'm *so* not listening
anymore."

Rosa touched Olivia's wrist to pry her hand from
her head. "It's not just Briar who's worried. I talked
to Cole. And Adrian's concerned, too."

Olivia balked. "Adrian called, too? For the love
of…" She threw her hands up. "Is nothing sacred
around here anymore?"

Rosa waited for her to wind down before she continued. "It's time to give your mama the skinny."

"Somebody hurt you, Liv?" Harrison demanded,
expression going from affable to fierce in a matter of seconds.

Rosa let out a mocking laugh. "Welcome to the
conversation."

Harrison ignored her and strung his arm around
Olivia's shoulders. "Your granddaddy's rifle still
behind the couch in the office? You tell me where
to find the bastard and I'll hunt him down. Hell,
I'll murder him."

Olivia ran her hands back through her hair in frustration. "Calm down, Daddy. This is exactly why I wanted to spend Thanksgiving alone."

"Harrison, she's right. Cool it before you lose the rest of your hair."

When her father had calmed down and both he and her mother were looking at her expectantly, Olivia sighed and lowered herself onto an empty tabletop. "I met a man in Vegas. We hit the liquor a little too hard and wound up in the honeymoon suite, married."

Harrison's face darkened. "I'm gettin' the gun."

Rosa planted a hand on his shoulder before he could rise. "Don't move another muscle." Swinging her sharp gaze back to Olivia, she said, "And? What happened next?"

Olivia shook her head. "Look, it's a long story. You just need to know…we might have had something. He tried to show me that we could have something. And I hurt him. I think I might have hurt him pretty badly." She lifted her hand, reaching for the right words for what she felt, for what she'd been able to make of her relationship with Gerald and what remained of it now with her in his absence…but they didn't come.

"He hurt you, too," Harrison deduced, frowning.

"No," Olivia said. "I just…maybe I shouldn't have pushed back. Maybe we did have something. Maybe there's something stopping me from letting him…letting any man in." When Rosa and

Harrison exchanged knowing looks, Olivia shook her head in automatic denial. "This is not about Rhodes."

Harrison's frown was deep. "You sure about that, Livie?"

"Like it or not," Rosa told her slowly, treading carefully on the past neither of them had spoken of since, "what happened with that boy changed you. It changed how you looked at life. Living. Men. It's got to be what's holding you back." She paused, scanning her daughter's face. "Did this British man make you happy?"

Olivia closed her eyes. And again, all she could see was Gerald. His face on the pillow next to hers. Then above her own, cresting over her as the heat of what was between them overtook them both. Dancing with her in the empty tavern. Kissing her in the rain. Playing with Rex. Reclined on the grass next to her, dirty, panting, smiling. Laughing with her in bed. Turning to her in the night....

She sighed and finally admitted it. "Yes. When I wasn't busy pushing him away, he made me happy."

"Did he hurt you?" Rosa asked pointedly. "Use you? Cheat you?"

Lifting a hand to massage her temples, Olivia shook her head. "I tried so hard to convince myself that he was...or he would. Down the road. But no. I don't think he would have. I think..." A sob escaped her and she clamped her mouth shut, unable to believe it had escaped. Harrison reached for her but she held up a hand to stop him. "No," she said in a ragged voice. "I'm all right. I'll be all right. It's just that I think I might have loved him. And, damn it, I got scared. I never get scared. What the hell's the matter with me?" she ended on a frustrated note.

Rosa reached for her hand. "It's simple, really. You haven't made your peace with what happened before. You've been carrying it around with you, using it as a block. A wall. In the case of this man you love, you used it as a shield. And, baby, if you're ever going to be happy, then you've got to find a way to move on. Maybe then you'll be able to figure out what it is you really want." When Olivia remained silent, frowning, Rosa added, "If what was between you and this man wasn't real, then why are you tearing yourself apart over it?"

Olivia swallowed. "You're right."

Rosa smiled and patted her hand. "Of course I am."

"Woman always thinks she is," Harrison muttered. But he reached out and touched Olivia's cheek. "I hate to see you hurtin', sugar bean. As much as it pains me to say it, your mother is right. It's time you stop letting that Phillips twerp get in the way of what is or should be."

Olivia licked her lips. "I know. Even if Gerald's already decided to move on from what we had, I need to make my peace with what happened before him." Taking a bracing breath, she said, "I want to show you something." Leading them back behind the bar, she reached underneath the counter and lifted the box another courier had arrived with the day before the divorce papers. Placing it gingerly on the bar, she pried back the lid and stepped away to let them both see what was inside. "He's a writer," she explained as they scanned the title page of the Rex Flynn book Gerald had been working on. "A really good one."

It was Harrison who flipped to the dedication page. Both of her parents smiled a little when they read the single line of text written there. "To my Olivia…" Rosa read aloud, "my touchstone." She glanced back at her daughter with a lifted brow. "If that doesn't put everything into perspective, I don't know what will."

Olivia nodded and let a real smile stretch across her mouth for the first time in a long time. "Yeah," she said, letting her eyes skim over the words she'd read a thousand times before. She sighed. "That it does." With her parents flanking her, and her husband's dedication in front of her, Olivia nodded, sure of herself for the first time in weeks. "I've got to call Roxie."

"Roxie?" Harrison asked, perplexed as both he and Rosa watched her walk, determined, to the swinging doors.

"Yeah," Olivia said, rushing to the door of her office. "She's got a wedding coming up and I'm going to need a big favor...."

CHAPTER TWENTY-TWO

THE TEMPERATURE HAD risen enough to allow for the guests at Roxie and Richard's extravagant wedding reception at The Grand Hotel in Fairhope to mingle outside. Olivia sipped champagne at the bar where all the other singles seemed to be hovering.

The entire setting was perfect. There was even fake snow—apparently Marabella Honeycutt had won that battle of wills against her daughter. And the wedding ceremony had also been perfect, the vows touching—and, if Olivia wasn't mistaken, both written by the bride's hand. There had hardly been a dry eye in the house. Olivia had sat with Briar, Cole, Adrian and Kyle, glancing over when her cousin gave several wet sniffles. Briar lifted her shoulders and whispered, "Sorry. It's the hormones."

Olivia had refrained from saying anything when Cole kindly handed his wife a handkerchief and cradled her fingers against his thigh.

When the ceremony began, Olivia had looked wildly around for a tall blond man in a tailored suit. She hadn't spied him. Neither had she seen him waiting in the receiving line…though she'd craned her neck every which way. For the first two hours of the reception as day began to give way to early evening and the light over the bay grew soft, she'd continued to search. Then resignation and grim understanding sank in along with the ache of her heart.

He hadn't shown.

Olivia sought the nearest waiter with the tray of champagne in his hand after Monica snagged her attention, and, beaming, lifted her left hand to wriggle the ring finger. Olivia's mouth had dropped at the diamond winking there. Skeet, proudly standing behind Monica, lifted his shoulders in a helpless gesture and slipped an arm around his fiancée's waist as Monica heralded the news, "We're engaged!" Olivia gave her congratulations, hugged them both around the neck and said, "I hope this means you've got a place of your own now and I won't catch you doing anything in my office. *Ever* again." They had a laugh and she went off to find a dim corner of the hotel garden to toss back the bubbly.

As she nursed her second glass of champagne, Olivia brooded. She'd clearly missed her opportunity. Gerald had apparently moved on, just as she feared. Or he hadn't found it in him to forgive her or give her another chance.

She had refused him far too many times, hadn't she? All because she hadn't been able to see through her past heartbreak to Gerald and the life they could have built between them. The love that lived there—or, *had* lived there. *Past tense, Liv.*

She brushed a wisp of fake snow off the rim of her glass and glanced around at Byron Strong, Briar's sexy accountant and the son of the inn's investors, who she'd forgotten was trying to carry on a conversation with her. He, too, apparently had arrived single. Though how that was possible, she wasn't quite sure. He was so good-looking, she nearly had to squint to look at him.

Damn it, she couldn't remember for the life of her what they were talking about. "I'm sorry," Olivia said, waving a hand in front of her face. "What did you say?"

Byron chuckled, knowingly. "Far away, are we?"

"Sorry," she said again, shaking her head to clear her glum thoughts. "Just distracted. You were asking if I knew the bride or the groom. Friend of the bride. You?"

"I've never officially met either," Byron admitted. "I'm a distant business associate of the bride's father."

"They spared no one the fake snow and icicles," she noted, sour.

He laughed fully now, looking around at the large crowd. "I have to say this is the most…elaborate wedding I've ever attended. Give me a deserted beach and flip-flops any day."

She raised her glass. "Hey, I'm with you." Only

her style was more the nearest, most deserted, fly-by-the-night chapel, wasn't it? Bitter, she drank deeply and finished off her second glass.

"Yoohoo, Liv!"

Olivia looked around and smiled as Roxie approached amidst a dazzling cloud of silk and organza she'd designed herself. Olivia lifted her arms and hugged her newly married friend. "The wedding, the reception...everything's great," Olivia told her. "You did amazing. And congrats, to both of you."

"Aw, thanks, hon." Roxie glanced over at Byron, her smile coy. "I hope I'm not interrupting something...."

"Ah, no, we were just talking," Olivia admitted.

"Then you won't mind if I steal her away for a moment, do you?" Roxie asked Byron.

He raised a hand and grinned. "Not at all, Mrs. Levy."

"Thanks, cutie-pie," Roxie said, answering the grin with a short wink. As she tugged Olivia away by the hand, full, frothy skirt rustling around her, Roxie glanced back at Byron. "Nobody told me Joe Manganiello was invited."

Olivia snorted out a laugh. "That's Byron. Strong," she added at Roxie's curious look. "The guy who saved the inn."

"He certainly looks the hero." Roxie stopped on the outskirts of the crowd. "Finally, a moment to breathe." She inhaled deeply despite the constraints of her tight bodice. "Ah…" she breathed as she let it out. "Better."

"If you need help practicing your Lamaze," Olivia said drily, "you should have hailed Briar, not me. As a birthing coach, I was terrible. I really just stood in the corner of the delivery room and cringed. Cole stepped up and got Briar through it."

"I'm fine now," Roxie assured her. She straightened, gripped both of Olivia's hands and dropped her voice. "I have a surprise for you."

"It's your wedding and you have a surprise for *me?*" Olivia questioned, unbelieving.

Roxie glanced, owl-eyed, over Olivia's shoulder in indication.

A thread of realization wove its way through Olivia slowly but surely. Her face fell in shock. For a moment, she could only stare at Roxie as her friend's smile turned mischievous. "He's here?" she breathed.

Roxie grabbed Olivia by the shoulders and turned her around to face the bay and the man standing before it, resplendent in twilight, a khaki suit jacket, vest, tie and…was that a kilt?

Frowning, Olivia measured Gerald's face. There was a smile there. Not just on his lips—in his eyes, too. She thought she'd robbed him of that smile. She was happy to see it. So happy.

Taking a bracing breath, she crossed to him, leaving Roxie and the party behind. Unable to find words, she simply stood, drinking him in, searching for something to say. Finally, she forced out, "I— Is that a kilt?"

Gerald looked down at the plaid wrapped around his waist. "Yes," he replied. "I told you I have family ties to Scotland. My mother's a descendant of the McLeod clan. The tartan is theirs."

"Oh." She blinked several times. He looked like some Highland version of Indiana Jones. *Okay, you can stop staring anytime, Liv.* It didn't work. Unable to help herself, she kept staring at him, entranced. "You came," she said, still not quite able to believe it.

"Roxie was kind enough to honor me with an invitation. I wondered if you were behind it." His smile faded away, those laugh lines around his eyes and mouth disappearing. She missed them instantly. "If you weren't, I figured it would be a good chance to talk to you about those divorce papers you never returned."

Olivia stilled. Divorce papers. He was here about them? Taking a deep breath, she gathered herself. No chickening out. Not now that everything she'd ever wanted was right in front of her. "Turns out," she said, taking a deep breath, "you can't divorce me."

The line between his eyes dug into the bridge of his nose. "What do you mean?"

Firming her lips, she realized they were dry. The words that tumbled out of them, at least, were steady. Strong. Sure. "In order for a divorce to

proceed, both parties have to be agreeable on th
point of separation," Olivia informed him. "I'n
not agreeable."

Something flashed in Gerald's eyes. A promis
ing gleam. Relief. "You're not?" he said simply
voice trembling.

She shook her head. Taking another bracing
breath, getting ready to dive in, headfirst. Hear
first. "No. I...I've missed you, Gerald."

His shoulders and chest lifted on a sigh. Whethe
it was from the relief she thought she saw on hi
face or weariness, resignation, she wasn't sure
"Olivia, you asked me to leave."

"I know," she said. "I thought that was what
wanted. But it wasn't. I pushed you away because
I was afraid. You were right. I was hurt in the past
I put my heart on the line once and had it flung
right back at me. I never forgot it. Unlike you,
never found the strength or the resilience to put i
behind me, to move on. I wasn't as strong as I'd le
myself to believe I was all these years. In a twisted
kind of way, the fear of feeling like that again—
alone, heartbroken, humiliated—made me what he
was. It made me hurt you. I did to you exactly wha
that guy in high school did to me. And for that I'n
sorry. I am so sorry, Gerald."

Gerald waited, watched, considered.

Olivia took a chance and moved closer, wanting
to be near him. The warmth of him, the warmth
she'd seen in his heart before she ruined it. "Once

I faced the past, I realized that the thing that I want most in the world is you. I want to move on, and I want you beside me. If I'm too late…if you can't forgive me for the things that I said, for pushing you away over and over again, I'll understand. I promise. But I also promise that if you can give it a welly and try to love me again at least, I will never push you away again. I'll never let you go."

As she watched his face in the wavering light of day, it softened gradually. Then the dimple in his cheek winked to life as a smile slowly spread across his face. Her heart skipped several beats and hope came alive inside her as he reached out to her.

She lifted her hand to his, the left one. His gaze snagged on the little gold band she'd placed there. She watched, letting her eyes fill with the tears that burned the back of them, as the muscles of his face grew taut and his shoulders lifted again on a quick inhale. When he lifted his gaze back to hers, there were emotions there, bright and burning. "You're wearing your ring," he said, smile reaching his eyes.

She nodded, not quite able to speak now as she watched forgiveness work its impossible magic in him. Biting the inside of her cheek to keep from weeping out loud, she lifted his hand and pressed it to her lips, lingering.

After a moment, he released her hand and raised both hands to her face, angling it up until he could see it. His eyes were soft and green and kind. "I've missed you, too," he whispered. "Even when I was angry at you and told myself there was no point...I missed you so terribly much, Olivia Rose."

She nodded her agreement, still unable to speak. The tears flowed now. She couldn't hold them back any longer. The dam that had held them back too long disintegrated at the onset of what he was offering her. His heart—all over again. What kind of man was he who would forgive her, then offer his heart to her on a silver platter all over again?

He was incredible. He was hers.

As she looked up at him, his expression faltered. "Olivia...are you crying, love?"

Love. There was that word. "Yes," she admitted, the word pushing out of her as her chest heaved. She stomped her foot as she raised her hands to her face to hide the flood of tears. "Damn it." She tried to turn away.

"Here," Gerald said, touching her arm and guiding her to a bench. From the inside breast pocket of his jacket, he pulled out a handkerchief and dried her eyes. When the tears only continued to pour, he gave up mopping them away and pulled her into his arms, rocking her, touching kisses to her face. "Shh, I'm here, love. I'm here, and it's not over." He pulled back slightly, using his thumbs to smear what was left of the tears on her cheeks. He grinned. "We'll marry again. Properly this time. All the bells and whistles, just like this." He indicated the reception that was still going strong into

he night. "It seems we'll have need of Roxie's ex-
pertise. Though waiting until she gets back from
honeymoon might just kill me."

Olivia smiled ruefully. "There's always Vegas."

He chuckled, brushing the hair back from her
face. "No. You deserve a real wedding with your
family, and I aim to give you one."

"I'm not sure I deserve it, or you."

"If I have to, love, I'll spend the rest of my life
convincing you that you deserve that and more."

She raised her lips to his, kissed him deeply. Taking a moment to breathe him in, she tasted him. He
was here. He was here in her arms and he wasn't
leaving. There was no way in the world she would
let him walk away again. "I don't need any of that,"
she told him. "You're it for me. You're all that I
need. Just you."

"Maybe not," Gerald acknowledged. "I hope you
don't mind, but I've spoken to your father. It's why
was late."

"My father?" She balked.

"Yes, I spent much of the morning at the bad end
of Betty trying to convince your father my intentions are honorable."

Olivia closed her eyes in disbelief. "I apologize
for him. He's sort of senile when it comes to my
mom and me."

"It was an interesting conversation," Gerald
admitted, grinning. "He told me this story about

you and some misguided bloke by the name of Phillip Rhodes?"

"It's Rhodes Phillips," she said after a moment's pause. "And, oh, no, he didn't."

Gerald's face sobered. "The story revealed more than I anticipated. I understand now more than I thought I could your reasons for keeping me at arm's length, for pushing me away." Before she could reply, he went on, "The reason I spoke to your father was to ask if he and your mother would be willing to sell Birdie's house to us."

Olivia's eyes widened. "What?"

"He said he'd give us a fair price."

Once again, she struggled for words. "Birdie's house?" she blurted. "But the apartment…"

"Yes, well, I figured we'd need more space," Gerald admitted. "I can hardly write on the kitchen table forever. And Rex needs room to run."

Olivia let out an incredulous laugh. "You mean turn around, stand up, sprawl out."

"And there's the children to consider."

She faltered, her gaze latching on to his face. "Children?" she whispered.

"I know it's early days yet for us," Gerald said as his thumb stroked the back of her hand, over the ring she wore there. "But at some point—down the road, perhaps—I'm hoping our minds are aligned on this."

Olivia's own smile bloomed slowly across her face. "Yes."

"Yes?" he asked. "To what part, exactly?"

"All of it!" she cheered, beaming. "The house. Rex. Kids. You. Especially you."

"Us," he corrected. "We'll make it work, Liv."

"We will," she said and she believed it. "I know because I love you. More than I've ever loved anybody else."

He sighed and, lowering his head to hers, kissed her again. "I love you, too," he murmured.

She'd wanted to hear the words again. They made her heart leap and her spirit soar. She took a deep breath, let it out and grinned like a fool. "About our wedding. I have one request."

"Go on, Mrs. Leighton."

Olivia's smile spread into a full-fledged grin. "Will you wear the kilt?"

Laughing, Gerald touched his brow to hers. "As you wish." They both looked down as he slipped his hand inside his pocket and pulled out another band of gold, one larger than her own. "Will you do the honors once more, love?"

She didn't hesitate to take the band and slip it onto the ring finger of his left hand. Holding the hand in hers, she looked up and tilted her head at the suggestive brow he had arched at her. "What?" she asked as a ready, familiar spark fired inside her.

Gerald grinned broadly. "I'm wondering how long I have to wait before throwing you over my shoulder and hauling you out of this place."

Olivia threw her head back and laughed uproari
ously. "Back to my bed?"

"The one you tend to hog, yes." He smiled.

Banding her arms tightly around him, she said
"We'll buy a bigger one. For our house."

"I like the sound of that." Gerald laid his chin o
her head and together they watched the bay rus
into the shore, listened to the whoosh of waves a
they met sand and rock. His voice carried over th
noise, warm, smiling, and it healed her. *He* heale
her. "So, stranger…how do you like your eggs i
the morning?"

* * * * *

LARGER-PRINT BOOKS!

HARLEQUIN *Presents*

PASSION GUARANTEED SEDUCTION

GET 2 FREE LARGER-PRINT NOVELS PLUS 2 FREE GIFTS!

YES! Please send me 2 FREE LARGER-PRINT Harlequin Presents® novels and my 2 FREE gifts (gifts are worth about $10). After receiving them, if I don't wish to receive any more books, I can return the shipping statement marked "cancel." If I don't cancel, I will receive 6 brand-new novels every month and be billed just $5.05 per book in the U.S. or $5.49 per book in Canada. That's a saving of at least 16% off the cover price! It's quite a bargain! Shipping and handling is just 50¢ per book in the U.S. and 75¢ per book in Canada.* I understand that accepting the 2 free books and gifts places me under no obligation to buy anything. I can always return a shipment and cancel at any time. Even if I never buy another book, the two free books and gifts are mine to keep forever.

176/376 HDN F43N

Name   (PLEASE PRINT)

Address   Apt. #

City   State/Prov.   Zip/Postal Code

Signature (if under 18, a parent or guardian must sign)

Mail to the **Harlequin® Reader Service:**
IN U.S.A.: P.O. Box 1867, Buffalo, NY 14240-1867
IN CANADA: P.O. Box 609, Fort Erie, Ontario L2A 5X3

**Are you a subscriber to Harlequin Presents books
and want to receive the larger-print edition?
Call 1-800-873-8635 today or visit us at www.ReaderService.com.**

* Terms and prices subject to change without notice. Prices do not include applicable taxes. Sales tax applicable in N.Y. Canadian residents will be charged applicable taxes. Offer not valid in Quebec. This offer is limited to one order per household. Not valid for current subscribers to Harlequin Presents Larger-Print books. All orders subject to credit approval. Credit or debit balances in a customer's account(s) may be offset by any other outstanding balance owed by or to the customer. Please allow 4 to 6 weeks for delivery. Offer available while quantities last.

Your Privacy—The Harlequin® Reader Service is committed to protecting your privacy. Our Privacy Policy is available online at www.ReaderService.com or upon request from the Harlequin Reader Service.

We make a portion of our mailing list available to reputable third parties that offer products we believe may interest you. If you prefer that we not exchange your name with third parties, or if you wish to clarify or modify your communication preferences, please visit us at www.ReaderService.com/consumerschoice or write to us at Harlequin Reader Service Preference Service, P.O. Box 9062, Buffalo, NY 14269. Include your complete name and address.

HPLP13R

LARGER-PRINT BOOKS!
GET 2 FREE LARGER-PRINT NOVELS PLUS
2 FREE GIFTS!

HARLEQUIN®

Romance

From the Heart, For the Heart

YES! Please send me 2 FREE LARGER-PRINT Harlequin® Romance novels and my 2 FREE gifts (gifts are worth about $10). After receiving them, if I don't wish to receive any more books, I can return the shipping statement marked "cancel." If I don't cancel, I will receive 4 brand-new novels every month and be billed just $4.84 per book in the U.S. or $5.24 per book in Canada. That's a savings of at least 19% off the cover price! It's quite a bargain! Shipping and handling is just 50¢ per book in the U.S. and 75¢ per book in Canada.* I understand that accepting the 2 free books and gifts places me under no obligation to buy anything. I can always return a shipment and cancel at any time. Even if I never buy another book, the two free books and gifts are mine to keep forever.

119/319 HDN F43Y

Name _____ (PLEASE PRINT)

Address _____ Apt. #

City _____ State/Prov. _____ Zip/Postal Code

Signature (if under 18, a parent or guardian must sign)

Mail to the Harlequin® Reader Service:
IN U.S.A.: P.O. Box 1867, Buffalo, NY 14240-1867
IN CANADA: P.O. Box 609, Fort Erie, Ontario L2A 5X3
Want to try two free books from another line?
Call 1-800-873-8635 or visit www.ReaderService.com.

* Terms and prices subject to change without notice. Prices do not include applicable taxes. Sales tax applicable in N.Y. Canadian residents will be charged applicable taxes. Offer not valid in Quebec. This offer is limited to one order per household. Not valid for current subscribers to Harlequin Romance Larger-Print books. All orders subject to credit approval. Credit or debit balances in a customer's account(s) may be offset by any other outstanding balance owed by or to the customer. Please allow 4 to 6 weeks for delivery. Offer available while quantities last.

Your Privacy—The Harlequin® Reader Service is committed to protecting your privacy. Our Privacy Policy is available online at www.ReaderService.com or upon request from the Harlequin Reader Service.

We make a portion of our mailing list available to reputable third parties that offer products we believe may interest you. If you prefer that we not exchange your name with third parties, or if you wish to clarify or modify your communication preferences, please visit us at www.ReaderService.com/consumerchoice or write to us at Harlequin Reader Service Preference Service, P.O. Box 9062, Buffalo, NY 14269. Include your complete name and address.

HRLP13R